THE MARSHAL'S LADY

LIBERTY VALLEY LOVE: BOOK 3

JOSIE MALONE

ISBN: 978-1-953735-89-8

Published by Satin Romance
An Imprint of Melange Books, LLC
White Bear Lake, MN 55110
www.satinromance.com

Published in the United States of America.

Cover Design by Lynsee Lauritsen

Dedicated to the horses I've known and loved through the years, especially my first Arabian stallion, the inspiration for the heroine's horse.

"Where no matter what, soulmates find each other."

PART ONE

"Action is the antidote to despair."

JOAN BAEZ

ONE

Friday, April 13ᵗʰ, 2018

RAIN DRIPPED FROM THE BRIM OF HER LEATHER COWBOY HAT AND splashed onto her gloved hand. Homicide Detective Beth Chambers peered through the misty drizzle. Did she see tracks from the horse ridden up this trail earlier in the day? Hunting Gary Smith, a suspected serial killer through Mount Baker National Forest wasn't one of her wiser decisions.

She knew he was a vicious monster even if nobody believed her. When she'd finally managed to get a search warrant last month, she'd discovered a cross belonging to one victim and an earring belonging to another in his car. The defense attorney claimed she'd gone beyond the scope of the warrant because it limited her to the house and garage that Gary rented in Eagleville. The prosecutor barely argued the case. Privately, he'd already told Beth all the work she'd done to close the murders in the three previous investigations was circumstantial. Nobody placed Smith at any of the crime scenes, although witnesses had seen him with various victims prior to their deaths. She hadn't found the knife or club he used on the women.

According to the lawyers and the judge, 'God in a Black Robe,' it didn't matter if the car was in the garage at the time. It'd been a calculated risk, but she was afraid he'd hide the rig, or have it detailed before she got back to the judge and had the warrant amended. Since it didn't specifically mention the vehicle, it made the jewelry inadmissible, *'fruit of the poisonous tree.'* As a veteran cop, she'd been chewed out by everyone from the lead homicide detective to the lieutenant to the police chief.

She refused to consider what the prosecutor or defense attorney would think of her taking vacation time to hunt Smith. If she'd gone 'by the book' he wouldn't have been loose to beat and rape her best friend. Remembering the sight of Nina's battered body tore at Beth's heart. He was the killer she'd sought for the past year when he'd started torturing and murdering prostitutes in western Washington. He had to be the one who'd dumped the bodies in and around Liberty Valley. The last three had been found near Eagleville, the small town where she currently worked at the 'cop shop.'

Was she paranoid to think he wanted to get at her? She scanned the path up ahead where her German Shepherd trotted in front of her horse. If it hadn't been for Luke, her retired K-9 partner, it would have been much harder to find the man she hunted. The dog picked up on Smith's scent almost immediately in the old ghost town of Monte Cristo. From there, Beth followed the trail into the Cascade wilderness.

At first, she'd worried Smith might cut across country, but obviously, he'd opted to cover as much ground in as short of time as possible. She suspected he was heading for the Canadian border. *I don't like the way the guy looks at me, which of course I can't tell the Lieutenant. There's way too much misogyny at the precinct and I can't say that either.*

The blatant contempt reminded her of what she'd seen during her Army tours in Afghanistan. Survival instinct warned her to be careful and watch her back, but if she mentioned it at work, her boss would insist she visit the department shrink again for more treatment of her combat-related PTSD. Smith had demanded a *real* cop interrogate him, contempt for her seeping from every pore when she interviewed him, and then he'd lawyered up as soon as one of the senior male detectives entered the room.

Beth leaned forward in the saddle and patted Tigger's sweaty gray neck. She and the purebred Arabian, bred for endurance, had won several trail-riding competitions. Usually, she opted for the shorter fifty miles in a day contests. Soft puffs of steam rose from the stallion's sculptured nostrils. He still arched his neck proudly, but white lather oozed under the leather breast-collar. "Poor guy. This is sure miserable weather for you and me."

She straightened in the saddle and felt her muscles leap in aching response. Sitting in an office chair this past winter hadn't prepared her for riding so much. She rose in the stirrups, twisted, and tried to relax. Tigger snorted. The loudness of the sound startled her. When had the woods grown silent? Large evergreens loomed closer to the narrow path. The trail was quiet, way too quiet.

Before, she'd heard birds and squirrels even when she rarely spotted them. An hour ago, the distinctive thumping of one of the state's helicopters conducting a routine marijuana search had disrupted the rainy spring afternoon. The oppressive silence reminded her of Afghanistan when death had lurked around each corner. Once Luke became her partner, she'd discovered the dog was more reliable than any of the men in the sheriff's department.

She suddenly realized she hadn't seen him in the last five minutes. Where was he? She reined Tigger to a stop and scanned the trail ahead. One gray boulder blurred into the next. Her apprehension grew. Where was Luke? Her hand fell on the butt of the rifle, and she slowly began to draw the 30.06 carbine out of the scabbard.

She continued to keep Tigger motionless, while she measured the giant first-growth cedars surrounding her and the path. Each tree was large enough to hide a man. Any of them would provide cover while Smith got a clear shot at her. But why wait so long? Why hadn't he ambushed her any time during the past two days? He must know by now that she was following him.

Her gaze narrowed on a brown, gray, and black shape near the granite boulders. It wasn't a rock. She knew in an instant. The limp, broken body was Luke. He was d...

Her brain refused to form the thought. At the same moment, she heard the whine of a bullet!

Beth spun Tigger toward the trees and spurred hard! The Arabian leaped forward, but it was too late. The leap changed into a rear!

She shoved the rifle back into its holder and concentrated on staying in the saddle. She threw her weight forward and to the right, hoping the shift in her balance would signal the horse to land on his front feet. Instead, the stallion continued to rise higher and higher.

No time to panic. She kicked her feet free of the stirrups, prepared to vault off the horse. *Not enough time*.

Tigger slipped on the granite. He lost his own balance, falling to the right. She saw the dirt approaching. Faster and faster. She threw herself out of the saddle, but the ground was too close.

The Arabian crashed over backward!

Beth tried to roll away from him – too little, too late. Her body slammed into the mud. Her head hit the granite boulder beside the path. She tasted blood, her blood. When she looked up, she saw Tigger falling toward her. Before she could move, he landed on top of her, crushing her beneath his thousand-pound body.

How many women had Smith killed? It wasn't the first time

Beth wondered that, but she knew it would be the last. Tigger still didn't move. The stallion couldn't. Her body felt as if it melted, sank in on itself. It was over. For a moment, she thought she heard someone nearby, but she didn't open her eyes. She couldn't.

Everything was over. *It's not fair*. So many projects she hadn't finished. She'd wanted Smith and so much more. A good man to love, one who loved her. Children.

That was gone. Only pain, unending agony now.

A prayer formed on her lips. "Just one more chance. Let me stop Smith. Please."

———

The sloppy wetness of Luke's tongue as he licked her face roused Beth. Her head spun. She struggled to lift one hand. She forced open her eyes and gently pushed the dog away. He whined and sat down beside her. She reached up, felt the bump on the back of her head where it'd hit a rock.

Remembering the sight of Luke's broken body beside the trail, she touched the dog, stroked his brown fur. He pressed closer, and she rubbed his shoulder. He'd been stunned, not killed. "Guess we both messed up, buddy. We've gotta be a lot more careful from here on out."

Luke growled and licked her hand. She risked trying to sit up. Her mind fogged and she almost slipped into welcome darkness. No time for rest. The accident had obviously been Tigger's fault. It wasn't the first time the stallion had thrown her. However, it was the first time he'd reared and gone over backward on top of her.

"Damned, stupid idiot. I ought to have bought a Quarter-horse instead of falling in love with a beauty like you when Nina took me to Xanadu Arabians. I shouldn't have listened when Audra bragged about how brilliant you are and your terrific pedigree."

From where he pulled at a few tufts of grass near a granite boulder, Tigger nickered in answer. Beth glared at the horse. A faint wisp of memory filtered into her mind, and she tried to follow it. She had fallen off him, hadn't she? Wasn't she pinned by the stallion for at least a moment or two? She must have passed out prior to Tigger standing up. No wonder she thought she was *dead meat*. For a moment, she recalled a sense of pervading peace, love, admiration, and acceptance. There had been all of that and yet something more.

The harder she tried to remember, the more the feeling slipped away. Reluctantly, she gave up the battle. She'd think about the accident later, after her head quit hurting. She hugged Luke tightly for a moment, then rested one hand on the German Shepherd's solid, eighty-pound body and struggled to her feet. Her ribs throbbed in protest. She must have cracked one, if not broken it.

Her head swam. She took a step. Her stomach rebelled and she barely made it to the side of the trail before she hurled, grateful lunch had only been beef jerky and water eaten in the saddle hours ago. Should she head home? Nobody would blame her if she stopped searching for Gary Smith, nobody but herself. She raised a hand to her forehead and felt for the cut she remembered. The blood had frightened her. She'd been so sure she was dying.

There was no blood on her face now and no sign of the injury either. She tried a cautious step. Her legs were fine. She could walk. Her hysterical fear during the accident prompted the notion it was the end of the world and her life. Nina often said, "*A good fall is one the rider walks away from.*"

Recalling her friend restored Beth's courage. She took a deep breath. Her body might feel a little sore, but she wasn't finished yet. Smith deserved to spend the rest of his life behind bars and justice must be served. She wouldn't wimp out now, not when she was so close to him.

"No." She petted Luke. "We're not going back yet. We're getting that scumbag off the streets and behind bars."

The dog pressed against her. She stroked his bristly short hair. "Come on, partner. Let's go look around."

Crossing to the Arabian, she took the rifle from its scabbard.

She checked the load and started up the path. The stud whickered and then trotted after her.

"Now's a fine time to tell me how much you love me." She swung around to catch the reins and tie up her horse. The sight of a bloody crease in the center of his forehead stopped her. A bullet wound. She was closer to Smith than she'd imagined. Tigger's spooking saved her life. She rested her hand on his gray neck. "I'll be more careful. I don't want you hurt."

The stallion nuzzled her arm and Beth changed her mind. She couldn't leave the horse tethered. If he were loose, he could run away from Smith, and since the Arabian was used to getting treats from her, he'd come when he saw her. She glanced at the trail, a thin scattering of dirt over granite.

She went to Tigger's right side. She opened the saddlebags and removed evidence bags and plastic gloves. Now, if she found anything, she would be able to use it against Smith. She worked her way through the overgrown salmonberry bushes and alder saplings, glad when she found her way back among the evergreens. Less than a hundred feet up the trail, she discovered the place where Smith had launched his attack. A few cigarette butts littered the muddy ground, and she recognized his footprints.

Removing her digital camera from a jacket pocket, she took pictures of the area then collected the evidence. No way she'd use her phone to take a video and risk losing it to the inept prosecutor. John Watkins, the lead homicide detective still complained about having to replace his smartphone when it was seized for evidence. She'd turn the cigarette butts into the lab when she got back to town. Tests would prove Gary Smith indeed attacked her, leaving her for dead.

The man was long gone. Did he think she was finished? Why hadn't he made sure? He generally beat his victims almost to death, then slit their throats to be certain they couldn't testify against him. Shooting her wasn't his usual M.O. Why had he changed? She shrugged. Everyone made mistakes. Smith was a human being, not only the monster she personally thought of him.

Slowly, she returned to Tigger, collecting her hat on the way. She replaced the rifle in the scabbard, checked the tack, and then swung into the saddle. For the next hour, she rode cautiously. She kept a wary gaze on the trail and often rested a hand on the butt of the rifle. Luke remained closer this time, a few feet from the Arabian.

Suddenly, the path opened into a small clearing. A hill rose before her, clawing into the sky. Even misty fog and slanting rain couldn't disguise the hazardous trail up the steep incline. She saw paw prints in the mud and knew Luke had already started the climb. She petted Tigger's neck, lingering to watch the moon rise above the giant cedars and hemlocks. Something in the atmosphere caused the bright globe to appear red tonight. It provided plenty of light to see the trail and that was all she cared about.

Tigger tossed his head and snorted, the loudness shocking her. She returned her attention to the mammoth slope in front of her. Huge granite boulders lined the path while smaller fragments awaited an unwary hoof. A light sprinkling of dirt covered the slick gray stone and a tiny evergreen clung precariously to the side of the hill. Fog shrouded the top of the ridge, hiding the steepest part of the ascent.

She took a deep breath and measured the climb again. Then, she urged Tigger forward. The gray stallion leaped up the rocky incline, scrambling for footing. Granite pieces fell behind them and she glimpsed another horse's hoofprint and a scrape on gray stone. So, Smith still had Wonder, an abused Appaloosa stallion he'd stolen from Nina Armstrong's horse rescue facility.

Nobody knew where the starved wreck of an equine came from almost two years ago, but Nina, a famous Washington State horsy do-gooder nursed him back to health. The woman had interrupted Smith when he'd absconded with the horse three days ago and she'd paid the price. Beth found Nina before she died. She identified Smith and asked Beth to return the stallion to her barn.

The drizzle grew heavier, silvery rain slashing down in a curtain of thread-like drops, streaming downward. Waves of water rolled, small drops followed by larger ones creating a hazy view, a thin fog-shrouded screen blocking most of the path behind them. Tigger collected himself for another series of leaps. When they gained the first plateau, she reined him to a halt.

Oddly enough she could breathe better up here, better than she had when she first mounted after the accident. Her ribs had stopped hurting. Her head no longer pounded like someone beat a jack-hammer against her skull and her stomach wasn't roiling. She truly had walked away unscathed. She'd have to tell Nina when they returned that her advice was correct as always. Of course, the younger woman would pitch a fit when she heard about the fall and lecture Beth for the hundredth time about keeping her heels down and staying balanced in the saddle.

She waited for Tigger to regain his breath. With a squeeze of her legs, she sent the horse forward again, grateful for the bright red moon lighting their way. More than once she heard his hooves strike small rocks. He jumped another log and came to a halt on the summit. She petted his steaming neck, scanning the top of the ridge. The evergreens which were so huge at the bottom of the hill had become tiny tips, like baby Christmas trees, insubstantial from this height.

Grateful the rain had stopped, she eyed the descent, stretching before her, down a winding trail. The path seemed clearer in the evening moonlight with none of the hazards they'd overcome on the ascent. She touched Tigger's sides with her legs and the Arabian headed downhill at a faster pace. When they reached level ground, the small stallion picked up a jog.

Suddenly, she heard a short yip. Luke had found something of interest. A low, menacing growl came next. It meant the discovery was male, a human male which the large German Shepherd considered fair game. His refusal to work with men had almost ended the canine's career with the department before it started.

"Luke, hold." Had she found Smith already? Why wasn't he shooting at Luke or her? She pulled her carbine from the scabbard.

Tigger snorted as they came around a bend. He leaped sideways as he caught a glimpse of the shadowy figure huddled near a boulder. Luke stood in front of the man, continuing to growl, hackles raised.

She cursed the dusk. The red moonlight didn't help her see much. She couldn't get a clear view of the man, but he appeared bigger than her suspect. "Smith?"

"No." The stranger groaned. "I'm hurt. Bad."

She shoved her rifle back into its holder. Her voice deepened with frustration and impatience. "What the hell are you doing here then?"

"Bleeding." Faint amusement filled his bass rumble.

TWO

"On Friday the 13th, if the moon is red,
  Follow the scarlet pathway to the Land of the Dead....!"

RULES OF CHRONOS

SHE SWUNG FROM THE SADDLE. HER PONCHO FLAPPED AS SHE landed, and Tigger tossed his head debating whether to spook or not. She ignored the horse and turned to the man. She viewed him dispassionately, cataloging his appearance. White, in his forties, approximately six-foot tall. He might be an inch or two more since he leaned against a rock.

Black, gray-speckled hair. Shoulder-length. Broad-shouldered. Wide chest, no extra fat, about 180 pounds. She noted the work clothes, a ripped wool shirt over a thick cotton one, pants, heavy coat, and boots – he'd planned to be out in the woods, and he wasn't a city slicker.

Pain-filled, navy-blue eyes stared at her. Bloody froth bubbled from his right lung, and she focused on the gunshot wound, a hole in his chest, approximately the size of a golf ball. For an instant, she remembered explosions, screams of injured soldiers and she shook her head. That war was behind her. She'd served her country, done her time. She was home now, safe in the USA, well as safe as a woman could be hunting a scumbag like Smith.

"What happened?"

"I got shot."

"I can see that." She glanced around, tried to pinpoint the best place for a shooter to hide. Too many trees and huge rocks. Anyone could be watching them. "Who did this? When and where?"

"Full of questions, ain't ya?"

"I want straight answers." She dropped to her knees beside him, the poncho swirling as it enveloped her. "Don't hold back." She peeled the shirts away from the wound, noticing the top one only had two buttons closing the wide neckline. He must pull it over his head when he dressed. "I don't intend to be the next victim because I'm helping you."

He'd already tried to stop the bleeding. The bandage torn from his shirt was soggy and wet with blood and rain. "Fella isn't around."

She stood, checking out the large evergreens and the narrow trail lit by the red moon. Luke had plopped down, lying on a bed of pine needles licking his paws. Well, if the dog wasn't upset or on guard, it probably was safe here, at least for now. She glanced at Tigger. The Arabian stood hip-shot, head down, eyes half-closed as he took a horsy nap.

The man gagged and turned his head to spit out a mouthful of blood. "This is where I came off my mare."

Beth took a deep breath. She'd seen worse injuries in Afghanistan. She didn't want to think about that, couldn't afford to remember those days right now. Medical procedures rattled into her mind. She needed to prevent shock. She opted for an authoritative tone. "I've got more questions."

"Save them. I'm dying. I know it." The man spat again. "So, do you." He coughed up more blood. "Nothing anyone can do. Thanks for trying."

"I'm not quitting yet." Beth stood and went after the first aid kit in her saddle bags. "Neither should you."

"The money from the bank robbery is on my horse. You've got to find her and take it back. The folks 'round here need every cent and Burdette can't afford to reimburse everybody with money in the bank."

"Bank robbery?" Beth swung around and noticed he was coughing again. She waited until he stopped choking and spitting blood before she asked. "Which bank did you rob?"

"I'm no thief, boy! I'm the Junction City marshal."

"Don't yell at me." Beth didn't bother to correct his assumption she was male. Her hat and loose poncho gave that impression. If he thought she was a man, he'd give her questions more respect. She returned to kneel beside him and swabbed at the blood on his chest. She had to keep him talking even if he began to babble. "The first thing you told me about was the robbery. What was I supposed to think?"

"Guess you're right." The stranger stared at her as she cleaned the area around the wound. "I don't know you. Where are you from? Just riding through?"

Beth waited until he spat again. "I was born in Seattle, but I've been around."

"Looking for work? I got a ranch outside of Junction City." He coughed up more blood. "Save me and you'll have a place for life."

Beth hid her amusement. "I've already got a good job, but thanks." She temporarily sealed the hole in his lung with a piece of clean gauze and decided not to tell him she was a cop too. At least, not yet. There wasn't a town called Junction City in Snohomish County, but perhaps she'd already crossed the line into Skagit. She'd check her map later.

For now, she helped him lean forward so she could clean the smaller entry wound in his back, then bandaged it. "What's your name, Marshal?"

"Morgan. Rad Morgan." The man waited. "And you? What's your name?"

She suppressed a smile and searched through the first-aid kit for a large bandage. "Beth Chambers."

"You're a woman?" Rad paused, spat more blood, then demanded. "What are you doing out here by your lonesome? This ain't a place for a lady."

"Spare me the trite, patriarchal lectures. If you needed a man to save you, then you should have put in your order before last Christmas."

He chuckled weakly. "Spunky, ain't ya, missy?"

She chose her sweetest voice, the one perfect for verbally disemboweling arrogant jerks in the Sheriff's Department. "You got a problem with that too, Morgan?"

"No, ma'am. I never did cotton much to sheep." Rad choked and coughed up blood for a few minutes. "I'm not belly-achin', but I purely hate dying in front of a gal. Are you pretty?"

With night fast approaching, he wouldn't know she'd packed an extra fifteen pounds on her five-foot, five-inch frame during this last stressful investigation. He couldn't see more of her face in the moonlight than she saw his. She mentally crossed her fingers and lied. "I'm beautiful, Morgan. Too bad you're planning to die. We could have had such a great future, or at least dinner. Who knows what might have happened afterward?"

That prompted another laugh and more choking. She unwrapped the covering on the bandage she'd removed from the first-aid kit. When he settled against the rock again, she smiled at him. "Okay. Exhale."

He looked confused. "What?"

"Breathe out as hard as you can." When he did, she quickly sealed the hole in his lung with the plastic wrapper from the

16

bandage. "All right. Hang onto this for me." She picked up his hand, professionally noting the clammy feel of his skin, and hoped he didn't go into shock before she'd finished. She placed his fingers on the wrapper. "Okay, you can breathe normally now while I do the rest."

She slid an arm under his shoulders, helped him straighten. Placing the bandage in the proper position, she put the thick pad of the dressing over the wound. Then, she wrapped the long ties of the bandage around his upper body. She secured the dressing and finished tying it into position.

She checked her knots. Nothing pressed on the wound. "Looks like we made it. How are you doing, Morgan?"

"Fine, ma'am."

"Don't call me that." She helped him lean against the granite boulder again. "My name's Beth."

"Wouldn't be proper for me to use your given name." He coughed up more blood. "We ain't been properly introduced."

The tension whooshed from her body. "Morgan, you kill me. Who do you figure will *properly introduce* us out in the middle of nowhere?"

Rad glared at her. "Someone needs to teach you manners, missy."

"What about you?" She pulled her survival knife out of the sheath on her hip. "Ever since you learned I was a woman you've been acting worse than my father. I don't take his disrespect. What makes you think you can get away with it? I saved your life. Be grateful."

"A man can only show gratitude just so long." He closed his eyes. "Don't push your luck."

When he remained silent for one long moment and then another, her concern intensified. "Morgan, are you all right?"

"I'm dying."

"No, you're whining again." She started to cut the bottom foot off her poncho for another bandage. "I'm here. I won't let you die,

Morgan. The one thing I can't bear is a whiny, sniveling coward. Get some guts."

"I'm coughing up blood. It'll kill me."

"Only if I leave you here alone." She finished cutting the heavy plastic piece she intended to use as another bandage. She laid the strip across the rock and went for her canteen. She needed to clean any dirt from the plastic before she put it over the dressed wound. "I won't do that. I'll get you to a hospital. You'll be fine."

"Doc's miles from here," Rad argued. "And why are you on this trail?"

Beth shrugged and opted for the truth. "I'm the lead detective on the Evergreen Murders and I'm looking for a suspect. He's escalated from when he started killing a few years ago. He's raped and killed at least six women in the past six months, but he made a mistake. His last victim survived and I.D.'d him. I'm taking Smith back to stand trial. If he's convicted, he'll spend the rest of his life behind bars."

"Looking for a killer ain't a job for a lady."

"Spare me." She folded the plastic into thirds. "The only thing I hate worse than whiny men are would-be Hollywood heroes."

Rad closed his eyes. "You don't hate men, missy."

"Really? Why not, Marshal Morgan?"

"Because you don't know any. I'll change that when I'm back on my feet."

"I thought you planned to die."

"It was *afore* I figured out I had to stick around and take care of you." He spat another mouthful of blood. "You must be pretty. You're sure enough spoiled and rude. The fancy fellers where you come from ain't done you no favors."

She glowered at him. "Now, we know why you're deep in these woods, Morgan. You're not allowed near civilization."

Beth dropped to her knees and used the strip of plastic from her poncho to cover the bandages she'd originally placed on his chest. The heavy waterproof material would create further pressure on the injuries. It'd stop the bleeding yet keep the wounds airtight at the same time.

Rising to her feet, she checked the precision of her handiwork. Each layer of the poncho piece overlapped the one under it. Together, they provided an even distribution of weight over the initial, padded dressings. Pushing what remained of her poncho to one side, Beth unbuckled the black web belt that held up her jeans. She slid the thin belt out of the loops on her pants and allowed the protective raingear to drape her again.

Then she knelt beside him once more. She extended the belt as far as it would go, holding the poncho bandage on his chest with the belt, fastening it at the top of the plastic. Going through her saddlebags, she found a second web belt and secured the bottom of the poncho piece with it.

She wasn't sure if the bullet had broken any ribs, but it was better to take precautions. She took a long roll of thick gauze and wrapped Rad's middle below the bandages she'd placed on his sucking chest wound. Now, what? She'd taken care of his injuries, but how was she supposed to move him somewhere safe? A cold breeze brushed her face, but at least it wasn't raining, and the ground was oddly dry here. Shouldn't it be muddy after raining all day? She decided to count her blessings instead of pitching a mental fit.

For the first time, she noticed the green stone attached to the chain he wore, and the strange designs etched into the small rock. *What was that about?*

Still kneeling beside Rad Morgan, Beth brought his blue shirt up to cover as much of his chest as possible. She adjusted his denim jacket. "We're almost ready to figure out what to do next. Let me put away my stuff." She suited her actions to her words, collecting all her first-aid supplies, even the used material.

Then she pulled out her flashlight and scanned the area, searching for any evidence that might tell her who'd shot Rad and left him for dead. He'd been right. There was nothing except a few tracks from his horse and she couldn't follow them now. His life had to come first. She had to stay here with him.

"You'll be fine." Her voice softened and she brushed a wave of black hair from his forehead. "I'll put my things away. Then, I'll get on my cell phone. We'll have you evac'd to the closest hospital before the hour's out."

"I'm tired, missy." He leaned his head against the rock. "If you won't let me die in peace, save the palaver."

"Okay, Morgan. I only have one simple question. Can you tell me what year it is?"

"1888."

Shock, she thought. She should have expected it. She reached into her coat pocket and pulled out the cell phone, turning it on to call for help. It came as little surprise when *'No Signal'* flashed on the screen. The situation reminded her of the song that her foster father, Will always sang. If it weren't for bad luck, she'd have none at all. Beth petted Tigger when he shoved at her with his muzzle. She turned off the phone and returned it to her coat. No point wasting power when she didn't have a way to charge the smart device.

She unfastened the tent and sleeping bag tied at the back of her saddle. "I'll get the tent up and over you, Morgan. We'll stay here until help arrives."

He blinked at her. "Stay here? You're loco."

"You're seriously injured. And I'm not moving you. We'll camp here for the duration."

He took a breath and then grabbed the rock behind him. Leaning on it, he struggled to stand. "Temperature's dropping. It'll snow before morning."

"What are you doing?" Beth caught his arm and steadied him. "Morgan, sit down. You'll hurt yourself even more."

"There's a cave."

"We can't make it." She wrapped her arm around his waist. "Lean on me, you macho idiot."

"Only a mile." He stumbled one step, then another. "I—can —do it."

"No, you can't. Nobody with two bullet holes in their body like you have should even try to walk a yard, much less a mile. You need to wait to be evac'd by Search and Rescue."

He ignored her. "Be faster if I rode. Get your horse."

She sighed. She had a feeling that he was more stubborn than she was. If she argued with him, he'd keep walking until he passed out. "Damn you, Morgan!"

"Angels ain't supposed to cuss." Rad stared down at her. "No ladies this far in the hills. You've gotta be from Heaven."

Tears burned behind her eyes. What was wrong with her? She never cried. "I'm no angel. Stop this, Morgan. Please."

"Get the horse," Rad ordered. "Man who shot me will be back."

That was a good point. Beth didn't want to take responsibility for moving Rad and endangering his life further. What if he died because he wouldn't take reasonable precautions? How would she live with herself? Then again, she didn't want somebody opening fire on them after dark. If the shooter returned, all their lives could be in jeopardy.

When he took two more steps, she made her decision. "All right. You win."

"Good one."

"I'm sure you think so." She guided him toward Tigger, measuring Rad's size and that of her small horse. She'd been right about his height and weight, six foot two and a hundred eighty pounds. There was no way the fifteen-hand Arabian could pack both of them and she wondered if the stallion would even be able to carry the man.

Feeling his weight sag on her more heavily, her knees buckled. She struggled for the strength needed to assist him in mounting Tigger. She helped Rad get his left boot in the stirrup. Before she could even try to lift him, he rested one hand on the saddle horn and the other on the cantle.

Then he swung up onto the horse's back. It was one of the most graceful maneuvers she had ever seen. Curiosity filled her. If he was this confident and self-sufficient after being wounded, what was he like in good health?

"Where's the cave?" Beth asked.

"Up the trail. On the right." Rad swayed in the saddle and then clamped his hands on the pommel. "Never say whoa in a bad place. Move out, missy."

"Yes, sir!"

THREE

"Friday the 13th, a Guardian may use Her Power to find what she truly seeks before the Midnight Hour....!"

RULES OF CHRONOS

Friday, April 13th, 1888

HE DIDN'T ANSWER. DID HE THINK SHE WAS TRYING TO BE POLITE? No, he couldn't be that stupid, could he? When she looked at him, she discovered he'd lost consciousness. His fingers still gripped the saddle, and she knew better than to try to get him off the horse. He'd made up his mind.

He was right about the risks they faced here, but she wished she knew more about this so-called cave. The hills around here didn't have limestone as a base. Most of them were volcanic in nature and granite in content. However, there were several old mine shafts in the Cascades and long ago the area had been famous for its silver. Rad Morgan had probably found an old shaft and camped in it.

Beth glanced at the man again. Worry wracked her. She took a step. Tigger matched it. Rad stayed in the saddle. Beth tried moving again. This time she took two steps. Rad didn't shift in his position. Had he died already?

She stepped back beside him and felt his pulse. He was alive. She forced down her fear. He was going to live. He'd made it this long and from here on in, the worst was over. At least, she prayed it was. "Okay, Tigger. We're on our own. Let's hit the road."

Tigger snorted. He gave an impatient tug on the reins and began to walk toward the path. Instead of his usual fast stride, the Arabian's pace was slow and easy, as if he knew an injured man rode him. Yet, Beth knew her horse hated wet weather too. He always fussed when she made him cross water or trek through mud. She turned him down the narrow track, leaving the huge ridge behind them.

She shoved at her leather cowboy hat, pushing it down further on her hair. Mud splattered her jeans and covered her boots. It wasn't raining now, but it'd done plenty of that earlier in the day. She should have put on the rain gear her foster father, Will bought her when he encouraged her to ride in endurance contests. Then she wouldn't get dirty. Oh well, she was washable and so were her clothes. Besides, the yellow pants and jacket always made her sweat like a pig, especially when she added the poncho.

Avoiding the question wouldn't get it answered. How was she going to leave Rad Morgan alone and go for help? She couldn't let him die, but she couldn't save him by herself either. She needed to ride somewhere she had cell reception and call the emergency rescue people. She would just have to cope until she had time to think. Tonight, she'd figure out a way to summon the paramedics.

Rocky slopes still surrounded the trail. Eventually, she found what she sought. Off to one side, there was a small opening. When she led Tigger nearer, she saw the cave Rad had spoken about. She just hoped it wasn't inhabited by man or beast. She tied Tigger to a nearby sapling, pulled out her flashlight, and went to explore. Luke took the lead, alert but not growling.

The entrance was barely four feet wide, but she'd be able to lead her horse inside. The cave turned out to be long and narrow, about half the size of the living room in her condo. A stack of firewood took up the right-hand wall. Someone, probably Rad dug a fire pit in the middle of the floor and lined it with rocks. She wondered why the place didn't fill with smoke. When she looked up to what she thought of as the ceiling, she spotted cracks in the rock that must allow the smoke to escape.

Obviously, this was Rad's home away from home. She went for her horse. Once she had the Arabian inside, she spread out her sleeping bag and blankets. She put her flashlight on a nearby rock, where it could provide some illumination. Then she grabbed Rad's wrist and gave him a gentle shake. "Morgan, wake up. We're here. I can't get you off the horse by myself."

Rad stirred. "Knew you'd do it, Miss Chambers. You're no tenderfoot."

His deep voice and compliment warmed Beth. She shook her head, trying to break his spell. She had to get her act together. "Right, Morgan. Now, bail off. I have things to do tonight."

"You're as shy as a green filly at a new waterhole."

Beth heard the amusement in his tone, but she also recognized his weakness. Despite all his talking, he was wounded. What was wrong with her? Was she losing her own self-control? She was attracted to Rad Morgan, and he could die at any moment.

His voice, his strength, his raw courage—he was more man than any she'd known in her entire thirty-four years. She felt as if she could drown in his blue eyes and listen to his lazy drawl for the rest of her life. Wait a minute! After listening to her foster father's constant lectures, she'd given up hanging out at the local cowboy bar, looking for a guy to keep her warm at night. Sex and alcohol dulled the memories of combat.

Since she'd begun spending more time with Tigger at the barn, conditioning him for the summer competitions, she hardly dated anymore. *Grow a brain. Help Rad Morgan live, and then you can jump his bones.*

Aloud, she said. "Come on, Morgan. I'll help you get into bed. Then you can sleep while I set up camp." No sooner had she gotten Rad Morgan off her horse than he fainted again.

Beth swore. She managed to half carry, half drag him to her sleeping bag, but he remained a collapsed hunk of manhood. She still had to take off his clothes. Amusement replaced her initial annoyance. It'd probably be easier to undress him when he was unconscious.

She knelt beside him and unfastened his jacket, easing it off his broad shoulders. Next came his shirt. Beth caught her breath at the sight of his wide, muscled chest that tapered down to a narrow waist. A V-shaped mat of black, curly hair teased and tempted her fingers, but she stuck to business. She unwrapped the bandage on his ribs to check for broken bones.

Damn, he had a great body. He was intelligent, and he radiated sex appeal. Why did he have to be hurt? Because if he weren't, Beth told herself sternly, she'd make a total fool of herself.

Wake up and smell the coffee, Chambers. He's hurt and he needs a nurse, not a horny cop who hasn't been laid in almost a year. That last time would have been better by yourself.

She glanced at his face. The dark blue eyes were still closed. High cheekbones, a blade of a nose that had been broken at least once, and a strong jaw with a sprinkle of beard stubble made him even more appealing. He wasn't a pretty boy, but what Will would have called, a man's man. She suspected he would have approved of Rad Morgan and the guy's attempts to take care of her.

Focus on the job at hand, Chambers. She checked the bandages on the sucking chest wound. They had held up well on the short trip to the cave. When she listened, she couldn't hear the horrible whistling, sucking sound that meant Rad Morgan's lung leaked air.

She breathed a sigh of relief. The classes she'd taken in the military and the experience she'd gained as an Army medic in

Afghanistan hadn't deserted her. So far, the man was alive, and she prayed he'd stay that way.

She unbuckled the gunbelt around his narrow waist and decided to examine the pistol later. It looked like an old Colt .45, an incredibly old model. A blush scorched its way into her cheeks as she unbuttoned his faded, mud-soaked jeans. She stripped the pants down to his boots, trying to keep her attention on the task, not on Rad's beautiful body.

Finally, she gave up the battle with her conscience and looked. His long red underwear didn't disguise any of his attributes. He was a big man.

After she finished taking off Rad's clothes, she tucked him into the sleeping bag and covered him with the extra blankets. She left him his long johns for modesty, not just his, but also hers. She spread out the jeans on a rock to dry, put his socks and boots nearby.

Crossing to Tigger, she quickly removed the saddlebags, then unfastened the Western saddle. She might need it to prop Rad up on his wounded side.

The idea seemed barbaric, but the Army taught her that if a lung-shot patient lay prone, his good lung could fill up with blood and he'd choke to death before he could be evac'd to the closest hospital. She had to keep Rad in a sitting position or make sure he stayed on his right side. She hoped it'd be easier than it sounded.

Beth petted Tigger's gray neck. "I don't know about this guy. Who'd turn his back on some idiot with a large caliber rifle?" Her voice trailed off, and she began to worry over the problem, the way Luke did a soup bone.

It didn't make much sense that there could be two people running around the National Forest with high-powered rifles. It fit another piece into the jigsaw puzzle making up Gary Smith's bizarre personality. For all that she was certain he was a serial killer, Beth had never discovered anything on him attacking a man.

He might have shot Rad Morgan from behind, just to get the

money. Of course, the same held true for the bank robbers Rad claimed to have pursued into the high country.

Beth sighed and lifted off the saddle. "Now, I have two leads I can't follow, Tigger. We've got to get help and have Morgan in the hospital ASAP."

Rad stirred at the sound of his name. "Doc Jenkins is in Junction City. That's more than a day's ride from here."

Beth glanced at the wounded man and hoped her tone didn't sound totally exasperated. "Is it still eighteen-ninety, Morgan?"

"Course not!" Rad's voice faded as he drifted back toward sleep.

Beth relaxed. "You'll be fine, now that you know what year it is."

"It's 1888."

"Bull!" Frustrated beyond human endurance, Beth led her horse out of the cave. An hour later, she was through with Tigger and Luke. The Arabian had been grained and groomed before she left him tethered outside. Luke prowled the perimeter. The two of them had taken out their share of criminals before the dog was shot that last time by a drug pusher. The serious injury forced the German Shepherd's early retirement. Although Luke recovered most of his strength, the Sheriff's Department hadn't wanted to push the issue, so Beth kept him at home. If anything or anyone came close, the animals would raise the alarm.

Meanwhile, Rad Morgan still slept. His pulse was strong. So was his breathing. Beth was almost positive he would live. She wished she had a guarantee, but she'd settle for a telephone that worked. Tomorrow, she'd ride out and try to get cell service. Then, she'd call in the help Morgan needed. She hadn't expected to find someone in dire straits, but she'd done the best she could, and she knew most of the detectives at the precinct wouldn't have been able to save Morgan.

Beth placed more wood on the fire. While it crackled into a good blaze, she opened a can of stew and made a pot of coffee. Then she went to check on Rad Morgan. He still slept, and she smoothed the blankets over him. He didn't stir, and she knelt beside him till she heard his next breath. He'd be okay. He had to be.

Slowly, she stood and crossed to where she'd left the gear from her horse. She peeled off her shortened poncho, carefully lifting it over her shoulder holster and personal weapon. She'd left the department-issued Sig Sauer in her locker at the precinct, but the pink Glock 17 she carried used .9mm rounds. If she had to shoot someone, she wanted that person to drop and stay down.

Rolling her shoulders, she put the now modified, much shorter poncho over a rock to dry, placing her hat beside it. She shrugged out of her black windbreaker and put the jacket near the poncho. She shook out her tent and went to hang the plastic over the channel to the outside. It'd help block some of the cold and allow the fire to heat the cave as much as possible.

Finally, there was time for her. Red-gold curls tumbled halfway down her back. Beth raked a hand through the tangles, pushing her hair off her face. One reason she wasn't taken seriously at work was her naturally curly hair. Another was what Will referred to as an *hourglass* figure. No matter how much she dieted, she never matched what society considered attractive.

Granted, when she was stressed, she junked out on chocolate. Will told her she was ravishing, but he had the typical father's prejudice. *Let it go.* She didn't have to be her own worst enemy. She had Gary Smith for that.

———

Rifle in hand, he'd stormed down the trail, bypassing the dog. He'd hit it with a rock, then slit its throat, and left the body to torment its owner. He'd meant to kill the horse, mentally drawing an X from each ear to the opposite eye and then planting a bullet dead center, but he'd intended for the woman to escape. Seeing her pinned under the dead stallion, he cursed.

Eight bad days in a row, beginning when she brought him in for questioning about the death of that whore. Somebody had to clean human trash off the streets. He should get a medal, not be thrown in jail with more scum. When he was set free to continue his work, he was interrupted with his next sacrifice.

And now this! He'd meant to take his time with the snotty detective, to enjoy cutting her to pieces before he killed her for daring to challenge him.

She'd died far too easy.

Blood covered her face. He saw her head, and neck, one hand, but the rest of her was pinned under the horse, crushing her body into the muddy trail. How could he shift the gray stud off her? Was there a way to lift a thousand-pound carcass off the woman? He shook his head. He couldn't free her from under the gray stallion or teach her the lesson she so obviously needed to learn. He contemplated crawling through the mud, close enough to cut out her tongue, his signature, but what was the point?

She was dead. She couldn't suffer or silently scream while he tortured her.

Frustrated, he turned. There were other women. He'd find one to take the cop's place. He'd done it before. He could do it again.

FOUR

"On the 13th day, in the light of the red moon, a Guardian's Power will last beyond the next noon...."

RULES OF CHRONOS

IT MUST BE A DREAM. THE LAST THING RAD CLEARLY REMEMBERED was lying in the dirt, bleeding to death. Now, he was warm. He hurt, but the agony that sliced through him with every breath was gone. He opened his eyes and recognized the cave he kept stocked as a halfway point between Junction City and the logging town of Portage. How had he managed to make it here?

He propped up on an elbow and looked around the dimly lit cave, smelling wood smoke.

Then he saw her!

She sat next to the fire, combing her hair. It was the same golden-red as the flames. He wondered if the hair warmed a man the way a fire did. He smiled when he thought of her sharp tongue, quick and mean for him, gentle and soft for the animals.

She wore a dark green shirt tucked into her pants and he wondered why she chose a shoulder holster for her pistol. Most folks opted for a gunbelt around their hips. He watched her finish braiding her hair and then pin it into a bun on top of her head. She was probably as surprised as he was to find someone out here in the middle of nowhere. He couldn't control the coughing a moment longer. He choked and tasted blood.

The woman jumped to her feet when she heard him. She slid one last pin into her hair as she crossed to him. "How do you feel?" She dropped to her knees beside him and pressed a hand to his forehead. "I wish my first-aid kit had an infrared thermometer. Then we'd know if you were running a fever."

"Isn't one yet." Rad couldn't recall how long it had been since a lady touched him. "I forgot your name."

"Beth Chambers. I found you on the trail."

"I'm shot, Miss Chambers, not stupid. I know where I was. It was no place for a lady. What are you doing out here by yourself?"

"I told you. I'm looking for someone, and I'll bet he's the one who shot you."

"That's right." He began to cough. "I remember now."

Beth rose to her feet and returned with an empty can. "Use this," she said. "It'll work as a spittoon."

While he coughed and spat up blood, she went to the back of the cave and gathered up her canteen as well as a small towel. She helped him rinse out his mouth and then let him wipe his face with the damp cloth. "Now, that you're awake, I'm going to lay out the ground rules."

"Say, please."

"What?"

"If you *ask* me, I'm liable to do most anything." He levered up so he could sit with his back to the rock wall. "You tell me, and we'll lock horns."

She planted her hands on her hips. "I saved your life, you arrogant, egotistical—"

"And now you're insulting me. I'm not the man to take it, Miss Chambers."

The flat statement earned him a long look before she nodded. "All right, Marshal Morgan." Her tone was sweet, too sweet. "This may come as a surprise, but somebody shot you—"

She was spunky and obviously had no intention of backing down. Amused by the notion, he shook his head. "I've known mules less stubborn."

She considered him in silence, then a smile dawned in her dark green eyes. "You're smarter than you look, Morgan." She paused again. "Let's compromise. You don't treat me like a brainless idiot because I'm a woman and I won't treat you like one because you're a man."

She wasn't very polite, but at almost forty-three, he'd been up the hill and over the mountain as the saying went. He'd take what he could get. "That's fine, ma'am."

"Okay. Well, first things first. Whoever shot you was behind you and on higher ground."

He coughed, spat into the can. "How do you know?"

"The angle of the bullet's penetration. I've seen a lot of gunshot wounds and I'm sure Gary Smith shot you. There probably aren't two men with high-powered rifles like his out here."

"Smith's a common name." Rad frowned, as he remembered the horse-thief who eluded him a few years back. "What's this fella look like?"

"He's mine." Beth held up a hand. "We'll talk about him later. There's a small entry hole in your back, but the bullet exited through your lung."

"And you're talking all around the subject, but I'm gonna die, aren't I?"

"Everybody dies, Morgan. The only question is when."

"I'm coughing up blood," Rad said. "That will kill me."

"Suck it up, will you? Whiners irritate me."

"I'm not whining. Men die if they're lung-shot."

"I wasn't there to save them," Beth said. "Granted, I'd like it better if I could get you out of here tonight to the nearest hospital, but it's not happening. You'll live unless you snivel at me too much. In that case, I might lose my temper and shoot you myself."

"No, you won't." She wanted to get a rise out of him, but he wouldn't give her the satisfaction. "You'd have left me to die if you were that kind of lady."

She glared at him. "You're going to be fine, Morgan. You'll be coughing up blood for the next few days, but I sealed your injured lung, and it will heal. There was a lot of blood. That would have scared anyone—"

"Not you." He grinned at her. "You'd fight bear with a stick."

"I'd win too." She folded her arms and eyed him sternly. "There will be infection and pain, but I have pills to thwart that until the Search and Rescue folks arrive."

He wasn't sure who she expected to come, but he wasn't about to tell her that they were on their own. Nobody except his best friend, the mayor of Junction City knew about this cave, and Connor was miles from here. As for Rad's younger brother, Kyle was fresh from the East. It was all the boy could do to saddle a horse by himself. Finding the back trail to Portage was beyond him.

Rad closed his eyes. He heard footsteps, boots on the rock before she knelt beside him. "What is it?" he asked.

"Marshal Morgan, you have to lie on your wounded side. Otherwise, your good lung will fill with blood, and you'll choke to death. Can you do it?"

"As long as I don't start a fever. You got pills for that too?"

"Yes, but you don't need them yet." She started to stand, but he couldn't let her leave him. Not yet. He caught her wrist.

"Let go of me," she ordered.

"No." He didn't open his eyes. He leaned against the wall and enjoyed the way she smelled. Soap, flowers, and rain-washed woman. He wished he had the strength to kiss her, but that would have to wait. "Stay here."

"What? Are you crazy? Feverish?"

He felt her hand on his forehead. "Doesn't say much for me or you, if I have to be sick or *loco* to want you close."

"You're grateful because I saved you. It wasn't a big deal."

"It was to me." He tightened his hold on her wrist so she couldn't escape while he slept. "Just not halter-broke. I'll see about that when I'm on my feet."

―――

"Damned stupid cowboy." Beth tried for what seemed like the millionth time to pry his fingers from her wrist. She paused and brushed the lock of black hair off his forehead. She couldn't believe that he decided to hold onto her because she saved his life. Talk about cupboard love.

He'd have to get that idea out of his head before help arrived. The other detectives would never let her hear the end of this contretemps. A smile teased her lips as she wondered how many times he'd been shot and saved by other women. Maybe, he had a harem already, a half-dozen sister-wives.

The frivolous thought cheered her, and she laughed. "You're such a jerk, Morgan." She adjusted her legs, changing her position beside him. All she had to do was wait for him to wake up, and then she'd be free.

An hour later, he woke as suddenly as he'd dropped off and she stared into the navy-blue eyes, so close to her own. Her pulses jump-started into life, and she shook her head. She lifted her chin, hoped she sounded more in control than she felt. "Let go of me."

"Don't worry. I've never broken any filly's spirit. I won't break yours."

"You're delusional." She jerked out of his grip, fully aware that he'd loosened his hold. "Bastard," she muttered. "Allow me to tell you what's going to happen when you're healthy, Morgan." She went over to the fire, added more wood to the blaze. "You're going to the hospital and if you keep up the loony-tunes act, you'll be in the mental ward."

"Ladies don't cuss." His deep voice held a warning. "Of course, if you keep doing it, that means I don't have to treat you like one."

"Don't do me any favors, Morgan. I'm a detective, not a lady."

"No reason you can't be both." He glanced at the fire and changed the subject. "What's for dinner?"

Beth blinked. She was still annoyed with him, and he wanted something to eat? That was a particularly good sign, and she shouldn't be yelling at an injured man. "I made stew and there's coffee. Can you manage that? Or shall I fix some soup?"

A faint grin tugged at the edges of Rad's mouth. "Reminds me of my brother. Any time something happens, he makes soup. And I could eat a horse. Where's yours?"

Beth couldn't help smiling at his weak joke, amazed he was in such good humor. Most men would have been moaning in pain and demanding she find a doctor out in the middle of the National Forest. His raw courage was admirable and the last of her irritation faded.

"Does that mean you want soup or something stronger? I'll warn you now I never bring liquor into the woods."

Rad studied her warily. "Reckon, I didn't ask, Miss Chambers. I wouldn't expect you to, but I could eat more than soup."

"Okay." Beth began to dish up the stew. Behind her, she heard him struggling to rise. "Wait a minute and I'll help you. It took long enough to stop the bleeding last time. I don't want it to start up again. By the way, did you see who shot you? Was it a short man with graying hair? Was he riding a palomino Appy stallion?"

"Miss Chambers, there aren't any Appaloosas in this country except for mine and Burdette's. The Army killed them all."

Beth frowned at the stew she was serving. "Bull, Morgan. I've listened to a lot of breeders, and I know the breed is restored. Granted, I wouldn't ride an Appy on a bet. The damned things have every conformation flaw known to man. I prefer a horse that looks like one."

Carrying the bowl of stew, she went back to him. She put the bowl to one side and helped him sit up. "If you don't want to tell me about Smith, that's fine. I'll track him on my own after I get you some help."

"How are you going to do that? The nearest place is Burdette's and most of the Lazy B hands will be hunting those bank robbers."

She sighed and picked up the bowl again. "Are you still telling the same story, Morgan? It's the middle of the Dark Ages in America, not the twenty-first century?"

"It's 1888." He accepted her help in eating. "How'd you make this when you didn't have time to hunt or roust up vegetables?"

She laughed. "It's canned. I don't cook. I don't need the aggravation."

"Guess you'd better learn. A man can die from canned food."

"Only if it's not done right." She steadied his hand as he dipped the spoon in the stew. "And I already told you that I'm not staying with you. I'll find help tomorrow and we'll have you taken to the nearest hospital."

"I'm not letting you go."

She tossed her head. "It's not your decision, Morgan. It's mine. The last thing I need is a man. I've got a fireplace that smokes, a dog that whines, a door that creaks, and an electric blanket to keep me warm. I like my freedom."

"You should have thought of that before you saved me, Miss Chambers. It's too late now. If I live, I'll probably have to marry you even if neither of us likes it."

"Morgan, stop it. Nobody is going to care if we spend tonight in a cave. Besides, tomorrow I'll find a way to call in the Park Rangers." She helped him finish the stew. "Do you want some coffee?"

"In a minute." He closed his hands over her shoulders and drew her toward him. "You sure are pretty."

"Back off, Morgan." She didn't want to hurt him, but there was no way she'd let him do this. When she attempted to pull free, his grip tightened, and his hands slowly shifted toward her neck.

She relaxed for an instant and then tried to yank away. To her surprise, she couldn't break his hold. One hand tipped up her chin and she glared into his face. "If Smith hadn't shot you, I would. Don't think you'll get away with this."

He chuckled and feathered his thumb over her lips. "And you say you ain't a lady."

She waited for the kiss, her pulses thudding. She could have freed herself if she weren't so concerned about not hurting him. Yeah, right. Maybe, she really didn't want to be free from his touch. "Morgan, don't."

He kissed her chin, then with deliberate slowness, he released her.

She stared into his face for a moment, before backing out of reach. "I thought you—" Her voice trailed off as she saw the knowing expression on his face. If he hadn't been injured, she would have thrown something at him, or she'd have thrown him out of the cave.

His mouth eased into a lazy grin. "Figured I'd hold off till I could do a lot more."

She tossed her head. "You'll wait till hell freezes over and the devil has a skating party."

"Ladies don't cuss." He glanced at the fire. "Reckon, I'll have to teach you that when I'm on my feet. How about a cup of coffee?"

She raised her chin and glared at him. "Only if you keep your hands to yourself. I don't like being pawed."

"You look like a wildcat with your eyes narrowed like that." His voice held admiration. "Does it scare them boys you know? Or did one of those fancy men in Seattle teach you to purr?"

The mocking question sent heat flooding into Beth's cheeks. Just because she'd stopped doing superficial sleepovers didn't mean she was frigid as John Watkins, the last cop she'd dated claimed. She wasn't a total innocent either, not after ten years in the Army and six in law enforcement. She'd lost her virginity in high school and that hadn't been a big deal either, only a rite of passage on Prom night. "Go to hell, Morgan."

Rad chuckled. "Telling a man to go, and making him do it are two different things, wildcat. I'll be the one to teach you to purr."

FIVE

"To fulfill Her chosen tasks, the Goddess will provide the Guardian with new talents when she asks…"

RULES OF CHRONOS

PURE FURY RACED THROUGH HER. BEFORE SHE ENGAGED IN another battle of wits with him, she spun and stormed from the cave into the night. It'd serve him right if she left him to live or die on his own. What a macho, arrogant, condescending jerk! She wouldn't allow herself to think about the way his smile lit up his features or how his dark blue eyes twinkled or the way his gentle touch had made her feel as if her backbone was melting.

Once out in the brisk April night, she found her usual calm returning. Granted she had a quick temper and little patience for fools, but she tried hard to control her emotions. She rarely displayed her feelings, and in the past few days, it had happened far too many times. First, she'd allowed her anger to push her into this suicidal hunt for Smith.

She still remembered the lieutenant's scornful voice when he demanded, "Who do you think you are, Chambers? Jane Wayne? What are you going to do, capture Smith in the high country? Will you get serious? You've contacted the RCMP and the Border Patrol. You've put the word out to local law enforcement, the Sheriff's Departments throughout the entire state, and the feds. Let other people do their jobs for once. Don't be stupid. Smith will get tired of hiding in the woods. He'll come back to civilization, and someone will arrest him. It doesn't have to be you. While he's out of the picture, work your other cases."

Smith would be back, Beth thought. To hunt again. To rape and murder. She hadn't been about to argue with her boss. If she had, he'd never have given her the time she needed to find Gary Smith. She didn't want to think about what the lieutenant would say when the first responders came into the woods to evac Morgan. There'd be more hell to pay.

She reached into her shirt pocket and pulled out the somewhat crumpled pack of cigarettes. She took one from the pack and lit her first smoke of the evening. Then she drew a deep puff of tobacco into her lungs. The cigarette eased her jangled nerves. She had to analyze the situation and find a solution.

Regardless of what Morgan said, the best place for him was a hospital. Of course, since he seemed to be hiding from society, it made sense he'd argue about medical treatment. She wouldn't be surprised if he thought the two of them could make it without a doctor. She'd bet it had been a long time since he'd seen a woman. No wonder, he claimed it was 1888, and she had to stay with him.

That brought back the question of who had shot him. Beth wondered if Smith really attempted to murder Morgan. He was enough to drive a saint to drink and she was far from that. Maybe he knew his assailant and all this garbage he spouted was to keep her off-track. It was a good thing she'd chosen to have a few moments to herself. She needed to collect her thoughts and regain her composure. Now, she could interrogate him and discover what he knew about the shooting incident. It was past time to show Rad Morgan *who* was in charge.

Why had he been shot? Had he stumbled on something in the National Forest that he shouldn't have seen? Beth took another puff from her smoke as she considered that idea. She remembered hearing from the Vice detectives that marijuana had been planted in the area and that it was even more protected than the legendary stills had been. Perhaps, Rad interfered with a would-be drug lord.

Then again, it could have been an argument over a poached deer, but few people would kill for that. Usually, the hunters would simply split the meat to avoid a controversy that might drag in the law. Of course, there were stills around the small town of Pine Valley. Even if Prohibition had ended long ago, it didn't make the moonshine legal, and *Everclear*, the homemade whisky was an ongoing problem. She hadn't even considered the possibility that he might have stumbled across a meth lab, although out here in the National Forest that was a bit farfetched.

Beth frowned as she finished her cigarette. She simply could not come up with a good reason for anyone to shoot Rad Morgan. Nothing truly fit the circumstances except Gary Smith was in the area and she knew she was prejudiced where the suspected killer was concerned. She'd rather believe that Smith had something to do with this than try to come up with another explanation.

Stubbing out her cigarette on her bootheel, Beth dropped the filter in her shirt pocket. She'd have to demand some answers from Rad and make sure he didn't sidetrack her by pretending not to know the year. She'd never let a man get the better of her when she was in the Army or the sheriff's department. There was no point in starting now.

"Miss, would you mind coming in here? It's not safe to wander around at night." Rad's deep voice interrupted her thoughts.

Beth reached for another cigarette. "Get some rest, Morgan. I'll be fine. I just want to check my horse and have a smoke."

"There's bears and Indians. At least come get your rifle. That pea shooter of yours won't kill a grizzly."

"Morgan, shut up!" Beth lit her cigarette. She hastily continued, trying to squelch her guilt. He was an injured man, and she should be kind to him. However, her patience was at the breaking point. "Go to sleep. Now!"

There was silence for a moment, then he drawled, "Reckon, you already know that ladies don't smoke. You need to learn manners, Miss Chambers, and I'm the man to teach 'em."

"Don't push your luck, Morgan." She stalked away from the mouth of the cave to stand under a cedar and watched the soft rain drift by her. The damp, cold mist brushed over her face, but the moisture didn't bother her. She saw a few white flakes and wondered if he was right about snow.

It was mid-April and that meant spring, didn't it? She sighed and shook her head. They were higher in the hills, but that didn't mean more than a light dusting of snow tonight. She'd been born and raised in Washington state and most of the natives on the wet side of the Cascades bragged about their webbed feet.

A smile tugged at her lips as she remembered Will's claim that Washingtonians didn't tan, they rusted. Her foster father had been a staunch supporter of *Lesser Washington*, even before the anti-growth groups. He always complained bitterly when more newcomers arrived from California or elsewhere.

She cupped the cigarette in her hand, so the glowing end couldn't be seen. Once again, she wished Will were here. If the old man had been, she could have trusted him to look after Rad while she went for help. As things were, she had nobody to depend upon but herself.

What was new about that? She'd been taught a long time ago not to count on others and then she was never disappointed. She frowned thoughtfully. Had Morgan learned the same lesson? Maybe that was the real reason he'd headed for the high country.

Will had several friends, other Vietnam veterans who hid out from the world in the woods. Morgan might be a survivalist freaking out from what he'd seen in combat. She'd served in the nation's longest war. He could have too. She always headed for the hills when her world got crazy, especially around the Fourth of July. Now, why hadn't she thought of that before?

She finished her smoke and went through the process of field-stripping the butt. She allowed the last of the tobacco to fall on the ground and then placed the filter as well as the paper in her pocket. She didn't leave a mess for other people to clean up. That was one of her rules for dealing with life.

She heard a soft rumble from Luke as she walked toward where she'd tethered the Arabian stallion. The dog's warning caused her to pause for an instant. She started to reach for her pistol, but there was no point in trying to shoot after dark. She couldn't remember seeing a night this black in a long time, not even in Afghanistan. Of course, she hadn't been camping in months, not since last November when she hid out from football season and the neighbors who shot off fireworks whenever the Seattle Seahawks scored.

Reaching down, she drew her favorite knife from the scabbard in her boot. Then she inched forward again. Comfort stole through her as Luke pressed against her side. She felt more than heard his growl this time. Approaching Tigger, she whispered, "Easy, son. You know it's us."

The Arabian snorted and nuzzled at her. She froze as she heard an answering whicker. What the hell? Who else was here? Did someone else know about the cave? Smith? She wished she'd gone back for her rifle. That carbine could do a lot of damage. The low whinny was repeated, and she realized it was coming from the thick salmonberry bushes. She took a cautious step toward them.

Suddenly, a black horse's head pointed out of the bushes and Beth saw a white blaze. She relaxed as she remembered that the stolen horse was a pale yellow. He would appear almost white after dark. This dark horse wore a leather bridle and the reins dragged on the ground. "Easy, love." Beth kept her voice soft, so she wouldn't spook the newcomer.

Taking one step forward and then another, she caught the soggy reins. She led the horse into the small pool of firelight that spilled from the cavern entrance. The light revealed a beautiful, black Appaloosa mare. Her hindquarters were white with a lovely pattern of black spots. Her dark legs ended in white socks and Beth had never seen such perfect conformation. The mare was almost as graceful as Tigger, but she was about six inches taller than the stallion and at least three hundred pounds heavier. She stood quietly while Beth put away her knife.

She caressed the ebony neck. "Aren't you pretty? But what did you do with your rider?" Touching the mare's neck again, Beth stiffened as her hand came away from a sticky, somewhat slimy substance. Blood! Was the mare hurt?

All at once, Beth's thoughts coalesced into order. Rad said he was riding an Appy. He'd been shot and fallen off his horse. The blood was probably his, not the mare's, but Beth's concern remained. She had to make sure that the horse was okay.

She removed the saddle. It was covered with more blood, adding proof to the theory that this was Rad's horse. Beth dragged the saddle into the opening of the cave and glanced toward the man. He leaned against the rock wall, his eyes closed. "Are you asleep, Morgan?"

No answer and she heaved a sigh. "Men."

She wouldn't be able to learn anything from him until he awakened. She went after her flashlight and returned to the mare to look for injuries. Other than a few patches of blood, the black Appaloosa seemed fine. When Beth inspected the bloody areas more carefully, she discovered the mare was uninjured.

Obviously, her rider had been hurt, not the horse. With that problem solved, Beth concentrated on grooming and feeding the new arrival. A pair of hobbles was attached to Rad's saddle, and she used them to secure the Appy near Tigger, a situation that pleased both equines.

When she reentered the cave, Rad was apparently still asleep. She should go over and help him lie down, but that might wake him. Instead, she'd search the saddle first. After she learned everything she could from his belongings, she'd take care of the man.

The saddle was almost as battered as hers. It had a huge horn and Beth knew that meant Rad was into roping. He'd claimed to have a ranch and men seemed to think dragging cattle around by brute force was a lot of fun. Her gaze fell on the long rope attached to the right side of the saddle. Beth ignored the rope when she spotted the rifle. It was an antique Winchester. "Wow." She wondered if she could convince Rad to trade it for her carbine. The rifle ought to be hanging on a museum wall, not inside a scabbard.

She turned her attention to the second pair of leather bags that hung on top of another set of saddlebags. The top set of bags was stuffed with money, both gold, and paper. She drew out one of the bills. The note was drawn on the First Bank of Junction City, dated 1887, and signed by Trace Burdette, bank president.

Beth stared at the banknote. Junction City? Where was that? She knew most of Snohomish County but didn't remember a town with that name. A bank that printed its own money – how could that be legal? She pulled out a second note. This one was dated 1886 and again signed by Trace Burdette. The signatures weren't identical but looked remarkably similar. Beth was almost certain that the same person approved both bills.

Was Rad Morgan correct? Had she traveled back in time?

"Get it together, Chambers." She pushed the note into the bag and pulled out a coin. It looked like real gold. Was she in a dream? No, all of this had to be part of Rad's delusion and somehow there had to be an explanation. She simply didn't know what it was yet.

Putting away the money, Beth studied the bedroll. It was a layer of blankets inside a canvas tarp. Interesting. Why hadn't Rad brought a sleeping bag? One of those would be much more compact than the blankets. She'd have to ask him.

Beth searched the other set of saddlebags. They contained extra ammunition for the rifle and his pistol. There were two empty burlap bags and she wondered how he'd planned to use them. She found a beat-up coffee pot and a sack of Arbuckle's coffee. Cans of beans, a slab of unrecognizable meat, and what looked like small gray, powdery rocks wrapped in paper took up what remained of the space.

"That's my gear," Rad said. "Did you find Nell? Is she all right?"

"Nell's your horse?" When he nodded, she smiled. "Then she's fine. She must have tracked us here. I didn't have time to look for her."

"She does follow me around a lot." Rad closed his eyes for a moment. "She likes biscuits. Did you find some for her?"

"No." She eyed the gray rocks again. "Not unless these are them." She held up one of the hard, powdery lumps again, and broke off a piece. "I can't believe you feed these to a poor, unsuspecting horse. What did you do? Forget the baking powder?"

"I thought you said you couldn't cook?"

She laughed. "Correction. I said I don't cook." She put the biscuit down and rose to her feet. "Are you tired? Would you like some help lying down?"

"I'd like some coffee first."

"Okay." She crossed to her own bags and removed a ceramic cup. Will had always told her that she ought to carry a tin one to be authentic, but metal absorbed the heat and she hated burning herself. The cup claimed, *"A Woman's place is in the House, the Senate, and the Oval Office."*

It ought to get his attention, she thought. *Or would he still insist it was only 1888?*

Before she returned to the fire and filled the cup, she heard the warning yip from Luke, followed by the low, rumble of his growl. She dropped the cup back in her bag, whirled to face the front of the cave. She slipped her pistol from its shoulder holster. "Morgan, your Colt is by your left hand. Get it."

"Why?" Rad asked, but he obeyed the instructions.

"Company." Beth started for the opening to the cave. "Smith shot you, he could have followed your mare—"

She stopped as she heard the crunch of footsteps on gravel. Instead of lunging for the only entrance, she moved against the side of the cave and into the shadows cast by the wall. Bullets ricocheted off the rock. *Bluff*, she thought.

"Keep messing with my horse and I'm gonna blow your guts into next week," Rad called. He didn't sound injured, just mean, and threatening.

She realized he tried to lure their visitor into a trap and admired the strategy. The footsteps paused on the gravel for a moment and then moved toward the cave. "I'm comin' in."

She didn't recognize the voice. At least it wasn't Gary Smith. She still didn't have any idea who had spoken, but she hoped it was a local person. Then she could send him for help while she stayed with Rad, or vice-versa. Before she asked if he knew their visitor, she saw the shadowy form of a man with a gun in his hand.

She raised her own weapon. "Drop it! Now!"

Her voice cracked like a whip and the stranger faltered. The tone was a signal for Luke and the dog attacked in the same instant!

The German Shepherd's eighty pounds knocked the stranger back and down. She followed them out of the cave as the man landed outside in the gravel. She kicked the pistol out of his hand. "Move and I'll let him rip your throat out."

She backed up a step or two and turned to look at Rad. He was leaning against the cave, his body shaking. After being ambushed by Gary Smith, it was little wonder he was frightened, and she pasted on what she hoped looked like a comforting smile. "It's all right, Morgan. He can't hurt—"

"No ma'am." Rad wheezed, and then began to cough and choke. When he regained control, he looked at her. "It's my brother." That set off the laughter again.

Beth swore. This time she didn't satisfy herself with a mere "hell," or "damn." She used the language she'd learned in the military as well as the cop shop. It felt good to cut loose with both barrels as Will put it. When she finished airing her opinion of both men, she called Luke off Rad's brother. "Get up and go in."

"What about my gun?" the man protested. "I need it."

"The hell you do. You can go in by yourself or Luke will help you."

The stranger eyed the snarling dog beside her and then walked into the cave ahead of them. He was a broad-shouldered man, slightly taller than Beth. Blond hair curled beneath a dark cowboy hat, wet with the rain. A jagged scar ran the length of his right cheek. He wore gray pants and a ragged gray coat.

"You all right, Rad?" the stranger asked.

Rad nodded. He placed his pistol on the ground next to him. "I'd be dead if it weren't for Miss Chambers. She found me on the trail. Patched me up. Brought me here—" His voice weakened, and he began to choke.

Beth glanced at him with quick concern, and then at the man in front of her. "Who are you?"

"Kyle Morgan."

Beth signaled Luke to watch the younger Morgan and put her pistol back in its holster. She picked up the coffee cup and returned to the fire. "Two of you."

"Yes, ma'am." Kyle smiled at her with practiced charm. "Thanks for helping Rad."

"Save it," Beth ordered. "I wouldn't have left a dog where Morgan was."

"You'd be nicer to the dog." Rad choked and coughed.

"I like dogs." She glanced at him. "Morgan, just cough up the blood. Stop being such a hero. You macho types are a pain in my..."

"He's coughing up blood?" Horror filled Kyle's voice as he interrupted. His handsome face paled, a greenish tinge around his mouth.

"If you're planning to throw up, do it outside. I won't clean up after you." She carefully filled the mug with coffee. "And for heaven's sake, grow a spine. Your brother's going to be fine. Like he told you, he got shot. I bandaged him. We'll get him into the hospital tomorrow. You can stay with him, and I'll go call for help."

"Told you already." Rad spat and then began coughing again. "Doc Jenkins is days from here."

"Then, we'll find someone else," Beth said, rising to her feet. "You'll do as you're told, Morgan. I'm in charge here."

Rad spat out a mouthful of blood and glowered at her. "No, ma'am. I am."

"Not hardly." Beth glanced at Kyle. "Take off your coat. Have you eaten? There's stew on the fire. How did you get here? How did you find us?"

Kyle Morgan blinked. "You surely do have a lot of questions, ma'am."

"And they're all too tough for you." Beth moved over to sit beside Rad and help him sip the coffee. "Okay. Here's another one for you. What year is it?"

"Told you already." Rad groaned. "It's..."

"Not you." She held the cup to his lips. "Your brother." She focused on Kyle. The younger man had an easy face to read. She'd know if he was lying. "When was the last time you saw Morgan?"

"A few hours ago," Kyle answered. "It's Friday, ma'am. April 13th, 1888."

SIX

"An Unaware Guardian may be baffled at the start, as her quest unfolds, and new talents emerge when she follows her heart…"

RULES OF CHRONOS

"WHAT DID YOU SAY?" BETH STARED AT THE YOUNG MAN'S FACE. Sincerity shone in his brown eyes. He believed it was 1888. Her hand trembled, and she almost dropped the mug.

Rad caught the cup before it spilled. "I told you already. And I said it more than once."

She turned on him. "You've brainwashed him. He doesn't know what day it is."

Rad took a swallow of the coffee. "He knows, ma'am. You don't." He glanced at Kyle. "She's not from here."

"I could have told you that," Kyle said. "Her horse is too gentle for a stud. He doesn't have a scar on him." He looked down at Luke who still guarded him. "Nobody trains a dog like this one."

"Trace Burdette does," Morgan said. "Didn't you see the one stalking you at the Lazy B?"

Kyle shrugged. "Thought it was because I fed it."

"No, it's because you called out Trace…"

Beth shook her head, held up a hand. "Called out?" It sounded like a possible crime to her, one that she should know about. "What does that mean?"

"I'm never gonna hear the end of it," Kyle complained. "Rad and I met up last summer after I was told Trace had murdered him."

"And he invited Trace out into the street and darn near got both of them killed." Rad sipped more coffee. "So, when we go to the Lazy B for Sunday dinner, Trace sets one of the dogs on Kyle to watch him."

"And you don't say anything about it." Kyle squatted beside the fire and scooped stew into one of the empty mess pans. "Some lawman."

"I choose my battles," Rad drawled. "And I figure it's better to have a dog follow you around than Mac or Gruber."

"Do they work for Burdette?" Beth asked. When Rad nodded, she continued. "Would they assault your brother?"

"Assault?" Rad considered the question. "I'm fairly sure they'd just slap him around a mite. They know better than to shoot him, and if they break any of his bones or leave bruises, Trace wouldn't be happy with them, since we'd have words then."

"Good to know." Kyle settled on a rock and started to eat. Between mouthfuls, he glanced at Beth, then asked, "What's going on? Where is she from?"

"Why don't you ask me?" She stood and went after her jacket. "I'm a homicide detective assigned to the sheriff's office in Eagleville."

"Where?" Kyle asked. "There's no Eagleville around here, ma'am."

"Why me?" She slid her hand into the pocket of her jacket and pulled out the case that held her badge. The sight reassured her.

She might be in a cave with two inept survivalists who claimed they lived in the 19th century, but after three tours in combat, she could cope. She knew what day it was, and she knew where she was too.

She opened her saddlebags and removed the map, opting for the paper one rather than the GPS on her phone. Since she didn't have that "current bush" her father joked about to recharge the device, it was best to save the battery. For now, she'd cater to a few of their delusions. "Look, I don't care about your fantasies. If you want to pretend to be cowboys from the olden days, fine."

Rad and Kyle traded glances. Then Kyle said. "We've been in the hills awhile, ma'am." He silenced his older brother with a look. "What day is it, really?"

She relaxed. "Great. At least one of you has some sanity. You were right about the day, but it's April 2018, not 1888." That settled, she demanded. "Can you get out of here tonight?"

Kyle shook his head. "No, ma'am. But I'll go at first light. Will you stay with Rad?"

"I'd better go, not you. If I call into the department, we'll get help a hell of a lot faster."

"He's no hand at doctoring," Rad interrupted. "All he can do is make soup, and most times we eat at the hotel, 'cause his cooking ain't that good. I'll do better with you, ma'am."

Beth frowned thoughtfully. Rad should be all right if she only went far enough to get a signal on her cell phone. But she was responsible for him. If she left and something happened, he might die before she returned. That wasn't happening on her watch, not again.

For an instant, she remembered other injured men, bandaging them and getting them out of the battle zone. She shook her head, forced away the memories. She didn't have time to think about that now, so she wouldn't. She'd been trained to compartmentalize, first in the military and then as a cop.

She took the map and went back to where Rad sat. She gestured for Kyle to join them. "When was the last time you were out of the woods, and don't give me a lot of garbage about Junction City. I'm sure it's a nice small town, but Eagleville is closer." She paused. "Actually, once you get into Pine Valley or even Monte Cristo, there ought to be phones and radios where you can call for help."

Kyle nodded, but his gaze was on the map. Beth unfolded the topographical *Metzger* and opened it to the correct area. "Okay. We're about forty miles into the National Forest. I came in on this trail that connects Monte Cristo and Pine Valley as well as the Armstrong's ranch."

"Who are the Armstrongs?" Rad asked. "I know most folks around here. Don't recall that name."

"Nina Armstrong runs a horse rescue at the Armstrong ranch. Smith attacked her and stole one of her horses. She's my best friend, so of course, I came after him." Beth adjusted the map so all three of them could see it. "If you ride southwest, this trail will take you to Monte Cristo before dark."

"Ma'am, I don't mean to be contrary," Kyle said, "but that town isn't there. Best thing for me to do is ride across country to the Lazy B and get Trace to send for Doc Jenkins."

"Think you can find the Burdette ranch by yourself?" Rad asked.

"Sure, if you draw me a real map," Kyle said.

"This is ridiculous." She stood and stalked to the front of the cave. "I always buy the latest maps before I come into the woods, and I'm surrounded by idiots." She headed out to check the horses and regain her temper.

———

"Want me to go after her?" Kyle asked.

Rad shook his head. "No, she's not the kind who wants company when she's angry." He coughed and spat up a mouthful of blood. "She's not from here. And if folks find out..."

"They'll think we're loco or she is," Kyle said. "What are we gonna do, Rad?"

"She's here, now. And I don't know a way to get her back where she came from. It could take nigh on two weeks for you to return with help. That means I may have to marry her. I can't have folks thinking I'm the sort of a man who'd dishonor a good woman."

"Nobody in Liberty Valley would dare insult you like that."

"Not to my face, but they'd talk behind my back. They'd raise a ruckus until the town council demanded a new marshal. Even Connor and Trace wouldn't be able to rein in the hotheads who might go to the governor."

"You're always thinking, Rad. I hadn't considered that." Kyle rose to refill the coffee cup, pausing to read the words on it. "I didn't mean to be rude, but those towns ain't here, not like that map shows or like she thinks."

"I know." Rad nodded. "Go to Burdette's. Bring back Trace, Prescott, and a posse for the money. Send for Connor too. He's the justice of the peace and he can marry us if it comes to that. I'm not waiting until the preacher rides through or Father Daniel comes up from Snohomish City."

"Want Doc Jenkins?" Kyle asked. "I can fetch him and Connor."

"Nope. I won't need him." Rad coughed again. "I'll either heal up *afore* you get back or I won't. Reckon, we should talk about if I die. The Bar M is yours. When you sell it, get a good price. Don't let the loggers steal you blind. Connor can help you with that."

Kyle nodded. "What about that herd of Appys? What should I do with them?"

"Take them to Burdette. I gave Trace a colt back when I got my first horses." Rad coughed and spat up another mouthful of blood. "Trace appreciates fine stock and will take good care of mine."

"I'll sell the cattle to the Lazy B too," Kyle said, passing the cup to Rad. "They can use the meat with all the orphans who live there. I'm sorry, Rad, but I'm no rancher. I want to live back East where things are civilized."

"I know." Rad wouldn't tell Kyle what a big disappointment he was or share the hopes he'd had last summer when the younger Morgan arrived. All Kyle cared about was reading or scribbling stories into his tally book. He'd written a few articles for the Junction City newspaper but turned down the job that the editor offered.

"If I don't make it," Rad went on, "take Miss Chambers to Matt Devlin down in Snohomish City. He'll help her find that man she's hunting."

Kyle nodded. "Whatever you want, Rad. Anything else you need me to do?"

Rad glanced toward the entrance of the cave and lowered his voice. "Get to the Lazy B and don't talk to anyone but Burdette's folks."

"Why not? I may find help closer than that. The Indians will be coming up to fish the river and they like you."

"Not this time, Kyle. I didn't tell Miss Chambers, but the fellow who shot me had one of their women, a special one. She was tied up and I was cutting her loose when he shot me in the back. He left me for dead—"

"And Miss Chambers found you?"

"Nell found me first. I came off her while I was tracking him and the shaman," Rad said. "Without me, the Indians won't trust you. 'Sides, that band of no-good bank robbers will be looking for the bankroll, too."

Footsteps crunching on gravel alerted them. Kyle rose to his feet, carried the empty cup over to the fire. "I'd better look after my horse. Shall I take the first watch?"

———

"I'll do it." Beth carried a saddle inside. "I don't plan on sleeping tonight. I already took care of your horse. You'd better get some sleep. I'll wake you at dawn."

Rad chuckled. "Anyone who thinks women aren't as strong as men hasn't met you, Miss Chambers."

Beth sniffed. "I already told you. It's Detective Chambers, and as the old saying goes, 'Women who seek equality with men lack ambition.'"

Kyle pulled out a pad of paper and a stubby pencil, obviously intending to write down the quote.

She scowled at him. "Marilyn Monroe said it."

"If what you say about where you're from is true, I'm guessing she ain't been born yet, so I can use it." Kyle began to write.

Beth looked at Rad, noting that he shared her exasperation with the would-be writer. "Hello! Marilyn Monroe and she wasn't the girl next door. Whether you admit the year or not, you have to know who she was."

The two men shared a look, and then Rad said. "Sorry, ma'am. We don't know her."

Beth flung her hand up in the air. "For heaven's sake, nobody knows her now. She's dead. And stealing her words is plagiarism."

That stopped Kyle in mid-sentence. "Oh, well. Nobody but the suffragists would believe it anyway."

"Wait a hundred years." Beth crossed to where Rad was sitting. "You'd better get some rest."

Rad nodded. "Will you stay with me?"

"Until Search and Rescue gets here, and you go to the hospital," she promised. "After I arrest Gary Smith, I'll come visit you." She moved the map and helped Rad lie down, careful to keep him on his wounded side.

She sat down beside him. It'd be fun to look him up after she caught Gary Smith. She'd show Morgan how out of date his ideas were and by the time he'd had an extended stay in the hospital, he might be ready to admit that civilization had its advantages. She brushed the lock of dark hair out of his eyes, and his hand gripped her wrist.

"I'll stay here," Beth murmured.

Rad closed his eyes. "I'll make sure of that."

———

No female could be trusted. His wife taught him that. He'd let her take a class at the college, 'for fun', she'd said. Next thing he knew, she wanted a job. Then she had rights and she was going to leave him.

And take his daughter. He'd had to kill them. And when he did, he realized the disease that destroyed his family was also destroying the entire country. Women everywhere were acting as if they were as good as men. Equal pay for equal work! Hah! No woman could work as hard as a man.

Other groups he'd joined had never understood it was women who ruined society, not minorities. Women had to be stopped or they'd break down the entire system. He needed a good group of men to follow his orders.

It was too bad he had to sacrifice Rad Morgan, but the marshal would never give up the money for a higher cause. To him, there were only the established codes that the people of Junction City, Washington Territory, and the federal government created. He insisted upon following them. The lawman believed in protecting the weak. He wouldn't have understood sheep were meant to be sacrificed and blood opened doors.

She was bad. Smith knew that, had known from the moment she fled into the woods away from her husband. So, Smith circled around and followed her. He'd forgotten how sensitive people were in this time, his own time. She'd heard him, seen him, then cried out for help.

Slowly, lovingly Gary Smith stroked the nightstick, a souvenir from the first cop he killed. He glanced at the young woman, huddled and silent because of the gag that covered her mouth.

She still watched him with huge, dark eyes. A bruise mottled one cheek where he'd struck her with his club.

The men from the tribe hurried to aid her after she helped his first choice evade him. They were good men, but she didn't deserve their consideration. Next time, she'd know to obey, to come when called. Even when he silenced her, it had taken most of the day to elude the Indians. And then the marshal found them. As soon as he'd seen this girl, Morgan tried to cut her loose and send her home. He never would have believed that she was evil.

She needed to be punished for that too.

It was safe now to treat this girl the way she ought to be treated, to teach her who was boss, what a woman's place truly was.

He'd teach her. First, fear. Then, respect. And then, he'd set her free.

Drawing his favorite knife, he started toward her. He smiled when she whimpered beneath the gag. She was learning already.

————

"I'm headin' out, Rad."

Barely hearing Kyle's whisper hours later, Rad opened his eyes. Beth lay asleep, her head pillowed on his hand where it still held her wrist. He'd made it through the night. Relief washed through him.

"Be careful. Watch your back. Don't skyline yourself. Look out for those bank robbers and the fellow who shot me."

Kyle nodded in silent agreement. Then he struggled to speak. "You've been the best brother, Rad. I—"

"Tell him, you love him and then ride like hell." Beth hastily sat up. "Or did you want something to eat before you go?"

Kyle shook his head. "No ma'am, I'll leave the food for you and Rad. I'll be back as fast as I can."

"Thanks," Beth said. "We'll be waiting. Do you need my map?"

"No, ma'am." Kyle turned and strode toward the opening of the cave. "I do need you to call off your dog. He ain't too fond of me, and I want to pick up my gun."

Beth glanced at Rad, her voice barely above a whisper. "Let go of me."

"Say please." Rad taunted.

"You son-of-a...."

Rad's hold tightened and he pulled her close. "I've told you before. Watch that cussing."

SEVEN

"A Guardian's Dreams reveal possible paths she might tread. Choices meant only to guide, not orders to obey or dread..."

RULES OF CHRONOS

SHE STARED AT HIM AND MOISTENED SUDDENLY DRY LIPS. HIS mouth was inches away from hers. She trembled. What was wrong with her? She couldn't let this macho cowboy know how he made her feel. She deliberately adopted the phony sweet tone she used to insult men. She knew Rad would recognize the act, and it would irritate him. "*Please* let go of me, *Marshal* Morgan."

He smiled and lowered his head. "One day, I'll kiss you the way you should be kissed."

She raised her chin, careful not to get too near. "One of these days is close to none of these days."

"True, but this is a promise and I keep mine." His mouth touched hers, and then he released her.

She didn't move for a moment. "Is that the best you can do? You brag better than you kiss."

"It's not a brag if I know I can do it." He glanced toward the entrance of the cave, his dark blue eyes narrowed. "Tell Kyle I want to see him before he rides out."

She rose to her feet and stretched. She'd camped out several times during the past four years, since leaving the Army. Although she enjoyed being in the wilderness, she'd never grown accustomed to sleeping on hard ground, but space was limited in the saddlebags. She hadn't packed an air mattress on her horse.

"Say please," she taunted.

"All right." His deep voice lowered to an intimate tone that teased her senses. "Please tell Kyle I need him."

"That's better." She evaded Rad when he reached for her and strolled out of the cave, fighting the urge to smirk at him. Wow, she loved it when she won!

The misty rain continued in the soft gray dawn. At least, it hadn't snowed. She'd keep the fire going most of the day. It was hard to remember Rad Morgan was wounded, even with the way that he constantly lost consciousness.

Luke joined her and led the way to where Kyle saddled his strawberry roan. "Rad wants to see you before you go." Beth glanced to where she'd left the other horses. "Did you take care of our stock?"

A flush reddened Kyle's cheeks. "I forgot. I'll do it."

"No," Beth said. "I will. That will give you and Rad some privacy." She debated telling the younger Morgan to trade off his horse for a new ATV, then changed her mind.

She'd wait until he returned with help and then she'd buy the horse. She frowned when she saw several scrapes and scratches on the gelding's shoulders. She rubbed his blazed face. "What happened to him?"

Kyle shifted, obviously uncomfortable at the censure in her tone. "We had to do some brush-popping yesterday to find Rad's trail. We ran into some devil's club."

The poisonous plant was best avoided. Large maple-shaped leaves dripped thorns and so did the stalks. Devil's club grew in patches. She'd found out the hard way how it burned the skin when she was a girl. Even now, the memory of those days when her arm swelled, ached, and throbbed made her heart hurt for the injured animal. "You washed out the cuts, got rid of the thorns, right?"

"There wasn't time." Kyle shrugged. "He'll be all right. He's just a horse."

She glanced at the bright red horse. His flaxen mane and tail had been a mess of tangles when she tried to groom him the night before. He'd tried kicking her when she cleaned his hooves. He was part Appaloosa. She could tell by the white hairs and peacock black spots on his rump. His light blue eyes and pinned-back ears gave him an evil appearance. "Go help your brother. I'll doctor your horse."

Thirty minutes later, Kyle swung into the saddle. The strawberry roan had tried to bite him when he mounted, swishing his tail, and stomping his front hooves. Kyle ignored the gelding's temper tantrum. "I'm sorry about your friend, ma'am."

Beth nodded. "Thanks. I worry about her. She's like a sister—"

He glanced at the cave. "I know how you feel. You'll take good care of Rad for me."

Kyle's tone made it a statement, not a question and she nodded again. She watched him ride away, his Appaloosa bucking the first fifty feet down the trail. She didn't blame the horse. The younger man said the right things, but obviously didn't consider animals had feelings. "When we see him again, Luke, you get to chew Kyle into little doggie pieces."

Luke growled in what she took as agreement and she petted him. Then she went to take care of Tigger and Nell. The rain-washed air tasted cleaner than it had in her memories last winter.

Sun broke through the clouds. Golden daylight gleamed off the evergreens, larger than any she recalled seeing. Sunbeams danced off the clear water in the small stream only a short distance away. She stopped at the creek first to splash the icy liquid on her face.

Next time, she'd have to bring a towel from the cave, but for now, her shirt sleeve sufficed.

Beth froze when she saw deer approaching. As the two young does came nearer, she stepped back to allow the visitors free access to the water and pulled out her digital camera to take a picture. Even after the deer had left, she could see their bounding movements. Next time she came into the woods, she'd have to bring her sketchbook.

She must be higher in the foothills than she usually rode. If the animals were accustomed to being hunted, they wouldn't have come so close to her. Tigger's impatient whistle gained her attention and she obediently turned in his direction. She had to water and take care of both horses. They were the only transport out of here until Kyle returned with help. She'd stop at the next town and restock her supplies.

Otherwise, Tigger would be stuck eating brush when the grain was gone. She hadn't planned on feeding two horses, but it wasn't Morgan's fault. He hadn't planned on being one of Smith's victims either.

She unfastened Tigger from the huge cedar and led him to the brook. When she called Nell, the mare followed them. Resting a hand on the Arabian's shoulder, Beth waited while he drank his fill. It took several minutes with the gray stallion testing the wind every few minutes.

She looked over the terrain once more and her smile widened as she recognized it. All this virgin timber meant she was in the middle of Mount Baker National Forest. No wonder Gary Smith managed to elude pursuit. From her frequent camping trips during the past three years, she was familiar with the few trails that honeycombed the vast acreage of evergreens, lakes, hills in the scenic Cascade Mountains.

She gasped when she saw a lazy bald eagle circle in the sky. The huge birds loved fish and could usually be found near streams or rivers, but this was the largest eagle she'd ever seen. Of course, it was the highest she'd been in the hills for quite some time. As the bird drifted out of view, she turned Tigger and led the Arabian back to the underbrush.

The stallion hesitated and she glanced over her shoulder just in time to see her horse limping. She dropped to her knees and inspected Tigger's left foreleg. It was swollen and hot to her gentle touch. It must have happened when he reared and went over backward. "Too bad you probably won't learn anything."

She sighed. She frowned thoughtfully at the creek. Cold water was bound to help her poor horse. If she soaked the Arabian's leg for a while, then the swelling and pain would ease. She'd get the bottle of liniment from the saddlebags and rub that in too. As she rose to her feet, she knew it was going to be a long day.

She took her horse back and tied him to another tree. Nell followed Tigger. Walking past the black, Appaloosa mare, Beth petted her neck. Both horses were ready for their grain. As she strode toward the cave, she glimpsed several broken branches lying on the ground. She gathered an armload of the hemlock and continued toward the cave.

In the daylight, everything appeared normal. The Morgans' story had been an invention of the night, and she'd been a fool to believe it for a moment. There was not one logical fact to support the theory that she'd ridden into the woods and found herself in the late nineteenth century.

The whole idea was ridiculous. Both Morgans definitely needed professional help, and she'd see to it that they received the aid. After she found Gary Smith, she could stop in at the hospital and visit the Morgans.

But she had to feed the horses and her patient. Then she needed to change Rad's bandage and treat Tigger. After that, she'd collect more firewood, get water into the cave, inventory her supplies and be ready when help arrived. Once Search and Rescue took responsibility for Rad, she could go after Gary Smith. Maybe someone would know Nina's condition. If not, Beth could charge her phone in one of the vehicles and call the hospital.

With her agenda in mind, she reentered the cave. She added a few chunks of wood to the fire. When she looked at Rad, she realized he was awake. His pants weren't on the rock, so he must have asked Kyle to help him dress.

"How do you feel this morning, Morgan?"

"Fair to middlin', Miss Chambers. How's Nell?"

Beth went in search of the food and her mess kit. "She's fine. I hobbled her last night and she stayed near Tigger. Where do you want me to have her taken when help arrives?"

Rad choked and spat out a mouthful of blood. "We went through that last night. There won't be any help today." He coughed again. "It'll take at least two weeks for Kyle to get back here with the posse."

"It'd better not. If he's gone more than thirty-six hours, I'm throwing his backside in jail. Once he gets to Monte Cristo, he can call in the Sheriff's Department and they'll bring in a helicopter."

Rad coughed, choked, and spit up more blood. "You're the most pigheaded woman I've ever met. How many times do I have to tell you? It's 1888. There isn't a town called Monte Cristo or one of those heli things."

"Bull. Time travel isn't possible yet, Morgan. So, either you're full of garbage or I am. And I don't think I've bypassed all the laws of science and nature."

Decision made about the year, she went through her supplies of dehydrated food and pulled out a package of freeze-dried sausage patties. Surprisingly, the baby food jar she used to carry eggs hadn't broken when Tigger fell on her and the saddlebags. "Don't sweat it, Morgan. Everything will work out the way it should."

"I hope so."

She came back to the fire. She placed her supplies next to it and reached for the coffee pot. It was warm and full. Obviously, Kyle had made a fresh pot before he left this morning. Maybe there was hope for him after all. She filled the mug and carried it over to Rad. "Drink some coffee and calm down. With as much blood as you've lost, you're going to need a lot of liquids."

"That makes sense."

She helped him sit up and he leaned back against the cave wall. "I just wish you'd listen to me."

She shook her head. "Sometimes I ask a man's advice."

"When? I want to see that."

"But I never take it," she finished. "Will says I'm contrary by nature."

"Who's Will?" Rad asked. "Your intended? You said you weren't married."

"My foster father." She returned to the fire and opened the small jar that she'd broken six eggs into when she left home. The dried ones always tasted like powder even after they'd been reconstituted with water and cooked. She'd hated them even before she joined the Army.

"What happened to your folks?"

She dumped the eggs into the pan. "My father died when I was four. My mother abandoned me when I was six, and I wound up in foster care. After I was bounced from home to home for eight years, I ran off. Life on the streets was better than what the state provided. Will and I met when I stole his wallet." Picking up a fork, she stirred the eggs. "He took me home with him."

"And you stuck around? Why?"

"It was the best place I'd ever lived." She tore open the plastic package that held the dehydrated pork sausage. "Will never—"

Her voice trailed away. How could she explain about developing a woman's figure at the age of eleven? It changed the way that everyone looked at her. From that time on, men and boys always tried to paw her, except Will. He was nice. He'd treated her with respect from the time she was a child and he always stood up for her, even when others in his family criticized her behavior.

"He's a good man." Rad guessed.

"The best." She dropped the sausage into a pan and added water. Then she changed the subject. "Are you hungry? Or feverish?"

"No fever yet. And I'm tired of batching it or eating at the hotel. Your food's a lot better than what I can cook."

"You'll change your mind. This is the last of the fresh food. From here on, it's dehydrated meals. Lucky for you I didn't go to the base and load up on M.R.E.s."

"De—What?"

"Prepackaged. Dried food." At the comprehension on his features, she knew he'd lied about the year. So much for all his stories. "Let's drop the formality, Morgan. Call me, Beth. I'd rather answer to that than Miss Chambers."

"A man doesn't call a woman by her first name unless they're married or promised, and we're neither."

Beth heaved a dramatic sigh as she dished up the eggs. "How could I forget? We're back to the *'Dark Ages'* in America again and it's 1890."

"1888."

Beth carried over his share of the breakfast and offered it to Rad. "Let's make a deal, Morgan. If you call me, Beth, I'll try hard not to shock you or your medieval sensibilities."

"Wouldn't be fair, ma'am. You think we'll be out of here in a matter of hours. I know it'll take Kyle the best part of three days to make it to Burdette's spread and another two to get help from Junction City and then at least two more for help to arrive. It'll be more than a week *afore* we see folks at the earliest."

"I don't think so." She laughed. "But I will say you know me better than most people and we only met last night. I'd keep my promise. I don't break my word."

"Tell me your real name then. I'll call you that."

"It's Beth. B. E. T. H." She measured the angled strength of his features, the combination of humor and mischief that lit his eyes. His broad chest seemed wider, accentuated by the ribbon of green plastic poncho over the bandage and the sleeping bag that hid everything below his narrow waist.

"I thought your name might be Elizabeth," Rad said.

"No. Just Beth. What's the matter? Is it too difficult for a cowboy to say?"

"It ain't." Rad teased. "What about Mary-Beth? Is that your name?"

"Nope." She cut up the meat on both of their plates since she only had the one knife. "My name is Beth."

"Funny." He held up the black case that contained her gold shield and identification. "That's not what it says in here, Miss Bethany Chambers."

She caught her breath at the sound of her old-fashioned first name. She jerked the case away from him. "How long have you had this?"

"Since last night." Curiosity seeped into his face. "Didn't you intend to show it to me? You're the one who brought it over with your map."

She shoved her identification into her shirt pocket and glared at him. "Nobody calls me anything but Beth."

"Reckon I'll call you, Bethany," Rad said. "Of course, I'll wait until it's proper."

She folded her arms and continued to glower at him. "What's your name, Morgan? Your real name? Rad's just a nickname, right?"

A hint of red tinged his cheekbones, and she knew she had him on the run. "If you call me Bethany, you're *'dead meat'* as soon as I learn your name."

He chuckled. "Yes ma'am, Miss Bethany."

"Didn't you hear me? I said—"

"I heard you," he interrupted. "And I figure I'm close enough to being '*dead meat*' that I can get away with it, Miss Bethany."

EIGHT

AFTER THEY'D EATEN BREAKFAST AND SHE'D CLEANED UP THE dishes, it was time to change Rad's bandage. She opened the set of saddlebags that contained the medical supplies and went to work. She pulled out the bottle of sulfa tablets she'd brought along in case she or Luke or Tigger suffered an injury on the trail. She hadn't expected a gunshot victim, but these would serve the same purpose. She wished she had something stronger than the codeine the doctor prescribed for her stress headaches, but the painkillers would have to do.

Carrying her canteen, she crossed back to where Rad leaned against the wall. She knelt in front of him. "Meds first." She held out two antibiotics and a codeine capsule. "Then, I'll change your bandage."

He eyed the pills dubiously. "What are they gonna do?"

"These big white ones will stop the infection." She deliberately didn't explain that the pills came from the veterinary hospital and were for Tigger. As the Army saying went, *'he didn't have a need to know.'*

"The other will ease some of your pain. I don't have enough to give you more than one every few hours, but the paramedics will be able to do more when they arrive."

70

He nodded, then took the pills. For once he didn't argue about her assertion that help was on the way. Maybe, he'd started to realize that her patience wasn't inexhaustible.

She unbuckled the two web belts that held the poncho piece secure and unwrapped the plastic layers, putting them aside. Then she removed the field dressing she'd put on the injury the night before. The wound was still sealed with the original plastic wrapper, and she didn't touch it. She wanted his lung to heal as quickly as possible.

She placed a new sterile bandage over the top of the plastic wrapper. "Lean forward so I can check the entry hole." When he did, she replaced the gauze pad on his back. "This wound will probably be the first to heal." She tied the bandages in place with the long strings that were part of the dressing.

"I helped out at a hospital during the war." Rad began to cough. When he finished spitting up blood, he continued, "The doctors were always digging out parts of bullets. I got any lead balls in me?"

She stared at him. "Are you serious?" She could tell by the sober look on his face that he was, so she answered the question with cool deliberation. "Nowadays, bullets are steel jacketed, Morgan. Whoever shot you, and I'm betting it was Smith probably because he wanted the money you carried, used a high-powered rifle. Smith carries a .30-.30."

"Because the rifle had more power, the bullet went through me?"

"That's right." She reached for the poncho strip and used it to cover his bandages. "And that's why you're going to live. If a lead ball had bounced around in your insides, you'd be—" She stopped, unable to finish her sentence.

"I'd die," Rad said, his tone flat with certainty.

"That's right." Tears stung behind her eyes, and she blinked them back. Why was she so upset? She'd done her best and he was going to live. She'd cracked jokes with the other detectives when they were trying to solve a murder, and subsisted on coffee, stale doughnuts, and cigarettes for hours, while they tried to figure out *whodunnit*.

She still saw the dead as real people. What prompted her emotional reaction today to his concern about his wound? Maybe, it was because she'd forgotten that he had mental problems for a moment. Everything seemed so normal while they ate breakfast together. But he obviously still believed it was the nineteenth century.

She frowned thoughtfully. He'd said he served in the war. He probably had ten years on her. She'd have to ask him how old he was. Then, she could lead the conversation to the places he'd seen while he served in the military. Once she got him talking about those experiences, she might be able to see why his time in combat prompted him to pretend he lived in 1888.

Then again, he could just be crazy. She'd leave the diagnosis up to the experts once they arrived.

"I'm tired, ma'am." His deep voice interrupted her thoughts.

"I'll help you lie down." She felt a new sympathy when she saw him wince, as he adjusted his position on the wound. She was beginning to recognize his pain, even though he tried to hide it.

She brushed his hair back from his face. "I know lying on this side hurts like hell. I wish I could do something about that, but we don't have the equipment they do in the hospital."

"I'd rather do this than die and you told me I'd quit spitting up blood real soon."

"That's right."

While she cleaned up the used dressings, she crossed her fingers. The Army had only taught her how to do emergency first aid. In the Middle East, there'd been helicopters so she could get Rad Morgan airlifted to the nearest Evac Hospital. She wasn't supposed to have to nurse him back to health like some pioneer woman.

She took a deep breath. Kyle had gone for help, she reminded herself. He ought to be back by nightfall at the latest. With searchlights and modern equipment, they could get Rad out of the foothills and into a hospital by tonight.

Everything's going to be okay. She glanced at Rad Morgan. He was almost asleep. "I've got to take care of the horses. Tigger hurt his leg yesterday."

"He's a game little beast. I was too heavy for him. Sorry I hurt him."

"You didn't! You weren't on him that long." Beth said indignantly. "I'd never overweight my horse. No, Tigger spooked yesterday before we found you. He saved my life."

"How?" Rad asked.

She bit her lip. She finished cleaning up and started for the entrance of the cave. "I'll tell you about it later. Get some sleep, Morgan."

"Not till you tell me what happened." He struggled up on one elbow. "Don't make me come after you."

"You couldn't. You're seriously injured, remember?"

"There's nothing wrong with my legs. Just my chest."

"Without a doubt, you are the most obstinate, egotistical, pugnacious—"

"That ain't the answer I'm lookin' for!"

She planted her hands on her hips. "And furthermore, you only sound like a hillbilly when you're angry. I've figured out that much."

"Yup. And I'm gonna get riled if you don't spill the beans. Talk, missy!"

She met him glare for glare. She admitted silently that the two of them were equally stubborn. Why did he have to be half crazy? He was as strong as she, and since she considered most civilian men were wimps, it was the highest compliment she could give him.

"Damn you, Morgan. All right, you win. Smith tried to ambush me a couple of hours before I ran into you."

"So that's why you wanted to know my name before you got

off your horse." Rad coughed for a moment. "Or you wanted to know I wasn't him." He spat into the can, then looked at her. "You told me I could take your word to the bank."

It took a moment before Beth understood that he was asking about her honesty. He wanted to know if she would keep her word. "Nobody questions *my* integrity."

"Good. Promise you won't go after that killer alone."

"What?" Beth demanded. "No way, Morgan. If I won't knuckle under to my boss or the captain, what makes you think I will when you give me an order? As soon as help arrives, I'm going after Smith."

Rad shook his head, worry in his face. "You fight the bit most of the time, Miss Chambers."

"What does that mean?"

"You're so ornery you wouldn't move camp for a prairie fire."

She glared at him. "I'm not stupid."

"Chasing that killer by yourself is as dangerous as walking in quicksand over Hades." He met her gaze. "You ain't learned what quit means."

"I don't quit." She lifted her chin. "Everybody else has. Smith must be stopped."

"I agree. Just don't leave me till help gets here."

"I won't." Her anger melted like spring snow in the sunshine. "Everything will be fine, Morgan. You'll see. Kyle will be back with the rescue team super-fast." She went to Rad's side, knelt, and adjusted the sleeping bag to cover his broad shoulders. "Get some rest."

She smoothed his black hair, noticing the speckles of gray, but they didn't take away from his appeal. "I'm going to look after Tigger."

He caught her hand. "Take your rifle. It'll hit further than that pea-shooter you pack."

She smiled, patted her shoulder holster. "This pea-shooter uses .9-millimeter rounds. It'll bring down a junkie on meth. I'll trust it. I'm a better shot with my Glock than I am with the carbine."

———

That evening, Beth glanced at her watch. It read 11:27 pm. She stalked toward the opening of the cave to stare out into the night. "When I get somewhere with cell reception, I'm getting a warrant for your brother's arrest. Do you know how long he's been gone?"

Rad yawned. "Only a day, ma'am. He won't get to Burdette's *afore* tomorrow night at the earliest."

She scowled at the brilliant white stars that decorated the ebony night sky. She didn't remember them being this bright before. "I'm BOLOing your brother and throwing his behind in jail."

"A what?" Rad asked.

"You said you're a cop. You know, a BOLO."

When he just stared, she sighed. "Okay, Morgan. It's a *Be On the Look Out* order." She almost said this was a life and death situation, then remembered that she didn't want to frighten him. Now, the man was positive he'd live. If she said anything that jeopardized his trust in her or himself, he might not struggle as hard to survive.

"Miss Chambers, it takes more time to get places than you're willing to give." Rad coughed for a moment. "It's late. Get some shut-eye. Everything looks better in daylight."

She frowned. He'd slept most of the day. She'd given him another two antibiotics and another painkiller when she changed his bandage this evening. His temperature was still normal, but there was bound to be infection with a wound this size.

What would she do when he began to run a fever? She'd deal with it. She didn't have much choice.

Kyle had been gone since early morning. It was nearly midnight. That meant he left almost eighteen hours ago. If he'd found help or called in, the authorities would have been here by now. That left two options. Either he hadn't called 9-1-1 when he got to a phone, or he hadn't made it out of the foothills.

With Gary Smith roaming around, and some would-be bank

robbers also in the forest, Kyle could have been ambushed too. If that was the case, then she and Rad were sitting ducks. All Smith would have to do was continue searching and he'd be bound to find them. She couldn't get Rad Morgan out of the woods without help, and Gary Smith might stumble over their tracks or the horses' hoofprints at any time.

She would have to go for help herself, she decided, two hours later as she stood outside the cave. She stubbed out the last of her cigarette on a boot heel and dropped the filter in her coat pocket. Then she went back into the cave and after the map. She'd find the most direct route to the nearest town.

That made the choice easy. She'd go to Robe and the Verlot Ranger Station. She'd be able to call for help, turn over the stolen money to the authorities, and organize a search for Kyle, all in one fell swoop.

"What are you doing?" Rad asked.

Beth went through the saddlebags, pulled out a protractor, a pencil, and the map. "Assuming the worst. Kyle's been delayed. That leaves you and me. You can't ride out of here. We need help and your brother obviously didn't find any."

"So you are riding out." Rad groaned. "Miss Chambers, you're more stubborn than a long-headed mule."

"Thanks." She went to where Rad lay. "Want to help?"

———

Rad considered his choices. If he were involved, he'd be able to steer her around trouble, direct her away from the Indian tribes and the logging camps. He liked the way she looked at him, how she filled out a pair of pants, the way the green shirt clung to her bosom, the wide green belt that made her waist look smaller.

Other men wouldn't see the fire in her eyes, or her spirit, or her courage. All they'd see was the body, and they'd attack her. If it came to that, Rad trusted the Indians more than he did the loggers. "Let me see the map. If I help, you'll be back sooner."

"That's a switch. What changed your mind? Why are you willing to help me now?" she asked, suspicion in her voice.

"You've got your mind made up, and when that happens, there's no point in arguing with you." Rad coughed and spat a small amount of blood into the can. He felt better and wished she'd give him the time he needed. He'd be able to ride out of here in a week or two.

"Thanks, Morgan." She pointed to a spot on the map. "If we plot a straight route to the Ranger Station and back, it shouldn't take more than six hours. I'll be here by lunchtime. And you'll be in a hospital by dinner."

Rad glanced at her head bent over the map. He touched her hair. "And what if you can't find the Rangers? What then? Will you believe me?"

She hesitated, then shook her head, staring at the map again. "I know it isn't 1888. I'm sure I can find help for you."

"And if you can't? You're fighting the truth worse than poison. I've got no call to lie to you about the year."

"Everybody has an agenda, Morgan. Mine is to protect and serve the people of Snohomish County. To take care of you I must get help. I know what you think the date is, and I know what I think too."

"Some things don't need all the thought you want to give them."

She gestured to the map. "Let's keep the peace, Morgan. Just tell me the fastest way to the Ranger Station. You probably know the area better than I do."

"I surely do. You've got nothing to fear, ma'am. I'll look after you."

"I'm not scared!"

———

A short time later, she sat next to the fire watching him sleep, and wondered if he was right about the year. The trees were all virgin timber, the animals weren't used to being hunted, the money in Rad's saddlebags was from the nineteenth century, his old Colt, and antique rifle—everything could be considered proof of the date.

She had collected sufficient evidence to prove it was 1888, but in her heart and soul, she hoped he was lying about the year. Granted, she'd lived through more hardship than most people. But she didn't want to think about traveling through time. That was impossible.

Even with all the technological advances in the past few years, time travel hadn't been invented yet. It was still just a fantasy that belonged in one of her foster cousin's books. She'd find Verlot and the Ranger Station in the morning. Then her usual nerve would return. In one way she could hardly wait to leave, but in another way, she dreaded the trip. What if he was right? What if she'd somehow traveled to 1888?

A few hours later, she rolled over and awakened as suddenly as she'd fallen asleep. Raising on an elbow, she saw Rad resting on the other side of the fire. The flames were at the same height they'd been when she'd drifted into slumber. Did that mean he'd added wood to the blaze?

She shook her head in baffled wonder as she reached for her leather boots. The only way Rad could move was by hitching himself around in slow, careful motions. Otherwise, he'd feel more pain and suffer more bleeding. Now, he seemed to be unconscious. She hoped he continued to sleep. Somehow, when he was alert, his curious certainty that it was 1888 came closer to reality.

Shaking out her boots, she pulled them on. She picked up her hat and jammed it on her head. Then she tiptoed to the back of the cave and sorted through the saddlebags for a clean, black tank top, soap, and a towel. She'd wash up, take care of the horses, and come back to prepare a meal.

After a breakfast of powdered eggs, dehydrated sausage, and canned fruit, she tidied up the dishes she'd used to prepare their meal. She smiled at Rad. "I'll bet you won't complain about the hospital food. It's better than this stuff."

"And my cooking," Rad said, not responding to the comment about the hospital. "Still heading out today?"

Beth nodded. "I have to."

"Your horse still lame?" He drank the last of his coffee.

"Yes." She took the cup from his hand and refilled it. "But I can make good time on foot."

"You'll do better on my mare."

"I planned to hike out. I never expected you to let me borrow your horse after our disagreements. Most of the detectives won't loan out their favorite department cars, much less their personal ones."

"I trust you. You know how to take care of a horse better than most men. And it'll be faster this way. You'll be back *afore* noon."

"Definitely." She flashed him a quick smile. "I'll heat up some chili for you before I go."

When he didn't speak, she tilted her head, eyeing him. "What's on your mind, Morgan?"

"You're wearing more than your *unmentionables*, aren't you? And putting up your hair?"

She glanced down at her black tank top. Since she'd intended to hike through the mountains for several hours, she hadn't wanted to wear too many layers, and this would keep her warm enough. "I'll take my coat. What's wrong with my hair? It's out of my face and that's all I care about."

"You're a grown woman. Pin up your hair. You want folks to know you're decent, especially since you're wearing pants and don't have a dress."

Beth folded her arms and looked him up and down. "This from a man who hasn't had a decent haircut or style in forever and hasn't shaved in two days. Get over yourself, Morgan. You're not the boss of me."

"Not yet, but if Kyle ain't back soon, I will be."

"What the hell does that mean?"

"I'll be stuck marrying you. *Taming of the Shrew* is entertaining to watch, but it doesn't add up to a peaceful home or life."

"In your dreams, Morgan."

"More like our nightmares."

NINE

LATER THAT MORNING, SHE STOOD IN A GROVE OF HEMLOCKS. HER words came back to haunt her. A creek bubbled at her feet, and she heaved a sigh while she watched Nell drink her fill. Beth wondered again where she'd gone wrong. Her map detailed the various landmarks, most of which she knew, but she hadn't found any of them. Suddenly, she realized she hadn't heard any heli-copters or off-road vehicles. Animals, yes. Civilized noises, no.

She'd used her compass to help plot out the various azimuths with extraordinary care. By her calculations, she should have wound up on the front steps of the Verlot Ranger Station. But, she hadn't. And no matter how many times she pulled her cell phone out of her jacket, turned it on, and tried it, the damned thing kept showing, *'No Signal.'* Of course, that meant the GPS didn't work either. She'd shut off the phone between times so she wouldn't use up the battery.

She seemed to literally be in the middle of nowhere. She couldn't text anyone and seek help that way. She was nowhere in the neighborhood of the Ranger Station. She couldn't be. She opened her map and studied the topographical features once more. Then she compared the map to the area surrounding her. Nothing looked right. For a moment, she considered the notion she *might be* in 1888.

She shook her head. In addition to her own efforts, Rad had given her explicit directions. Had she really traveled through time? Of course not! She dismissed the ridiculous idea. She wished she'd brought Luke with her instead of leaving him to guard Rad Morgan. The dog would have sniffed out any humans in the surrounding woods. She sighed again. Her map and compass hadn't worked. Now, how was she going to find help? Obviously, she couldn't depend on Kyle. The man seemed to have disappeared into thin air.

She glanced at the sun. It was close to the midpoint in the sky, so it had to be almost noon. She verified the time by checking her watch. She'd promised Rad that she'd be back early. She needed to backtrack to the cave. Suddenly, aware of the hills grown silent, she returned her attention to the black Appaloosa mare. She tightened the cinch and swung into the saddle.

At the touch of her heels, Nell moved forward willingly. Beth struggled to curb her impatience. It had been kind of Rad to loan Beth his horse, especially since she was aware of the fondness he had for the mare. But, after riding Tigger, every other mount was a distinct disappointment.

Her steel gray Arabian was so responsive that all she had to do was shift her weight. The slightest touch of the reins, caused the stallion to turn, stop, or back. Combining signals made him perform difficult dressage maneuvers.

Beth reached to pat the mare's black neck. Nell was nice and dependable. She never spooked or bolted, never even tried to act up. She climbed every hill without faltering, but she was sufficient to convince Beth that she didn't want an Appaloosa or any horse like this calm, steady mount.

As they approached the river the horse tensed, her ears pricked forward. Beth reined the horse to a stop and listened. After riding Tigger, she knew better than to discount what the mare's body language transmitted.

She heard splashing and then the sound of voices. Could it be swimmers, she wondered? But it was too cold to even ride without her jacket. She'd seen snow on some of the higher hills. What fool would be swimming in the river? Kids, she decided. And where there were children, there should be adults nearby. Adults that she could send for help.

She urged Nell forward and around the last bend to the river. There were boys on the far riverbank, teenagers spearing fish. Wait a minute. The rivers around here had short seasons for sport fishing, only two months, usually December and January. She remembered Will griping about that last Christmas. So, what were these kids doing? Poaching?

Before she called out to them, one of the boys spotted her and Nell. He yelled something to the other kids, and they all turned in her direction. For the first time, Beth realized they were Native Americans, wearing little more than loincloths. Then she saw a woman on the far shore back in the trees, again in a native costume, gesturing to the boys.

"Hold it!" Beth urged Nell into the water.

The group of boys turned. They hurried up the gravel bar to the far riverbank, and into the cedars, vanishing from view.

The Appaloosa mare could only move through the icy water just so fast. When Beth reached the far bank, the group was gone. She reined the mare into the trees behind the Indians, but there was no sign of them. They'd melted into the woods. Where had they gone and how could she find them?

Why run from her? What could she do to them? Beth pondered the questions as she turned Nell back to the riverbank and rode upstream to the point where she had crossed earlier in the day. The group outnumbered her, and she didn't pose a threat to them.

Without a radio or cell phone reception, she couldn't call in for help. And it was the Department of Fish and Game who looked out for rivers. She really didn't have a lot of authority out here in the woods. So, what frightened the Indians?

And how was she going to find them to arrange for help?

There was no way possible. An hour later, Beth still puzzled over the costumes they wore, the spears and nets they used for fishing. She rode up the gravel bank that opened into the trail to the cave. She saw the hoof-prints Nell had left behind earlier that morning, overlaid by another set of tracks.

A distinctive set of tracks— Beth jerked Nell to a stop and vaulted from the saddle. The tracks were from Wonder. Gary Smith had been here.

When?

She remembered Will saying something about being able to feel the heat if the horse hadn't been there that long ago. She bent and checked the dirt. The clay was cool to her touch. However, the tracks were sharp, clearly cut into the dirt, aiming upstream.

She had to follow the trail. This was the closest she'd been to Smith in two days, ever since she'd found Rad Morgan. The thought of the man she saved stopped her. Morgan counted on her, she knew that. He expected her to come back. If she went after Gary Smith now, there was no telling what would happen to Rad Morgan.

Bull. Beth knew exactly what would happen to the man. Morgan would die. Obviously, his brother wasn't coming back with help. It was all up to her and if she chased after Gary Smith, Morgan was a dead man. So, she had to go back. She didn't have to like it. She had to do it. She couldn't put Gary Smith first and let Rad Morgan suffer the consequences of that decision.

What would a *real* homicide detective do? What would a man do? Would he go after Gary Smith or return to take care of an injured civilian? Beth eyed the tracks again and the direction they pointed. She wanted to pursue the killer, not act as a nursemaid, but she knew the rules of her job. It was more important to save Rad Morgan's life than it was to act like a macho detective and hunt Gary Smith alone.

She had already been ambushed. It was pure luck that she hadn't been killed outright, and if she got hurt now, nobody would ever find Rad Morgan. She couldn't count on that moronic twit,

Kyle. If he'd intended to return in a timely manner, he'd have been back yesterday afternoon or last night.

And she'd shown what a fool she was. She'd come into the woods alone after a man who was armed and dangerous. He'd shot at her, hitting Tigger instead. He'd already wounded Rad Morgan and the survivalist could die. If Gary Smith had seen that band of Indians, he would have attacked them too, or at least he'd have gone after a woman or a girl.

She had to be responsible. Shoving a toe into the stirrup, Beth mounted the Appaloosa and swung the mare to the right and up the trail to the cave. She'd do what was right. She'd save Rad Morgan's life first. Then she'd go after Gary Smith, and when she got cell reception, she'd call in and tell the sergeant about Kyle. There was nothing wrong with that boy a week or two in the local jail wouldn't cure.

She arrived at the cave two hours later. Reining Nell to a halt, Beth swung from the saddle. She petted Luke when he came to greet her. Then she stepped into the cave and checked on Rad. He was still lying on his wounded side. Was he awake? She couldn't tell if his eyes were open. "Morgan, I'm back. How are you?"

"Fine," Rad said, but he didn't look at her. "You find what you were looking for, Miss Chambers?"

Beth frowned and dropped the reins on the ground. She hurried across to him and touched his forehead. His skin was warm, but not hot, not yet. "No. I didn't find the Ranger Station. I saw some Indians fishing."

"They see you?"

"They ran from me." She watched Rad's features. "Why would they be scared?"

Rad tensed under her touch. "How many were there? What tribe?"

"Native Americans. Indians. How should I know their tribes, Morgan? I'm not stationed at the res. They have their own police force. And I don't have enough rank to get sent there as a liaison."

"How many Indians did you see?" Rad repeated, trying not to shiver.

Beth rose to her feet and went after his bedroll and the extra blankets. "Six boys between the ages of eight and possibly fifteen. One woman."

"No men?" Rad demanded. "They wouldn't be fishing alone."

"They were." She returned with the two blankets and covered him. "I don't lie."

Rad began to cough. He spat up a small amount of blood. "The men probably went hunting."

"That wasn't all I saw." She crossed to where Nell patiently stood just outside the cave entrance and began to untack the mare. "Gary Smith is in the hills. I spotted tracks of the horse he stole from Nina."

"You didn't go after him?"

"I wanted to!" Beth snapped. "But your rotten, measly life came first."

"Thanks."

Beth tied up the breast collar and cinch. Then she pulled the saddle and pads from Nell's back. "And furthermore, your directions stunk. I didn't come close to finding the Ranger Station."

"I told you it wasn't there. If it's where you say you come from, it won't be for at least a hundred years. You had to find it out for yourself." He paused, then offered his brand of advice. "Ma'am, kicking up a storm never gets a body anywhere, unless it's a mule."

"If you don't quit comparing me to a mule, I'll give you a lesson in animal behavior." She spun around and stalked out of the cave to lead Nell toward the trees where Tigger was staked. "Men. When God made them, *She* was only joking."

She hobbled Nell near the Arabian stallion. "Everybody lies."

Why had the first tenet of homicide investigation come to mind at this moment? Because she hadn't found the Ranger Station. And the reason she hadn't come across it was that she depended on

Morgan's directions after her map and calculations failed her. How could she have been so stupid?

She'd trusted him to tell her the truth about the location of Robe and Verlot even when she knew it wasn't on his personal agenda. The last thing he wanted was help. He ran away from civilization, and she forced him to face his fears. Why had she expected him to help her?

She wasn't an innocent, but she certainly acted like one this morning. She led Tigger down to the creek and watered the stallion. He limped beside her, although he wasn't as lame this afternoon as he'd been the day before. After she finished taking care of the horses, she stormed toward the cave. Enough was enough. She'd let Rad Morgan know exactly what she thought of him.

Unfortunately, he was asleep. That prevented her from carrying out her plans. Well, she'd wait, she told herself. When he woke up, she'd chew him up one side and down the other. By the time she was through with him, he'd know better than to mess with her mind.

He slept for the remainder of the afternoon. She rebuilt the fire, brought in more wood, carried in water. Finally, she curled up beside the campfire with the map. She carefully went over the topographical details, sure she could pinpoint their location and the nearest town if she relied on her own skills. No more asking for help. She had the reputation for being the lone wolf in the department. From now on, she'd remember that.

After she laid out the course to the nearest town, Beth folded up the map and stored it in the saddlebags. She didn't dare leave Rad at this time of day and most of her chores were done. She needed to feed him supper and change his bandage, but he had to be conscious for both things.

That meant it was a case of '*hurry up and wait,*' as they used to say in Afghanistan. Beth pulled a fantasy paperback out of her saddlebags and returned to sit by the fire. She would read away the afternoon while he slept. It didn't take long to become involved in the story of shape-shifters from dueling families or packs.

She barely noticed when Luke began to carry in rocks and pile them at her feet. The German Shepherd never went after sticks. He preferred baseball-sized stones perfect for sharpening his teeth and playing fetch.

Close to dusk, she built up the fire and went to look after the horses again. She carried in firewood. The clouds held a soft purple, gray tinge, reminding her of what Will called a snow sky. It was April, she thought. Winter was over and even if the nights had been cold, it was the wrong season for snow.

Still, better to be safe than sorry, as the saying went. She'd stockpile firewood tonight to keep them warm. With that in mind, she pulled a packet of dehydrated lamb stew from her saddlebags. She'd serve it, the package of crackers and cheese and for dessert, they'd split a chocolate bar.

"We eating soon?" Rad asked.

"In about twenty minutes or as soon as the stew's warm." She glanced at him, adding water to the powdered mixture in the mess kit. "Ready for coffee? Or would you prefer water?"

"I need to take a walk first, ma'am."

"That's not happening, Morgan." She put the pan where it could heat on the flat stone near the fire. "You have a hole in your chest, remember?"

"No, I don't. You patched it up." He struggled to sit upright.

She hurried over to help him, but he made it without her.

He leaned against the stone wall, coughed, and spat. He rested for a few moments, then pushed the blankets aside. "Shake out my boots for me."

"What are you doing? You can't go anywhere."

"Ma'am, if I don't go outside, we'll both be sorry."

Beth stared at him for a moment. Comprehension dawned and she felt a blush scorch into her cheeks. He truly did need to go outside, or she should make other arrangements. "That's why you wanted Kyle yesterday. Have you been going outside all this time?"

He barely nodded and she realized he was as embarrassed as

she was by the subject. It didn't make a lot of sense, she thought. Hadn't she seen everything possible as a detective? In a warzone? Or for heaven's sake on T.V. and in the movies? And discussing his toilet habits made her uncomfortable—she was so losing it.

"Okay, Morgan." She grabbed one of his boots and tipped it upside-down. "But I think it'd be better if you used a can and stayed inside. What do you folks in the olden days call them, oh yeah, chamber pots?"

"I'm not that helpless."

"Close to it." She eased the first boot onto his foot, shook out the second, and put that one on too. She slipped an arm around his waist. "Lean on me."

The two of them maneuvered out the entrance and she guided him into the trees. When he leaned against one, she stepped away and turned her back. She searched the grove and found a short, thick branch to serve as a cane for him. Maybe, she had traveled in time. She couldn't imagine any of the men she knew acting like Rad Morgan if they'd been shot in the chest.

When they returned to the cave, the stew was ready. She divided it and took the larger portion to him. He eyed it dubiously. "I always heard the prettier the gal, the worse she cooks, but I thought it was just a story."

"And I heard real men don't whine, so I guess we're both disappointed," she retorted, passing him a spoon. "If you think this is bad, wait till the chicken soup."

"Since we don't have any chickens out here in the woods, I reckon I'm safe until we get to the Lazy B or Junction City."

She laughed. "Don't count on it, Morgan."

TEN

AFTER SUPPER, RAD DRIFTED OFF TO SLEEP AND BETH OPTED TO play solitaire with the deck of cards from her saddlebags. It allowed her time to think. If he hadn't lied about the trail, she should have wound up on the steps of the Verlot Ranger Station this morning, and he'd have been evacuated earlier today.

Unless it really was 1888, and she'd traveled through time. Then the two of them would have to deal with this alone, without help from a civilized society. Still, the idea was ridiculous. For one person to travel through time was fantasy, but she and Gary Smith were both here. That made it totally outrageous. Yet she had the three things needed to solve a case, evidence, witnesses, and her own professional observations.

Physical evidence included Rad's clothes, supplies, weapons, and the tack on his horse. She had that horse, one with fine conformation, unlike any Appaloosa she'd ever seen before. All the ones Nina had taken her to see when they shopped for a horse for Beth to buy were tall, rangy, and showed the sleek lines of the Thoroughbred crossed with Quarter Horses. None of them looked like Nell.

For witnesses, she had Rad and Kyle Morgan, if she didn't include herself. Both men swore it was 1888 and their stories never changed. If this had been a homicide investigation, she would have continued to interrogate them and tried to learn the truth. But what they claimed was too bizarre, too improbable.

Her own observations came into play. What about the Native Americans? They'd been fishing with spears and long-handled nets for heaven's sake. The boys wore loincloths, and the woman held a blanket like a shawl over what was probably a long dress. Hadn't there been a skirt touching the ground? Beth considered the river again. She'd forded it at least a hundred times, riding in the hills, and rarely spotted a fish. Today, the water had been full of them, and it wasn't spawning season.

She had everything she needed to solve this case, even if she didn't like the answers. *Where am I really? I know that trail. I've found my way home from the National Forest hundreds of times before.* What went wrong today? Mentally, she reviewed the clues she'd glossed over once again. She stood, went to examine Rad's antique Winchester, his battered saddle, and the banknotes again.

She turned, aware he was watching her. *I'm a detective, damn it. And I'm not where I should be, am I? If I'm in 1888, how did I get here?*

"I don't believe you, Morgan. I won't believe you." Was that weak, reedy voice hers? She lowered her tone, hoping she would sound stronger. "It's not 1888. It can't be."

"It is. Don't worry, Miss Bethany. I'll take care of you."

Beth raised her chin. "I can take care of myself." She went after her own saddlebags. "Let's get that bandage changed."

"You did that this morning."

"And I'm going to do it this evening too." Beth retorted. "So, stop complaining."

"I don't bellyache."

"All men do, regardless of what year it is."

She opened the bag and checked the remaining stock of her medical supplies. She only had three large bandages left. What would she do when they were gone? Improvise. She'd brought several white t-shirts. She'd tear up the cotton shirts and add the cost to Rad Morgan's bill. By the time help arrived, she'd probably be out of all her supplies.

———

Kyle scowled into the darkness. He was still at least a half day's ride from the Lazy B. Between cutting the trail of that back-shooting killer, and almost riding into a band of armed men, undoubtedly the bank robbers, it'd been hard to make any time at all. Then there were the Indians. The peaceable sort, just up for the fishing, but he hadn't wanted to trust them. Not after what Rad said about one of the women being attacked.

He wasn't Rad. His older brother spoke better *Chinook* than most people, even better than the preachers. He liked the Indians and said he'd learned a lot from them about living out here.

Kyle eyed S.O.B., his strawberry roan Appaloosa. His brother was a hard act to follow. Most men wouldn't have traveled to Oregon to buy horses from the Nez Perce tribe. Rad was as touchy as a teased rattlesnake most of the time. Grown men walked well around him and more than once during this past winter, Kyle had heard his brother called a bad man to cross.

Even Trace Burdette, Junction City's famed gunfighter treated Rad with cautious respect. Rad was strong, too tough to die from a coward's bullet.

Only Kyle had a hunch that his brother was a goner regardless of what the woman said who rescued him. No man could live with a large hole in his lung. Kyle stared into the night, waiting for the moon to rise. If he was careful, he might be able to make it to the Lazy B by dawn. Of course, he'd have to wait near the gates until the sun was well up before Gruber or Mac would allow him to see Trace.

———

It had begun to rain an hour before, a fine mist that developed into a steady downpour. Beth wanted a cigarette, but she wouldn't smoke around Rad, not when he was recovering from a sucking chest wound. "Want to play a hand of poker? I'm bored."

He chuckled. "You're as jumpy as a long-tailed cat near a rocking chair." He coughed and spat into the can. "I'm purt near useless so come tell me about this killer you're tracking."

She crossed to the fire and filled the coffee cup. "I've got pictures."

"Save them till tomorrow. I can't sleep when I think about blood or when I see it."

She carried over the coffee cup and sat down beside Rad. "Where should I start?"

"At the beginning," Rad said. "When did you find the first body?"

"It began five months ago, just before Christmas. We expected the usual, suicides, accidents, family homicides, the works. The death rate is always high around the holidays. Then we were told about this girl. She was twelve, although she looked older. Her foster parents reported her missing. She already had a record for prostitution." Beth took a sip of the coffee, then stared into the dark liquid.

"He'd killed her. How?"

"First, by beating her with some kind of club. We didn't find it, or the knife he used to torture her for hours." Beth left out the worst of it, the multiple rapes. She couldn't talk about those, not when the young girl's face still haunted her sleep. "Finally, he finished her by slitting her throat, but not till he'd cut the skin off her in pieces."

"You saw her?" Rad asked. "That's no sight for a woman."

"It's my job," Beth said. "I'm a homicide detective. Granted, I just got promoted to the division a year ago, but I wanted it. I worked hard for it. I figure out who did the crime and bring the person to justice." She took another swallow of coffee, wishing she'd brought along some liquor. "It was my case, and it was far too gruesome for what I normally see."

"I was in the Calvary," Rad drawled. "I've seen what some white men did to Indian women during those slaughters. What did this killer do that worried you?"

"He was too efficient, too professional. I could tell by looking at this girl's body that it wasn't his first murder, that he'd done it several times before." Beth shook her head, trying to dismiss the memory. "When I went back to the office, I started running numbers through the computers."

"What's a computer?" Rad asked.

She gave him a sideways glance. If it were really 1888, he wouldn't know and if he was a survivalist, he might not be familiar with everything that technology could do. "A machine that helps solve crimes. I entered the facts that I had and asked for other murders that had the same characteristics from across the Northwest."

"Did you find any?" Rad took the cup from her hand before she spilled the coffee.

"Too many. My supervisor took one look and almost lost his mind. I had one body and I was calling the guy a serial killer. Watkins said I was hysterical, and I should concentrate on the crime at hand."

"Reckon you was relieved to find you weren't as crazy as a duck in the desert." Rad turned the mug and swallowed some of the coffee. "This feller did all that killing, right?"

"I'd rather spend the rest of my life in a mental hospital than be right about Gary Smith." Beth jumped to her feet and began to pace the narrow confines of the cave, once again wishing she could have a smoke. "Do you know how I felt reading all the reports and seeing a trail of murders from clear across Washington, Oregon, and Idaho? I found some files that had been open for twenty years."

"How old is he?"

"Fifty-four." She swung at the entrance of the cave and stomped over to the fire to add more wood to the blaze.

"Then he's been killing longer than that," Rad said. "A man, crazier than a *loco* bedbug had to start when he was weaned, or even *afore* that."

"Why?" She turned to look at Rad.

"A *real* man protects women. This fellow's got something against them. Figure out what and you'll know who he's after. Then you can catch him *afore* he does in the next one."

"That's an interesting concept." Beth pulled out her cell phone, turned it on, and brought up the list of murdered women. She'd downloaded some of the information in the files onto her phone, names, ages, professions, and the locations of the victims.

She frowned thoughtfully. Normally by now, the battery on her 'smart' phone would be close to dying since she didn't have a way to charge it, even though she didn't leave it on for an extended period of time. She took a moment to check for emails. None showed up in her mailbox. Another oddity. She didn't mention it to Rad, but she'd forwarded her information to an old friend at the F.B.I.

Fletcher contacted her on a regular basis, every time he came up with more useful info. Granted, he'd originally assumed she wanted more than help with a case, but once he realized murder was the priority, not renewing their sexual relationship, he was on-board. The two of them always agreed justice should prevail over personal desires. They'd met in the Army and went their separate ways after their hitches ended because neither of them were ready for lifetime commitments.

She decided to think about the emails and Fletcher later and focused on the case. "Race doesn't count. He doesn't care what color they are. He's murdered women from every ethnicity."

"How about age? He kill little girls?"

She sat down next to Rad and began to study the screen. "That's odd. It looks like he hasn't killed anyone under twelve."

"What about old women?" Rad finished the last of the coffee. "How did they earn their livings? Any of them no better than they should be?"

She frowned at the phone in her hand. Before she assessed the facts before her, he shifted onto an elbow. As she watched, he crawled toward the fire. "What the hell are you doing, Morgan?"

"Fetching a cup of coffee."

"Stay still." She snatched the mug from his hand. "Honestly, Morgan. I didn't patch you up so you could kill yourself. I'll wait on you till you're healthy or until help arrives."

"I'm just shot. I don't have a broken leg or arm. I can get my own coffee."

She rose to her feet and stalked toward his battered tin coffee pot. "I'll tell you what I don't understand. Why is a man like you running around loose? You'd think some woman would have snagged you years ago."

"I'm not ready to be roped and hogtied."

She stopped pouring the coffee and stared at him. She could see the sincerity in his blue eyes and etched on his rugged features. For a moment, she wanted to forget everything she had assumed about him. He was so mentally incompetent he didn't know what year it was, she reminded herself. She had met him barely three days ago and she was falling in love—

She shook her head and forced away the ridiculous idea. She liked Rad Morgan. He was different from the men she worked with at the department. He reminded her of some of the career soldiers in the military, not the by the book guys who'd become so indoctrinated they couldn't think without regulations, but the others like Fletcher Gaines. They were the ones she admired and respected, the survivors who knew how to win wars but had sacrificed pieces of their souls in all the battles.

She finished filling the mug and returned to where he lay, holding the cup out to him. "You're different, Morgan."

"Is that good or bad?"

"I haven't decided yet."

When a smile tugged at the edge of his mouth, she grinned back at him. So, he was crazy. He apparently didn't lie or cheat or steal. He told her exactly what he thought, whether she liked it or not.

She had to admire him, even if she told herself sternly that she didn't believe it was 1888. Or was it?

She put another piece of wood on the fire, then returned to sit beside him and read the police files. "One more thing, Morgan. I'll do the chores around here. You concentrate on getting well."

"It's not fittin' for a woman to boss me around, but I'll let you be in charge when I'm asleep, Miss Chambers."

"Thank you, Marshal Morgan." She kept her tone super sweet but knew the sarcasm didn't pass him by.

PART TWO

"It is better to die on your feet than to live on your knees."

DOLORES IBARRURI

ELEVEN

It was the first woman he'd savored in two years. This time he didn't have to worry about being interrupted. It wasn't like when he hunted in the cities and back alleys. And he didn't have to bury the body. He could leave her for the coyotes and other scavengers to eat.

Someone might find her bones eventually, but it wasn't likely, not when he was back in his 'old time,' his favorite place for hunting. Only that female detective dared to question him about the matches she'd found in her computer. But even she hadn't imagined the true scope of his genius. It was too bad she'd died so quickly when he shot her horse. He hadn't expected the animal to rear, to fall on top of her so he couldn't get to her. He'd wanted to tell her she'd missed out on so many of his trophies.

He'd been hunting a long time.

He laughed softly. Hundreds of years, but nobody would believe that. No one knew he could open the Portals of Time with blood sacrifices, and escape from one world to another where more disobedient women waited.

And he knew he'd continue hunting until he saved the world, made it the way the Bible said it was supposed to be, until men ruled, and women were the subordinate, submissive servants they were born to be.

Taking care of the Indian woman was the right thing to do. Her death - a suitable sacrifice. He'd realized that this morning when he went to water the stallion he rode and saw the tracks of the black Appaloosa mare. Her hoof prints overlaid those of his horse.

He spotted small boot prints, from her rider, too tiny to belong to Rad Morgan. Either the big man had help and was going to live, or somebody had stolen the mare and the money. He hoped that the first scenario was the case, and the lawman had survived. Men weren't his enemies and Gary Smith already knew he could outsmart the marshal. He had before.

When he finished watering his horse, he rode up the trail after the mare. The tracks faded into a mush of others from the animals that had come to the river earlier in the day. He wasn't surprised. After all, he'd sinned by shooting a man, a member of the higher order. And by breaking his own code, he'd have to pay.

———

RAD SIPPED AT THE WARM, WEAK BREW. HE PREFERRED HIS COFFEE strong enough to float a horseshoe. He put down the cup, still baffled by the way it was made. How could someone put writing on a coffee cup? And a photograph of a real person?

He recognized the woman as the one who'd voted in a presidential election a few years back and been arrested for it. He supposed she'd agree with the sentiment etched on the cup. *"A woman's place is in the House, the Senate, and the Oval Office."*

Many men would take offense at the notion of women holding public office, but if it were the law of the land, Rad knew he'd uphold it. Having women on the Town Council worked in Junction City and he didn't know why they couldn't do more. Heck, most of 'em were smarter than the fellows he had to deal with every day.

Lizbeth Quinn, the madam of the parlor house in Junction City often consulted with him, the mayor, and Trace Burdette on local issues at her tea parties. Lizbeth used flowered china cups on those occasions, a gift from the mayor. Still, Rad had never seen or heard anyone speak of a cup like the one Bethany brought with her into the woods.

He glanced at the top of Bethany's head, bent over the little machine. "Need your help, missy."

She looked at him. "Why?"

"I want to sit up a while."

"Sure." She put the contraption to one side. Then she slid an arm around his shoulders and helped him lean back against the saddle behind him. "How's that?"

Before she could step away, his hand closed over hers. He drew her near. "Come here."

Her knees gave way and she almost tumbled against him. But he stopped her, holding her a careful distance from him.

Slowly, his hands slipped up her arms, and his mouth touched hers, barely brushing her lips. The kiss was innocent, soft, and gentle. His lips left hers to tease and torment her eyebrows, her nose, her cheeks in a series of light butterfly kisses. When his mouth caught hers again, her lips parted. Before he deepened the kiss, he lifted his head.

She opened her dark green eyes and stared into his. "Was that it?"

He chuckled. He released her and leaned back against the rock. "A wild filly can't be tamed the first time out."

She tossed her head. "I'm not a horse. Damn you, Morgan. Why light a fire if you aren't man enough to put it out?"

He laughed again. "When I'm working a horse or dealing with a woman, I take it slow and easy. Worst thing is to rush them."

She lifted her chin. "I think it shows you don't know what you're doing. Maybe you need lessons in kissing too."

His gaze narrowed on her finely boned face. He saw the mischief and daring in her wildcat eyes and realized why she was taunting him. "Think what you like, Bethany." He picked up the coffee cup. "Reckon, we'll work it out later."

"You bastard." She jumped to her feet and stormed toward her coat.

"Yes, ma'am." He took a swallow of the coffee. It was cold and bitter, just the way he felt. "And was your pa formally introduced to your ma? Or were they doing business and she got caught?"

She gasped. "You miserable son of a—" She yanked on her coat. She stomped toward him, rage in every step. "Who the hell do you think you are?"

"I know who I am. And I'm not the man to take your sass, Miss Chambers. Told you that already."

"Oh, I remember everything you told me."

"Then your cussing and smoking are *gonna* stop?" Rad asked. "Or are you planning to run wild till I'm on my feet?"

"Go to hell! I wish I'd left you on the trail." She cut loose with a stream of cusswords, some of which he'd never heard before. If it had been summer, the words would have burned the grass for yards around.

He waited till she'd run out of breath. She certainly had a colorful way of expressing herself. "Reckon, you'd make a mule skinner blush. I'd better invest in a case of store-bought soap if we're forced to get hitched."

She bent and grabbed one of the rocks her dog left in the cave. She hurled it in Rad's direction, almost missing him. The stone knocked the ceramic mug from his hand. The cup shattered on the cavern floor. The dregs of the coffee splashed into the dirt.

She stared at the broken pieces of the cup scattered on the floor. Tears filled her eyes and she fled from the cave into the night.

He scowled. If he didn't have this hole in his lung, he'd go after her, but he was as weak as a sick cat. It was all he could do to get himself out of the cave twice a day to tend to his own needs. Now, he knew more about Miss Bethany Chambers.

For all her spunky talk, she bolted like a jackrabbit in tall grass

104

when she got hurt. He'd have to be more patient with her, not get testy when she riled him.

———

By the time she arrived where Tigger was staked, Beth controlled the urge to cry. Some wounds went too deep, and bawling wouldn't mend the broken cup. Of course, she hadn't just thrown away the gift from her best friend, she'd also destroyed any hope of a relationship with Rad Morgan.

No man would tolerate having rocks thrown at him, and she couldn't blame them. Beth shook her head. No matter how hard she tried to control her emotions, she always blew her own act. She wouldn't blame it on the P.T.S.D. She'd had a short fuse before she went to war. She fumbled in her pocket for the package of cigarettes and shook one out of the pack. She lit it with the gold lighter, a gift from Will last Christmas.

Like Rad inferred, she was illegitimate. Her parents had been so busy finding themselves that neither of them had time for the child they created. Why had she blamed herself for not winning their love and approval? She was older than both of them and she still struggled for self-acceptance. Would she ever find that core of self-assurance she so desperately wanted?

Beth smoked a second cigarette, and then a third. When she finished her fourth, she was ready to brave the mixed rain and snow to check on Tigger and Nell. The horses were fine. Luke paced beside her as she walked toward the cave. Snow misted across her face, hit her shoulders with a new velocity. Flakes landed on her coat and didn't melt.

The fire blazed and she frowned as she realized that once again, Rad had added more fuel. She turned to scold him, hesitating when she realized he was reading her book. Beth went to the back of the cave and slid out of her black jacket. She placed it on the edge of the rock to hang and dry. She wasn't ready to face him yet. She pulled out her hairbrush and used it to straighten out her damp, tangled curls.

Finally, she couldn't dawdle any longer. She went to sit beside the fire, pleased when Luke came to curl up next to her. She concentrated on the dark exit into the night, refusing to look at Rad. "Good book, isn't it?"

"It's a different way to tell Romeo and Juliet," Rad said.

Beth stared at him, surprised by the parallel he'd drawn between the book and a Shakespearean play. When she got back to civilization, she'd have to tease Will's niece, the author and her favorite adopted cousin, about it. "Anything else?"

"What makes them turn into wolves?"

"They're shape-shifters," Beth said.

When he didn't answer, she flicked him a glance. His steady gaze was her undoing. Tears bubbled into her throat. "I'm sorry," she choked.

"Come here and say that." Rad laid the book aside.

"Why? Does it add to your pound of flesh?"

"Nope. You come now. I'll come later when it doesn't hurt like this."

Beth rose and crossed to stand in front of him. "I apologize for yelling at you and…"

Rad smiled and tugged on her hand. He pulled her down to rest against him, on his good left side. "Miss Chambers, I've been through the war. Reckon I can stand a little hollering."

She couldn't hold in her emotions any longer. Tears slowly slipped down her cheeks. She struggled to pull away, but his hold tightened, and she turned her face against his shoulder. "It's Detective Chambers."

He stroked her hair. His deep voice softened. "Names hurt, don't they, Bethany? And I'm no fonder of being called a bastard than you are. 'Course, neither one of us got to pick our folks, did we?"

Beth lifted her head, ignoring the tears that continued to rain down her cheeks. "You mean you're—"

At his nod, she asked, "But, what about Kyle? He's your brother?"

"Same ma." Rad gritted. "Different pa. We got in her way when she did business. I was thirteen when he was born so I looked out for him as much as I could. When a customer killed her, we ended up in an orphanage. He was barely three, still in short pants. They found him a home and I lit out."

"I'm sorry." Beth apologized again. "To me, it was just a word, and I was so angry and frustrated—"

He wiped away her tears with his thumb. "You ought to remember that words have meanings. Think *afore* you insult me next time."

"I won't do it again," Beth promised. "I don't know why I lost my temper like that."

"We strike sparks off each other." He brushed a kiss over her forehead. "Both of us are so tough, we've got horns. We're bound to lock 'em occasionally."

"I've never heard it said like that." She rested a hand on his beard-stubbled jaw. "You certainly have a way with words, Marshal Morgan."

His arm tightened around her shoulders. "I figure there will come a time when we get along like two cats by a warm fire."

"I'd like to see that."

"You will."

———

Rad awakened early the next morning. It was almost dawn, the gray half-light before the sun rose. It was the time of day when the deer and elk came to water when birds just began to flutter from their nests. The hint of light filtering through the entrance of the cave told him he'd lived through another night. It was the time of day he'd learned to love during the war.

Rad looked at the sleeping woman, resting so close beside him. Sometimes, he felt as if her strength poured into his wounded body. He'd been shot before, but never recovered so quickly. He shook out his boots, then slowly drew them on.

He struggled to his feet. Breathing came easier with each day. He no longer felt as if a red-hot knife was stabbing into his chest. He lingered long enough to cover Bethany with the blanket that slipped off her and left the cave.

The dog greeted Rad when he left the cave. Snow dusted the trees. A scant inch covered the ground around the cave. The big brown and black dog growled a warning as he approached the horses and Rad stopped.

Another growl and this time the dog's hackles rose.

Rad turned to lean against a rock, rubbing his thumb over the green stone he'd worn since last Christmas when old Fremont gave it to him. "Reckon when a man thinks he's as thorny as cactus, he oughta try ordering around somebody else's dog. It's a downright humbling experience."

The dog tilted his head to one side, then sat down and watched Rad. He returned the favor, unsurprised when the big animal showed his teeth in a dangerous grin.

———

It was morning. Beth opened her eyes and saw sunlight at the entrance of the cave. How could she have slept so long? She glanced where her patient should be, surprised he hadn't awakened her with his movements. Then she stiffened! He was gone!

Where? She tossed the blanket aside and rolled to her feet. Where was he? When had he left? Why?

Had Smith found them? No. If he had, they'd be dead. She hurried out of the cave and gazed around. She scowled at the snow on the ground. It was April, damn it! And it should be spring. Was this more proof that she'd traveled through time? No, she decided. She was higher in the foothills than usual. Of course, it snowed up here when the temperature dropped.

Then she spotted Rad Morgan. He leaned against a rock, Luke

in front of him. Beth strode swiftly toward the two of them. "What the hell are you doing, Morgan?"

"Had to see a man about a horse." Rad drawled, holding the stick she'd found for him the day before. "I did. Dog wouldn't let me back inside."

She stared at him. Then she looked around. "What man? Who was here?"

He chuckled. "Never mind. I'll explain it to you later."

She frowned and checked the ground. There were faint indentations in the snow, but the only tracks she could see belonged to Rad and Luke and her. "Come on, Morgan. Let's go inside. I'll make breakfast. Then I want to change that bandage."

"You fuss more than the doctors in the hospital during the war." Rad stumbled to his feet. "'Course we called them butchers for a reason."

Beth put an arm around his waist. "What reason?"

"They got paid extra for cutting off arms and legs. So, most of 'em didn't bother bandaging us. No money in it."

Beth guided Rad toward the cave. She didn't know how to answer him. If he'd been right about the year, she might have believed him, but she'd been in Afghanistan. She knew how hard the medical people worked over there. And there was no way that the military paid bounties for amputations, not today.

"What's for breakfast?" Rad asked.

"Cereal, I think." Beth mentally tallied what was left of her supplies. "We're out of eggs."

"Good," Rad said. "They tasted like they didn't know what chickens are."

"You didn't complain about them yesterday."

"I forgot. Never josh with cooks or mules. They have no sense of humor."

TWELVE

"A Guardian trains to Protect and Keep Others from harm, in the city, country, house, home, ranch, or farm..."

RULES OF CHRONOS

AFTER A BREAKFAST OF COOKED GRANOLA WITH DRIED APRICOTS, and coffee, she changed Rad's bandage. To her amazement, the entry hole in his back was almost healed. When she checked the large exit hole in his lung, she could see the wound beginning to close under the plastic. There was hardly any drainage from the injury.

"How do your ribs feel?" Beth asked.

Rad shifted an inch or two, testing them. "Fine, Miss Chambers. I've felt worse after a horse stomps me. You have magic in your hands."

"I'd rather give the antibiotics the credit." She opened the last bandage and put a clean dressing on the wound. "From now on, stay in the cave. I don't want you moving around. If we have company, I'll take care of them."

"It's not fitting."

"What's not? I'm a Homicide Detective with the Snohomish County Sheriff's Department and I worked my way up to that slot, Morgan. Between that and being an M.P. in the Army before I became a medic, I've handled just about every kind of criminal the system has thrown at me. Who was here? Where did he go?"

He frowned at her, obviously trying to follow the conversation. "Nobody was here."

"You said you saw a man—" Beth reminded him. "Who was it? A friend of yours? Did he go for help?"

"Miss Chambers, what do those detectives call it when they got to be alone? For personal reasons?"

She allowed the silence to build as she considered his questions. The two of them had been alone for almost four days. The only time she helped him with what he called his *personal* needs was yesterday, and there wasn't a toilet in the cave.

Obviously, he'd been going outside into the woods at least once a day. That was nearly enough to make her believe they were in 1888. She couldn't think of any other man who would be able to do so much with such a serious gunshot wound. "You're different, Morgan."

"Yes, ma'am."

"It wasn't a compliment."

Okay, I'm lying but he won't know. She finished changing the bandage and cleaned up the old dressing, putting it with the others she was saving for the medics. She scrubbed her hands, then opened the bottle of antibiotics and handed him two pills, along with her canteen.

"You gonna ride out today?" Rad asked.

She frowned. "I should, but I'm having a few qualms. With Smith riding around in these hills and being close to the cave, I don't want to risk running into him. If the snow continues, it would be easy to track me here."

"Don't blame you for being scared." Rad agreed.

"I'm not frightened," she snapped. "I can take care of Smith. But if something happened to me, you'd die."

He grunted, clearly not believing a word she said. "I appreciate you looking out for me. I'll help you catch that killer when I can ride."

"Thanks." She meant it. He was the kind of man she wanted to have with her. He'd back her up without question and be better than any of the cops she'd worked with in the past. "How many people know where this cave is, Morgan?"

"Just me, and Connor Riley," Rad said. "We found it when we were hunting bear five years ago."

"You find the bear?" Beth asked.

"Yup. Connor shot it and then walked up on it like a dude."

"What an idiot!" Beth headed for the saddlebags to gather the supplies she needed to take care of Tigger's leg. "Were you there in time to rescue him?"

"Got there *afore* the bear killed him, but it did a fair country job of mauling him. Danged fool had read somewhere that he should play dead and the bear would quit. Only that grizzly hadn't read the same book."

Beth spun to confront Rad and call him a liar. There were few grizzly bears in the foothills, and most had been transplanted from Canada. They were rarely seen. In fact, she couldn't even recall seeing tracks when she rode these trails during endurance contests.

"Morgan, there aren't any bears."

"Maybe, not where you come from, but we still have too blamed many. Burdette loses almost a dozen calves to them and the cougars every year. Told Trace more than once to start raising deer and elk."

"Not a bad idea," Beth agreed. "I know a man who raises them and buffalo. Back before I was promoted to Homicide, I worked in Animal Control. He called me when some teenagers started poaching."

"They hungry?" Rad asked. "Folks will do just about anything to keep from starving."

"No, these kids were just mean. They got new rifles for Christmas, so they started hunting the tame deer. It was easier to shoot those than to go out in the woods. The first thing they shot was this guy's pony, the one he kept for his kids to ride."

"Doesn't sound like they were old enough to pack rifles. Their pa should have taken away the guns and used his razor strap on them."

"I understand the feeling, but some do-gooder would have screamed child abuse." She pulled out the bottle of liniment so she could doctor her horse. "I arranged for the parents to pay for the deer, the boys to help butcher them, and for the rifles to be sold to pay the veterinary bill for the pony. She didn't make it."

"Poor critter."

Beth nodded and returned to the subject most on her mind, the safety of the cave. "Does anyone besides you and your friend know about this place? How did your brother find it?"

"Nobody knows about the cave. I stocked it and have been using it for the past few years. Laid a few traps, but nobody ever sprung 'em. Reckon, it's as safe as anywhere else." Rad yawned. "I'm about ready for a nap."

"How did Kyle find it the other night?"

"His horse knows it. I used to ride S.O.B. on my circuit around Liberty Valley until I broke out Nell a couple of years ago. He'd have brought Kyle here."

"Then we'll stay close and leave as few tracks as possible till Kyle gets back. I just hope he made it to town."

"He should be at the Lazy B by now," Rad said. "And they should be here *afore* the next week is out."

"Before then or I swear he's going to the local jail."

Rad chuckled. "I look out for him. Most folks around here figure Kyle has enough charm for both of us."

"Charm doesn't pay the bills unless you're a used car salesman," Beth said. "He should grow up. How old is he?"

"Just turned thirty. And I'm not locking up my brother. He'll bring help."

"I'm sure he will." As soon as the weather warmed up, she should try riding out to the nearest town again, except she'd begun to believe he was right about the year. She wouldn't tell him that, but there was too much evidence to disprove the idea. *Okay, I've been in this cave too long. I've got to find a way home.*

She frowned thoughtfully at the photos on her digital camera. "Feel up to looking at a picture of Gary Smith? Can you I.D. him and tell me if he's the man who shot you?"

"Thought you were certain that he was."

"I am, but a witness statement would be better."

She set up a series of six pictures on the same screen, wondering what he'd think of the small color images. Would he still pretend it was the 19th century? It didn't matter if he did, not if he identified Smith. She stood, crossed to Rad, dropping to her knees beside him and holding the camera so he could view it. "Do you see the guy who shot you?"

Rad's eyes narrowed. He pointed to the center photo and scowled up at her. "How did you get this picture? It's Gary Smith Senior. I've been hunting that horse thief for more than two years."

"What?" She stared, baffled. "How on earth can you be hunting him? Why would you even know him? You said this was 1888. Make up your mind, Morgan. How could we both have come here from the future?"

"Well, it'd explain how he disappeared into thin air when I was tracking him *afore*."

———

Snow melted into the mud of the trail and Kyle rode toward the back gate of the Lazy B ranch. Giant cedar logs served as a barrier to keep the Burdette stock where they belonged. Only a fool would trespass. The ranch hands tended to shoot first and then bring the bodies into town since Trace refused to have a cemetery on the spread.

A tall, burly Irishman stepped forward at the gate, cradling a rifle in his arms. "What do you want, young Morgan?"

"Rad sent me for help." Kyle reined his horse to a stop. "He's been shot, and he's hurt bad, Mac."

"Wait there. I'll signal Burdette at the main house."

In a few minutes, a stocky, older man came from the line cabin on the other side of the gate. "Get down and come inside. There's coffee on the stove."

"Thanks, Gruber." Kyle swung out of the saddle, dodging S.O.B's kick. Damned Appaloosa could both cow and horse kick. He led his horse to the hitching post. His hands felt numb, and he stuffed them into his coat pockets. "Have you seen anything of the posse?"

"They rode back into town a few days back. Said they didn't have any idea of where to look without your brother to lead them. He didn't show up where he was supposed to meet them. What happened?" Heinrich Gruber took the reins. "I'll put up your horse this time. Where's the marshal?"

"In a cave in the hills." Kyle lowered his voice. "We got the bankroll from the thief. He was barely fifteen and Rad ordered him out of the territory before Burdette got ahold of him."

"Fair enough." Gruber started for the shed behind the cabin. "Go get warm. You can tell me the rest when I come inside."

"All right." Kyle headed inside. He carefully closed the door and scanned the room. It was small. A coffee pot sat on the wood-stove, and he looked for an extra cup. Four bunks lined two of the walls. Clothes hung from pegs on a third wall. Canned food lined the shelves on the wall next to the door and he spotted a blue enamel cup.

He filled it and went to the table near the stove. He shrugged out of his coat, hung it where it could dry. Then he sat down and let the cup warm his hands.

The door opened with a blast of cold air. Gruber kicked it closed behind him and carried an armload of wood over by the stove. "When was the last time you ate?"

"I had some jerky on the trail."

Gruber grabbed a plate and dished up beans from the pan on the stove. He put it on the table in front of Kyle. "Burdette and Prescott are on the way up with the Swensons. Fill your gut. We'll be riding out to fetch your brother when they arrive."

Kyle dug into the beans decorated with chunks of ham. He was hungrier than he'd thought and finished the food in minutes. "Rad wants Connor there. Somebody needs to ride into town and fetch him."

"Why?" Gruber poured a cup of coffee for himself. "We don't need the mayor."

"Rad and I split up in case the thieves tried to trail us. Someone shot him in the back and a woman found him. She got him to a cave, and she's been nursing him. She wants the doctor for him, and right before I left, he reminded me to fetch Connor. Rad says he'll have to marry her. They've been alone for days by now and she's a decent woman. She says the fellow who shot Rad is the same one who killed her sister."

Gruber shook his head. "Only the marshal could find a woman in the backwoods of nowhere. I'll tell Mac to ride into town now." He stood, picked up Kyle's plate, and refilled it. "You eat more and then sleep till we're ready to ride."

Kyle hesitated. "Rad wanted Matt Devlin to come. The girl says she's going after that killer by herself, and if he don't make it, Rad wants Matt to help her."

"Cross that bridge when we come to it." Gruber pointed to the plate. "You eat. I'll tell Mac to bring back a posse of loggers and shingle weavers from town. If your brother is as bad off as you say, the sooner we get to him, the better. He won't be able to protect that money for long."

"Rad told me to fetch suitable clothes for her, at least one store-bought dress." Kyle drank some coffee. "I'd better go with Mac. I surely hope Rad makes it, cause if he don't, she's pigheaded enough to bring that money into town by herself, and then hunt down the man who shot Rad."

Gruber chuckled. "No wonder your brother says he has to wed her. The two of them are tougher than a basket of rattlesnakes. Mac will bring women's garb from the mercantile unless you're determined to go with him."

"I'm going."

Gruber gestured toward one of the bunks. "Sleep and I'll roust you when Mac's ready to ride."

———

Rad Morgan was asleep when she came into the cave after taking care of the horses late that afternoon. Beth nodded in satisfaction and went back out to bring in firewood and water from the creek. They'd been careful about noise, but she would take extra care when she went for a smoke break at night.

It was warmer outside, so the snow had melted. She hoped that meant winter was truly over and spring was underway. Returning to the cave, she added a log to the fire and went to inventory the contents of her saddlebags. What food did she have left? There were packages of soup mix, dehydrated meals, coffee, and joy of joys, two cans of *Sterno*. Now, she could heat small amounts of food without having to build up the fire.

She laid her carton of cigarettes to one side and opened the other half of the saddlebags. Inside were more prepackaged meals for hiking and camping. So were her first aid kit and extra white cotton t-shirts. She'd start tearing up them for bandages today.

She'd fed the last of the grain to the horses this morning. From here on, they'd have to be content with brush and she'd be careful where she staked them, so nobody saw Tigger or Nell. Luke would continue to hunt for his food, and she'd supplement his trophies with leftovers.

She had the two paperback novels written by her adopted cousin. If worse came to worse, she could use them for fuel to start the fire or to heat meals, but she hated the thought of destroying the books especially since Audra signed them.

Granted, I'm the only one who knows she and erotic romance author, Destynee LaFleur are one and the same. She'll give me more copies when I return home, but I don't want to tell her I had to burn them.

Beth grimaced. She also hated the idea of leading Gary Smith to them, so she'd have to get her priorities straight. There was a deck of cards, but she doubted they would burn easily. She checked her supply of matches. Plenty, in case her lighter failed. She also had soap, toothpaste, a hand towel, and a washcloth.

"What are you doing, Miss Chambers?"

"Looking over our supplies, Morgan." She replaced the toiletries in the saddlebags. "I want to be sure we make it until Kyle returns."

Rad nodded but continued to study her with a narrowed gaze. "Think Smith is that close, missy?"

Beth bit her lip. She'd spent too long in combat, three tours in the Middle East and she had to listen to her own sense of situational awareness. How could she explain it to a civilian? "I feel he is."

"A person's got to trust their hunches." Rad drawled. "Besides those bank robbers are up in these hills too. They're likely to have their eyes peeled for a sign."

Beth studied her patient. "Tell me something, Morgan. How did you get the money away from the thief?"

Rad shrugged one shoulder. "Just told him to fork it over. He was only a boy, old enough to carry a gun, but too scared to use it. I took the money back and read him from *The Book*. He wasn't much of a crook. I hope he changes professions *afore* he gets his neck stretched. He didn't seem like a bad sort, just related to bad company."

Beth frowned. "Did you turn your back on him?"

"I'm no fool. 'Course I didn't." Rad yawned. "Told him it was pure luck I found him, and Burdette didn't. If the Lazy B hands ran across him with the bank money, he'd hang higher than a Christmas tree ornament and if they fetched up with his kin, they would too. That bunch isn't worth the powder it'd take to blow 'em to—"

Beth sighed. "Your stories sure don't fit in with the norm. You almost make me believe it is 1888." She opened the extra set of saddlebags and closed them up again when she realized all they held was another heavy shirt, socks, and underwear. "I wish I knew why you're so determined to fake me out, Morgan."

"I'm not faking!" Rad retorted. "I've told you more than once. It is 1888. And you ain't the only one with a complaint. If I had to be rescued by a woman, then why couldn't she dress and act like one? Why did it have to be a wildcat that's garbed like a boy and thinks she can hunt bear with a stick?"

"Wait a minute, you drugstore cowboy! I'm not the crazy idiot running around pretending he doesn't know what year it is." She glared at him before common sense took over, and she stopped speaking. Why was he so eager to squabble with her now when he'd been polite and extremely patient with her before?

He'd always listened to her side of any argument, and he'd never been this rude. She stomped over to him and jerked the blankets over his shoulders before she bent to place a hand on his forehead. His skin was hot to her gentle touch. "Damn it, Morgan. Why didn't you tell me you were running a fever?"

"Didn't know I was."

"Well, you are." Beth hurried back to the first-aid kit and sought out the aspirin. "This is all I have to help cut the fever."

Rad studied the pills suspiciously. "It's not morphine, is it?"

"No," Beth said. "Why?"

"Saw men in the hospital who depended on it."

She poured water into the cap of the canteen and helped him take the aspirin. "I didn't bring any morphine and you won't get addicted to these pills. I'm going to give you more antibiotics."

After he'd taken the pills, she picked up her mess kit. "I'm going to the creek for water. We've got to break this fever."

"Yes, ma'am."

"And you've got to stay on your wounded side. I'm not big

enough to force you to do it, Morgan. So, you've got to remember to do it regardless of how high the fever gets. I'm counting on you."

"I'll do it."

"You'd better."

THIRTEEN

"Talents of a Guardian include the Power to Heal those with good hearts, any who ask,

However, the health and safety of women and children are a Guardian's main task…"

RULES OF CHRONOS

BETH HURRIED TO THE CREEK WITH LUKE AT HER HEELS. SHE filled the largest pan with cold water and glanced toward the two horses. They were grazing and didn't need any attention. She quickly returned to the cave to keep watch over Rad Morgan.

That became the pattern for the next three days. She didn't have time to go anywhere. She hardly had the time to take care of the horses. Instead, she heated soup and coaxed Rad to drink it. She changed his bandages several times, tearing up her white, long-sleeved t-shirts when she ran out of first aid bandages.

Somehow, she forced liquids, aspirin, codeine tablets, and antibiotics down him. The hardest part was keeping Rad up on his wounded side even with their two saddles between him and the cavern wall.

She had to give him credit for trying, but whenever the fever soared, he tossed and turned. On the third day of the war to keep his temperature down, she felt exhaustion taking its toll. She'd have loved to get some sleep, but her presence was all that kept him up on his wounded side.

She added more cold water to the bottom pan of the mess kit and began to bathe his face again. She brushed a tendril of red-gold hair from her face and pinned the strand in place. She didn't have time to fuss over her appearance. Shades of her days in the Army, she kept her hair a bun on top of her head. He'd have appreciated it because of his claim that it was 1888.

More and more, she found herself believing the assertion even if she couldn't explain why Gary Smith had traveled to the 19th century too. Both of them must have landed here, but how? She wanted an explanation and wished she had brought one of her cousin's earlier books, one that used time travel as a plot point. *Too bad, too sad, Chambers. Cope with 'what is', not 'what could be.'*

Glancing at Rad, she noticed the blankets had slipped and she reached to pull them over his shoulders. When she gazed into his face, she realized he was conscious.

"Sure, is hot in here, ma'am."

Beth flicked a glance to the mouth of the cave. Another downpour added coolness to the spring air, and the fire didn't do much to warm the area. "You've got a fever, Morgan." She sponged off his face again before she offered him a drink of water. "There's soup. Are you hungry?"

He shook his head. "No, ma'am. Reckon I'm more tired than anything."

She watched his eyes close. Slowly, she replaced the cap on her canteen. Worry swamped her. If he wouldn't eat, his fever must be worse than she thought. She was almost out of antibiotics. When she ran out, what would she do? Cope, she told herself. All she could do was continue fighting the fever, the infection and pray for him.

Next time she came into the woods, she'd bring along a short-wave radio. Then she wouldn't have to leave to find help when the cell phone didn't work. Tears of weariness stung her eyes and she forced them away.

He began to toss and turn, rolling onto his back. She grabbed his shoulder, yanking him into place on his wounded side. "Lie still, you damned fool!"

He opened one eye. "I told you, missy. Ladies don't cuss."

"Yeah, right. Well, a gentleman doesn't lie." Beth snapped. "If you aren't perfect, then you shouldn't expect me to be."

"I'm no liar."

"You promised you'd stay on your wounded side. Every time I turn around, you're on your back. Your good lung will fill with blood, and you'll get pneumonia."

He smiled, a faint twist of his lips. "And you'll leave my carcass to stink when I die. I remember you saying that. You're a hard woman, missy."

"A weak one would let you die." She brushed his hair off his forehead and wiped his face with a cold cloth. "And you told me you'd eat. You aren't doing that either."

"I ate yesterday. At least I think it was—"

It'd been two days before. "Well, I made you some soup. The least you can do is try and drink it." She helped him sit up and lean against the wall of the cave. Then she lifted the cup of soup off the can of fuel.

"What kind of soup is it?"

"Chicken noodle."

"Where'd you find a chicken out here? Or is this more of your fake food?"

"If you're going to complain, you'll hurt my feelings." She held the cup of steaming, yellow broth to his lips. "It's not too bad."

He wrinkled his nose in disgust. "I don't think a chicken even saw this."

"Morgan, the next time you get shot, you oversee the catering. I'm doing the best I can. I'm sorry the meals don't match up to what you expect."

He finished the hot beverage before he spoke again. "Sorry, Miss Chambers. I'm as thorny as cactus when I'm poorly. I didn't mean to hurt your feelings."

"It's all right." The apology touched her heart, and she took a moment to brush his hair back. "I don't like instant soup either. It's difficult for a woman like me and a man like you to get along at the best of times. We've done well so far, Morgan. Now, why don't you get some sleep? And stay on your wounded side, okay?"

Once he was lying down, she covered him with the blankets. Her tone softened. "You're going to be fine. You'll see."

He caught her fingers for a moment. "Reckon, your bark is enough, and you don't need to bite."

She laughed. "You're just sick." She wiped his face with the damp, cool cloth. "I'm always nice to sick people, children, and animals. When you're back on your feet, I'll give you hell."

"First thing I'll teach you is not to cuss at me."

"Don't bet on it. No man orders me around. I've been smoking, drinking, and cussing for years, and I plan to keep on doing it."

"Not for much longer."

———

The next day she continued nursing him. He awakened and swallowed some soup, this time without complaint. His meek acceptance of the medications, and water worried her even more. How long would he be so well-behaved? What would she do if he died? Where the hell was Kyle and the help he'd gone to find? Even in the olden days, it couldn't take this long, could it?

Her eyelids drooped and she shook her head, forcing herself to stay awake. She could sleep when the fever broke, not before. She reached for the cloth in the pan of water and began to bathe his forehead, occasionally sponging off his face and neck. She made sure to wet his lips as well.

Wringing the cloth out in cold water again, she closed her eyes for a moment. Sleep almost captured her mind, but she fought for awareness. She felt herself losing this battle and rebelled against surrender, but the exhaustion won.

Two hours later, she awoke. Somehow, her short nap didn't leave her refreshed. She would have sold her soul for more rest. She gazed at him. He appeared to be sleeping naturally for the first time in days.

Damp sweat beaded his forehead, and she whispered a fervent prayer of gratitude. His fever had broken.

He was going to be all right. She wiped his forehead and his face gently with the cloth. She couldn't restrain her grin when he opened his eyes.

"Get some shut-eye, Miss Chambers. You look awful."

She laughed, her exhaustion giving her the same euphoria a good bottle of wine would have. "What are you in charge of? The complaint department? Your fever broke. How do you feel?"

"Weak as a sick cat." He smiled. Faint amusement deepened the lines around his dark blue eyes. "Reckon, I been giving you a hard time, Bethany."

"Don't apologize." She managed to keep her own smile, even at the sound of her dreaded and hated name. It didn't sound as bad as she remembered. Perhaps, it had something to do with the way he drawled it. "Now, that you're better, my name is Beth."

"I know." Rad teased. "Else I'm *dead meat*. I'll be fine, missy. You go rest."

"I will." She found her canteen and offered him a drink of water as well as more pills and antibiotics. She had more sense than to tell the man he was taking the horse's medication. If he asked, she'd tell him later. And when help arrived, she'd tell them.

Beth stood and stretched. She gathered up the cloth and the pan of water. She carried them outside and dumped out the water, hanging the cloth to dry in the bushes. Then she checked the horses. After she led them to the creek, she tied them in the bushes where they'd be hard to see.

She petted Luke. He wagged his tail and followed her back to the cave. He came inside, plopping down beside her when she sat on the blankets she'd been using because Rad Morgan had her sleeping bag. The poor animal had missed her usual attention.

It felt wonderful to pull off her boots for the first time in days. She unbuckled her shoulder holster and put the Glock where her hand could fall on it at a moment's notice. She unbuttoned her heavy green shirt. Sliding out of it, she tossed the shirt in the direction of the saddlebags. She glanced at Rad. He appeared to be sound asleep.

Good. She unfastened her jeans and slipped them down her long legs. Her black tank top felt scummy as if she'd worn it forever. She opened the saddlebags and pulled out the red Washington State University football jersey she couldn't tear up for bandages.

She looked at Rad again. He was still asleep. She sighed, gripped the hem of her top, and drew it off, over her head. Then she reached for the clean, red, mesh-style, Washington State University football t-shirt. The cotton netting reminded her of fishnet. Beth pulled on the long shirt. It fell to her thighs.

She fumbled underneath it for the hooks on her bra and unfastened it. She wanted a bath in the worst way, but she was just too tired. It'd have to wait. As she slid into the bedroll, exhaustion claimed her. Beth struggled to open her eyes one last time and check Rad. He was resting too, and then sleep conquered her.

———

Rad slowly released the breath he'd been holding. She must have thought he'd passed out. He'd never tell her otherwise, well at least not until they were hitched good and proper. It wasn't as if he had a choice since they'd been alone together for more than a week.

He still saw her long, pale legs, the flare of hips that

narrowed into a waist he could almost span with his hands. He'd gotten the barest glimpse of her breasts, just a flash as she changed shirts. He muffled a groan as his body stirred at the memory.

He had to wait till they were married. He repeated the words to himself again. He'd wait till they got hitched. But Connor had better not waste any more time finding the cave.

———

Dusk had fallen and they set up camp before full dark. Kyle toted his saddle to the wagon and put it with the gear that belonged to the other men. They'd ridden out Wednesday morning to bring in Rad and Miss Chambers, but the problem was the snow that buried his trail. He couldn't find the way back to the cave and the other men barely hid their contempt.

Well, all except Zebadiah Prescott. The big, blond cowboy was always friendly, and that made Kyle feel even worse.

"Ready for coffee and grub?" Prescott asked, passing over a tin cup of coffee.

"I guess." Kyle stared morosely into the depths of the coffee. "I'm sorry."

"For what?" Connor Riley sauntered over to the campfire and filled a plate with beans. "Hell, *boyo*. You've barely lived here six months and you made it all the way to the Lazy B on your own."

"I figure we'll find a few more tracks tomorrow," Prescott added. "We should be with the marshal by nightfall or Monday at the latest. Sure as sugar, we ain't goin' back without him. Trace would skin us alive."

"And you'll already be having your hide nailed to the barn wall," Connor taunted. "Leavin' Trace behind on the Lazy B is a donnybrook in the making. How do you plan to face that, Zeb?"

"With a good distraction," Prescott said. "Trace told me to bring home that gal who rescued the marshal."

"But Rad plans to do the right thing and marry her," Kyle

protested. "It's why we waited for Mayor Riley. He's the justice of the peace."

"Well, what Trace wants, Trace gets," Prescott drawled. "And Trace wants to see if this woman is suitable for the marshal. If she's not, she'll be downriver before the week's out. But I promise not to let her be sent to China."

———

She woke when warm sunshine caressed her face. Luke still slept next to her. She petted the dog, then raised up on an elbow to check Rad. She froze. His bed was empty. He was gone, and so was the tent she'd used to block the doorway of the cavern.

She threw the blankets to one side and leaped to her feet. She raced from the cave.

"What's wrong?"

Beth gasped at the question and swung to face Rad. He was sitting on a huge granite boulder with Nell standing beside him, nosing his arm. Beth scowled at the pair. "What are you doing?"

"I was enjoying the sunshine." Rad drawled. "Now, I'm enjoying the view."

Beth felt a blush scorch her cheeks as she realized just what *the view* was. The fine mesh of her red t-shirt played peek-a-boo with her skin. Her flush intensified when he studied the curves of her body. It was as if he traced every line of *her* with his gaze.

She started to turn away, to go back into the cave and dress. Then she stopped. Turnabout was fair play, so she focused her attention on him. It was as though she saw him for the first time. Even sitting down, he looked tall. Broad shoulders and a wide chest filled out the plaid flannel shirt she'd washed but she could see the bandage still wrapped around his wide chest and the green stone at the end of the chain he wore. Faded blue pants encased his long legs, and he'd pulled on his leather boots. She must have been asleep longer than she'd thought.

Not only had he dressed, but he'd also had the time to shave.

His shaggy black hair was still too long, but it was clean. He must have bathed in the creek. She frowned at him. He was doing far too much, far too soon. "Come on. You need to rest."

"I can rest out here in the sunshine. I'm staying put, Miss Chambers."

"The hell you are!"

"You're in a sod-pawing, horn-tossing mood, but I'm not hurt now." He stopped to listen. "Company's coming. Get in the cave. Find your britches and that peashooter."

"How do you know?" She flicked a glance at Luke and noted the warning the dog's stiff posture gave. She hated admitting the man was right.

"Damn you, Morgan!" She started for the cave, hearing the distant sound of gravel crunching and Kyle's voice. "Aren't you going to need a weapon?"

Rad gestured to the rifle propped beside him. "I already have it."

"Men!" Beth tossed her head. "What I need is a cigarette." She stalked toward the cave, pausing to listen again. This time, she didn't hear anyone, but she knew her dog had keener senses than she did.

Rad stood and followed her. "Miss Chambers, you slept two full days."

"What?" Beth spun around and gazed up at him. She'd forgotten he towered almost a foot above her own five feet, five inches. "Bull! I went to sleep last night after your fever broke."

"Friday night." Rad corrected. "It's Monday morning now. You were plumb tuckered out, missy. You didn't even hear me when I lit the fire, or rustled grub, or fed that dog of yours."

"That means," Beth began to count the days aloud, "we've been up here for ten days. Four before your fever started, four while I nursed you through it, and two while I slept. And you're telling me Kyle is finally back with help?"

"No, ma'am."

"I'm definitely throwing his scrawny behind in jail. He's as useless as a—"

"Knot in a stake rope?" Rad quirked a brow.

"Exactly!" She heaved a sigh. "Now, I'm going to have a smoke. I hope you realize the sacrifice I made while I was nursing you through that fever. I was too busy to have a single cigarette then."

"You shouldn't smoke at all. It *ain't* fitting, and I don't like it."

"Spare me. I've heard it all before. I know cigarette smoking causes lung and heart disease. I didn't do it around you because of your injury. But I've been smoking for years, and I don't plan to quit unless I start having kids. It's bad for them."

"Sounds like it's bad for you too."

"Well, it's my life. I'll throw it away if I want to. And right now, I'm having a smoke."

He followed her to the opening of the cave. "No, you aren't."

"Why not?" Beth asked, in her sweetest voice. "Are you planning to stop me, Marshal Morgan?"

"Already did." His tone was low and amused. "I burned up your smokes while you slept. You never even stirred."

She glared up into his rugged features. His jaw seemed as if it'd been sculpted from stone. "You didn't?"

"Yes, ma'am. I sure did."

She whirled and raced into the cave where she'd left the saddlebags. It didn't take much searching before she realized the cigarettes were gone. "You destroyed the entire carton?"

"I told you more than once. Ladies don't smoke."

"You are a miserable, sorry excuse for a man! How dare you?" She jumped to her feet and grabbed her windbreaker. The package of cigarettes she'd had in the right-hand pocket was gone too.

"Of all the arrogant, macho disgusting things to do. I saved your life. I didn't have a single cigarette for three, no make it five days, and this is how you repay me. That's it. I'm so outta here."

FOURTEEN

"Chosen by the Goddess, a Guardian serves her whole life long,
guiding, protecting, healing, teaching the weak to be strong…"

RULES OF CHRONOS

"Where you headed?" He'd figured she'd rant and rave about the tobacco. Anybody would, but he was ready to rein her in now.

Beth glowered at him, and he saw tears glimmer in her eyes. "Go to hell, Morgan." She opened the saddlebags and yanked out clean undergarments. "You miserable son-of-a-"

"Told you, missy. Ladies don't cuss either." Rad held up a hand when she spotted the pile of rocks the dog had heaped up near her bedroll. "And if you chuck one of those at me, you'll eat your next meal standing up."

She jerked on her jeans. "Don't you dare threaten me, Morgan. This time I'll shoot you and I won't play around like Smith did. No man lays a hand on me." She pulled on heavy wool socks, and then her boots. "Not unless I want them to."

"That explains it," Rad said.

"Explains what? You finally figure out something with that pea-brain of yours?"

"Doesn't take a college degree to know some man beat you." Rad's voice lowered, filling with menace. "Did you kill him? Or leave it for me to do?"

———

The question hung in the air. She slowly turned around. Across the cave, she saw his face and the sincerity behind the question moved her troubled heart. Will had stood up for her like that and offered to protect her from all comers, acting like the father she'd always wanted. In Luke, she'd found someone else who would give his life for hers. Her lips trembled into a shaky smile.

She could just imagine Rad's reaction if she compared him to an old man or her dog. "Stop it, Morgan."

"Stop what?"

"You're making this harder than it has to be. You're okay. I'm okay too and now I can go after Smith. He must be stopped before he kills somebody else."

"I promised to help you find him."

"You don't have to." She began to pack what remained of her supplies into the saddlebags. She stopped when she realized that the filthy tank-top, she'd taken off two days before had been washed. "It's my job, Morgan. I'd rather do it by myself."

"I'm going with you." He leaned the rifle against the stone and crossed to her. Catching her hand, he pulled her up and into his arms.

"I don't want you." She lied, drowning in his heated gaze.

"Yes, you do." He bent his head. "That's why you're so scared, Bethany."

His mouth captured hers in a kiss that claimed and soothed her tormented soul. This time he wasn't gentle or slow, yet she knew if she struggled at all, he'd immediately release her. The knowledge eased her fears, the ones ingrained from childhood, and she allowed passion to tempt her.

She rose on tiptoe, pressing her body against his lean strength. She threaded her fingers into his dark, shaggy hair. She opened her mouth under the pressure of his and traced his bottom lip with the tip of her tongue.

The invitation was sufficient, and Rad took the initiative. His tongue slid into her mouth, exploring the soft interior behind her teeth. Then he coaxed her tongue into what seemed like a game of tag, taunting, teasing, and finally demanding a response that left her clinging to him, her mind in a fog.

Luke's yip followed by a fierce growl roused Beth from her daze. She pulled back to look up at his rugged, albeit strongly carved features. *Stupid*, she told herself. *I'm being stupid.* "Company."

"Yes." He rubbed a thumb over her lips. He bent and touched his mouth to hers again, just for an instant. "I'll take care of it. Get dressed. Pin up your hair."

For a moment, Beth wanted to protest, to argue with him. He had no business ordering her around. Then her gaze fell on the clean top. She'd never known a man who would do his own laundry, much less hers. Even Will expected her to do what he considered *women's* work, the cleaning, cooking, washing, and that was on top of outside chores when she was a kid.

After she returned from Afghanistan and left the Army, she went to work on the county police force. She still spent her days off at Will's, doing what he didn't want to do.

Beth shook her head. Her football t-shirt ought to be modest enough, but she felt uncomfortable with the idea of wearing it where any man, other than Rad, could see her. And she didn't want the medics leering at her. They'd be so busy doing that, they'd forget they were supposed to be taking care of Rad Morgan.

Of course, he was almost well. That reminded her. She'd been asleep for two days. And he hadn't had his bandage changed during that time. She glanced at the opening of the cave.

Nobody was in sight. Wait a minute. How did she know help had arrived at long last? It could be the bank robbers or Smith. She hastily stripped off her red jersey and put on her bra and the clean tank-top. She'd used almost all her t-shirts for bandages. She added a heavy green blouse. Tucking both shirts into her jeans, she wrapped her olive-drab, web, pistol belt around her waist. After ten years in the Army, it only took a few more minutes to quickly braid and pin her hair into a bun.

She picked up her shoulder holster and the pink Glock. It should be loaded. She checked anyway. It was. The feel of the plastic grip gave her courage and she crossed to the opening of the cave, pistol in hand.

Luke stood beside Rad. Beyond them, she saw a group of men, including Kyle Morgan. She relaxed the hold she had on herself. Everything was finally all right. At long last, help had arrived. She holstered the weapon. "Well, it's about time."

Rad shook his head. "Miss Chambers, you'd kick if you were hung with a new rope."

"Indubitably." Beth petted her dog and encouraged him to sit next to her. Luke's hackles were still raised, and the German Shepherd wasn't likely to calm down until they left the men behind. She scanned the group again.

There were ten men, in different styles of rugged outdoor clothes. Some wore short logging pants. Others had on bib overalls. Their footwear ranged from cowboy to logging style boots. A few even wore suspenders over their solid, dark shirts.

All in all, they were a motley crew. They didn't look anything like the emergency teams she'd seen in her years at the Sheriff's Department. None of them wore Search and Rescue or law enforcement uniforms. Her concern grew when she noted the horses the men rode. Where were the four-wheel-drive, emergency vehicles? The A.T.V.s? The ambulance?

There should be at least one or two. As a matter of fact, why were they all milling around like so many sheep? The medics should be here with Rad, asking a ton of questions. She glanced down the trail and spotted two other horses. These were hitched to an old-style buckboard, like the kind she'd seen in museums, the ones the pioneers used.

Pioneers. The nineteenth century. Her thoughts jumbled together like ingredients in a blender. Rad. The money, hand-written banknotes, and gold coins. The old weapons. His clothes. His attitude. No helicopters or vehicles or real roads. The missing Park Ranger station.

What the hell happened? How did she end up with all these antiquities?

Only they weren't old. Not for here. Not for now! She stared at the group of men again, realizing one additional quality she hadn't noticed before. Most were short, not much more than her own height. Short to her, but not for today. And today was—

"1888," Beth whispered.

"Yes," Rad answered in low tones. "I told you, missy."

"How did this happen?" She cautiously pinched her arm. "Ouch." That hurt. It meant she wasn't dreaming. She knew she wasn't. She might have fantasized about a man like Rad, but she wouldn't have had him severely wounded. Especially not when he stirred her with only a look.

O.M.G., it really was 1888.

How had she gotten here? Beth shook her head. She didn't know. Snapping her fingers at Luke, she retreated inside the cave. It had almost become home in the past ten days. Now, she wouldn't have to look at the living history display outside. She could try and assimilate the information she had and plan some possible solutions.

Time travel? How was that possible? Why was she here? This was real life, not one of Destynee LaFleur's fantasy romances.

Beth sank down on her sleeping bag. Luke curled up beside her, his head on her knee. He growled. She rested a hand on his brown and black head, ruffling the fur on his neck. "Why are we here, partner?"

Smith, she recalled suddenly. The suspected killer was here

too. She'd seen the tracks from his horse. She'd followed him. Her job wasn't finished. She had to find him, had to stop him from hurting anyone else. She had to heal the injuries he caused. The feeling of peace, warmth, and love she associated with her own accident swept over her. What was she doing here? Why had she come? And how was she going to get home?

———

"Well, you ain't dead, old son." Connor Riley strode over to Rad. "Kyle said you were a goner. I figured you were too damned stubborn to die."

"Got that right." Rad gripped his friend's hand. The two of them were closer to fifty than thirty and had arrived in Junction City about the same time. Connor worked as hard as any of the loggers he hired and didn't dress much fancier.

Rad jerked his head toward the cave behind him. "Miss Chambers went out of her way to save my life."

"Kyle told me about her." Connor's eyes twinkled with good humor. "He said she was prettier than any of the gals around here, even my daughter."

"Reckon, she'll do."

"That's what Kyle said. She doesn't take any sass from anybody, not even you. And she's a good cook. Kyle says she made a dandy stew the first night he met her."

"Kyle talks too much." Rad frowned at his best friend. He and Connor had ridden together in the war, had worked ranches down in Texas, and driven cattle across the country to points east, before they moved north to Washington Territory. Connor was one of the few men in Liberty Valley who wasn't afraid to josh him.

"Kyle said she was sweeter than the bee trees around here, that she made his ornery horse purr like a kitten."

"Sounds like Kyle didn't have to do much to roust all you fellas out of the saloon." Rad drawled. "Is that why you got such a big posse? They all planned to court her if I saddled a cloud and rode to the great beyond?"

Connor sobered. "I was headed for Portage to see if you made it there when Kyle rode in and brought me word. He already had the buckboard. He told me that you wanted me to marry or bury you. We got to your office just as Doc finished swearing-in my loggers as deputies. We didn't have any trouble rounding up a posse. Everybody wants their money back."

"And a new pretty gal in town didn't have anything to do with it?" Rad asked. "Women are scarcer than upper teeth in a cow around here, only Miss Chambers is more than that. She may act as sweet as sugar, but she wouldn't give a man standing room in hell. She nursed me day and night after Kyle left and I'm not the soul of patience."

"To put up with you, she'd need more sand than a desert." Connor reached for the plug of chewing tobacco in his vest pocket. "It takes guts and gumption for this country." He bit off a chunk of tobacco, then offered the plug to Rad.

"Not for me." Rad drawled. "My chest won't take it yet."

"Hurt bad?"

"Not like *afore*. Then I wanted to die, so I didn't feel ripped apart."

"Kyle told us you were lung-shot." This time it was a big burly man with a warm grin, who approached. "So, did he know what he was talking about?"

"He knew, Doc." Rad's gaze narrowed on the man in the dark coat and matching pants, black because then the blood didn't show when he operated. "And I told him not to bring you. You're needed in town."

"Doc saved my life six months ago." Kyle pointed out as he came over, followed by Zeb Prescott. "I knew he could help you."

"I still don't need him. Miss Chambers did all that was necessary."

"Did I hear my name?" Beth stepped out of the cave and eyed Kyle. "Well, it certainly took you long enough."

"Yes, ma'am." Kyle smiled with practiced charm and tipped back his hat. "Thanks for saving Rad's life."

"I did it for him, not for you." She turned her attention to the older gray-haired man. "Did I hear correctly? Are you the doctor?"

"He sure is," Rad answered, "Miss Chambers, this is Doc Jenkins. He's the finest sawbones in these parts and he goes everywhere."

Doctor Jenkins removed his hat and bowed. "Actually, I'm the finest practitioner in the whole Territory."

"That's right," Beth muttered. "Washington isn't a state yet."

"It will be," Connor said, eyeing her curiously. "One day."

"Sooner than you think." Beth focused on the doctor again and smiled at him. Then she used her sweetest voice. "Doctor, would you consider looking at Marshal Morgan? I'm not sure I did everything right."

"'Course you did!" Rad drawled. "I'm alive, ain't I?"

Beth gave him a stern look but kept a smile pasted on her face. "Yes. I still want the doctor to check your injury. Why? Who knows, Marshal Morgan?" She mimicked his southern drawl to perfection. "I coulda made a mistake. Mixed in some sulfur with that poultice, perhaps."

Doctor Jenkins winked at Rad. "I'll get my bag." He hurried toward the wagon.

Connor choked on his tobacco. "Now, ma'am. We didn't mean for you to overhear—" He started sputtering and coughing,

"I'm sure it was a compliment." Beth's voice was as sweet as honey.

Rad grimaced. "He's gonna poke and prod me forever and a day. I'm fine, Miss Chambers. What did you do that for?"

She dropped the sweet facade. "You deserved it, Morgan." She turned to Kyle. "Get some hot water and make sure that doctor scrubs his hands. Otherwise, he could infect the wound."

"Yes, ma'am." Kyle hurried away, obviously relieved to be out of the battle between the woman and his brother, but Zeb Prescott lingered to watch the show.

"You're like a barb-wire fence, Miss Bethany," Rad said. "You got your good points, but patience *ain't* one of 'em."

She lifted her chin, so their gazes met and clashed. "Call it a lesson you needed to learn, Marshal Morgan. Payback's hell. And I don't get mad. I get even."

FIFTEEN

"A Guardian chooses a life partner to be a forever mate, not to follow, or lead, but to walk beside her, sharing the Guardian's fate ...."

RULES OF CHRONOS

AFTER SHE WENT BACK INTO THE CAVE, RAD WAITED TILL CONNOR finished coughing and spitting tobacco juice. "You all right?"

Connor shook his head. He lifted off his hat, raked a hand through faded red-brown hair, and replaced the hat. "I never saw the like, Rad. She doesn't know about you, does she?"

"Reckon she knows enough. We've been alone for ten days."

"She don't know when you yell, everybody runs for cover." Connor whistled, softly. "She'll make you toe the mark. She's got more courage than most folks around here."

"She and Trace will get on like two pups on the same trail," Zeb commented, pulling out the makings to roll a cigarette. "Neither of them say whoa on a go-ahead show."

"And they're not meeting until after I marry her," Rad said, his tone even.

Connor eyed him. "But you don't have to marry her."

"I don't?" Rad asked. "I was alone with her. She's a lady."

"Kyle said you wanted me to look after her if you didn't pull through. Now that I've met her, I'd be happy to do it."

Rad chuckled. "Hands off, *amigo*. I saw her first."

Kyle came back to the three of them. "Doc's ready for you, Rad. And Mayor Riley can marry you and Miss Chambers soon as Doc's finished."

"Good." Rad waited. His brother had something else on his mind or he wouldn't stand around. "Speak your piece, boy. I got no secrets from Connor."

Kyle looked at the cave and then lowered his voice. "It's about her. I told the folks in town she's hot on the trail of that man who shot you. She found you in the woods and brought you here."

"Nothing wrong with telling the truth." Rad gripped his brother's shoulder for a moment. "That comes close enough."

"What's not true about it?" Connor asked.

"Before he shot Morgan, he nearly killed my best friend and stole her horse," Beth deposited Tigger's saddle in the dirt by the front of the cave. "This eavesdropping is getting to be too much of a habit for my taste and I don't like it. Move your conversation elsewhere." Turning, she strode back toward the cave.

Rad shook his head and strolled toward the wagon. Sooner or later, he'd have to sort out his differences with Miss Bethany Chambers, but for now, he'd give her time to simmer down.

"Do you want me to look at you, Rad?" Doc Jenkins asked. "I will admit I'm curious about what she did. I've seen men survive when bullets touch their lungs, but I've lost patients when it's more serious."

Rad shrugged. "You can look."

"Well, remove what remains of your shirt then."

———

In the cave, Beth collected her saddlebags. She'd inventoried the supplies she had on hand, a minimal amount of dehydrated food, her W.S.U. t-shirt along with an extra work shirt, socks, underwear, the two Destynee LaFleur erotic romances, a deck of cards, a small pad of paper, and a pencil. She turned toward the entrance when she heard footsteps and recognized the man who'd been speaking to Rad outside. "And you are?"

"Connor Riley, ma'am. I'm the mayor of Junction City." He removed his hat. "I want to thank you for taking such good care of Rad. He's a decent man."

"I know that," Beth said. "He just talks too much."

"Do you have any sisters, Miss Chambers?"

"No," Beth said. "Only Nina. She's closer than any sister could be." Her voice trailed away.

Connor nodded, sympathy on his face. "My family's back in Ireland. I haven't seen hide or hair of 'em in more than thirty years, but Rad Morgan has backed me in more than one donnybrook."

"And you're good friends," Beth finished. "I'm glad."

"What happened to your friend was bad, too bad," Connor said. "A man would ride far to find a gal like you." He hesitated. "Miss, what you heard Rad say. He didn't mean nothing bad. Out here, a man needs a woman to ride the river with, a gal who can paddle half the canoe. Pretty isn't enough."

"I see." And she did.

She watched the mayor leave the cave, admiring the way he defended his friend. Then, she turned back to the sleeping bag, her bed that Rad Morgan had slept in for more than a week.

She had to find Gary Smith, but would she ever forget Morgan? Not likely.

Why had she traveled this far except to track down a killer? She couldn't allow the temptation to stay with a man she'd just met to keep her from doing the job. Besides, Rad would find a real woman soon enough, one that could fulfill the demands of life in 1888. It wasn't her.

She had to find Gary Smith and drag the man home, in chains if possible. She wasn't staying here in Podunk Hollow. Before she rolled up the sleeping bag, Luke growled. She saw the young blond man enter the cave. He carried an armload of firewood and she gaped at him. "What are you doing?"

"If Marshal Morgan needs this place again, it better be restocked." He stacked the wood neatly beside the firepit. "I'm Zebadiah Prescott." He smiled, sky-blue eyes friendly. "Trace told me to offer you the hospitality of the Lazy B."

Beth blinked. "Morgan said it was the closest place. He told Kyle to go there for help."

"He did well for a city slicker fresh from the East. Impressed Trace for the first time in months."

"I heard they had issues," Beth said, studying the young man. Something about the way he carried himself reminded her of the Army Rangers she'd known in Afghanistan. He was too alert, too ready for any battle. And her dog had stopped growling at him. Instead, Luke leaned against Zeb Prescott, enjoying the way the man petted him.

She frowned at the gunbelt that circled Zeb's lean hips. His coat was pulled back so he could easily reach the pistol. "That's odd. I thought cowboys always wore two guns."

"Trace does, but one is all I've ever needed." Zeb winked at her. "Invite's open, ma'am. I'll fetch the rest of that wood."

"Thank you." Beth tilted her head to one side. She should accept or decline the invitation in person. "Which of the men out there is Trace Burdette?"

"None of them," Zeb answered. "Trace doesn't hunt vermin anymore. That's my job." He chuckled suddenly. "We still argue about it. I'm hoping that guarding the Lazy B will keep my wife busy long enough for us to get the bankroll home and she won't come looking for us with the rest of the hands at the Lazy B."

Beth caught her breath. She nearly said what she thought. From what she'd learned in school, women stayed home, and men did everything in the old West. "I didn't know women packed guns out here."

"Trace got hers from her grandpa when he died. Come visit us soon." Zeb gave Luke one last pet before exiting the cave.

Beth wondered who'd be the next to introduce himself. She had to admit that the idea of a woman in charge of a ranch baffled and interested her. Visiting the Lazy B had just become more of a priority, even if it had nothing to do with finding Gary Smith.

———

Rad suppressed a groan when Doctor Jenkins unwrapped the poncho piece over the bandage. The man wasn't rough, but Bethany had a gentler touch.

"Interesting. I've never seen anything like this before." He peeled back the cloth dressing, gazing at the wound. "You *were* shot in the lung. How many times did she change the bandage?"

"At least twice a day." Rad shrugged one shoulder, then winced when the gesture pulled on his chest. "Why?"

"Too often, but I can't blame her for fearing infection. What else did she do?"

"Fed me pills and made me lay on my hurt side till I prayed to die. She didn't want my good lung to fill up with blood. Said that would kill me."

"I don't know about that." Doctor Jenkins mused. "Never read anything like that in the journals. I need to talk to her and learn more." He opened his bag. "Well, I'll wrap you back up again. You got a good nurse there. I'd let her finish what she started."

"Works for me." Rad nodded at Kyle when he came to join them. "I'm proud of you. I wouldn't have thought anyone could get a wagon up here. You're a better man than I am."

"It was Trace's idea," Doctor Jenkins said. "If you were dead, it'd be disrespectful to toss you over your horse and take you home to bury, but Kyle was the one who rented the buckboard from the livery and was determined to get it here."

Their praise obviously stunned Kyle. He walked to the front of the wagon and grabbed a small paper package. "Got you a new shirt, Rad. Man doesn't get hitched every day. And I got something for her too, but you have to get her to wear it."

"What is it?" Rad eyed the large package Kyle held.

"Those clothes for her you told me to fetch." Kyle crossed back to where his brother was standing. "I even got her a fancy dress and all the trimmings. Call it a wedding present. I did my part. You've got to get her to wear it."

Rad opened the small package that Kyle had handed out first. Inside was a dark blue shirt. He pulled it on, easing it over the long underwear and the sore side of his chest, tucking it into his pants. Then he fastened the buttons. "A man couldn't ask for a better brother."

"You joshing me?" Kyle demanded.

"Nope. I'm straight with you, boy. If I were any prouder of you, I'd bust. I gave you an impossible job to do, and you did it." Rad picked up the large package wrapped in brown paper and tied with string. "You got through this country and didn't get killed by that back-shooting coward who plugged me. And you didn't get ambushed by that band of cutthroats who robbed the bank or the Indians, Miss Chambers ran across."

"They were just up for the fishing," Kyle said. "I didn't have any trade goods. And you said to keep clear of them."

"And you sure remembered everything when you got to the Lazy B. You got the doc like Miss Chambers asked and Connor like I wanted. And you managed to get a wagon clear up here where no roads go. You're a hell of a man, Kyle."

Rad tucked the large package under his arm. "Now, I'm *gonna* try to convince Miss Chambers that we can get married right here, right now."

"Don't be surprised if she holds out for a real preacher," Doctor Jenkins said. "It amazed me when Trace insisted on having the priest from Snohomish do the honors instead of Connor. Women are notional."

"But if anyone can hold a wedding up in the middle of nowhere, Rad can," Kyle said. "I'd bet on it."

"How much?" Doctor Jenkins asked. "I got a sawbuck that says he can't pull it off."

"Ten dollars is a bit rich, but count me in," Kyle said.

"Me, too," Connor reached into his pocket. "What about you, Zeb?"

"I'll hold the money, but it's too close a contest to call."

———

Rad glanced around the cave as he entered. It looked different already. The bedrolls were both tied and stacked in a corner. The fire was out, and the pit was cleaned. He put the package down and looked at the rear of the cave.

Beth glanced over her shoulder at him. "I've looked all over the place, but I can't find the bandages I was saving for the medics. Of course, that doctor may not need them, but it'd be good to get rid of the evidence."

"I already did." Rad drawled. "I had a good bonfire while you were asleep. I burned the bandages, that big map and most everything people would question. Couldn't bring myself to destroy the books or the food or your special contraptions about Gary Smith Senior."

Beth rose and held out her hand. "It's been entertaining, Morgan. I don't know how I got here, but I must stop Gary Smith. I know that."

Rad took her hand and drew her close, putting his arms around her. "Miss Chambers, will you marry me? You know the worst about me already. I'm not much of a bargain. I got a hardscrabble ranch outside of Junction City and being the marshal doesn't pay much. We won't live high on the hog, but I can provide for you."

She closed her free hand around the one that was holding hers. She lifted his calloused fingers to rest against her cheek. He saw tears in her eyes.

"I can't, Morgan."

"Rad."

She repeated the name softly. "Rad, I can't marry you. I've got a job to do."

Rad brushed his lips over her eyelids, then her lashes, tasting the salt of her tears. "Like I said *afore*, I'm willing to help you, Miss Chambers."

"Beth," she corrected, softly.

He kissed away the tears again. "I want to help you, Bethany. I'm eager to help you."

"I don't know how I got here and I'm not staying." Beth lifted her chin, so their gazes met. "I'm going home as soon as I arrest Gary Smith. This is your time, not mine."

"You have to marry me. I've been the marshal in Liberty Valley a long time, but I won't be if folks hear I ruined the good name of the woman who saved my life."

"I already told you. I'm going home."

"We'll worry about that later." He kissed her gently. "Let's get hitched, Bethany, and not let yesterday or tomorrow use up today."

She shook her head. "No, Morgan. It's a crazy idea and I'm not taking part."

SIXTEEN

"A Guardian renders aid to the helpless, the dying, the unborn. She celebrates life and grieves with those who mourn..."

RULES OF CHRONOS

SHE SLIPPED HER ARMS AROUND HIS NECK. SHE SURRENDERED TO the magic of his kiss, but only for an instant. Then, she pulled back. How could they be married today? They hadn't applied for a license. Even if he'd arranged to have someone say the words, it wouldn't make the ceremony legal.

I like him, she thought, *okay, that's not completely honest*. She admired and respected him. But they'd met just over a week and a half ago. She didn't really know him. Still, she didn't want to see him blamed because they'd spent so much time alone in the past few days. Like they had a choice. He'd have died without her and both of them knew it.

She'd read enough books to know 19th century morality was totally different from that of the 21st century. *Hell's bells and cockleshells. If I didn't, just listening to one of Will's lectures about what he considers appropriate behavior is enough to show the way society has evolved in the past fifty years.*

In his day, girls wore dresses everywhere and he totally freaked the Sunday she showed up in her jeans to drive him to church. She needed Rad's help to find Gary Smith in 1888. She didn't have a clue where the killer was hiding, and this was a whole new world to her. How could she track him down in the middle of the Old West when she was accustomed to hunting suspects in 2018?

She gazed up into Rad's face. "This isn't fair to you when I'm leaving A.S.A.P."

"What does that mean?"

"As soon as possible."

"I don't think so. You're here for a reason. I'll bet you're here to stay." His mouth teased hers in light, butterfly kisses. "Let's get hitched, Bethany, and put out this fire so neither of us shock folks."

She gave in to the magic of his kiss and let her mind drift away on a cloud of passion for a moment. "Marriage isn't my be-all and end-all. I have a job to do."

He snagged her chin, lifted it with a calloused thumb. "Those men out there will force the issue if we don't make this our choice, not theirs. If it becomes a shotgun wedding, the town council will fire me at their next meeting. Even Connor and Trace won't be able to stop them."

"Crap on a cracker." She heaved a sigh. "The things I do for my job and other LEOs suck. Okay, Morgan. I'll marry you, but I damned well won't promise to obey you."

His lips claimed hers once more before she could add to the list of things, she wouldn't do for him. The kiss ended and she rested her cheek against his broad chest, listening to the steady beating of his heart. "How are we going to get married without a minister or a license?"

"Connor's the local justice of the peace and the mayor of Junction City." Rad stroked her hair. "He'll do the honors and he'll have the license with him. We'll do it now. We've got a ten-mile ride over rugged country to Burdette's spread and it's almost another ten miles to town. My spread's on the other side of Junction City."

Beth frowned. "Morgan, that's damn near a day's ride. You're barely healed. We'd better stay here another night and leave early in the morning."

"We're riding out, Bethany. I need to get the bankroll back to town and see how things are before we put a posse together to hunt Gary Smith."

Beth pulled out of Rad's embrace and backed up a step. She planted her hands on her hips. "Morgan, you're pushing yourself too hard. You've only been out of bed for two days." She raised her chin. "I'm not going anywhere this afternoon."

"You don't have a choice." His tone lowered and became menacing. "I'd rather you come peaceably. But, if you won't, I'll drag you outta here."

"Damn you, Morgan. Just tell me why!"

"Because that posse out there left more tracks than a herd of buffalo." He turned and strode to the entrance of the cave. "We're leaving, Miss Chambers, as soon as the wedding is over. Will that horse of yours let you ride him in a skirt?"

"Of course not!" Beth tossed her head. "I wouldn't even try committing suicide that way."

"Should have known." Rad glanced over his shoulder. "Kyle brought you a dress. Leave it for later. You can wear what you got on—"

"The hell I will!" Beth flashed. "This may be the only wedding I ever have."

"Count on it."

"Stop growling. You sound like a grizzly bear. And I'm damn well wearing a dress to my wedding whether you like it or not." She glared at him. "I can't take a bath in the creek with all those men out there. So, you'd better bring me a bucket of water."

"Say, please." He came toward her, graceful as a cougar. "No woman orders me around."

She raised her chin even higher. "And no man tells me what to do."

A faint smile twisted his mouth. "Then I reckon we both better put on our company manners and say please and thank you."

Beth's anger melted into bare amusement. She laughed, just for an instant. "You're right, Morgan. Will you *please* bring me some water so I can clean up?"

"Be happy to, Bethany." His smile broadened and he feathered a soft kiss over her lips. "I don't want to get pinned in here by that pack of two-legged coyotes who robbed the bank. This time we'd both get killed."

Beth stared after him as he left the cave. He was right. Why hadn't she thought of the jeopardy, or the danger posed by the bank robbers as well as Smith? Rad considered the idea almost as soon as their would-be rescuers arrived. Why hadn't she? Even if he was the local marshal, she was a police officer too.

She hadn't seen Junction City yet, but it couldn't be that big of a town or it would have rated a mention in the local history section of one of the county libraries.

And the man wanted to take her to his ranch. She sighed. She had to turn her brain back on and get with the program. Taking care of Rad Morgan provided a nice vacation from her *real* job, but the holiday had ended. She went over to the package he left and pulled a knife to cut the string that secured the brown, wrapping paper.

When she folded back the paper, she spotted the heavy material of a dark blue dress. It looked like satin, and probably was, she told herself. There weren't any synthetic materials in the late 1880s were there? Under the elaborate dress were several sets of underwear that reminded her of the camisoles and other lingerie sold in department stores back home, pantaloons, stockings, and garters. Obviously, nobody had invented nylons yet.

She poked cautiously at the leather button-up shoes. They must be for dressy occasions, she decided. Nobody could wear them for work. She continued to examine the next items. They were two weird pieces of long material with what felt like spokes sewn inside and more strings to tie around something.

Odd, she thought and was glad to recognize a heavy canvas divided skirt, then a second one made of soft leather, followed by several blouses, two vests, and a coat. Kyle had gone hog-wild at the stores in town. Who did he think was going to pay for all these clothes? They probably wouldn't take her Visa at the shops.

She glanced over her shoulder at the sound of footsteps. Rad entered the cave, a bucket of water in hand.

She smiled at him. "I've got a big problem, Morgan."

"Told you already." Rad set down the pail. "Wear pants."

She picked up the spoked material. "What's this?"

"A corset." A hint of red crept along his cheekbones. "You wrap it around your middle on top of your unmentionables and tie it. Gives a woman a slender waist."

"Not me," Beth said. "I read an article about these instruments of torture a couple of years ago. It said that the reason women fainted all the time and had trouble carrying children was because of corsets. I like my body the way it is."

"So do I. Leave it off."

It was her turn to blush. She tried to ignore the heat in her cheeks. "Get out of here, Morgan. I need to change and we'd better hurry before the wedding turns into a massacre when those bank robbers arrive."

———

Rad inclined his head in acceptance and left the cave. Outside, he crossed to where Connor Riley waited near the back of the wagon. "Connor, Miss Bethany ain't partial to obedience. Reckon, you'd best leave that part out of the ceremony."

Connor frowned thoughtfully. "Tisn't her place to dictate the wedding vows."

"What if you don't rub her nose in it?" Doc Jenkins offered Connor a drink from his flask. "If Rad gets her to wear a dress to this shindig, then it seems to me, he's shown who will be wearing the pants in his house."

Rad was grateful Bethany couldn't overhear the conversation. If she did, she would come out swinging, and it'd make his job harder. He'd been training horses for a long time, gentling them, not rough-breaking like most men did. He'd learned over the years, it wasn't *what* he said to a horse, but *how* he said it. "I figure a filly is well-trained when *she* wants to do what I *tell* her to do."

"A woman isn't the same as a horse." Connor pointed out, a smile sliding into his eyes. "Most the ladies in town would skin you alive if they heard you, Rad."

"If more men treated their women as good as they do their horses, I'd have less work to do." Doc took a swig of his whisky. "I'd enjoy the peace and quiet."

Before the argument progressed any further, Bethany came out of the cave.

If she was lovely in her men's clothes, in a dress she was beyond beautiful. Her flame-colored curls were pinned in a bun on top of her head. The dark blue dress fitted every curve. Her waist looked smaller than ever. Even though the dress covered her arms, and buttoned tightly to her throat, it was as if he could see her entire body. The full skirt floated around her, as she came toward him. Rad caught his breath.

———

Beth deliberately took small steps so the skirt wouldn't sway too much and give anyone a view of her petticoats. She'd seen enough old movies to know how women moved in these dresses, and she had to admit privately that it was fun to wear something more elaborate than her usual work attire.

As she drifted toward Rad, the rest of the men turned to look at her. Their talk stilled and then began again in whispers. She smiled at the doctor when he came to join her.

The physician winked at her. "I don't recall seeing a prettier gal anywhere. What if you tie-up with me, and we'll let Rad eat our dust?"

"Even after I stayed alone with Morgan?" Beth widened her eyes in false innocence. "Why, what would people think?"

"Whatever is the most wicked." Doc pronounced. "I been up the hill, over the mountain and fought the varmint, ma'am. You can't live your life by other folks' lights."

"I couldn't agree with you more," Beth said and took his arm. "My father isn't here. Will you give me away?"

"I'd be honored." Doc walked beside her.

When they were in Rad's earshot, Doc asked again. "You sure you want to settle for him when you could have a grown man like me?"

Rad took a step forward, good-humored menace filling his eyes. He smiled, but his deep voice carried a threat. "You've been in this country longer than the mountains, Doc. I saw her first."

Beth laughed. "And he asked me first, too." She tilted her head to one side and teased. "Of course, I'd be willing to bet that Doctor Jenkins would never give me orders."

"Wouldn't dream of it." Doc winked again. "A man who don't respect women ain't much of a man in my book. She is mighty pretty, though. And you're gonna have to fight off all comers, boy, so you'd best marry her." Ceremoniously, he traded places with Rad.

Beth trembled when she met his gaze. All at once, the wedding seemed profoundly serious. "Are you sure about this?" she whispered.

Rad nodded and closed his hand over her elbow. "You'll see, missy. We'll get along as good as two six-guns on the same belt."

Connor began the ceremony. Beth listened intently to the words. They sounded real enough. Just before he asked them to make their vows, the man leaned forward and asked, "What are your full names?"

"Bethany Rose Chambers."

"Radolf Doyle Morgan."

Beth suppressed a giggle. What a name! She'd have a way to harass Rad now. All she had to do was call him by his full name when he annoyed her. The rest of the wedding only took a few moments. She knew she had to be dreaming when Connor only asked her to love, honor and cherish Rad, not to obey him. Well, she wouldn't push her luck and ask the mayor why he'd deleted that portion of the vows. It was supposed to be 1888, wasn't it, and wives were supposed to defer to their husbands, weren't they?

When the ceremony was over, Beth waited for Rad to kiss her. He didn't. Instead, he just looked at her. The expression on his face made her knees quiver, she had never seen a tenderer glance. The two of them turned to face the other men.

Kyle approached them and bent to kiss Beth's cheek. "Welcome to the family."

"Thank you." Beth clung tightly to Rad's hand for a moment longer. "I didn't expect this to happen."

"Rad did." Kyle mimicked his older brother's drawl. "He told me to bring back Connor."

"You talk too much." Rad gestured toward the brush where his and Bethany's horses were tied. "Get those animals saddled. We've been here too long. It's no place for an ambush."

Beth frowned, studying Rad's broad chest. Something was wrong with his shirt. Suddenly, she realized what it was! Blood seeped into wool, creating a stain, obviously from his wound. "You're bleeding."

"I'm all right."

She gripped his muscled arm and urged him toward the wagon. "Don't be silly. Did the doctor change your bandage?"

"Nope."

"Men!" Beth snapped. "You macho types are a pain in my—"

Disgusted with the bunch of them, she turned and stomped toward the cave, muttering swear words. She stopped next to Zeb Prescott and asked. "Could someone bring a bucket of water? Morgan's bleeding again."

"Sure, Missus Morgan." Zeb gestured to one of the loggers. "Mac would be glad to."

She felt a blush seep into her cheeks. She hadn't expected to be called by Rad's name. After all, she had a perfectly good one of her own. Going into the cave, she gathered her medical supplies. She'd have to use the remains of her last t-shirt for a bandage.

Doctor Jenkins was helping Rad remove the new wool shirt when Beth returned. She glanced at the physician. "Are you going to assist me with this procedure?"

"Well, I know better than to tell you I can bandage him." Doctor Jenkins replied. "Rad may have you in a dress for the wedding, but he hasn't tamed you yet, not by a long shot."

———

The previous night he'd returned to the site where he left the last yapper, just so he could remember and relish every moment of her training, but now it was time to leave her for the coyotes. He glanced up the trail and heard voices, male voices to his right. It was also time to get help to complete his mission.

Turning the stallion, he rode in that direction. He stopped as the other riders spotted him. He recognized the boy who had surrendered the money to the marshal. "Morning."

"Howdy. Who the hell are you?" One of the older men spurred his horse forward. "What are you doing here?"

"The same thing you are. I'm looking for the man I shot, the one who got away with your money."

"I 'spose you was going to return it." This time the boy spoke.

"No. I'm going to keep it." He studied the band of men, all of them in ragged clothes and on scrawny horses. "I guess we could split it. I get half."

The older man laughed. "You got sand. I'll give you that, mister. Why should we share our takings?"

"Because I'm the reason you've even got a chance of getting

some of it back. I shot the man who took the money away from your boy. All I have to do is find that damned black Appy mare and the cash is mine."

"A black Appaloosa?" This time a different man whistled softly. "Mister, you've got more guts than sense. You shot Rad Morgan? You'd best pray he's dead because if he comes hunting, you won't have time to talk to your Maker."

"I got him through the lung."

"Then, he's a goner," the leader said. "Mister, I reckon we'd be honored if you rode with us. Never thought any man could kill Morgan except maybe Burdette and that breed wouldn't draw on the marshal. What's your name?"

"Smith. Gary Smith." At long last, he had the respect and admiration he deserved. Soon, he'd make these men into the followers he needed, and then, he could really change the world.

For the first time in years without a yapping bitch to see him, he smiled.

———

Rad frowned at Doc. The physician's sense of humor tended to rile folks and it wouldn't take much for Beth to realize she'd been manipulated into wearing a dress for their wedding. Hopefully, Connor and Zeb wouldn't point that fact out to her.

While the men prepared to ride out, Beth used white strips from the t-shirt to make a bandage. With a gentle touch, she sponged off the blood on his chest. "You've got to be more careful, Morgan."

"I'll keep that in mind, Missus Morgan." Rad glanced past her to Kyle who lounged outside the cave entrance. "Did you get our horses saddled?"

"Not yet, but I will right now."

"Well, stop," Beth ordered. "I'll saddle my own and there's no way your brother can ride without tearing up his chest."

"I can ride," Rad said. "I've felt worse and stuck in the saddle."

"In the wagon." Beth dumped out the water. "We'll use the blankets to make up a bed for you."

"I ain't ready to be buried yet," Rad said. "I'll ride my horse."

She shook her head and heaved a sigh. "In the wagon. I'll stay with you, but I have to say that you take a lot of looking after, Morgan." She turned to Kyle. "Come along. You can help me clean out the cave. Everything's ready to be loaded and your brother wants out of here so we're in a better spot if we get ambushed by those bank robbers."

Doc Jenkins watched and waited silently until Beth was out of earshot. "Was keeping her in a dress worth the bother of riding in the wagon, Rad?"

"I reckon so. We'll be at the Lazy B by dark and I don't want Mrs. Sims finding fault with my wife. Bethany's chock full of pride—"

Zeb chuckled. "Can't have any more than Trace and if Ma Sims isn't able to keep her in dresses, you're fighting a losing battle, Marshal."

"Trace doesn't live in town even yet," Rad said. "If those church-going ladies look down their noses at her, Bethany's liable to tell them to go to hell in a heartbeat and I'll be moving on to Portage. I can set up my office anywhere in the valley."

SEVENTEEN

"A Guardian brings to justice those who hurt, maim, and kill. But allows those who harm none to do as they will…"

RULES OF CHRONOS

THEY WERE ON THE TRAIL TO THE LAZY B LESS THAN AN HOUR later. One rider led Tigger and another ponied Rad's mare. It wasn't Zeb Prescott or the two men who obviously took orders from him. He'd given them special instructions. The young, dark Irishman he'd sent for water was behind them, watching for anybody on their back trail.

The second, a big blond had slipped into the woods parallel to their group, ready to warn them if anyone approached from that side. Meanwhile, Zeb was in front of their group and something in his manner reminded her of Afghanistan and a soldier leading a combat patrol.

Connor Riley drove the buckboard, Doctor Jenkins on the seat next to him. Both men seemed as wary as the rest of the posse. Beth sat in the back of the wagon beside Rad, his rifle close to hand, and her carbine next to her, but she had her pistol in its shoulder holster.

She'd made up a bed for him. He didn't use it, opting to lean against the back of the bench seat. Before they left the cave, she'd changed to one of the divided skirts and a blouse rather than dirty the fancy blue dress. It felt wonderful to have something clean to wear, not the jeans she'd worn the last ten days.

My vacation is over. Finally, she had time to think about Smith and the women he'd probably murdered. He'd left three of them in Eagleville, but those victims weren't his first prey. She frowned, recalling the number of similar crimes on the computer. How many women had he killed and why?

I'm the last person to demand justice for them, to make sure they didn't die in vain. But they did. How could they threaten Gary Smith? What did they do?

"What are you cogitating about?" Rad asked.

"Smith. Why would he kill so many women?"

"Which Smith?" Doctor Jenkins asked. "There's a lot of men who use that name."

"Gary Smith Senior," Rad said, obviously choosing his words with care. "And if a man thinks a woman who can rope steers, ride broncs and chase the wind is too much for him, he's right."

"From what I remember of him, Smith was afraid of most everything that wore a skirt," Connor said. "Sure, and he acted tough around them and tried to scare them."

Beth blinked, glanced at Rad, and then at his two friends. "Let me get this straight. All of you know the man I'm hunting. How many women did he kill when he was around here? And how could this happen?"

"I'm not sure how it happened that you know the man we do," Doctor Jenkins said. "But he had to go somewhere when he left town with Trace Burdette's horse. As for women, he, Lew Williams, and Kirk Dahlberg were partners in more ways than one."

"Where do I find them?" Beth asked. "Maybe, they'll have a lead on locating Smith."

"Williams and Dahlberg died in a fire last fall," Rad said.

"You could talk to Hannah Ortiz," Doctor Jenkins suggested. "She ran the bordello for Dahlberg and knows where most of the gals went who worked there."

"A bordello?" Beth eyed Rad dubiously. "Prostitution is legal in *your* town?"

"Most of us are liking the parlor house a lot better," Connor said. "Trace still keeps Lizbeth in meat and John Lee's the best cook in town, but don't be a-tellin' my daughter I said so."

Beth shook her head. She had a lot to think about. It sounded like things were far different in the *Old West* than she'd ever believed. She still didn't know how Gary Smith managed to make it here and it sounded like there were a lot· of witnesses she'd needed to interview. Trace Burdette Prescott would be at the top of her list.

As the hours passed, Beth grew weary of riding in the buckboard. It jolted and bounced across the grassy meadows and was even worse in the woods. The only good part about the wagon ride was that Rad could rest and not fall from his horse onto the ground. He slept heavy, his head in her lap and she stroked his black hair.

"He must still be awfully weak." Doctor Jenkins said in a low voice, clearly pitched so Beth could hear and Rad wouldn't awaken. "He hasn't complained once about losing his hat. Kyle didn't mention it, or I'd have brought him one for town."

"We'll get him one later." Beth smoothed Rad's black hair again.

They were crossing a huge grassy meadow. A line of blue spruce trees towered on the far left of the field. Luke jogged alongside the wagon. As she watched, the dog smelled something.

Then, he tore off toward the trees. Beth caught a whiff of the same scent for a moment, sweet, yet unspeakably foul. In that instant, she knew! It wasn't reason that drove her, but pure instinct. "Stop the wagon!"

When Connor reined the horses to a halt, she eased away from Rad. She grabbed her jacket, sliding her arms into the sleeves. She had her phone, digital camera, gloves, and a few plastic bags for evidence. Then, she was out of the buckboard, running for the trees where Luke waited.

The odor hit her nostrils again.

A dead body.

She pushed the bags into her skirt pocket. Drew her pistol and ducked under the long boughs that draped onto the ground. She scanned the shadowy darkness, ready to shoot if necessary. A crumpled heap across from her. Luke growled.

She studied the area again, then slowly approached the woman.

Young, barely out of her teens. Five feet, two or three inches. Slight, a hundred pounds. Jet black hair, tightly braided. Brown eyes stared, wide open, fixed on nothing. Broken teeth...from repeated blows to the mouth. Crushed nose. A shattered cheekbone protruded through the face. Clothing cut away...

Even with bits of flesh and blood in what must once have been a puddle of blood under her head, the woman had been pretty. But not anymore. Not after what Smith had done to her.

She must still have been alive when she arrived here. Until he slit her throat and she bled out.

Even though Beth was certain this was Smith's work, she still had to check for his trademark torture. She drew on a pair of plastic gloves, opened the mouth, and saw the ragged cut. The missing tongue was taken this time while the victim was alive. That was different. Normally, he took them after he administered the *coup de grâce*.

"Bethany?"

"Stay there." She peeled off the gloves, tucking them into her pocket. She flipped open her notepad and quickly sketched the scene. Then she pulled out the digital camera and took pictures of the crime scene. Once she finished, she backtracked carefully toward Rad, watching for evidence.

"What is it?" Rad asked. "A deer?"

"I wish." Beth returned to the wagon and opened her saddlebags for her flashlight. "Did you get rid of my light?"

"Yes, ma'am," Rad answered. "I'll get you a lantern."

"That'll do." Beth went through the saddlebags where she'd packed her jeans. "Sorry about your caveman sensibilities, but Smith just had one hell of a good time playing hack and slash on a Native American woman. I'm guessing, but I'd say she's somewhere between twenty and twenty-five. I'll know better in a little while." She glanced at the physician. "How strong is your stomach, Doctor? I need your help."

"What do you want me to do?" Doctor Jenkins asked, climbing down from the wagon.

"Give me a time and place of death," Beth said. "Tell me what injuries happened first, if she was raped, and how he did it. I need facts and I don't have the qualifications you do."

"Bet you'd like an autopsy too," Doctor Jenkins said. "I'll do the best I can, Mrs. Morgan."

Beth slid her pistol into its holster and swung to face Rad and Kyle. "I don't want anybody under that tree until I'm through and the doctor is too. Otherwise, I could end up with extra footprints, misplaced evidence, and a screwed-up crime scene."

"I've got a feeling we're spending the night here," Kyle said. "Can we defend ourselves, Rad?"

"We'll have to," Rad said. "Get some of the men to stand watch while the others set up camp. I'll do some scouting and see what tracks are around."

"Good idea." Beth nodded in agreement. "Most serial killers return to visit their victims and Smith isn't any different. Let me know what you find."

Darkness had fallen by the time she completed her preliminary investigation. She'd gathered every piece of evidence she could find, cigarette butts, two shell casings, and a few scraps of paper.

Why hadn't Smith cleaned the area? He'd never have left a mess like this in Eagleville. Maybe, he didn't expect anyone to find the body.

While the doctor examined the body, Beth walked the perimeter. She located the spot where the stolen horse stood for hours, if not days. Every bush had been stripped of leaves and the tree was totally barked. It'd drop in the next windstorm. It wasn't much fodder for a stallion that topped eleven-hundred pounds and she winced. Wonder had been starved before. The poor Appaloosa was being abused again and there was nothing she could do about it.

Reluctantly, Beth left the doctor to finish his work. She saw a small campfire on the other side of the meadow and smelled meat cooking. The scent nauseated her. She couldn't even think about food, not after seeing a battered, broken body. And there was no way she would be able to suffer companionship, especially that of men. She wanted to scream at them, to yell, to shoot everything male for allowing a crime of this magnitude.

Finding a rock to sit on, Beth put the lantern beside her. She put the evidence bags on the ground beside her. Obviously, Smith had taken his time killing the girl. She'd been with him for hours, if not a day, possibly two. Beth pulled out her notebook and eyed the sketch she'd made of the body and its position under the tree. When the doctor completed his autopsy, she'd interview him and discover what he knew.

It was time to start writing up her notes for what would eventually become part of her report and she removed a worn pencil from her shirt pocket. Of course, she could do it on the phone if the battery held up, but she wasn't trusting it since she hadn't been able to charge it in the past ten days. Granted, she hadn't kept it on twenty-four-seven the way she did at home. Of course, if she used it for her report, the lawyers would demand it for the legal case and that so wasn't happening. Not when the "contraption," as Rad called it, was her personal property and expenses always took forever to be reimbursed by the county.

She remembered her supervisor, John Watkins complaining he

still hadn't been paid for his "smart phone" when the judge ordered him to give it to the defense team and the rest of the detectives laughing at him. The lieutenant had pointed out they'd been told repeatedly to take notes "old school" style. She'd drawn a series of sketches that showed the entire crime scene as accurately as possible, backing them up with her digital camera. She could give up the memory card to the prosecutor and buy a replacement. It was much cheaper than losing her cell phone and all its contacts.

———

"Not much of a wedding night." Connor gazed at the tree, then across the meadow where Beth sat by herself, head bent over a notebook. "Reckon, she's even thinking about your marriage?"

Rad shook his head. "Nope. She's all tangled up with that dead girl."

Connor jerked his head toward the tree. "You see her?"

"Not yet," Rad said. "Reckon, I will when we bundle her up to take her back to her people. Do you have that whisky bottle you carry most of the time, Connor ?"

"Sure do. Need a swig?" Connor held out the flask.

"Thanks." Rad took the small bottle and headed toward Bethany.

"Drinkin' near a decent woman is purely foolish," Connor advised. "Sure, and I remember it stirs them up worse than a nest of hornets."

Rad nodded and kept walking. He'd found tracks from the killer's horse. If she knew about them, she'd light out after Smith. Rad sat down next to Bethany. "How bad was it?"

"Bad enough." Beth concentrated on the pad of paper in her hands. "Don't worry about me, Morgan. I'm fine, just not sociable." She shuddered as memories obviously crowded into her mind. "Not hungry either."

"Thirsty?" Rad held out the whisky bottle. "It's Connor's I'm not much of a drinker anymore, but Prince Beauchamp owns the local saloon. He makes it strong enough to cure what ails you."

Beth slowly laid her notebook aside. "I thought you told me ladies didn't drink or smoke."

"Reckon, most ladies don't have to take care of a dead girl either, 'specially not after that butcher." He pried the cork from the bottle.

Beth nodded. "You're all right, Morgan." She took the bottle from his hand. "I never told you that we used to go out for a drink after the bad ones. How did you know?"

"During the war, and right afterward I tried drowning myself in liquor. It didn't help for long. My troubles swam better than I figured they could."

"And you stopped drinking for good?"

"No, but I cut back. I may have a couple of glasses when we're playing poker, but that's all."

"You're a brave man, braver than me. I need help to face my demons." She lifted the bottle to her lips and took a swallow.

She coughed once, twice, then surrendered to the choking fit that left her breathless. He patted her back, and finally, she raised her head. "What the bloody, blue hell is in this crap? It tastes worse than paint thinner smells."

"Have another drink." He guided the bottle to her mouth. "It gets better."

"The hell you say!"

A short time later, Rad replaced the cork in the bottle. She'd passed out after only a few swallows of the whisky. Despite what she claimed, she wasn't much of a drinker.

He picked up the notebook and flipped through the pages, stopping at a picture of the girl under the tree. She had been gutted worse than a deer. He frowned. Somehow, he had to find a way to protect his wife, but he couldn't get her drunk every night. She was brave, had guts, and demanded a man's respect, but she was also out to stop a monster. And she couldn't do it alone, even if she figured she could.

Rad closed the notebook and turned down the lamp. Putting them together, he lifted Beth into his arms. She'd fuss at him if she knew he intended to carry her to the wagon, but it was only a few steps away and he was well on the mend.

Connor met him at the buckboard. "She all right?"

"Asleep." Rad put her on the bed in the back of the wagon, removed her boots, and then covered her with the blankets. He returned the whisky to his friend. "Thanks."

"You're never touching Prince's brew," Connor said, his brogue thickening. "So, what have you been a-doing?" He eyed Rad, then turned his attention to Beth, obviously smelling liquor. "Why you're slicker than cow slobber, *boyo*. She'll be spittin' tomorrow."

"But she'll sleep tonight."

EIGHTEEN

*"Respecting all life is a lesson a Guardian teaches.
She leads by example and rarely preaches…"*

RULES OF CHRONOS

IT FELT AS IF SHE HAD A CEMENT BLOCK ON HER FACE. SHE struggled to open her eyes and groaned as the light hit them. She remembered this feeling, but she hadn't experienced it in almost three years. The department shrink advised against self-medicating with alcohol for PTSD, saying it would make the nightmares worse.

Will had suggested she find different hobbies. She should stop drinking at the local bar and picking up the wanta-be cowboys. She'd tried taking a few college and Community Ed classes, but that got old in a hurry. Then, her foster father suggested she buy a horse and start endurance riding.

She rubbed her aching forehead. She'd gotten drunk on only a few sips of whisky. Of course, the homebrew was stronger than anything she could buy at the neighborhood liquor store. It sounded like Rad was the marshal of an interesting town. Brothels, bootleggers – what else was legal in the Old West?

She felt the warmth of a body beside her and remembered the strange wedding ceremony the day before. She was married. Maybe she was still single in real life, but here on the other side of the rainbow, she had a very sexy husband. No wonder she had someone sleeping with her. Okay, so maybe she was a bit callous since she still thought of this as a temporary arrangement while she was here, but she'd been straight up with Rad Morgan before the ceremony. He might think she was here for the duration, but she didn't know about that.

Without opening her eyes, she reached out a cautious finger and touched the person beside her. Fur? Weird. She cautiously slit one eye and saw Luke lying next to her. She giggled and her head throbbed in response. Slowly, she rested a hand on the German Shepherd and tried to rise. Hadn't she been through this before? Yes, when Gary Smith ambushed her on the trail.

Where was Rad? She slowly lifted her head and looked around the campsite. She saw blanket-covered forms and counted them. Six. Where were the rest? Counting her husband, there should be five more men.

She eased out of the blankets and sat on the tailgate. She spotted a canteen next to her saddlebags. She pawed through and found a first-aid kit. Aspirin. A daily vitamin. Next, she opened a packet of powdered orange juice and dumped it into the canteen, shaking the container to mix the two. She washed down the pills with the juice and felt almost human.

Luke stood and shook. He jumped down from the wagon and waited in front of Beth. She slowly slid to her feet and petted the dog. "Remind me never to drink that garbage again."

She reached for her boots. She shook them out, drew them on, and headed for the bushes to take care of what Rad referred to as her *personal* needs. Smiling, she shook her head. There had to be a better way.

Her good humor faded when she saw the tracks. The distinctive hoofprints from Nina's Appaloosa headed north into the woods. Beth swore. Last night it had been too dark to see Wonder's trail, but now she had daylight on her side. She'd pursue Gary Smith and stop him before he killed anyone else.

Hangover forgotten, she hurried back to the wagon. She yanked out her saddle, pads, sleeping bag, and other gear and left it in the back of the buckboard. Taking the bridle, she went after Tigger. She'd put her horse together and then find Rad. He could either come with her or she'd find Smith on her own.

She'd groomed and cleaned Tigger's hooves by the time Kyle stirred, sitting up in his blankets. Beth wasn't concerned about the younger Morgan. She cared more about hitting the trail behind Smith. She picked up the saddle blanket and pad, sandwiched together, putting them on Tigger's gray back. When she turned for the saddle, the stallion reached around and pulled off the blankets, dropping them on the ground.

Beth put down her saddle, grabbed the blanket and pad, shook them, and started over. "Smarty-pants! It'd serve you right if I rode without them."

Tigger nuzzled her arm this time, and Beth watched the Arabian closely as she lifted her saddle.

Kyle yawned as he came nearer, rolling his shoulders. "What's going on?"

"Not much." Beth flung the heavy Western saddle onto her horse's back. "I found Smith's tracks. I'm going after him."

"Does Rad know?" Kyle took off his cowboy hat, ruffled his dishwater blond hair, and then replaced the hat.

"I'll tell him before I leave." Beth walked around the horse and let down the cinch on the right side. Then she went back to the left and unwrapped the latigo, so she could fasten on the saddle.

"A wife generally asks her husband before she does something important like chasing after a back-shooting, woman-killing coyote." Kyle's tone was polite and unassuming.

"I'm not from here." Beth reminded him. "And I don't ask any man's advice because then I might have to take it."

"Yes, ma'am." Kyle watched her finish saddling. When she began tying on the rest of her gear, he walked away.

Beth scowled after him. She'd wanted to ask where she could find Rad, but she didn't want to look desperate or needy. She shrugged and returned to the task at hand. It was time to go.

———

Kyle hightailed it to where Rad was standing guard. "She's pulling out."

"What?" Rad swung around to eye the camp. "Damned if she ain't. That woman beats a mule for stubborn." He tossed his rifle to his younger brother. "Stay here and keep watch."

Before Kyle answered, Rad strode down the short hill and into the camp. He walked around the sleeping men, sure they were playing possum. There was no way they'd sleep past sun-up. "Where do you think you're going, Bethany?"

"After Smith." Beth checked her rifle and then put it in the scabbard. She found her shoulder holster and strapped it on, then added her pistol. "Want to come?"

Rad drew a deep breath and took a step closer to her. "No. And you aren't either."

"Oh, but I am." Beth checked the knots that fastened on her saddlebags. She picked up her bedroll. "I thought you promised to back me up."

"I did," Rad said, taking the roll of blankets from her and dropping them back in the wagon. "And I will, but not today. Prescott can track a whisper in the wind. He, Mac, and Olaf left last night to trail that hombre and see where he ends up. I gave my word to Zeb. We're taking the money to Trace and that gal you found to her family. Once that's done, we'll catch up with Zeb and hunt down the man who shot me."

Beth scowled. "It's my job, Morgan, not Zeb Prescott's, and I'm leaving today."

Rad's hands closed over her shoulders, and he pulled her to

him. His voice lowered to a menacing rumble. "Listen to me, Missus Morgan, and listen good. Even that dog of yours has more sense than to chase a coyote into the back country. I won't let you ride into an ambush."

Beth tried to wriggle loose. "Smith won't know I'm coming."

"He'll expect somebody after the way he stalked and tortured that girl." Rad's hold tightened. "He won't spot Prescott or his men, but they won't be looking for you, and I don't want them to shoot you. So, you're not leaving, Mrs. Morgan. We'll just let Smith simmer a while. Then, when he doesn't expect us, we'll ambush him. Turnabout is fair play."

"The hell with you!" She glared up at him. "I'm going after him now, Morgan. Not when you finally get around to it!"

"The hell you say, Missus Morgan." He leaned closer to her, his tones lower and even harsher. "Things are different here. You married me yesterday of your own free will. I have plenty of witnesses to it."

"So what?" She tossed her head. "You don't own me. We're just married, that's all."

"You're wrong. Far as the law's concerned, I do own you. If I must rope and hogtie you to get you to the Lazy B, not one of them men will protest or even blink. And if they heard the way you sass me, they'd expect me to tan your backside. Lucky for you, they're asleep."

Beth gasped before she raised her chin in defiance. "I've been beaten before. If you ever lay a hand on me, I'll shoot you!"

Despite his own attempt to cow her, Rad was annoyed. He'd never strike her. He wanted her to think, not rush into danger. Well, if he was going to be hung out to dry, then he might as well go all the way. "As long as I'm reading you from *The Book*, I may as well finish the job. You put on one of those skirts Kyle brought and pin up your hair. No wife of mine wears pants!"

———

Beth took a deep breath, as the tension between them mounted. Using self-defense techniques, she'd learned in the Army, she could break his hold and kick his macho backside to the curb. Well, okay there weren't any curbs here, but she had choices. Did she want to end this relationship now before it even started? Or did she want to work out their differences? If they had a knock-down, drag-out fight, she wouldn't have the back-up she needed to go after Smith.

She met his gaze evenly. "I think we both better stop before we say things that are unforgivable, Morgan. I don't take crap worth a damn and neither do you."

"That's true." He feathered a calloused thumb over her lips. "Shall we start the morning over again?"

"Works for me." She rose on tiptoe and brushed her mouth lightly across his. "What if we have breakfast and you tell me the instructions you gave Zeb Prescott?"

Rad nodded. "All right. Will you trim my ears if I say that you'd look mighty pretty in one of those skirts Kyle brought?"

"No." She laughed. "I'm not that big a witch. But I won't take orders, not even from my husband. Got it?"

A smile dawned in his dark blue eyes. "I've been running in single harness for a long time, Bethany, but I can learn to be part of a team."

"So can I."

Leaving him with Tigger, she collected clean clothes and went into the bushes to change out of her dirt-stained jeans and heavy cotton shirt. When she returned, she saw her horse grazing by Rad's mare while he saddled up. The other men were breaking camp and Connor stood near the small campfire doing something with a coffee pot. It looked like they'd be on the road before too much longer.

The afternoon sun was high overhead as they wound their way through yet more giant evergreens, grassy meadows, and occasional stands of second-growth cedars. When the trail bordered the river, she heard the regular splashing of fish and frequently spotted bald eagles overhead. The regular appearance of wildlife gave more credence to the year as if she needed it. Rad had taken the front for their group, riding point and she pretended she was glad that the other men avoided her too.

She'd had most of the day to think about the scene with Rad, and suspicioned she'd been played. He'd backed off way too quick on his ultimatum that she was *his wife* and would wear what he felt was suitable. It didn't make much sense for him to *wimp out* on an argument. Will always quoted his favorite TV judge and said, *'if something doesn't make sense, then it isn't true.'*

Beth might have changed to a heavily divided skirt this morning, but only because she didn't want to wear her jeans all day, not after she'd investigated a crime scene in them the night before. It had nothing to do with his ultimatum, she told herself again, but didn't he think he was all that and a bucket of clams? He was hot, but either he mellowed out for real, or she'd find a way back to civilization.

There had to be a pair of ruby slippers somewhere.

She leaned forward and petted Tigger's neck. "We're not in Kansas, Toto, but we'll get home somehow."

Doctor Jenkins rode up beside her. "Thought I'd tell you about the woman."

"That's fine," Beth said. "What did you see?"

"She fought him as much as she could. Broke her nails and he's bound to be scratched up." The physician continued listing the injuries. "All of them happened before he killed her, and she died hard."

His voice faded and Beth eyed him. "I know he did worse, Doctor. You don't have to protect me. He raped her."

"I'm not even thinking about that." Doctor Jenkins lowered his voice and glanced toward Rad. "Marshal Morgan will take her back to her people, but they're gonna be up in arms. She was a shaman. I met her when I went to take care of a sick child."

"What?" Beth stared at him. "I don't understand."

"As the saying goes, there's more that happens in this world than we're aware of, Missus Morgan. And that girl must have cursed her killer. He cut out her tongue, but his days are still numbered. And when her people see how their medicine woman was dishonored, they'll be hunting him."

Beth tensed. "Morgan said that Zeb and his men followed Smith's tracks. Will they be in danger?"

"Not from the Indians. Mac speaks Chinook nearly as well as Rad."

Beth frowned and then eyed the physician again. "He's done it before."

"What?"

"Smith always cuts out their tongues," Beth said. "He usually waits until the end, after he slashes their throats. He did this one earlier. We haven't been sharing that detail with anyone."

"You want me to keep shut about it?" Dr. Jenkins asked.

Beth nodded. "I'll tell Rad. Other than that, nobody else needs to know."

"All right. I'll need to tell him the rest of it. He's the law."

Beth hesitated, wishing there was a way to keep the majority of the gory details away from Rad. "Smith didn't stop at rape, did he?"

"No, he dang near tore her apart with some sort of club. And I've seen that before in town when a couple of the gals from the bordello died."

"What about his wife? Did he hurt her?" Beth asked.

Dr. Jenkins shook his head. "Kind of strange when you think on it. Vera was a tiny thing, frail, and she doted on him. She'd keep his meals hot and never fussed when he spent nights at Dahlberg's saloon. Did laundry for the loggers…"

"And her wages?" Beth asked.

"Went to him, of course. She never held back a cent."

The words were measured and careful, but Beth could tell by the tone that the physician hadn't liked Smith's wife. "There's more to it, isn't there? You had issues with her."

"Vera Smith didn't eat until he came home and had the best of the food." Dr. Jenkins glared into the distance. "One thing for a grown woman to do that, but she wouldn't feed her children even when they cried and begged. And she whipped them if they stole candy from the mercantile or if the church ladies fed them. She said not eating a meal or two wouldn't kill them, but I think they missed more than the occasional dinner."

"How many children?" Beth asked gently.

"Four. Smith was enraged when the two older boys and the girl lit out and Rad refused to look for them. Said they were old enough to choose and they had."

"Where did you send them?"

When he didn't answer immediately, she waited, aware she was the focus of his narrowed gaze and then a faint smile lightened the man's face.

"What? You didn't think I'd know who rescued the kids?" Beth asked. "I'm a detective, Doctor. I'm not stupid."

He chuckled. "You're the only one in town who ever wanted to know. Trace's grandpa and I sent them to my sister in California. Rad suspected what we'd done, but he never asked, and we didn't tell him. Those youngsters grew up fine. I can't say the same for the youngest boy. Junior was his pa's shadow and struggled to be just like him."

"What happened to Junior?" Beth asked.

"Tried to bushwhack Trace one time too many and Prescott took umbrage at the notion."

"I'll bet," Beth said. "He seemed the type. And Junior?"

"Oh, Trace paid for the funeral. Told Rad it'd lure out the fellow who hired him since Junior didn't have brains enough to pour piss out of a boot if there were instructions on the heel."

Beth frowned. Would she ever become accustomed to this world, or would it always seem foreign to her? Zeb Prescott had killed a man, and obviously he hadn't stood trial or served any prison time. Instead, he was considered a hero.

With another chuckle, Doctor Jenkins swung his horse around and headed back toward the wagon. Beth frowned. Obviously,

Smith's fury had escalated. He'd never stopped any of his victims from screaming before. What had this woman done? It must be something different, and somehow, Smith felt attacked. Why had he vented his spleen on the captive, taking her tongue before he finished torturing her?

NINETEEN

"To do HER Sacred Work, SHE chooses a Guardian then creates a hallowed place, despite Time and Space...."

RULES OF CHRONOS

HOURS PASSED. AS THE SUN SANK LOWER, THE TRAIL WIDENED. Giant evergreens lay end to end, making a solid barrier beside what could be considered a narrow, one-lane track.

"This is the start of the Lazy B," Rad said, reining Nell beside Tigger. "We'll spend the night here and take the woman the rest of the way to her folks tomorrow. Trace and Gruber can return the money to the bank. The loggers will guard them."

"It sounds like you want Connor and Doctor Jenkins with us," Beth said. "Will that be enough to show respect for her?"

"I'll ask Trace's godfather to come, too," Rad said. "Fremont Goodman speaks for her on formal occasions."

"That should do it."

Ahead of them, the group came to a stop, and farther up the trail, she heard Kyle greet someone. A horse squealed and Beth saw a big bay shouldering through the posse who respectfully backed their mounts off the trail. As the rider approached, Tigger laid his ears back and snorted a challenge.

Beth tightened her reins and corrected the Arabian. "Friend of yours?"

Rad chuckled. "It's Trace, and she rides a stud too."

The other stallion wasn't the only intruder. Luke growled at the dog that trotted behind Trace's Appaloosa.

Beth studied the other woman as she neared. At least five-feet-five, slender despite the layers of clothes. She wore a heavy black duster over dark clothes, pants, a shirt, and a jacket. High cheekbones, long black braids, obviously part Native American. As Zeb had said, she also packed two pistols on her hips.

"Marshal." Trace pitched her voice low, but every word carried. "Good to see you alive and kicking. Where's Zebadiah?"

"He, Mac, and Olaf are trailing Gary Smith Senior."

"He the one who bushwhacked you?" Trace asked. "You tell Zebadiah not to kill him? That he's mine."

"No, he's not," Beth interrupted. "I've chased him this far and I'm taking him back to stand trial."

Trace frowned. "And you are?"

"Homicide Detective Beth Chambers."

"Bethany Morgan," Rad said. "My wife uses my name."

"Wrong. I have a perfectly good name of my own that I've used for thirty-four years, and I'll keep right on using it, Morgan."

"We'll discuss it later when we're alone, Bethany."

Amusement flickered into Trace's face, for an instant, then faded as she looked beyond them and into the buckboard. "What happened?"

"Smith." Beth followed the other woman's gaze. "He likes to rape and kill. We're taking his latest victim home."

"Tomorrow's soon enough for that, Trace. Can we park the wagon up by the gate, so the children don't see her?" Rad asked.

"Yes. I'll ask Gruber and Lars to stand watch, so you can tell her folks that we honored her as much as possible." Trace waved a greeting at Connor and Doctor Jenkins, before swinging her horse around to ride beside Beth. "So, where are you from, Detective?"

Beth blinked at the abrupt tone. It was the same she'd have used to interview a suspect. "Why do you want to know? Is it a requirement for camping on your property?"

"I'm curious about you," Trace admitted. "Zebadiah says it's because I own everything around and I always want to check everyone's back-trail."

"Be a bit difficult to check mine," Beth said. "I followed Smith here, but you wouldn't believe me if I told you where the trail started."

"You'd be surprised," Trace said. "My grandfather had a lot of stories about these mountains and special places in Liberty Valley."

"You've never shared all his stories with me," Rad said. "Why not? We've talked about most everything under the sun."

Beth looked at the man on her left, then at the woman on her right. Did they have a past? And did she want to ask? Maybe not here or now, but she'd find out the truth from Rad later.

"I'll share them with the detective," Trace said. "She can decide if you have a need to know."

Beth blinked at the phrase, one common in her time, but not one she expected to hear in 1888. "Oh, I'm definitely interested in those stories now."

"Thought you might be." Trace left them to ride forward to where the men waited outside a gate. "I'm back, Gruber. Let us in and signal Ma to have a guest cabin made up for the marshal and his deputy."

"Wife," Rad said. "She's my wife, not my deputy."

"I own Junction City." Trace glanced over her shoulder. "You've been griping about a deputy for the past three years, Morgan. You have one who will ride with you now, while Cal watches over the town. You can stop trying to get Zebadiah to take the job."

Rad winced when Trace rode away. "I knew she'd be out for

blood if Prescott didn't come back with us. I just didn't expect it to happen so quickly."

"I have a job," Beth said. "No offense, Morgan, but I'm not working for you."

"None taken." He urged his mare closer to Tigger and the Arabian didn't object. "I'm glad that we'll have privacy tonight."

She struggled to ignore the heat that warmed her face and trembled when he leaned close enough to catch her chin with his fingers. "What about you and Trace? Have you known her for a long time?"

"Since her grandpa brought her to town when she was a tyke who threw rocks like they were baseballs." Rad chuckled. "Would have been better if he'd told us she was a girl-child instead of leaving us to find that out last year."

"No way." Beth gaped at him, then glanced after the younger woman. "And your brother got into a fight with her?"

"Yes, and she won." Rad's deep voice gentled to a murmur. "It may make the two of you madder than rained-on hens, but I'm keeping you safe from that killer. He comes near you, Bethany, and I'll make him a free lunch for the coyotes. He's not doing to you what he's done to those other women."

"And what about Trace?"

"She has Prescott. And there won't be enough left of this Smith to scrape up if he's stupid enough to come on the Lazy B, like his son. His pa left him behind when he took off with Trace's horse."

"What?" Beth gaped at him. "Dr. Jenkins mentioned, but—"

"Gary Smith Junior," Rad said. "Prescott shot him."

"You knew about it, and you didn't arrest him?" Beth asked. "Why not?"

"Why should I? It was a fair shooting. Junior came looking for trouble, and he found it."

"I see," Beth said. "And his mother? What happened to her?"

"Died of a fever five years ago," Rad said. "Doc took care of her. She's buried in town."

"Good to know." Beth made a mental note to visit the grave and see if Gary Smith Senior stopped by to pay his respects. Who knew? Maybe the man would take her flowers.

When he released her and backed Nell away, Beth rode beside him through the gate. Once the wagon was safely inside, Connor turned the buckboard to face the main track beyond the fence. Then, he and the older man that Trace called Gruber began to unhitch the team.

"Go on down to the main ranch," Connor said. "I'll be along later."

"I'll have Lars bring you a horse." Trace led the way along the ridge to a path that wound downhill. "Missus Sims will save you a plate, Mayor. She made a dried apple pie today since it's the marshal's favorite and she knew he'd be coming for supper."

"Good thing I lived," Rad said. "Her pie is as close to heaven as I want to get."

Smiling, Beth followed them down the narrow trail. Dusk made it hard for her to see, but Tigger had no such problems. When they reached the bottom of the hill, the trail widened to a wagon track, and she saw the shadowy shapes of buildings.

Trace reined up in front of the first house, a small cabin that was set off to the right side of the road. A grizzled old man and a red-headed teenage boy stood by the nearby corral. "Fremont and Shawn will look after your horses."

"Thanks, Trace." Rad swung out of the saddle. "We'll see you in the morning."

Beth watched as the rest of their party followed Trace down the track in the direction of the largest structure. There would be time to look around tomorrow. She glanced back at Rad, then dismounted. She staggered for a moment and leaned against her horse until she had her land legs. Wow, that was a long ride, and she hadn't expected to be so stiff.

"Detective Morgan, this is Fremont Goodman," Rad said, "and Trace's adopted son, Shawn. This is my wife. She found me on the trail after I was ambushed and took care of me."

"It's nice to meet you." Beth passed Tigger's reins to the boy. "Thank you for meeting us."

"Don't worry about doing the pretty tonight, ma'am," Fremont said. "You look tuckered. Get some rest and we'll meet and greet tomorrow in the daylight."

Halfway to the cabin, she stumbled on the rock-strewn path. She caught her breath when Rad swung her up into his arms and carried her the rest of the way. "Put me down. You can't do this. I'm too heavy and you definitely shouldn't be carrying anything when you're still healing from that gunshot wound."

"You're not as big as you think you are, Missus Morgan." He pushed open the door. "And I'm not a city slicker."

"That's for sure." She turned her face into his shirt, listening to the steady heartbeat. She slid her arms around his strong neck and pressed nearer.

His arms tightened around her. She trembled when he dropped kisses on her hair, then her forehead. He didn't grab at her or act as if she were a machine that needed to be poked, prodded, pushed into sexual action. Just having him touch her with respect had to be the biggest turn-on she'd ever known.

Inside the cabin, light from the lamps caught her attention and she glanced around. There was only one room, and it was obviously intended for eating and sleeping. A large bed covered with a red blanket took up most of the left wall. A small wood-stove heated the cabin and on top of it, a covered kettle held what must be their supper. It smelled like homemade stew or soup.

A table in the middle of the room had been set for two. She saw a loaf of sourdough bread, butter, and a jar of homemade jam as well as a pie. "Looks like supper is waiting for us."

He slowly released her, and she leaned against him. She pulled his head down so their lips met in a kiss, slow, gentle, and oh, so soft. The sweetness of the embrace sent shock waves thudding through her. She moaned, a whimper of pleasure as the kiss continued, still tender, innocent. She threaded her fingers into his hair, teasing his mouth with her tongue. She felt him smile before he ended the kiss.

His lips roved across her jaw to nip at her ear. "Easy, Bethany. We have all night and the rest of our lives."

"So, what are you saying?" She tipped her head to one side. "We have to wait?"

"Yes." He framed her face with his hands, dropping tiny butterfly kisses on her forehead, brows, and nose. "I can kiss you as much as I want. And I will, but not till we have supper. We're taking our time tonight."

She began to unbutton his shirt. "Want to bet?"

He captured her wrists, and his lips teased the pulse in her throat. "Slow down, Missus Morgan."

She gasped when his mouth explored the line of her neck. "How much do you think I can stand, Morgan? How many of your kisses?"

"I don't know, but I reckon we'll both find out."

She shuddered when he kissed her ear, along her jaw, over her chin. It felt as if her nipples stood to attention, pushing against her bra. "No more. Please."

"Why?" His mouth was barely an inch above hers. "Thought you wanted me?"

"I do, but I can't wait forever. I'll die."

"We'll just have to see."

His mouth claimed hers and she surrendered eagerly, silently chanting, *'Yes, yes, yes!'*

She clung to him, pressing into the lean strength of his body. The hell with dinner. She'd have him now and food could just wait. When he traced the line of her lips with his tongue, she opened her mouth, enticing him into a passionate duel. At last, at long last, he would make love to her, real love.

Instead, he pulled back and nipped at her bottom lip.

Frustrated, she pushed him away. "Damn you, Morgan. What are you trying to do to me?"

"I'm gonna know you, wildcat. I'll know every inch of your

body with my eyes, know how you smell, how you taste, how your skin feels when I touch you with my hands, with my mouth…"

Heat flooded into her face. Her knees didn't feel as if they'd hold her much longer. "I can't wait much longer."

"Oh, you'll wait." He rested a hand on her shoulder, guided her to the closest chair. "And after I know all of you, Missus Morgan, I'll take you."

She clenched her fists, nails biting into her palms. Would she even survive until morning? She'd never had a man make love to her like this, using words to seduce her. How was she supposed to wait for him now? She watched as he picked up the plates and carried them over to the stove to fill them with stew.

"I can't believe you expect us to eat dinner first."

"Here, we call it supper. We eat dinner in the middle of the day." He winked at her. "And I plan to keep you busy all night, Missus Morgan. So, you better eat, or you'll be out of spunk well before dawn."

"Want to bet? I'll make you beg for mercy in less than an hour if we ever get to bed."

He chuckled. "Oh, we'll get there, but not for a while."

An hour later, he brought in wood for the stove, then went back out to carry in their saddles and other gear. Beth scraped what was left of their stew onto one plate and added the heel from the loaf of bread. On the porch, Luke accepted the offering as if it were his due and she dropped to one knee to pet the large dog while he ate.

Surprisingly, he hadn't lost much weight during this adventure. He'd probably hunted the rabbits to extinction around the cave. She glanced up at Rad when he came out of the cabin, holding a set of saddlebags. "What's going on?"

"I need to take this money to Trace. I'll be back in a few minutes."

"I'll be here," Beth said.

When he walked away, she stood and went inside the cabin. She shifted her saddle and opened the bag that held her clothes, removing the red WSU t-shirt. He'd enjoyed seeing her in it yesterday morning. Hopefully, it would entice him into making his move. He'd like the picture she presented, she'd see to that.

There wasn't a closet in the cabin, so she hung the blouse on the pegs near the bed, tucking her bra underneath it. She removed her boots, putting her socks in them. She drew on the mesh t-shirt and unfastened the buttons on the skirt. She glanced over her shoulder at the sound of footsteps.

Rad came inside. He stopped and stared at her. Then, he picked up a piece of wood and barred the door. He started toward her. "Have I told you how much I like that shirt?"

"I seem to remember something like that." She slowly slid out of the skirt and her panties, went across to hang them on a peg. "But I've been wrong before."

"Not this time."

When she turned, he was there. He reached for her, pulled her to him. Her pulses thudded in excitement. She smiled up at him. "You're wearing too many clothes, Marshal Morgan, but I can fix that."

"Oh, I'll bet you can." One of his hands twined into her hair and he lowered his head.

She rose on tiptoe and their lips met. A long slow kiss that made her senses spin, as if she rode a roller-coaster of emotion.

When he lifted his mouth from hers, she focused on unbuttoning his shirt. She unfastened the first one. "There's something I haven't told you about me."

"Probably a lot of things, Bethany. We've only known each other a few days, and we'll be learning a lot about each other over the next fifty years."

"That long?" She undid the second button, then the last one. "I should have told you before the wedding. You won't be the first man…."

He tipped up her chin and she met his steady gaze. "What are you going to say about that, Rad?"

"I'd much rather be your last."

"I can promise you that." Her breath escaped in a sigh, and she stepped forward to rest her cheek against his wide chest. "Will you promise me the same thing? Will you be faithful to me as long as I'm here?"

"Definitely." He stroked her hair. "Were you fretting over what I'd think of you?"

"Yes, but I'm not going to worry about it anymore." She helped him lift off the shirt, admiring his broad shoulders. She ran a finger over the green stone on his necklace, then smoothed her hand over the chest hair and eyed the bandage he still wore. "I don't want to hurt you."

"It'd hurt more if we didn't finish what you're starting."

She tipped back her head. "Then kiss me again, Rad. And take me to bed."

TWENTY

"On Friday the 13th, if the moon is red,
Follow the scarlet pathway to the Land of the Dead....!"

RULES OF CHRONOS

HIS MOUTH CLAIMED HERS AND ONE KISS MELTED INTO THE NEXT. When he cupped her breasts, she shuddered with wanting. His thumbs rubbed her nipples and she moaned. The pleasure of finally having him was going to kill her before morning. She just knew it.

She pressed against him, felt the hardness of his body rub against where she wanted him most. She reached down, touched him through his pants, and felt the leap of his response. Oh yeah, he was so ready for her.

He ended the kiss. "Slow down and wait for me."

"For what?" She unfastened the first button on his pants. "You want this."

Bending his head, he flicked her nipple with his tongue, through the netting of her shirt. She gasped when he slowly drew her nipple into his mouth and sucked. She tangled her fingers in his hair, holding his head exactly where she wanted it.

His hands slowly explored her back, sliding down to her hips. She parted her legs, hoping, praying he'd know what she wanted. She was so wet.

"Please." She bit his ear. "Do it. Do it now."

"This?" He trailed a line of kisses to her other nipple, swirled his tongue around it. "Or this?" One large finger slid deep inside her, followed by a second and he began a steady rhythm.

She wanted to climb him like he was a tree, push him onto the bed, rip off his clothes, and demand satisfaction. But he wouldn't move. Instead, he held her in place in front of him, while he tormented her nipples with his mouth, rubbing the t-shirt over her breasts. At the same time, he continued the movement of his fingers inside her.

She tried to torture him as much as he did her, kissing the strong line of his jaw, his cheek, his ear.

Then, his thumb found her, rubbed lightly while he kept sliding his fingers in and out. She couldn't take any more. She couldn't. Pleasure seized her, rocketing through her. Knees buckling, she gripped his shoulders, his arms. "Oh, God!"

"No. I'm Rad."

She managed a weak laugh, pulled him back toward the bed. "Take me now."

"Soon."

He followed her down onto the bed, pushed her legs apart, his head between her thighs. His mouth teased her, replacing his fingers. She twisted beneath him and felt his smile against her before he stroked upward with his tongue, flicking gently and then slowly explored the folds of skin with soft strokes. He licked and then slowly deepened the intimate kiss.

She gasped when his tongue drove into her. How did he even know about this? It was the nineteenth century, and she'd never had the kind of sex she enjoyed reading about. Never, until now.

And he kept lapping, licking, and then he finally drew her clitoris into his mouth and sucked. And she came apart.

She convulsed, screaming.

He was lying beside her when she felt normal again. Well, at least as normal as a woman who'd had two amazing climaxes could be. Finally, he was naked. She rolled against him and smiled when he shuddered in response. She was ready and eager to take him and ride, ride, ride.

She slid her hands over his broad chest, watching the bandage so it didn't slip, glad he wasn't bleeding, grateful he wasn't in pain. She brushed her lips across his. "Now, Rad."

"Not yet."

This time when he kissed her, she tasted herself and almost came again.

"Soon," he said. "We have all night and a bed, not a rock floor."

"It's better than the cave for this," she admitted.

More kisses, more touches as they came to know one another. She worked her way down his body, determined to return the favor and give him the same pleasure he had her.

But he wouldn't let her. He drew her back beside him. "Not tonight."

"Be afraid, Morgan. Be very afraid." She kissed him, nibbling at his ears. "I'll do it."

He chuckled and pulled her toward him. "We'll save it for later."

She caught her breath when he rolled on top of her. "Well, it's about time."

"Whatever you say, Bethany." He laughed and parted her legs with one of his. Keeping his weight on his elbows, he drove deep into her.

One long stroke, then another. She dug her nails into his back, rose to meet him. "Faster."

"No." He kissed her. "My way, not yours. Not tonight."

He knew just how to do it. Long, steady strokes alternating

with short, fast ones until it felt as if they'd both fly among the stars. And more kisses. She met him, kiss for kiss, thrust for thrust, hips clashing, determined to show him that she was the boss.

But she wasn't. Not tonight. And suddenly, she realized that she moved as he directed, responding to his touch. Rising and falling, the way he wanted. She stopped for an instant. "No."

His jaw tightened, his eyes darkening with fierce passion. He was hard inside her. "Yes. You're mine."

And he began to move again. He lowered his head, and his mouth captured hers, his tongue plunging deep. And she answered the claim he staked, mirroring the movements he made. It was a dance. He led and she followed, but just for tonight. Next time, she'd be in charge.

They took the path to the stars, climbing ever higher, each thrust taking them farther and farther. And then he drove her past the sun as they flew, exploded together.

Afterward, she lay in his arms. Nice. It was nice to be held and snuggle against him. "That was amazing. You're amazing."

"Didn't know I married a screamer." He tightened his hold on her. "I'd say you're the amazing one."

She giggled and nipped at his chin. "Just you wait, Morgan. You haven't begun to see all the amazing things we're going to do."

She wasn't inexperienced, but she'd never known sex could be like this, she thought, three hours later. His lovemaking was different from any other man's, tender yet exciting. She'd had her share of the 'wham, bam, thank-you ma'am' boys. Thank heaven that was over. She had a 'real' man now, one comparable to the fantasy guys in her cousin's books.

Beth rested her cheek on his chest, listening to the steady heartbeat. She smoothed her hand over the tangled V of curly black hair above the green poncho bandage. He'd more than satisfied her before he fell asleep, but she wanted him again. Her fingers searched out his nipple and she teased it with her tongue.

His arms tightened and he pulled her to lie on top of him. "Reckon, I didn't wear you out after all. I'll have to try harder."

"Are you planning to kiss me again?"

"I'll do what I have to do." He threaded his hand into her hair, drawing her mouth down to his. The fierce kiss sent shivers down her spine. A lifetime later, he released her, and she tried to remember how to breathe.

He smiled up at her. "Your turn."

She leaned down, brushed his lips with hers. "Let's see if I really can make you beg."

Daylight crept around the edges of the shutter and across the room to tease her face. She sighed, rolled over, and tried to slip back into slumber. Stretching out an arm, she felt the emptiness beside her. Where was he?

She opened her eyes and looked around the room. He wasn't there.

He'd gone somewhere, but she didn't remember him saying anything about it last night. She slipped out of bed, pulled on her t-shirt, and went to the table. No note. Nothing.

There was a pot of coffee on the woodstove. She picked up a cup from the table and poured a mug. Sipping the thick strong brew, she scanned the area. The stack of horse gear seemed different, and she realized what was wrong. His saddle was missing, along with his rifle. He'd left her here with these strangers.

She picked up her watch. Almost noon. Okay, so she'd get dressed and take charge. She was a homicide detective and she'd do what she had to do. When he returned, she'd kick his butt from here to Eagleville. Hello, they were married, at least in this century! What was he thinking? Had he gone after Smith without her?

It didn't take long to dress. She opted for a clean blouse and an ankle-length, divided skirt. She fastened on her shoulder holster, slid the pistol into place. She brushed her hair, braided it back into a pony-tail. Remembering where she was and *when*, she paused, then coiled it into a bun and pinned it up. Like he'd told her, she wanted people to know she was a *decent* person. Boots and her police jacket and she was ready to go. She left the lapels down so the identification couldn't be seen on the coat.

She stepped outside into a glorious spring morning. Cool, yet sunny. She saw Tigger and Nell in the corral, sharing a big pile of hay. Luke rose off the porch and escorted her to the drive. She glanced up the road, lined by several buildings, barns, cabins, and one huge house. And where there were houses, she'd find people. She started walking.

As she neared the house, she saw a garden. Seven children worked, a couple hoeing the dirt while others pulled weeds. The three girls wore long, bright dresses, and the four boys were in work shirts and pants. Beth spotted Trace on the porch. The other woman wore dark clothes, black pants, a dark shirt, a bandanna, boots, and still packed pistols on her hips.

"Morning," Beth called.

"Closer to dinner time," Trace said, but her tone was friendly. "Come on up and set with Ma and me."

"All right." Beth followed Trace around the house and in the back door. "Where is Rad?"

"He headed out bright and early to take that shaman to her folks," Trace said. "The tribes in these parts like to bury their dead straight away and she's waited too long. It's disrespectful."

"What Smith did to her was worse." Beth paused, as they entered the kitchen, and she spotted an older woman and three young girls, one Asian, one Hispanic, and a tiny blonde preparing a meal. She wouldn't bring up the subject in front of these people. It was cop business and discussing a gruesome murder wouldn't be appropriate with civilians.

"Ma, this is Beth Chambers Morgan," Trace said. "Beth, this is my housekeeper, Missus Sims. The children call her, Ma, and the rest of us have gotten in the habit."

Mid-fifties, brown hair now lined with silver pinned at the nape of her neck, honey-brown eyes, approximately five-feet-three inches tall. A solid hundred and sixty pounds, Beth judged. Missus

Sims wore a blue dress covered by an old-fashioned white apron. She returned the assessing gaze and didn't speak.

"It's nice to meet you," Beth said. "The stew was wonderful last night."

"Did the marshal share the pie with you?" Missus Sims asked.

Heat crept into her face as she remembered just what they'd done with the pie, and she hoped they didn't see her blush. She smiled. "It was amazing."

"They taste even better for breakfast." Trace walked over to the table and pulled out a chair. "Come and sit. I'll get you a piece of that pie now."

"She'll spoil her appetite for dinner," Ma scolded. "And it's just beans and ham hocks. Nothing fancy."

"And your cornbread," Trace said. "That's high on the hog for us. When the men get back, we'll have more on the table."

Beth sat down.

A Chinese girl brought over a cup of coffee, putting it in front of Beth. "Do you need milk or honey? It is strong."

"Thank you." Beth watched the girl move around the room, then eyed Trace. "You certainly have a lot of kids here."

"The orphanage burned down a few years back," Trace said, sliding a saucer with a slab of pie to Beth. "So, I brought Ma and her brood here to live. I'll show you around after we eat."

"We have a new school." The blonde carefully put a small pitcher of cream on the table near Beth. "Our Jenny teaches us every day, 'cept we never get to sass her when we're learning to read, write and cipher."

Beth smiled at the youngster who couldn't be much more than seven or almost eight. "What subject do you like best? I love reading stories."

"Me, too." The little girl beamed at Beth. "I'm gonna learn to read *Huck Finn* by myself. Pa, I mean Trace told Jenny that I can."

Beth watched the child lean against Trace's chair. While she seemed to be all joy and light, there was wariness in the little girl's light blue eyes that were the same color as her dress.

"You know my name," Beth said. "What's yours?"

"Becky." She pressed closer to Trace. "But I've been good so the marshal can't take me 'way."

Trace sighed, then scooped the child into her lap. "Daughter, we've talked about this for nigh on the past year. Nobody is taking you from me."

Beth cut into her pie. "That's for sure. I'm not ready to have kids yet."

"Really?" Becky asked, peeping around Trace's shoulder. "And you won't let him give me back to them mean folks?"

"I found Becky in the woods almost three years ago after she ran away from her adoptive family," Trace explained. "And I brought her here to stay with Ma and the other orphans and me."

"Looks like a match made in heaven." Beth focused on the pie. The flaky crust fell apart at the touch of her fork. The apple slices were sweet, yet tangy. It was the perfect breakfast. "I wouldn't move her either. She already has a family."

"Well, there you go." Trace helped the girl slide down. "Now, you need to help Ma finish dinner, or the boys will be in here, claiming they're going to starve before too much longer."

An hour later after the meal, Beth left with Trace to see the headquarters of the Lazy B. "Who rode with Rad to the reservation?"

Trace blinked. "You mean the Indian villages? They're nowhere near the reservation. That's miles west of here. Marshal Morgan took her to the fishing grounds. Connor, Doc, Fremont, Lars, and a couple of the loggers went with him. He's plenty safe enough."

"Until he gets back here, and I skin him alive," Beth said. "He knew I wanted to talk to the victim's family."

Trace shook her head. "Wouldn't work. They won't talk to you any more than they'd talk to me."

"Why not?" Beth asked.

"Their women aren't like you and me," Trace said. "The tribe will figure we dishonor our husbands by being warriors. Then, they won't tell Morgan anything either, because you're nearly as big an embarrassment as I am, so I asked my godfather, Fremont to speak for me. We've done it this way for years."

"They so have to get a life." Beth lifted her chin. "Well, at least that tells me what Morgan was thinking and why he left me behind."

"Nobody says you have to stay and wait for him." Trace grinned, mischief sparking in her green eyes. "I have another, better idea if you're game."

"What?" Beth asked.

"We spend today here. Then first thing tomorrow, we ride into town with Gruber and get the money back to my bank manager. He'll be glad to see it. My uncle Roy frets something fierce over every cent and he took it personal when we were robbed."

"Okay, I can see where that makes sense," Beth said, "but I can tell by your tone that you have something else in mind. What is it?"

"You can settle in at the marshal's office," Trace said, "and look at all the wanted posters and such. It'll give you a few ideas where to look for Smith and I'll help you hunt for him."

"Why?"

"Because he stole my best stud, Emancipation. I raised him from a foal after his mother was killed by a cougar. Morgan gave him to me, and I want my horse back."

This bunch was more talk than action. They'd ridden up to a one-room shack in the middle of nowhere and called it their hide-out. The boy slept inside, but the rest of the men camped outdoors. It probably smelled better than the cabin. Their hobbled horses grazed in the clearings, around the trees.

If it bothered the hardscrabble bunch that he left his stud tied to a tree with nothing to eat, nobody said anything. It was a hard time and none of these wanta-be outlaws whined about critters having rights. The youngster might be too scared to sleep outdoors, but he didn't hide out during work-time. He looked after the stock, fetched wood and water for meals, was the first to jump when his pa, Jake Dawson gave an order. The boy offered to tote water to the stallion more than once, but Gary put a stop to that the first day.

He scowled. He didn't know what that yapping bitch had done to the horse when the Appy wintered over at the do-gooder's barn on the Other Side for the last couple of years, but the horse had too much spirit to suit him. Regular beatings and lack of water and food would break the stud's mind, the same way it broke the yappers. It hadn't worked yet, but then again, he hadn't had much time to train the beast.

The men clustered around the campfire, drinking coffee and swapping lies about the crimes they committed. Dawson signaled and Gary went over to him. "What?"

"We're planning to rob the Granger store. He has money in the safe. Folks bank there who don't want to go to Portage or Junction City."

"Sounds interesting. What's the place like?"

While they took turns answering, describing the layout he looked around. Where was the youngest boy? Not in sight.

Suspicions raised, he stood. "Be right back."

He circled into the woods, so they'd figure he was answering a call of nature, careful not to make noise. He spotted the pale yellow of the stud first, then glimpsed the boy who stood at the animal's head.

Young Dawson had loosened the rope that snubbed the stallion to the tree. He held a pail for the horse to drink.

Gary stormed toward them, loosening the nightstick. "You little bastard. I told you to leave him alone."

"He'll die without water."

"And you'll die for giving it to him." Gary slammed the club into the boy's arm. The bucket fell and the boy screamed. Like a girl!

Thoughts jumbled in Gary's mind. The boy sleeping alone. Taking care of chores.

Protected by his pa. Nobody angry because the kid lost the money to the marshal. Hell, no wonder. The snot-nosed punk was a girl.

Gary kicked the little yapper on the ground, then yanked away the kid's hat. Long brown hair fell over the little bitch's face. "Time for you to learn a lesson." He raised the club.

She tried to roll away, but he followed. He brought the club down hard on her hip. "Never touch..."

A scream and she kicked at him with her other foot.

He hit her knee. "My horse."

Another yell of pain and she scrabbled away like a crab on her hands and good knee, dragging her broken leg behind.

He went after her. Struck her across the back. Killing her was going to be so much fun and it'd teach the gang of thieves not to lie to him. They'd learn who was in charge.

PART THREE

"If you obey all the rules, you miss all the fun."

KATHARINE HEPBURN

TWENTY-ONE

They'd followed the tracks the marshal pointed out Sunday night. It hadn't been that difficult at first. Smith made no effort to hide his trail and the hoofprints were easy to distinguish from those of the wild animals that crisscrossed the paths. When he forded the creeks and crossed patches of gravel, it made finding him that much harder.

Still, Zeb persisted. Olaf and Mac hadn't protested at all, even when they rode into a rainstorm. Once they heard about the Indian gal, they'd pretty much thought the same thing he had. It could have been Trace. And Zeb would make damn sure it wasn't.

Yesterday, he'd found where Smith had joined up with a bunch of riders. That made it easier to follow him.

Olaf rode up beside him. "Can't figure why anyone would let that crazy man into their outfit. Shoot him? Yes. Accept him?" He shook his head.

"I'm a-thinking it's the Dawsons, the same ones as robbed the bank," Mac said, his brogue heavier than usual. "Who else would be out here?"

Zeb nodded. Good point and it meant they needed to take care if there were other armed men around. He heard a distant scream. A woman or a panther?

He reined his horse to a halt and listened. After a moment, another cry of mortal pain. Then, a third. And a gunshot.

He glanced at the two men. "Sounds like we found Smith. But let's ease up on them. Olaf, can you cause a distraction?"

The big Swede flinched at the next scream. "You betcha. You mind if anyone dies?"

"Not when they're letting Smith cut up a woman. You kill whoever gets in your way." Zeb eyeballed Mac. "I'll cut loose on Smith and draw his fire. You snake out the woman. Least we can do is keep her from dying any harder."

———

Rad stopped the solid palomino gelding he'd borrowed from the Lazy B remuda on the ridge overlooking the summer village. Dogs barked a warning and he continued to wait until they'd been seen. Then, he urged the horse to a steady walk. He slowly rode toward the older man who stood in front of the largest summer house. Cattails woven into giant mats attached to poles created the walls and roof. It was bigger than the cabin where he and Bethany spent the night before.

Not time to think about his wife, Rad decided. He needed to focus on the job at hand. He tightened his grip on the reins and the horse stopped again. He glanced quickly over his shoulder and saw the wagon Connor drove directly behind him, flanked by Doc Jenkins and Trace's representatives.

Rad turned back around to face the tribal leader and spoke in Chinook. "We brought home your lost shaman. I tried to save her but—" He paused when the head man raised a hand.

"The Evil One uses blood to cross between worlds. He will pay for choosing one of ours to open doors."

The name fit Gary Smith. He was purely evil. And it sounded like there was more to learn here than he'd originally believed, so when the invitation came to remain overnight, Rad accepted.

Beth reached into her coat pocket, started to pull out her phone to show Trace a picture of the horse Gary Smith stole, then hesitated. It was 1888 and while she didn't remember when people started using telephones, the one she carried was brand new in 2018. Luckily, she'd barely turned it on, so it still had some power left even if she couldn't charge the battery. It wouldn't go over well in the back of the beyond. Rad had accepted what he called her 'contraptions' fairly easily, but it didn't mean others would be so open-minded.

"What does your horse look like?" Beth asked. "How big is he? What breed?"

"Emancipation is a real light palomino Appaloosa, blazed face, two white socks, seventeen hands," Trace said. "His mother died when he was only three months old, and Morgan gave him to me. He was the start of my Appy herd. The horse I rode last night, Deuce, is one of his sons."

"Does Emancipation have peacock spots on his hind-quarters?" Beth asked.

Trace stiffened. Just for an instant, tears shimmered in her green eyes, then she blinked them away. "Yes. So, do all his foals. You've seen him, haven't you?"

Beth nodded. "Smith stole him from my best friend, Nina Armstrong who runs an equine rescue facility. She took him in almost two years ago. She fed him up, got him looking like a horse again instead of a skeleton."

"What happened to her?"

"Smith raped her. He'd have killed her, but I interrupted the attack. He fled before I arrested him, but I got help for her before she died. The doctors expect her to make it and I promised I'd find Wonder. That's what she calls him because it's a wonder he survived."

"I appreciate her looking after him."

"Nina always goes the extra mile for her horses. Taking him

was another of Smith's mistakes. He never should have assaulted her, much less stolen such a famous animal. His story made the local papers when he was originally found, and Nina still uses him to raise money to feed her projects. People owe her favors, and she won't hesitate to call them in to save Wonder, even if she has to do it from a hospital bed."

"I want him back, but maybe she'd accept one of his foals."

"Well, let's find Smith first and rescue the horse," Beth said. "We'll figure out where he'll live once he's safe."

"Sounds like a good plan to me," Trace agreed. "Now, let's take a walk."

Touring the Lazy B took up the afternoon although Beth didn't see the entire ranch. Something about the layout of the various cabins, barns, and other buildings bothered her, but she couldn't quite solve the puzzle, so she let it simmer in her mind.

Red Hereford cattle grazed in some of the pastures. She hadn't realized they were in western Washington at this time but didn't reveal her ignorance. Bay, black, buckskin, and sorrel Appaloosas from youngsters to mature mounts roamed different fields, divided by split rail and log fences. They'd seen a few Quarter horses and met Trace's favorite old mare, Ginger in her own paddock, accompanied by her last two foals, twin yearling palominos. They were more sunshine gold than Wonder, the horse Trace claimed was their sire.

A metallic clanging disrupted the peace of the afternoon.

"What is that noise?" Beth asked.

"Supper," Trace said. She led the way back to the large house where they'd started the tour and around to the backyard. "We wash up here."

Beth glanced at the group of children. The girls wore long bright dresses. The boys were in pants, boots, and what had to be homemade shirts. Kyle Morgan waited his turn to clean up with a Hispanic man about his age and the red-haired teen she'd seen on her arrival.

"Where's the posse?" Beth asked. "I thought they were supposed to take the money to town with us."

"Two of 'em complained about eating with women and children at the table," Trace said. "So, I told Morgan to take them with him when he left this morning. Gruber told me the marshal sent them off to town after he chewed their ears for embarrassing him. Granted, my foreman tells me that some folks don't like my rules for adopting the orphans, so they stay here until they're grown."

"What are your rules?"

"Three meals a day, two sets of new clothes a year, a bed to sleep in with blankets, schooling, no beatings."

Beth nodded. Those standards seemed reasonable to her, but then again, she wasn't from here and when she was in foster care, if she'd had a home with those rules, she'd have been in hog heaven as Will said. She wouldn't have run off and ended up homeless on the Seattle streets.

"Where were the kids supposed to eat?" Beth asked. "Outside with the dogs?"

"It wasn't where," Trace explained. "It was *when*. Most folks expect children to eat after the men. Women eat after everybody else because they must do the cooking and serving. But we don't do that on the Lazy B. Everybody sits down together. It's my place and I do as I damn well please."

"Works for me," Beth said. "Of course, I've always felt that some people are just too stupid to live."

Trace laughed. "Got that right."

Beth headed over to wash her hands. If Rad Morgan thought he'd receive that kind of subservient behavior from her, he'd better reconsider. She was his wife, at least in this time, and no way in hell would she act the part of a servant. She'd do just about anything to capture Smith but crawling to some man wasn't on her agenda. Now she knew Vera Smith's behavior wasn't unfounded or unacceptable regardless of what Dr. Jenkins thought.

"Are we taking the bankroll to town tomorrow?" Beth asked,

lingering while Trace dried her hands. "Or are we waiting for Morgan to return?"

"We'll go bright and early," Trace said. "Kyle and Gruber will ride with us. Pedro and Shawn will watch over things here. We can come back tomorrow night or stay in Junction City."

———

It was almost midnight, but she couldn't sleep. She'd grown accustomed to having Rad nearby during the last few days and she missed him, not that she'd ever let him know that. She sat on the porch steps watching the stars overhead. Luke slept on the ground near her feet.

Quiet reigned. So quiet—she could get used to a world without traffic or airplanes. Or bombs, or IEDs or wounded soldiers screaming. Occasionally, she heard the yip and howls of distant coyotes along with the warning barks from the ranch dogs. The wind rustled in the trees and occasionally, the spring breeze brought the scent of the river that flowed nearby.

But she didn't feel as if there would be an attack at any moment.

Gravel crunched. Luke lifted his head, growled. She pulled her pistol. "Who's there?"

"Me," Trace said, stopping a few feet away. "This a private party? Or do you want company?"

Beth shrugged, holstering the Glock. "Pull up a step and join me."

"Sounds good." Trace drew out a tobacco pouch and papers. "A smoke always makes me relax. How about you?"

"Now that makes the night even better." Beth laughed and reached for the papers. She hadn't rolled her own cigarettes since she was a teenager, but the skill quickly returned. Unfiltered tobacco was always sharper than what she usually smoked, but a cigarette at night soothed jangled nerves.

"Okay, so maybe I'll survive back here after all," Beth said.

"When Morgan decided to do the macho routine and burn up my ciggies, I just wanted to shoot him."

"I've been there." Trace sighed and leaned back against the post that held up the porch roof. "There are times when Zebadiah makes me want to ship him to the South Seas again. He gets real quiet when the steamboat's in town."

Beth stared at the younger woman. "Say again. What did you do?"

"Had him shanghaied when he irritated me one time too many last summer." Trace drew on her cigarette and exhaled. "Now, that we're hitched, he threatens to make me eat my dinner standing up if I try it again. But he knows it'd be as dangerous as being up a tree with a grizzly, so it's all hot air."

Beth nodded. It sounded as if Trace and her husband had a good relationship based on mutual respect. "It surprised me when he left to trail Smith."

"It annoys me Morgan even asked him," Trace admitted. "Of course, Zebadiah being Zebadiah, he could have volunteered too. He always looked out for his sisters and tried to protect them."

"From what?"

"Their pa tended to beat on all the children. Zebadiah got the worst of it since he sassed the Reverend constantly, but it kept the girls safe."

"And nobody stepped up to stop the abuse?"

"My grandfather did when we moved to town, but it cost him. The Reverend owned the mercantile, so we had to buy our supplies in Snohomish City and pack them to the ranch."

Beth took the tobacco pouch Trace passed and rolled another smoke. "You said he had stories about these mountains. Strange ones?"

"He called the people who came from far away, *Journeyers,* and said that he'd met an incredibly special one, a *Guardian*. She lived with my grandmother's tribe for a while."

"What made her so special?" Beth struck a match and lit her cigarette. "What did she do?"

"Taught the shaman some special medicine and healed a warrior who should have died from his battle injuries," Trace said. "Fremont knows her too, but he says it isn't proper for him to tell her stories. He doesn't go to town, but when he returns home, you should talk to him. He'll tell you how to find her."

"I will," Beth said, returning the tobacco. "Maybe he can also tell me how I got here."

"Are you going to tell me where you're from?" Trace asked.

Beth looked up at the stars. "The question is whether you'll believe me or think I'm crazy."

"Then wait until you trust me to believe you." Trace stood. "Morning comes early on the Lazy B. I'll see you at breakfast."

———

She slept deep and woke when Luke barked a short, sharp sound. No nightmares or memories. She saw Shawn walking purposefully in the direction of one of the barns. Out in the corral, Tigger, and Nell happily munched grain from two buckets of feed. A large pile of hay was between the two horses.

"Do these people ever sleep?" Beth asked Luke, but the dog just flopped back down with a low growl. What had she expected? A doggie speech?

After she washed and dressed, she toted her saddle and pads to the corral rail. She made a second trip to the cabin for the rest of her belongings, almost feeling as if she was checking out of a motel. She groomed her horse, then tacked him for the trip to town.

Before she finished tying on her equipment, she heard the clanging of the iron triangle. "Breakfast for me," she told the horses. "I'll be back and we're off on a new adventure."

After breakfast, Shawn accompanied Beth back to the corral. He haltered up Nell and led her off to the paddock with Ginger and the yearlings. Beth bridled Tigger and took a few minutes to check the equipment tied to the saddle. Then, she led him through the corral gate, swung into the saddle, and rode out to meet Trace who was on a different bay Appaloosa stallion, one with a circular-shaped star in the middle of his forehead. A wolf-dog cross waited behind the pair.

With Luke trotting ahead of them, they headed up the road to the back of the farm where Kyle waited with a distinguished-looking man in his mid-forties. Beth swept him with a cop gaze, judging height. Approximately five feet, ten inches, a solid hundred-fifty pounds, graying black hair, gray eyes, gray mustache, matching scars on his cheeks. What was that about?

"Heinrich Gruber, this is Marshal Morgan's new deputy," Trace said. "Detective Chambers."

"Morgan," Kyle added. "She married my brother."

"Ma'am." The older man tipped his hat. "Welcome to the ranch."

"Thank you." Beth continued to study him while he went to get a solid brown gelding. Gruber still had a faint German accent and she'd bet he'd moved here from Europe as a young man.

Once he was in the saddle, they followed Trace to the gate. She swung it open, and they went through. Gruber locked it behind them, and they headed west on a well-marked trail.

Diamond dew glistened off the grass and on the salmonberry bushes adjacent to the gate. Trace set a good pace down the track, a steady mile-eating walk. Beth glanced at Kyle who rode beside her. "How far is it to town?"

"We'll be there by dinnertime."

Beth winced. A day in the saddle didn't sound like much fun, then she remembered that around here, the people didn't eat lunch. They called the noon meal, dinner. She checked her watch. It was barely seven in the morning, so they only had a four or five-hour ride to the nearest city. She could handle it. But she missed her Jeep and its heated seats. Regardless of how much she loved her horse, she had to admit that Tigger's saddle wasn't nearly as comfortable.

An hour passed as they rode, mud squelching beneath the

horses' hooves. Beth stretched and looked around. Giant cedars, hemlocks, and other evergreens marched beside the trail. Moss dripped from the trees. Clumps of huge ferns reminded her of the rainforest on the Olympic Peninsula.

A branch snapped in the woods. Luke's head came up and he veered to stand between Beth and the evergreens. She reined Tigger to a halt, pulled her Glock from the shoulder holster.

Trace spun her own stallion to face the shadowy depths of the forest, just as quick to reach for her pistols. Gruber's rifle was across the pommel of a saddle and even Kyle held a gun.

Beth caught a glimmer of something white, then it melted into the trees. What the hell? She swung out of her saddle, passed the reins to Kyle. "Be right back."

Trace was behind her, and they entered the woods together, fanning apart. Beth slipped to the right and saw the other woman ease left, the two dogs on patrol.

A dash of white on the far side of an evergreen and Beth spotted a hoofprint in the mud. She knew that mark. It came from one of Wonder's distinctive shoes. Now, where was Gary Smith?

Glock tight in her hand, she followed the tracks.

The evergreens parted into a small clearing, and she heard a soft nicker. Then, she saw the giant light palomino Appaloosa.

He wasn't alone.

He stood in front of Trace, his huge head buried against the woman's chest, her arms around his muscled neck. The stallion was obviously by himself. An empty saddle, broken reins trailing, a hobble around one front foot.

Where was Smith?

Beth scanned the woods, but she didn't see any footprints from another human, just hers and Trace's. "How did he get here?"

"He came home," Trace said, tones muffled.

"Yes, but what did he do with Smith?" Beth asked, still watchful.

"I don't know, but when I find him, I'll kill him."

TWENTY-TWO

"To fulfill Her chosen tasks, the Goddess will provide the Guardian with new talents when she asks…"

RULES OF CHRONOS

BETH NODDED AND DIDN'T SAY THAT MURDER WAS AGAINST THE law or any of the other things she thought. She'd arrest Smith and take him to stand trial, the same as any perp. She frowned as she approached Wonder. "What the hell happened to him?"

Bloodstains covered his shoulders and chest. More blood on his neck. Something slashed his right ear—a knife? A large lump above his right eye and he could barely open the left. Gashes up and down both front legs.

When Trace turned toward the main trail, Wonder limped after her, dragging one hind leg. Was it broken? Or had he popped his stifle?

"We'd better go back to your ranch," Beth said. "We can doctor him there. For now, let me check his hindquarters before we make him walk the rest of the way."

"That works," Trace agreed.

Late that afternoon, Beth had a better idea of everything wrong with the Appaloosa. She still thought of him as Wonder, even if Trace insisted on calling the horse, Emancipation. But it wasn't worth arguing about, not when his life came first. Beth cleaned all the injuries and bandaged the worst of them. She mixed sulfa with grain and the stud slicked the meds right down as if the mash was a treat. He'd been struck in the face with some sort of club. He hadn't been hungry long enough to loosen that many teeth.

She'd checked his stifle, but the joint hadn't popped on his rear leg. Maybe staying in a stall would heal whatever happened to his left rear leg. She wished she had access to a veterinarian and a portable X-ray machine. Failing that, she'd have to do her best to save him. Leaning against the stall door, she watched him slowly chew a mouthful of hay.

She'd make another mash for him at bedtime and then in the morning. Oddly enough, the bottle of sulfa tablets remained full despite the fact she'd used several pills for Rad. She had plenty for the huge horse. Things were strange here, or perhaps she was the strangest of them all.

"Ma says leave him and come for supper." A child stood safely at the barn door.

Beth glanced over her shoulder and saw Becky. "Be right there. You can come closer. He won't hurt you."

"I'm not scared of him," Becky said, indignant at the insult. "We have horses all over the Lazy B and Trace teaches each of us to ride. When we're old enough to take care of it, we each get a horse of our own."

"Well, you can't be scared of me." Beth latched the stall door and left the stud to pull hay from the manger. "I told you the marshal and I wouldn't take you away."

Becky eyed her warily. "And if I told you I wanted to stay here with Ma and the rest of my family, you wouldn't let nobody steal me?"

"That's right." Beth followed the girl from the barn. "Who wants you?"

The small blonde hesitated, then swung back to whisper. "The bad man took Trace's horse. He tried to take me again, but I runned away and hid."

"The bad man?" Beth froze, putting two and two together. She hadn't heard of Smith going after a child, but why wasn't she more surprised? She pulled out her camera and brought up the picture of Gary Smith Senior. "Is this him?"

"Yes, but I'm good at hidin'."

"Stay that way." Beth tucked away the digital camera before the child asked about color pictures. "Why did he want you?"

"He bought me for five dollars. He said he'd teach me to be a *good girl,* only I didn't want him touching me, not after... So I runned 'way. And Trace found me."

"And brought you here," Beth said, in an even tone. There was more to the story, but she'd have to wait to interview the child until the girl had at least one advocate, either Ma or Trace with her.

"Let's go have supper," Beth said, patting the little girl's shoulder. "I don't want Missus Sims mad at me for letting her food get cold."

"She really scolds when that happens," Becky said, "and then you get extra chores."

"Well, we don't want that to happen. I have enough work to do now."

Becky giggled. "That's the same thing Pa, I mean Trace says. And she gets Fremont to do her chores. Maybe, he'll do yours too."

Later that night, Beth sat on the porch of the cabin, watching the stars glitter and the clouds roll by. Tigger munched hay in the adjacent corral, content to have Nell with him once more. There would undoubtedly be a foal next spring and she hoped Morgan wouldn't be too upset about the addition to his horse herd. Luke lifted his head and growled a soft warning as Trace approached.

"Neither one of us sleep much, do we?" Beth smiled at the other woman. "Pull up a step."

Trace passed over the tobacco pouch before sitting down. "I figure Emancipation will be happy to spend the next few days eating. He's dropped a couple of hundred pounds, but that's not the worst of it. Got clubbed hard around his face and ears."

"I don't think he'll lose that eye," Beth said, rolling a cigarette. "I'll doctor him in the morning. Then, I'm going to backtrack him and see if I can find Smith."

"Make that we," Trace said.

"What?"

"We'll backtrack him and find Smith." Trace struck a match and lit both their smokes. "Gruber and Kyle can take the money to town without us."

"All right." Beth drew on the cigarette and debated silently. Finally, she added, "I need to talk to Becky tomorrow before we ride out and you should be there."

"Why?"

"She knows Smith. He bought her from that family you spoke of, and she ran off before he could *train* her. How old is she?"

"Almost eight," Trace said, obviously mentally calculating the child's age when she was found three years before. "What kind of degenerate buys a little girl?"

"Smith, and I'll bet there's more to the story." Beth exhaled. "Becky must have seen something pretty awful, or she wouldn't have booked it."

"Booked it?" Trace asked.

"Ran off," Beth said. "If you and Ma are there, then you'll know what happened and you can convince her that she was right to escape. Otherwise, sooner or later, he'd have killed her. She's a spunky kid, too spunky for his taste."

"Apples don't fall far from some trees," Trace mused. "She might have seen him hurt somebody in her family. She never talks about having relatives, but she had to come from somewhere."

If Smith murdered the girl's mother, that could be why Becky didn't mention it, Beth thought. *The child might be hiding what she witnessed.*

Beth grimaced. Just the notion of Smith buying a five-year-old was enough to nauseate her, never mind what he planned to do to the little girl. Gary Smith Senior had probably killed a lot of women, but there had never been any sign that he was a child molester. So, why would he insist on having the girl and claim that he planned to *teach* her, or *train* her to be a *good girl.* Good for what? Had he intended to sell her as a child prostitute?

Focusing on Gary Smith made it easier to avoid worrying about Rad and the stress that the trip might have taken on his injuries. She knew better than to love anyone, especially some tall, ruggedly handsome, arrogant drink of water who left her behind instead of treating her like an equal partner. So, she'd contemplate what she learned about Becky instead.

Questions about the girl remained in Beth's mind for the rest of the night and through breakfast the next morning. When the rest of the children left the room, she stayed at the table with Becky, Trace, and Missus Sims.

The little girl eyed the three of them warily. "Am I in trouble?"

"No," Trace said. "Not unless you've done something Ma and I don't know about yet."

Becky heaved a sigh. "I hid from Manda yesterday and played with the kitties 'stead of sweeping the school. She told on me, huh?"

Beth suppressed a smile while a few other misdeeds came to light and Missus Sims rendered justice with well-chosen words and extra chores. Once that was finished, Beth said, "I need your help, Becky."

"My help?" Light blue eyes widened in surprise. "But you're big and I'm little."

"Yes, but you know about the *bad* man, and I don't," Beth said. "I want to catch him and put him in jail, so he never hurts anybody again."

Becky tilted her head to one side as she considered what must be a strange idea. "By yourself?"

"I'll help her," Trace said. "But can you tell me why he wanted you?"

"He tooked away Sorry first," Becky explained. "I cried and cried and ran after them. I was goin' too, but the lady whipped me and locked me up in the trunk for bad girls."

The knowledge that they'd been right about the child suffering some type of abuse made Beth wince and she shared a long look with Trace. "Who is Sorry?"

"My real big sister. The one who tried to keep the boys away from me, 'cause they did bad things to me like my uncle did bad things to her." Becky climbed down from the chair and went to Trace, crawling up in her lap, whispering something in the woman's ear.

"I'll tell Detective Beth," Trace said, a soft, lethal promise. "You don't have to talk about that, Becky."

Missus Sims rose and brought over the coffeepot. "Did anybody say what happened to your sister, Becky?"

"He told us that she runned away, so he come'd back. He was real mad 'cause he said the boys wrecked me and I wasn't worth ten dollars, so he made their pa give him back some of his money. And he was even madder 'bout Sorry, 'cause Uncle Walt did things to her to make her have babies. But she didn't."

Five dollars for a little girl who'd been attacked and raped by at least two boys. What kind of parents would allow their sons to molest other youngsters in their care? Monsters. Beth closed her eyes for an instant before she asked. "Then what happened?"

"It was nighttime. He said I had to eat supper with him. Then, he made the lady give me a room with a door that locked so the boys couldn't get me, and he said he was taking me away in the morning. And he'd teach me to be a *good girl* so I could grow up right. He said he was goin' to send me to a special school too, only I didn't want to go with him. He was scary."

Beth stiffened. It was beginning to sound more like a rescue than abduction. Now, she was more curious than ever about the older girl. What had Smith done with her while he went after Becky? Had she been murdered or truly escaped from him, or had he sent her somewhere? Would Morgan know when he returned?

"Where did that man go, then?"

"To read the Bible to them mean people. He said they wasn't doing good things, so he'd learn them better. And he told me to go to bed. He wouldn't let nobody in the room with me."

The rest of the details that Becky revealed were ones Beth already knew. The girl climbed out of the window while the rest of the family slept and fled into the woods. Trace discovered her and brought her back to the orphanage at the Lazy B, then drove the would-be adoptive family out of the area since that was the only recourse.

Beth waited until they were on the trail leading off the ranch before she asked. "Why didn't Morgan step up and protect Becky?"

"Children belong to their parents," Trace said. "And when those folks took in the girls after their own kin died, well they had all the rights under the law."

"How old were the boys who assaulted Becky and her friend?" Beth reined Tigger closer so they could converse in low voices. "Over eighteen?"

"No. If they'd been grown, I'd have killed them. The oldest was about fifteen and the other two were a year or so younger. Twins and purely as evil as their pa who had also used Becky."

"She didn't mention that." Beth made a mental note to add it to the file she'd created on Gary Smith. "What happened to her foster mother?"

Trace's gaze narrowed. "I offered the woman a refuge if she wanted to leave them, but she'd have to tell Morgan the truth so he could arrest the menfolk. She chose to leave town with her man and boys. There's a special place in hell for a mother like that who won't guard all her children and raise them proper."

Beth agreed silently with the assessment but knew she'd have taken the entire family into custody. It seemed as if she and Morgan had some serious sorting out to do when he returned. He undoubtedly upheld the laws of his time, but he certainly hadn't served justice when it came to Becky or her sister.

How many times had he looked the other way? How could she tolerate or even remain married to a man who did nothing to protect victims of heinous crimes? Yet hadn't Dr. Jenkins said that Morgan stepped up when Smith's own children fled from him? Who was the real man? How would she find out?

It reminded her of Will's favorite quote. "All that's necessary for evil to exist is for good men to do nothing." Of course, she'd always tweaked it and said, "All that's necessary is for good *people* to do nothing."

Tears burned and she blinked them away. Today, she missed her father more than ever and wondered if she'd ever see him again. How was she going to get home? She didn't have any ruby slippers or ruby cowgirl boots. Would she be stuck here in the land that Time forgot for the rest of her life?

Later that morning, Beth watched Kyle Morgan and Heinrich Gruber head for town with the bankroll. Then she swung Tigger in the direction she and Trace had taken the day before, Luke trotting ahead of the Arabian. They reached the grove where they'd discovered Wonder in less than an hour. Despite the mist that drifted through the giant evergreens, the distinctive hoofprints showed in the mud. They were easy to follow.

The stallion had walked or rather limped for hours, dragging one leg behind him. Breaks in the vegetation showed where he'd stopped to graze. He'd obviously been alone. No boot prints could be seen near his tracks. So, he'd left Smith somewhere. How?

"Did he buck off Smith?" Beth asked. "Or spook and dump him?"

"No sign of that yet," Trace said.

They rode on. Beth scanned both sides of the path, knowing that Trace was undoubtedly doing the same thing with one of her wolf-dogs tracking behind the other woman's horse. Beth still didn't see any evidence of other humans near the Appaloosa stud's hoofprints. Chills crept along her spine. She didn't like this. Where was Gary Smith? Could he be planning to ambush her again?

No. He doesn't know I followed him here. Wake up and smell the latte, Chambers. You're not on your own. You have back-up and it won't be impossible to find Smith, not here and not now.

TWENTY-THREE

"An Unaware Guardian may be baffled at the start, as her quest unfolds, and new talents emerge when she follows her heart..."

RULES OF CHRONOS

THE SUN CREPT HIGHER, AND THEY STOPPED AT NOON FOR A BRIEF lunch break. Unsaddling the horses, they allowed the stallions to graze while they ate some of the food Missus Sims sent. Leaning against her sleeping bag, Beth eyed Trace speculatively. "Do you want to go back to the Lazy B tonight or keep hunting?"

"We haven't found him yet," Trace said. "If we return to the ranch, we'll just have to start over tomorrow. Let's ride on."

"Works for me," Beth agreed.

Lunch break over, they continued the search. An hour later, they found a small creek trickling down a steep hillside. A large portion of dirt had fallen beside the water. Beth swung out of the saddle and studied the landslide. Wonder's hoofprints revealed the rest of the story. The stallion had stopped to drink, and the land gave way beneath him. "Lucky he didn't break his leg."

"And that the wolves, bears, and such didn't find him," Trace said.

"Definitely." Beth checked her cinch, tightened it, and stepped into the stirrup. She guided her horse around the slippery terrain and on up the slope.

Suddenly, Luke gave a low growl. The other dog followed the German Shepherd's lead and they headed off into the woods. Beth pulled her Glock. "Company."

Trace pushed her long black coat out of the way, so she reached the pistols on her gunbelt. "Smith?"

"One can only hope." Beth urged Tigger forward.

She used the shelter of the trees to ease up after the dogs, pausing when she heard the short sharp bark that signaled Luke's favorite prey. A man!

Slipping from the saddle, she ground-tied her horse. He could run from Smith but would wait for her unless something or someone really frightened him. Out of the corner of her eye, she saw Trace copy the action. Beth worked the left side of the trail, while Trace took the right.

The cedars parted into a small clearing and Beth recognized three of the men sitting on their horses, Zebadiah Prescott and the two fellows who had gone with him to find Smith. They weren't alone. Three scrawny young men, barely out of their teens rode with them. One of the spare horses towed some sort of stretcher carrying an injured person. It must be the old-time version of an emergency vehicle.

"And you give me hell for bringing strays home to Ma," Trace said. "What is this, Zebadiah?"

"What remains of the Dawson gang." Zebadiah swung down from his horse and strode toward Trace. "The littlest one could use some doctoring, Missus Morgan. She has a busted leg, ribs, and sleeps more than I like."

Beth nodded. "I'll take a look."

"Fair enough. Trace and I will fetch your mounts," Zebadiah said, "and she'll tell me why you're both out here instead of home on the Lazy B where I told her to stay. Where it's safe."

That didn't sound too promising for a marriage, more like a father-daughter relationship, Beth thought. The two walked past her and around a bend in the trail. When she looked over her shoulder, she saw the pair kissing as if they'd been apart for years, rather than days. She hid a smile.

Men! Why couldn't he just say he wanted a moment with his wife?

The unconscious girl lying in the stretcher was young, probably about fifteen or sixteen. Slight, molasses brown hair, a hundred and ten pounds. Bruises on her face, a swelling on the left side of her head, so whoever clubbed her was right-handed. Her left leg was splinted, and someone wrapped her ribs.

"Who did this?" Beth asked.

"I doctored her as best I could." The big, blond man leading the horse hitched to the stretcher spoke up. "The feller we were hunting did the damage. She said she fed and watered his horse and it angered him."

"He shot Pa." A teen who bore a striking resemblance to the girl dismounted and came close, holding a canteen. "Want some, Mina?"

"Yes." A bare whisper.

Beth took the container and dropped to one knee beside the girl. "You're going to be fine." She caught her breath when she saw the golden-brown sugar eyes. Familiar eyes. "I know it."

"Better than I do." Mina took a small sip. "Who're you?"

"Beth Chambers. And I'm going to see to it that you live."

"Are you a doctor?"

"In a way," Beth said. "That's how I know you'll be fine."

And the other way she knew that Mina Dawson lived was because of the old family Bible her great-grandson kept as a memento. Whenever Beth was in trouble, she had to copy verses from it, so she'd studied the family tree too many times to forget her foster father's ancestors.

She closed the canteen and passed it back to the boy. "I suggest we head for the Lazy B and get your sister to Missus Sims. Once she's in a real bed and eating real meals, Mina will heal up a lot faster."

Relief replaced worry and the boy nodded. "Yes, ma'am."

Beth headed over to her own horse and took the reins from Trace. "So, what happened to Smith? Where is he?"

"Hightailed it into the trees after shooting the kids' pa," Zebadiah said, holding Trace's horse for her to mount. "We didn't chase him any further. He'd lit out one way and your Appy bolted the other. Did he make it home ahead of us?"

"Yesterday," Trace said. "So, Smith's afoot?"

"Yes, but there are ranches around here and folks who should be a-watching their stock, and their families." A dark-haired man reined his horse to the front of the line. "I offered to go after him, but Prescott refused."

"I'm glad, Mac." Trace shared a look with Zebadiah, before she added, "Never chase a coyote over a hill. He'll attack when you least expect it. And Zebadiah needed you to help bring these youngsters home safe."

The statement was more tactful than Beth expected the younger woman to be, but it didn't require a comment from her. Once in the saddle, she rode behind the stretcher so she could keep an eye on Mina. The young woman didn't stay awake long. The jolting of her makeshift bed caused her to faint again. That must be a mercy.

Memories stirred as she watched the sleeping girl. Shortly after Beth began to live with Will, he'd encouraged her to join a local 4-H group, the Silver Flying A's. She'd made new friends in the band of young girls and boys, especially the Dawson girls. One teen, a petite brunette, Audra had been the spitting image of Mina, and Beth smiled at the memory.

So now she knew why her adopted cousin looked so different from her sisters. She was a definite throwback to her relatives here.

However, Beth wasn't about to share what she knew from the future with the people who lived in Liberty Valley in 1888.

The afternoon dragged by. Since they had to keep the horses to a slow walk with Mina in what Trace called a *travois,* they couldn't make good time. As the day warmed, Luke trotted in Tigger's shadow part of the time. In the early evening, Beth recognized the trees and trail. They were close to the Lazy B.

"Almost home," Trace said. "Keep a sharp lookout for an ambush."

As if her warning was the clue he needed, Luke yipped, then tore ahead of their party. Beth reached for her pistol. She paused when Tigger tossed his head and nickered in welcome. He wasn't frightened, but glad to see whoever approached.

Excitement trickled through her when she glimpsed the black Appaloosa mare jogging in her direction. Rad lingered long enough to speak to Trace and Zebadiah, then rode toward her.

He glanced at the three strangers and Beth knew he saw everything, the same way she always did, a cop's once-over of the situation. He reined Nell in next to Tigger. Beth nodded in greeting. "Learn anything we can use?"

He chuckled. "I missed you too, Missus Morgan."

In less than two hours, they arrived at ranch headquarters. Beth supervised Mina's transfer into the house and onto a bed. She and Missus Sims undressed and gave the girl a sponge bath, then eased her into a nightgown. During the process, Beth inspected the injuries. There was no need to change the splint on her leg or the bandages on Mina's ribs, but it proved necessary to clean the wound on her head.

Beth diluted two sulfa tablets in water, flavored the medicine with honey, and convinced the young woman to sip the concoction. "You'll feel better tomorrow."

Mina managed a weak smile. "I already do."

"Well, as soon as you drink this willow bark tea, you'll be able to sleep," Missus Sims promised, holding a china cup. "And I'll sit up with you for a while. When I need a rest, Jenny will be here."

"I'll take a turn too," Beth said, gently smoothing the girl's hair from her bruised forehead.

Rad loomed in the doorway. "Tomorrow, but not tonight. We need to interview the other Dawsons, and you'll want to hear what I learned about the shaman."

"You got that right." Beth smiled at Mina. "I have high expectations for you. We'll discuss them in the morning."

"Does that mean no more bank robberies?" Mina asked, leaning back against the pillows. "Tell my brothers we're going straight."

"Oh, I will," Rad said. "I think Trace plans to hire them. The Lazy B needs more hands to work cattle."

Collecting her jacket, Beth shrugged into it. She watched relief ease the tension on the girl's features. Now, Mina really would sleep. And in the morning, they'd discuss Gary Smith. There had to be a way to find the man before he hurt someone else.

Rad stepped aside so she could step out into the hall. Beth frowned up at him when he closed the bedroom door behind them. "What?"

"This." He pulled her into his arms.

She laughed when he lowered his head. He brushed her lips with his in the softest of kisses. She tangled her fingers in his hair, tiptoed up, and caught his mouth with her own. Before the kiss deepened, he lifted his head.

"Why stop?" she asked. "I haven't said, 'no,' Morgan."

"Later," he said. "We do things differently here."

"Funny. I didn't think times had changed that much." She led the way to the stairs, slightly baffled. She knew he wanted her, and a kiss was only a kiss, wasn't it?

Or was this going to be one of those nights when he told her what a woman could and couldn't do and bitched about her jeans? If so, all they'd be doing was sleeping in the cabin—well at least he'd be sleeping. She'd probably sit up on the porch, watch the stars and try not to think about Afghanistan or the way wounded men screamed.

The three Dawson boys sat in the kitchen with the burly blond man that Trace had introduced as her foreman, Olaf Swenson, and his carbon copy of a brother, Lars. However, neither Trace nor her husband was in sight. They had undoubtedly opted for privacy and wouldn't be seen again before dawn.

Beth glanced over her shoulder at Rad. "So, which one do you want and where do you want to talk to him?"

Humor crept into Rad's dark blue eyes. "I'll take the oldest out to the porch. You take the youngest to the parlor and the middle one can sit here with the Swensons. Whoever finishes first can interview him."

"Works for me." Beth signaled the boy who'd given water to Mina on the trail. "Let's go."

"Why?" He looked more scared now than he had earlier. "What do you want?"

"Detective Morgan wants to know what you saw, and she doesn't want you and your kin conjuring up tales," Rad said. "We'll see if we get the same story from the three of you and then Olaf can decide if you're worth straightening out or if we should just host a necktie party."

She almost asked what a "necktie party" was and decided to wait when the youngest boy stumbled to his feet, brown eyes wide with fear. The phrase must mean something different than the shopping trip it sounded like, but she'd ask Rad later. She'd get more from the boy if he were frightened, rather than overconfident. He walked ahead of her into the empty parlor. She pointed to a leather chair and sat down across from him in the matching one. A lamp on a corner table provided enough light so she could watch his facial expressions.

Reaching in her jacket, she pulled out her pad of paper, flipped through to an empty page, and began to make notes. "What's your name?"

"Nolan David Dawson."

"And how old are you?"

"Thirteen last fall."

"How many people rode with your family?"

Nolan relaxed a little and rattled off a list of names that included his father, two older brothers, his sister, uncle, and a pair of cousins. He described meeting Gary Smith who'd wanted to ride with the Dawsons, but the younger members of the family weren't as impressed as the older ones.

"He said he shot the marshal and Mina told me she thought he was a liar. Nobody's ever walked away from a gunfight with Marshal Morgan. Pa said it was just bad luck Mina lost the bankroll to him, but Smith was all riled about it."

Beth nodded. *Good information to have.* "And what happened to your father?"

Tears swam in the boy's eyes, and he blinked hard. "Mina got caught watering Smith's horse. He started whaling on her and Pa tried to stop him. Smith yanked out his rifle and shot Pa dead. I never saw a rifle shoot that fast. He killed Uncle—"

More tears shone and Nolan's voice faded into silence. He buried his face in his hands.

Beth leaned over and rested a hand on his narrow shoulder. After a while, the boy continued, describing the way his uncle fell. And how Zebadiah Prescott showed up with help, rescuing Mina from certain death. Smith ran off into the woods and Nolan's cousins went to find him, threatening to kill him.

"I'm plumb worried about them," Nolan went on. "They're tough, but they ain't mean, not like Smith. He could shoot them too."

"We'll keep an eye out," Beth promised. "If they're willing to go straight, we may be able to find them honest work."

She waited until Nolan calmed down, then took him back to the kitchen. She'd finished her interview while Rad completed the one with the last teenager. She met his gaze. "You and I need to talk, Marshal."

"Yes, but there's no reason these fellers can't hit the hay, Olaf.

Why don't you take them out to the bunkhouse? We'll palaver in the morning after breakfast when Trace and Prescott are here too."

Olaf stood. "Fair enough. Let's call it a night."

"Daylight comes early," Lars agreed. They ushered the boys out the door.

TWENTY-FOUR

*"A Guardian's Dreams reveal possible paths she might tread.
Choices meant only to guide, not orders to obey or dread..."*

RULES OF CHRONOS

WITH LUKE SHADOWING THE TWO OF THEM, BETH WALKED BESIDE Rad toward the cabin they'd shared one night. "So, what did you find out while you were gone?"

He chuckled and grasped her elbow, pulling her closer to him. "Is work all you think about?"

"Well, you weren't interested in anything else." She hid a smile. "Were you?"

"Oh, I can think of a few things." He guided her up the steps to the cabin, his deep tones amused. "What about you?"

She pushed open the door and scanned the empty room, lit by a lamp on the table. "Alone at last," she taunted and slid her arms around his neck. "So, do we talk now about the cases or wait a while?"

He lowered his head. "I'm voting for later."

She tiptoed up and brushed his mouth with hers. "Much later."

"Sounds good to me."

When he deepened the kiss, she sighed and melted against him. Oh yes, this was what she'd been thinking about and dreaming about for the past two days. Between kisses, she managed to push his coat off the broad shoulders and began to unfasten his shirt. He hadn't removed the bandage and she decided to take care of that in the morning. He must be well on the mend since she didn't see any seepage from the wound.

She caught her breath when he unbuttoned her blouse. Turnabout was obviously what he had in mind, and she was so ready for that.

He nipped her ear. "Bet I can make you scream tonight, Missus Morgan."

"I wouldn't be surprised."

He trailed a line of kisses along her collarbone toward her throat, and she bit back a moan. "Can you just hurry up, Morgan?"

"Maybe in a year or two, but not tonight."

Two hours later, wrapped in his arms and lying close to him, she felt safe enough to sleep. No nightmares, she thought. She pressed her ear to his chest and listened to his heartbeat through the bandage. "I did miss you," she whispered.

"I know," He stroked her hair. "I'll bet you were riled as hell that I left you behind. If you'd come with me, nobody would have spoken to us."

"Trace explained the situation," Beth said. "So, what did you learn?"

"The woman who died was a shaman and she knew Smith came back, said she felt it on the wind when he arrived. She argued with the head man about staying upriver to fish and hunt. She wanted the families to return to larger settlements where they'd be safer."

"Smart woman," Beth murmured. "So, how did he catch up with her?"

"One of the younger gals ignored the shaman's warnings and

wandered off. The medicine woman went to find her. The girl returned, but the shaman didn't."

"That's why we found her." Beth propped up on an elbow and leaned over to kiss him. "And you took her home. I'm glad."

"Me, too."

"So, are the Indians going downriver?"

"No, but they're being real careful until Smith is stopped, and the head man offered to send help if I needed it."

She eyed him warily as he took up most of the bed. Would he try to leave her behind again, or was this just a one-time occurrence? She was a trained law enforcement officer and she'd be a partner while she was here but trotting after him like some kind of servant wasn't her style. "Do you need help, Morgan?"

"I've got it." He feathered his thumb over her lips. "I've got you."

"Right answer." She kissed him again.

Sunlight glinted through the windows when she woke. It was barely dawn. He still slept beside her, and she smiled. At least this time he hadn't ridden off without her. She trailed a hand over his dark chest hair. Early morning sex would delay their departure, but they had time. She'd make time for this, for him. She leaned over, brushed her lips across his, and felt the response as he awakened. "Good morning."

"Now, it is." He chuckled. "I've never had a woman like you."

She smiled into his dark blue eyes. "And you never will have another one. I don't share."

"Fair enough. Neither do I."

"Good." She pressed close to his side, eying the bandage on his chest. She'd really like to have sex on top of him, but she didn't want to hurt him, and she wasn't sure how much pressure he could take. She kissed his beard-stubbled jaw. "I have a few ideas, but I don't want to shock you."

"Go ahead and try," he teased. "I can take it."

"Just remember you said that." Her mouth found his.

When she woke the next time, she was alone in the bed. She

could tell even before she opened her eyes. Her shoulder holster, complete with pistol hung from the nearest bedpost. Light flooded through the windows and for a moment, she missed her condo with its blinds that would allow her to sleep the day away.

Where was he? Had he left her again?

She reached for her watch to check the time. It was two-fifteen in the afternoon. No wonder she'd slept so late. Her body demanded payback for staying awake most nights when he was away. No mystery there. Sleep was hard to come by since Afghanistan. She usually stayed up several days in a row and slept a few hours only when she couldn't last any longer without rest.

The door opened and she reached for her pistol, then stopped when she recognized Rad. He carried in a metal washtub, like those most people used for watering livestock.

"What is that?" Beth asked.

"Your bath. It's the only chance you'll have to take one for a week or more." He put down the tub, then went back to the porch to carry in buckets of water. "We'll ride out in the morning. It's too late to go anywhere today."

She leaned against the headboard, pulling up the blankets, and watched as he filled the tub, hiding a smile. "You do think you're the man in charge, don't you, Morgan?"

"Somebody has to be." He grinned at her. "Or did you want to stay at the Lazy B awhile longer?"

"I like the people here." She drew up her knees and rested her chin on them, "but I'm ready to hunt down Gary Smith before he hurts someone else."

"Sounds fair." Rad poured another bucket of water into the tub, the steam rising. "What did the youngest Dawson boy tell you?"

She took a deep breath and brought him up to speed on what Nolan said about the attack on his sister. Afterward, Rad told her what he learned from the older boys. The major points of the attack were the same. She frowned thoughtfully. "Did the older boys shoot at Smith? Is he injured, on foot or did he steal one of their horses?"

"He left on shank's mare," Rad said, "but he's probably stolen a horse by now. We need to pass the word around and have folks keep an eye out for him."

Beth nodded in agreement. "They'll want to watch over family members too. Since he didn't get to kill Mina, he'll be frustrated and looking for a new victim."

"Zeb already told Mac and Gruber to watch for strangers."

"Good idea to lock down the place. He tried coming after Becky once she ran off. He's bound to do the same thing if he figures out that Mina's on the Lazy B."

Rad put down the bucket and turned to face her. "Which one is Becky?"

Beth studied the concern on his rugged features. "She's the little blonde chickee, eight years old. Smith bought her from her foster family." She continued filling him in on the details she'd learned about the man. "So, I'm wondering what happened to the other girl, Sorrel."

"She waits tables and dances a bit up in Gunny Creek."

"What does that mean?"

"She's a dancehall girl in the saloon." Rad carried the kettle from the woodstove over to the washtub. "I talked to the owner because she seemed a little young for what she was doing, but he told me that she doesn't work the line yet. And she said she was there willingly. So, there wasn't anything I could do except leave her. She claimed she didn't have any family."

"Work the line?" Beth propped her chin on her fist. "What is that?"

"Some of the hurdy-gurdy gals sell themselves, not just watered-down whisky." Rad poured hot water into the tub. "And we call that *working the line*."

Pulling the top blanket from the bed around her, Beth stood. "I'd like to talk to her about Smith. According to Becky, he was determined to remove them both from their foster home when he found out what was going on there."

"That was decent of him, but it's kind of a surprise."

"You're telling me."

Smith's streak of morality was still confusing, Beth thought as she soaked in the tub a short time later after she washed her hair. She wouldn't have figured he'd do anything to protect anyone, much less two young girls. Yet how had Sorrel ended up a prostitute? Who took her to the saloon? Or had she found it on her own? And where the hell was Gunny Creek?

Beth sighed and wished her phone still had Internet access. There was no way to pull up map coordinates and locate the settlement. She'd have to wait until Rad took her there. She grimaced. Being helpless didn't appeal to her. Maybe, Trace would draw a map of the local area.

Bath finished, she wrapped her hair in one of the towels and dried off with the other. She opted to wear a blouse and skirt to supper to what Trace called the Big House. It seemed like the least she could do when they'd be riding out in the morning and she'd be back in her jeans, now clean. Thankfully, Missus Sims had insisted on washing their laundry, but Beth did her own underwear since she didn't want to shock the older woman. It was 1888, after all – even if she wasn't one-hundred-percent sure how she had arrived in such a strange place.

Rad returned in time to drag the tub outdoors and dump the water. He'd obviously had a chance to bathe and shave today. He wore a favorite blue shirt, black pants, and boots. They weren't the only ones who dressed up for dinner or supper as Rad called it. Beth slipped her pistol in the pocket of her skirt and was ready to go.

Trace and Zeb met them on the way to the Big House. The other woman wore a light blue dress. Her hair was neatly coiled in a bun and for once she didn't have the set of pistols on her hips. Zeb not only packed a pistol. He also carried a rifle. Even at home, he still felt the need for protection.

At the house, Beth recognized the older man who'd traveled with Rad to the Indian village. Trace introduced him as Fremont, her grandfather's best friend. Before they could chat, supper was served.

It was a simple meal, or so Missus Sims said, but the home-made meal seemed anything but plain to Beth. Beans cooked with chunks of bacon and onion, boiled potatoes, fresh-churned butter for the slabs of cornbread and drop biscuits, coffee for the adults, and milk for the children. Three pies sat on the warming oven, ready to be sliced for dessert.

Beth savored every mouthful. "Wow, I wish I could cook like this."

"So, do I," Rad said.

Beth shot a glare at him, then smiled at Trace. "You'll have to expect us to visit whenever Morgan decides he wants a home-cooked meal."

"You're always welcome," Trace said. "The Lazy B wouldn't have made it this long without Missus Sims' cooking. I can't afford to pay my men much, but she feeds them better than they eat in any of the logging camps."

"Or that we ate on any of the cattle drives I ramrodded," Zeb drawled.

Missus Sims carried around the pot of coffee, topping their cups. "And you men will say anything to convince me to make doughnuts."

"Whatever it takes," Fremont agreed.

Beth glanced down the length of the table, amazed at how quiet the children were. Sometimes, she even forgot they were at the table. They passed around the food and the older ones helped serve the younger ones. Becky smiled, a sunshine grin and Beth winked at the little girl.

"So, when is doughnut day?" Beth asked. "I'll definitely come for that."

"Next time you visit," Missus Sims promised. "Plan to stay a few days then too."

———

She left Rad sleeping and wandered out to the porch to mull over the questions that continued to torment her. How had she arrived in a place that not only allowed prostitution but legalized it? Why did she care about a man who didn't intervene when a young girl sold her body in a bar? Even here, wasn't it a crime against a child? Shouldn't anybody who slept with that teenager be jailed as a pedophile, not ignored?

No answers, at least not yet. She sat on the step and petted Luke when he came to lie beside her, watching the stars play peek-a-boo through the clouds. What if she rode away tomorrow and gave up on the quest to stop Smith? Could she find her way home? What did she need? A pair of red slippers or cowboy boots?

She certainly wasn't in Kansas anymore, much less Snohomish County or Washington State for that matter. Still, nothing in the way of answers popped into her mind. Will always said that the solution lay within the problem. Well, she had lots of problems, but no solutions. And remembering her foster father only added to them. Had he known where she would end up? Why hadn't he said anything?

Of course, she undoubtedly would have thought he was ripe for the insane asylum if he had. Why hadn't he told her the truth about his family, that he was descended from outlaws and bank robbers? Time travel to 1888? Chasing a suspected rapist and serial killer into the Old West? It sounded like one of the fantasy novels Audra Dawson wrote as Destynee LaFleur, not reality.

Beth heard footsteps crunch on rock and looked toward the gravel road. It wasn't Trace and her cigarettes, but the old man from dinner, Fremont Goodman. He sauntered toward her and Luke. The dog lifted his head but didn't growl or bark.

"Mind if I join you?" Fremont asked.

"That's fine." Beth hitched over a bit, closer to the dog, and made room on the step. "Couldn't you sleep either?"

"Tonight, there's just too many memories of places I've been. Folks I've known, loved and buried. I've outlived most of my friends." Fremont pulled out a small buckskin pouch. "So, why are you awake, Detective Morgan?"

She shrugged. "They say it's a symptom of P.T.S.D."

He rolled a cigarette and passed it to her. "What's P.T.S.D?"

"Post-Traumatic Stress Disorder." At the incomprehension on his wrinkled features, she added. "I can't sleep. Saw too much in the war."

"Me, too." He sat down next to her and struck a match, lighting both their smokes. "I've ridden a lot of miles, seen a lot more battles than you have. Been alive almost seventy years, but I'm not ready to cash in my chips yet."

"Me either." She remembered the department shrink telling her the suicide rate was on the rise among Afghanistan War vets and how pissed she was when he shared that with the lieutenant. Of course, then she heard rage was one more symptom and justifiable anger wasn't considered normal.

"Trace told me that you need to hear my stories, the ones only she and I know. The ones I lived with her grandpa."

"What stories?"

"Those about the *Guardian* and what she does." Fremont drew a flask from his other pocket. "That's gonna be you, sooner than you think."

"What's a *Guardian*?" Even as she asked, she knew.

She remembered riding out of Monte Cristo just over two weeks before. The silent woods and large evergreens looming over her, and everything quiet, too quiet. The world holding its breath. And then looking for Luke – she hadn't seen him for so long, at least five minutes.

Her gaze had narrowed on a small gray, brown and black shape near the granite boulders. The limp, broken body of Luke. He was d...

The whine of a bullet!

She shook her head, forced away the memory. She put an arm around the dog's neck and held him tight. "Smith shot at me—"

"Was that all?" Fremont asked. "Or did something else happen?"

She nodded. "My horse spooked, reared, and fell on me. But I was okay."

"Kinda strange, don't you think?"

"Yes." She remembered more.

She'd thought everything was over that afternoon. So many projects she hadn't finished. Tears stung, burned her cheeks. And the crushing pain, unending agony as she lay beneath her dying horse. She'd begged for help, prayed for it actually. *Just one more chance. Let me stop Smith. Please.*

"Somebody heard me. Something or someone changed the outcome," Beth said slowly. "I don't know who or what. Universe, maybe. Some kind of Power. Maybe God."

"That's what Padden said when she saved me." Fremont opened the bottle and passed it over. "She'd faced death, her death, and wanted a second chance. She got one, but she had to pay for it."

Beth smelled the whisky, then tasted it. Definitely homemade, but it went down smooth, sending warmth through her body. "And you think that's what happened to me?"

"You have the same look she does like she's seen what lies beyond this world. She came back with a healing power. I should have died, but I didn't, thanks to her."

Beth took another sip of liquor, then returned the flask. "What happened to you?"

"A battle with another tribe over stolen horses." Fremont drank. "I took a spear through the gut saving my best friend. She healed me, but I have the scar."

"Rad would have died if I hadn't found him."

"And nobody else could have healed him." Fremont passed back the whisky. "The rest will come to you in its own time, but you have work to do here. Things to change."

Beth frowned. She hadn't considered that. She could make a difference here. She already had when she saved Morgan. And

Mina. Wasn't the girl intended to die? At least, she would have if Zeb Prescott hadn't interrupted Smith. And Prescott wouldn't have been there if Morgan hadn't sent him to trail Smith, and Morgan couldn't have sent him if he'd died of his injuries.

She shook her head. Circles within circles. Everything seemed connected.

She watched Fremont rise. "Where are you headed?"

"Back to the bunkhouse. Dawn comes early on this spread. And you folks will be riding out to pass the word about Smith." Fremont paused. "Tell Morgan to take you to see the sheepherders. You'll want to talk to Padden."

"A lot of people have sheep. Where's this Padden?"

"Not at ranch headquarters and not now, Detective Morgan. The marshal will take you there." Fremont turned back. "He's your forever mate, and that's the way it's been for Padden and me. I was on my way here to look after Trace when her grandpa died, and Padden rode north with me."

"A 'forever mate'?" Beth shook her head. "But he doesn't do things the way I do."

"But he gets them done anyway," Fremont said. "It's why I chose him to carry on for me. He's one of the few men around that doesn't just look. He actually sees. And it's past time for Padden and me to let somebody younger fill our boots. She'll be glad you finally arrived."

TWENTY-FIVE

"There are laws a Guardian may not break or bend.
*These include Time, True Love, Life, Death and Events
beyond her ken."*

RULES OF CHRONOS

BETH STARED AFTER THE OLD MAN AS HE WALKED AWAY. SHE HAD too much to think about. A *Guardian*, she mused. So, she did have a job here, but just who or what was her new boss? What was her assignment? How was she supposed to carry it out in 1888 Washington Territory? And what would happen when she returned home to 2018 where she belonged?

The door opened behind her, and she glanced over her shoulder at Rad. "You were asleep."

"Heard voices." Wearing pants and a flannel shirt, he carried a blanket. He came outside and folded it around her shoulders. "You don't sleep very well, do you?"

"Too many nightmares." She leaned into him when he sat

down next to her, enjoying the warmth of his body. "You were a soldier. What changed things for you?"

"Time." He put an arm around her shoulders. "You want to talk about what you saw before you came here? Are you thinking about those dead women?"

"No." She turned her face into his neck, breathing in the scent of his skin. "I joined the Army seventeen years ago as soon as I graduated from high school. I was a military cop then trained as a medic and ended up in the Middle East during the war. Too much blood. Too much death and dying."

He nodded. "You probably saw more of it than most."

She'd never thought of that, but he was right. She spent her time treating injuries, so the wounded survived until they reached the doctors. When the department shrink suggested she saw more blood in a day than a combat soldier did, she dismissed him as a civilian who couldn't find his butt with two hands and a roadmap. Maybe, he'd had a point.

She sighed and relaxed even more. "We could probably think of something to do in that bed."

"Sleep." He dropped a kiss on her hair. "We've got a long ride ahead of us today if we want to make it to Junction City by nightfall."

"Well, that wasn't what I had in mind."

"Save your ideas till we get home."

"I need to change that bandage in the morning."

"You can do it before we ride out."

She nodded and pressed closer to him. She heaved another sigh, then fought back a yawn. With him on one side and Luke on the other, she felt surprisingly safe. She closed her eyes for a moment, letting her mind sort through the information she'd learned from Fremont. She hadn't written out anything he said.

She needed to do that, add it to her notes. There had to be a reason why she was here. More importantly, there had to be one for Smith to be in 1888. And she would have to learn why he was here, how he managed to travel through time to capture him.

Tomorrow, she told herself. She'd sort it all out tomorrow.

———

After breakfast, she checked on Mina. The young girl still slept between meals, but she was on the road to recovery. Beth had drawn a picture of crutches and Fremont agreed to have them ready when Ma Sims said the girl could leave her bed. When she finished with the teenager, Beth insisted Rad join them in the kitchen. She wanted to change his bandage before they headed to town.

Missus Sims proved an able assistant which wasn't a shock since she had obviously nursed the children and others on the ranch for years. She had clean cloth for bandages, hot water from the kettle on the stove, and what she called, 'tincture of arnica' for pain. When Beth unwrapped the poncho piece, she was pleased to see the entry wound had healed. She still put a clean dressing over the spot where the bullet penetrated his back.

Next came the hole in his chest. Surprisingly, it had nearly closed, but she still didn't trust it. She left the small plastic sheet that sealed his lung in place, washed the area around it, reminding herself not to drool at the sight of Rad's muscled body. She took the folded clean cloth that Missus Sims passed her and put it over top of the plastic.

"When will you stop fussing?" Rad asked. "It looks fine to me."

"It's not fine." Beth used the long strip of rag that Missus Sims handed her to tie the padding into place. "It needs another month to finish closing and you should stop stressing it."

"What does that mean?"

"It means not lifting anything, Marshal Morgan, and letting other people look after you." She picked up the poncho piece and wrapped it over top of the initial dressings, strapping it back into place with the web Army belts.

As he pulled on his shirt, he considered the idea. "I'm not dead yet and I saddle my own horse."

"What's the point in asking my advice when you won't take it?"

"I'm a grown man. I'm the territorial marshal in East Liberty Valley, not just Junction City and I look after others. Since I have a wife, I take care of her too."

Beth nearly rolled her eyes at the stubborn look on his face. If they were alone, she'd have told him he was also a pigheaded idiot, but she wouldn't chew his ears in front of Missus Sims. Putting the extra bandages in her saddlebags, she drew out the bottle of sulfa tablets. "And now, you'll take two of these and some of the arnica, so you'll be able to ride all the way to town without me pitching a fit."

"I don't need medicine. Save it for someone who does."

"Morgan, if you've never heard my father's saying, 'happy wife, happy life,' then it's time you did."

Missus Sims smiled appreciatively and handed a glass of water to Rad. "Are those the same pills you said to give to Mina?"

"Yes, but she only requires one in the morning and one at night." Beth put away the bottle. "The marshal is bigger, and his wound was worse, so he needs more." She glanced at Rad. "When will we be back this way? I want to see how Mina does."

"In about two weeks."

"Good," Missus Sims said. "We'll make doughnuts."

———

The trail wound through the evergreens, widening as the hours passed. Now, it was a narrow track, almost a one-lane road. She could even have squeezed her Jeep through parts of it. Tigger pranced eagerly beside Rad's mare.

He reined to a stop on a small rise and gestured to the cluster of buildings off in the distance. "Junction City."

Beth gazed at him for a moment, then eyeballed the town

again. It didn't look like much to her, but he sounded proud. As far as she could tell from here, it had a main street that stretched more than a half-mile and approximately three other roads that branched off to the left and right. Most of the buildings were single-story, built out of wood, and covered with cedar shakes.

She tried to remember if she'd ever driven through the town before, but it didn't look familiar. To the far left, she saw the glimmer of the river and a boat dock. "Is that for real?"

He followed her gaze. "Trace has supplies shipped up from Snohomish City for her businesses. She owns almost the entire town. And what isn't hers, she holds the paper on."

Beth shook her head. Wow, a woman owning a town, and Trace didn't look like the snobby rich bitch type. "She's so young. How did that happen?"

"She invested the money her grandpa left in the town and built onto it." Rad gestured to the buildings at the far end of town. "That's the bank. The mercantile is next to it and then there's the newspaper office. If the judge made it to town, we'll get a warrant for Smith and have Paul print us some wanted posters."

"Well, yee-haw." She couldn't help it. Rad sounded so much like an old-time lawman off television. She watched a smile tug at the edge of his mouth. Amusement glinted in his navy-blue eyes. She took a deep breath and glanced at the town again. "So, educate me. What's a mercantile?"

"A store. Susanne Prescott manages it for Trace. They sell everything from clothes to boots to food and hardware. I have an account. You can buy what you need before we head out to my ranch."

Beth almost said she had money and more importantly a credit card, then recalled she was in 1888 and her funds wouldn't be accepted here. She nodded in agreement. "Well, let's head on into Dodge City, Marshal."

"It's Junction City."

"Oh yes. I forgot. We need to do something about your sense of humor."

She rode beside him toward the town. Men dressed in tradi-tional logging attire streamed in and out of the closest building and slowly she realized it was a bar. Well, they probably called it a saloon, but it was still a place where men congregated to drink.

And fight.

Two of them tumbled through the door into the street, rolling in the dirt. Tigger snorted, then reared, as three more loggers jumped into the fray. Rad swung out of the saddle, dropping his reins, and waded into the fracas, ducking as one man aimed a punch.

No way she'd let another LEO get his ass kicked, even if that lawman were from the 19th century. Vaulting free from Tigger, Beth grabbed her rifle. She leveled the carbine at the biggest man and yelled in her loudest street cop voice. "Stop that!"

———

Rad blocked a blow, then back-handed the man who'd thrown it. The young logger fell back into the mud. "Up against the hitch rail. All of you."

"You heard him. Move."

He flicked a glance over his shoulder and saw her. Beth held a rifle. The dog stood beside her, eager to jump somebody. Teeth bared, waiting.

"Now, ma'am. It was just for fun." The biggest man grabbed his buddy by the suspenders and backed cautiously toward the boardwalk.

"And when Detective Morgan shoots you, she'll enjoy it." Rad bent, pulled the last man out of the mud. "What's this about?"

Silence as they looked at him, then at Beth, and back at him. He suspected they'd been fighting over one of the saloon girls, but none of them wanted to share that truth with Beth for an audience.

A young man strode out of the shadowed entrance to the saloon. He was tall, lean with a handsome face but cold hazel eyes. He introduced himself to Beth. "Prince Beauchamp."

"He owns the Cedar Stump," Rad finished. "So, do you want to tell me what this is about?"

"Not particularly." Prince tipped his hat. "Ma'am, the boys will pay for the property damage they caused, and we'll work that out on our own."

The five loggers looked at each other, then nodded in agreement. "That works for us, ma'am," the biggest one said.

"I don't think so," Beth said. "You fought in front of us and we needed to settle it, so tell us the cause."

Rad pointed to the youngest logger. "Talk now or I'll send for the mayor."

The threat to call in their boss solved the problem. The boy eyed the other loggers and then said, "There's this new girl."

"And she set you fellows up to war over her." Beth heaved a sigh. "Men. Can't live with them and just can't shoot them. Did any of you think with the heads on top of your necks?"

Rad choked back a grin as she put away her rifle. "Fetch the gal, Prince. Somebody's going to jail, and it looks like it'll be her."

The saloonkeeper nodded and returned inside.

"Marshal, no," the oldest logger said. "Don't do that. All she wanted was for the fellow who had her first to take a bath and then it was whoever paid the most. And we can settle that amongst ourselves without arguing. Else, we'll be back in the woods tomorrow."

"And it'll be two weeks before we get back to Junction City."

"By then, you may have some manners and know how to conduct yourselves in my town." Rad frowned when Prince escorted out a small girl in a short, tight blue dress. The low-cut neckline revealed her bosom and striped stockings flaunted shapely legs. The last time he'd seen her was in Gunny Creek, so why had she moved on to Junction City?

He glanced at Beth and saw anger flicker into her face. He turned his attention to the hurdy-gurdy gal again. "You're coming with us, Sorrel."

"Why?" She tossed her head and bright red curls flew. "I ain't done nothing illegal, Marshal."

"Because you're not old enough to sell yourself in a bar," Beth snapped. "Now, move it. And as for you, Beauchamp, I'll be back tomorrow morning to talk to all your women and they'd better damn well be able to provide proof of age."

"How old do they have to be?" Prince asked, cautiously.

"More than twelve." Beth retorted.

Rad watched her cross to the gray Arabian and remove her coat from behind the saddle. She wrapped it around the girl, then urged her to walk toward him. The loggers moved out of the way.

The biggest man finally spoke. "Honest, ma'am. We didn't know her real age."

"Next time, open your eyes and look."

Prince ushered the loggers back into the saloon and for a moment, Rad wished he could go with them. Instead, he collected his horse's reins and led the way to the stone house that served as the town jail. Connor and Trace had insisted that the Madison home was the perfect replacement when the original marshal's office burned down and since they ruled the town council most of the time, it was a done deal.

Rad wrapped his horse's reins around the hitch rail. He studied Sorrel's pretty face, trying to see her features beneath layers of paint. How did his wife know what he didn't, what he hadn't even suspected?

"I'm not twelve," Sorrel finally said. "I'm sixteen."

"In four years," Beth said. "I just spent days out on the Lazy B with your younger sister. Do you think Becky didn't tell me how old you really are?"

"She doesn't know anything. She's just a tyke."

"Really?" Beth arched a brow. "You expect me to buy that load of crap?"

Rad opened the front door and waited for Beth to propel the girl inside. He caught Beth's arm for a moment. "Is she actually twelve?"

"Possibly thirteen, but no more than fourteen," Beth whispered. "Becky wasn't positive about Sorrel's age, but she had to be young for Smith to 'rescue' her three years ago."

Rad nodded. "Then, we'll keep her with us for now and take her out to the Lazy B later to live with the other orphans."

"Like they'll have me." Sorrel narrowed stormy green eyes. "I've been working saloons for ages and none of them fancy do-gooders will take in a girl who's done that."

"Trace Burdette will insist you move in with them," Rad said. "She likes to reunite families and since Becky is there, you'll have a place to eat and sleep. There will be chores and schooling—"

"What if our uncle shows up?" Sorrel demanded. "They'll give us back to him and his family, won't they?"

"Is that who Smith rescued you from?" Beth asked.

When the girl nodded, Rad said, "He won't set foot on the Lazy B. Trace wanted to shoot him after what he'd done to Becky and your uncle knows better than to be on Burdette property."

"Well, he didn't know better than to show up in Gunny Creek and tell Mr. Jackson to put me *on the line* because Uncle Walter wanted the money and me to share his bed when he was in town." Sorrel looked around the large main room and then went to sit at the table near the cook-stove. "So, I hightailed it out of there. If I must be a whore, I get what I earn."

———

The marshal's office and jail weren't much to write home about, Beth thought, but Rad certainly seemed proud of it. Three small cells opened off the main room and he told her that they had once been bedrooms for the Madison girls, Zeb Prescott's half-sisters. Since his stepfather dreaded fires, a constant hazard during the dry weather, Reverend Madison insisted on building the one-story house out of river rock.

Rad left to visit the mercantile and bring back suitable attire for Sorrel. While he was gone, Beth slowly surveyed the largest room of the house. It was obviously an office with a desk and chair, a kitchen with counters, cupboards, woodstove, table, and chairs. She sent Sorrel to nap in the curtained-off alcove that held a bed and a smaller table with an oil lamp. Men's clothing hung from hooks on the wall.

If he thought they were living here for the rest of their lives, he'd better think again, Beth told herself. No way could she survive in something this small. She heard footsteps on the boardwalk and swung around as the door opened.

Kyle Morgan sauntered inside, accompanied by an older, white-haired man in a black suit.

Beth rested a hand on Luke's head and eyed Kyle. "Well, look what the cat dragged in. I wondered why you stayed in town when Gruber came back to the Lazy B."

TWENTY-SIX

"A Guardian trains to Protect and Keep Others from harm, in the city, country, house, home, ranch or farm..."

RULES OF CHRONOS

Kyle shrugged. "Thought I'd stay in town and help out Cal for a while."

Beth studied the older man and realized he'd returned the favor. On the far side of fifty years old. Six foot, a beanpole in the black suit, he wore two pistols with rounds of ammo on the gunbelts and carried a rifle in his right hand. Gray hair hung to his shoulders and his coal-black eyes were as cold, as empty as a rattlesnake's. "I don't think he needed you."

Cal smiled, but it was a bare quirk of his lips. "Neither did you."

"Good point." Beth inclined her head toward the alcove. "I sent Sorrel to sleep back there. I didn't want to put her in one of the cells."

Cal hung his rifle on the rack by the front door. "Ran into the marshal at the she-bang and he mentioned it."

"She-bang?" Beth asked. "What's that?"

"The mercantile." Kyle crossed to the stove and filled cups with coffee. "Rad told us you'll be having a meeting of the minds with Prince Beauchamp tomorrow. You should know that the age of consent is fourteen in Washington Territory and girls have to be ten according to the federal government."

"Never did agree with that," Cal said. "When they're little, they should be playing with toys, going to school, and doing chores, not be around grown men in saloons." He opened a tin of milk and put it on the table. "You may want your coffee a bit weaker, ma'am. Most womenfolk do."

"Thanks, but I drink it straight unless there's *Bailey's*."

"What's that?" Kyle asked, mimicking her question from before.

Beth eyed him narrowly. Sooner or later, they'd have it out. She let the silence drag on too long before she said, "Irish cream, strictly alcoholic and medicinal for when I have to tolerate two-legged jackasses."

Cal choked back an appreciative grin. "Too bad I'm riding out. I think you and I could get along well with each other."

Beth glanced at him, then at Kyle. "What's up? Why are you leaving?"

"The marshal doesn't need me to run the jail when he has a wife to cook for him and the prisoners, or to watch over the town when he's out riding his circuit," Cal said. "So, I'll leave in the next couple of days."

"No." Beth pulled out a chair and sat down. "I don't cook. I'll be riding with Morgan, not sitting around town waiting for him to return. I'm a detective. I sure as sugar won't ever take care of things here or people in lock-up."

"Not unless she can put her dog on 'em," Kyle said. "Told you she had it attack me, Cal."

"He didn't draw blood," Beth said. "So, quit whining." She

turned her attention back to the older man. "Any other stuff we need to discuss?"

Cal slowly shook his head. "No, ma'am. I wouldn't dare dispute what you say."

"Good."

The opening door drew her attention and she frowned as Rad entered, pushing Sorrel ahead of him. "Now, what the hell is up with that? She was taking a nap."

"Not for long. She climbed out the window and was headed for Snohomish City on your horse," Rad said. "Guess we'll have a necktie party soon as the judge gets here."

Beth watched the girl's eyes widen with fear and asked. "What's a necktie party?"

"Hanging," Kyle said. "Should I round up a few men to build a gallows, Rad?"

"Need to have a trial first." Cal filled another cup with coffee. "We're civilized here."

Beth nearly said that she didn't think killing a child for taking a horse was particularly civilized but thought better of it. Instead, she stood and walked over to one of the small bedrooms and opened the wooden door. Bars on the window on the far wall allowed in some daylight. "So much for trusting you, Sorrel. Put her in here, Rad. How's my horse?"

"I didn't hurt him," Sorrel said, indignant at the insult. "I would have let him go as soon as I got downriver a-ways."

"Doesn't mean I'd have him back, does it?" Beth scanned the room. A cot, table, and one chair made up the furnishings. There were blankets on the bed, so the girl would be warm enough. "You and I will talk later and you're not going to be a happy camper. Can you read and write?"

"I'm not stupid. Of course, I can."

"Good." Beth glanced at Cal. "Would you find her paper and a pencil? Writing an apology will give her something to do before supper."

Sorrel lifted her chin, defiant to the end. "What if I don't?"

"Then, you'd better have it done by breakfast if you want to eat in the morning."

"Starving me is against the law," Sorrel protested, stomping into the cell.

"Not my law. This is my town." Rad chuckled. "And you stole my wife's horse. Missing a meal won't hurt you, not when there are worse consequences." He shut and locked the cell door.

"Where is Tigger?" Beth glanced up at Rad before she headed out to the street. "Is he really all right?"

"He's fine. I tied him next to Nell again." Rad pulled out a chair. "We can take them to the barn soon."

Beth returned to the table to drink her coffee, hoping she didn't look as irritated as she felt by Rad claiming her as a possession. She was her own person and Tigger was her horse, not Morgan's. "Does that mean you'll want to hang Gary Smith for stealing Wonder?"

"We'll try him first," Rad said. "And since the stallion belongs to Trace, it won't take long for the jury to convict him, especially in Junction City."

"What about the woman he killed?" Beth asked. "Murder should take precedence over theft."

"You're right." Carrying his coffee, Kyle moseyed over to the stone wall behind the desk and began to look through the wanted posters. "It should, Missus Morgan, but since it was an Indian, he'd have to stand trial in a federal court, and a conviction isn't guaranteed."

Well, that was crap, Beth thought. Smith would get off because the victim would be on trial, not what he'd done to her.

"Is this Smith?" Kyle came back to the table. "Or should I say, is this the right Smith? It's a common name."

The poster provided a written description of the man she pursued and a thousand-dollar reward. She glanced thoughtfully at Rad. "Why isn't there a picture?"

"Why should there be? We know what he looks like."

"I see." Beth read the charges dating from several years before.

They included horse theft, robbery, cattle rustling, arson, and murder. "Who did he kill if women don't count?"

"Not all women," Kyle corrected, "just those who make their livings in an un-Christian manner."

"This one just digs that hole deeper and deeper," Cal commented. "Amazing no woman's shot him yet or busted him upside his head. Reckon I'll fetch paper for the young gal before I begin cooking supper. It was before my time, ma'am, but Smith was suspected in the orphanage fire that killed both the preachers."

"I'm fairly sure it was Dahlberg who actually set the fire," Rad said, "but Smith did work for the man."

"Is that all?" Beth finished her coffee. "I can't believe that was the extent of his crimes."

Rad stood, picking up the poster. "Could have been more but I didn't have any victims who'd press charges. We'll talk about it later. Now, let's go walk around town and take the horses to Connor's barn. We'll stop by the paper and have Paul print off more of these. Then, we can spread them around the area."

It lent a new meaning to putting out a BOLO for a suspect. Beth shook her head ruefully, longing for the days to come. It would be so easy if she had a computer, but those wouldn't be around for years. "Telegrams. Can we send his description to other towns?"

"We're not that fancy up here, Detective Morgan, but we'll send the posters by steamboat downriver to Snohomish. The next boat will take them to Seattle. And from there, the description will go by telegraph to all the other major cities in Oregon and California."

Luke followed them out to the horses. Tigger didn't seem the least bit upset by his adventure but stood contentedly by Rad's mare. The only adjustment Beth needed to make was to the stirrups. Sorrel had obviously shortened them to fit her legs.

"Newspaper office first," Rad said. "Then, Paul will start on the posters tonight and we'll have them next week before we leave town for the Bar M."

Beth sighed and shook her head. Obviously, the days of desktop publishing were far in the future. She nearly asked what was so complicated about printing a page that didn't have any pictures. Instead, she unfastened her sleeping bag and saddlebags. "We aren't leaving our personal gear in the barn, are we?"

"It'd probably be safe enough at Connor's, but then I'd have to go over later if you wanted something."

"Or I would."

"Not the way we do things here, Detective Morgan."

Beth heaved another sigh as she watched him tote her personal items into the jail. Everything seemed so strange in this year and place. She was accustomed to looking after herself, not having a man wait on her. And what a man!

She allowed herself to admire his tall, lean figure and broad shoulders. She couldn't decide what she liked better, the way he filled out his dark blue shirt or those long legs and the tight butt. Then again, there were the navy-blue eyes that were the color of the night sky right before sunset—hmm, no wonder she couldn't make up her mind.

It only took a few minutes to drop off the poster at the newspaper office. She swung into the saddle and reined Tigger to walk beside the Appaloosa mare. "What are we going to do while we wait forever for those notices?"

"Need to introduce you to folks around town and then we'll ride out to the ranch. You haven't seen your new home yet."

Beth checked out the small wooden houses that lined both sides of the muddy track. How many rooms did they have? Probably enough for the people who lived in them, but why did she have such a feeling of claustrophobia? Granted, her one-bedroom condo had to be at least three times the size of one of these cabins.

Rad guided his horse toward the large two-story house that stood at the far end of the street. "Cal will find extra copies of the poster in the office. We'll put up a few here and pass out the rest on the way to the Bar M."

"Bar M? Is that the name of your ranch?"

"Yes, but it's your spread too now."

It was a new idea, one that touched her heart. She'd never actually had a home to share with another person. Even when she lived with Will, the cabin was still definitely his home, and she was just a long-term visitor. It still sounded like everything from travel to notifying the locals would take an incredibly long time. What would Gary Smith do while she was stuck here in Mayberry? Kill another woman?

She followed Rad behind the house to a barn. "Who lives here?"

"Connor and his daughter." Rad dismounted. "It's where I always keep my horse when I'm in town. She gets good feed and good care."

Every time she thought she had a clue about life in the "olden days," things changed. She hadn't considered all the requirements of Horse-keeping 101. She slipped out of the saddle, letting Tigger stand beside Nell.

She moved to the Arabian's left side, undid the latigo. She always tied up the breast-collar and cinch on the right. It took a few extra minutes, but it meant her saddle wasn't trashed. Rad returned from the barn, lifted off the tack, and walked away.

"Wait a minute," she protested. "I told you earlier that you shouldn't be stressing yourself. I can carry my gear."

Too late. He was long gone. Men! He needed to be careful, not hurt himself. Had he forgotten he had gotten shot barely two and a half weeks ago?

———

Once they got the horses settled, they left the barn and headed toward the house. Rad glanced at Beth. Even with her hair coiled in a bun, wearing a divided skirt and the short black coat, she didn't look like a woman from Junction City. She was a lady, but she had an edge that reminded him of Trace Burdette.

He hadn't expected help when he confronted the loggers, much less for his wife to pull a rifle and back him in a fight. He reckoned he could get used to a deputy like her, but at times she still seemed a stranger. Especially when he woke at night, and she was long gone.

Connor greeted them at the door. "Saw you bring up the horses, so I put on the coffee. Kate did some baking, but she's off and away to visit Ursula and the babe at the newspaper."

"Who's Kate?" Beth asked.

"My daughter. She teaches school." Connor led the way to the kitchen. "She's talking about a box social to raise money for a new roof. Be warned, Missus Morgan. She'll be asking you for help."

Rad watched wary concern flicker into Beth's eyes. He pulled out a chair for her to sit down. "We're headed out to the ranch and to warn folks about Gary Smith. We'll be back for the social, but we have other business."

"I heard my loggers were squabbling about a new hurdy-gurdy gal." Connor filled three cups with coffee from the pot on the woodstove. "Would that be the fight over to Prince's place today?"

"Yes, and we have the girl," Beth said. "She's not old enough for what she wants to do."

"And Detective Morgan will be talking to the other gals to make sure they are," Rad finished, "but I think Sorrel is the youngest I've ever seen on the line. Detective Morgan says she's no more than twelve years old."

"I'll ask Lizbeth to meet you at the saloon in the morning, Detective." Connor brought over the cups. "After that, you'll be wanting to meet her ladies from the parlor house."

Beth stirred cream into her coffee and reached for one of the sugar cookies on the platter in the center of the table. "What's a parlor house?"

Connor sputtered into his cup, unable to answer.

"A high-class fancy-house," Rad said, watching Beth nibble at the cookie. "Lizbeth opened it when she came to town fifteen years ago."

"And a fancy-house? What's that?"

"A brothel," Rad said, "but don't call it that when Lizbeth can hear you. She runs a decent place, pays her taxes, and her women are full-grown."

"Not like the ones at the last saloon who robbed my loggers blind," Connor added. "Good to see them move on to Snohomish City after the Nugget burned down last summer."

Beth nodded, amusement trickling into her green eyes. "Don't worry, guys. We had prostitutes where I lived before. I can handle it as long as there aren't any kids selling themselves."

Three hours later, Rad strolled through town checking on the activities at the saloon, parlor house, and mercantile. Everything seemed peaceable, just the way he liked it. He entered the jail to see Beth and Sorrel sitting at the table. Leafing through a stack of papers, Beth drank coffee while the girl ate supper.

He wasn't surprised his wife had shown mercy to the youngster. Beth talked tough, but she wasn't cruel to children or animals, and she wouldn't let the girl miss a meal, much less leave her locked in the cell. He hung his rifle on the rack by the door. "Anything happening I should know?"

"Not really." Beth smiled sweetly. "You have a problem if I draw pictures of Smith on some of these posters?"

Rad considered the idea while he crossed to the stove and the battered coffee pot. "Might be a good idea. We have some new folks around who won't know him from Adam's ox."

"Okay, then." Beth stood and went to the desk. "Works for me. I'll find a pencil, but a pen would be better."

Sorrel glared after her, then turned in the chair. "Well, what do you two plan to do with me? She says you're not hanging me."

"*She* has a name." Beth didn't raise her voice, but it still held a threat. "So, manner up, missy. And all I said was that you wouldn't die for trying to steal my horse if your apology met my criteria. Since you misspelled half the words, you've got some serious rewriting to do."

Rad hid a smile behind the tin coffee cup. The two of them had a lot in common, but he knew better than to say so. He listened to the girl gripe and complain about the essay while she finished eating. She stormed off to the cell, paper in hand, still muttering.

"Can't leave her with Cal, so what are we going to do with her?"

"Take her with us to the ranch I guess." Beth frowned. "How do we keep her there when we go to hunt Smith?"

"Turn her over to the housekeeper." Rad sat down in the opposite chair and enjoyed the opportunity to sit and watch his wife. "Hannah and Gabe Ortiz will take good care of her."

"What if she tells them about selling herself?"

"Won't bother them. Hannah worked in the parlor house before she married Gabe."

PART FOUR

"The way I see it, if you want the rainbow, you gotta put up with the rain."

DOLLY PARTON

TWENTY-SEVEN

THEY'D ATTENDED CHURCH AT THE HOTEL, WHICH WAS YET another shock to her system. Beth assumed there would be a formal place to get that "old-time religion," and never expected that most of the people in town would show up to hear the mayor read from the Bible and listen to a choir of schoolchildren sing.

They'd had dinner as Rad called the noon meal with Connor and his daughter, then walked the town that had pretty well rolled up the sidewalks to observe the Sabbath. It meant her meeting with the local prostitutes was the highlight of the afternoon. She'd spent the evening drawing more pictures of Smith on the back of wanted posters, grateful for the high school art teacher who'd insisted on students learning to use a fountain pen.

Sorrel sulked in the cell she used as a bedroom. When she wanted privacy, she closed the door, but since she wasn't locked inside, Beth didn't feel too badly for the tween. Both of them had survived worse abuse. Writing and rewriting the apology for attempting to steal Tigger wouldn't hurt the girl, where hanging her definitely would. She finally surrendered and asked Cal for help. The old deputy corrected spelling, punctuation, and grammar, and then the teen copied the pages again. It gave the girl something to do since video games hadn't been invented yet.

The highlight on Saturday had been their shopping trip to the mercantile where Sorrel now had appropriate clothes instead of the costumes she wore at the saloon as a *hurdy-gurdy* girl or prostitute. One of the new dresses even had lace trimmed, Italian sleeves, something the storekeeper called the latest fashion. Sorrel wore it to church and Sunday dinner at the mayor's. The girl demanded three full pinafore style aprons so she wouldn't get any of the dresses dirty doing chores.

Meanwhile, Beth refused to allow the tween to walk around Junction City alone. There were too many loggers who knew she'd intended to sell herself in the saloon and she might be assaulted. When Sorrel whined about being bored staying in the marshal's office, Rad handed her a copy of Blackstone's Commentaries. The lawbook kept her occupied for the next two days until they left town.

———

One side of her saddlebags held a stack of posters ready to be handed out to anyone they met. Beth grimaced. It sure would be a lot easier in a hundred years to get the word out on a perp or unsub. She didn't say that to Rad. He obviously figured they were doing their best to find Smith and Paul Levine at the newspaper had promised to have more posters ready when they returned to town. These would have pictures too.

Sorrel rode a small paint gelding Rad bought from Connor for her. Red hair in braids, wearing pants under one of her new dresses, and a wool, store-bought shirt, the girl looked younger than ever without cosmetics. Mentally, Beth subtracted another year. Sorrel couldn't be much over eleven. Saddles creaked as the horses slogged through spring mud on the trail.

Beth glanced at Sorrel when the girl rode closer. "What?"

"That's my question. What do you plan to do with me?" Sorrel asked.

Beth shared a look with Rad, then said. "Keep you until you're old enough to go to college."

Tears shimmered and Sorrel bit her lip. "I think maybe I want to be a lawyer."

"Good God! Why?" Beth demanded. "You can do anything. Why be a shyster for hire? You'll be putting low-life scum back on the street after I lock them up."

"Could be she wants to help folks who need it." Rad winked at Sorrel. "Next time we're in town, I'll take you to meet Mr. Vance. He's the one to tell you about law school."

"And you'll stay while they talk," Beth informed him, shaking her head. "I don't know that man and she's not to be alone with him. I don't believe it. A lawyer in my family. Ick!"

"What does 'ick mean?" Sorrel tilted her head to the side. A smile tugged at her mouth. "At least, you didn't tell me I'm a stupid girl and all I'm good for is making babies."

"Now, who'd be stupid enough to say something like that?" Beth's hand tightened on the reins and Tigger danced underneath her. She forced herself to take a deep breath and relax so the stallion could. "Smith?"

"No. Uncle Walter. He told the schoolmarm that back in Oregon when she wanted me to keep learning readin', writin, and cipherin'. He told her girl-children should know to cook, clean, and mind little-uns because they'd just be wives and mothers and leave extry book-learnin' to men."

"He's a fool," Rad said. "If a man wants his children to be smart, then he needs a smart woman to ride the river with."

Beth flicked a sideways glance at him and decided he was sincere. He'd already told her that "pretty wasn't enough," that he wanted a partner. And she had guts enough for that. "What about Smith?"

"Oh, he agreed with Uncle Walter about the schooling, but Mr. Smith said I was too young to be sharing my uncle's bed, so he took me away. And when I told him that they'd just make Becky do it, he asked me how I knew."

Beth watched a muscle twitch in Rad's cheek, and his jaw tighten before she asked. "And what did you tell him?"

"That my cousins were already messing with her, and their pa would be next. Mister Smith, well he cussed a blue streak and went back for her."

At the Lazy B, Becky had shared most of the story with her, but a few details still bothered Beth. "Smith told them that you'd run off and that was why he wanted Becky."

"Well, kinda running and going where he told me." Sorrel leaned forward to pet her horse's neck. "He said for me to go to Gunny Creek and work for the lady at the boardin' house. When I arrived, she said she'd only pay me a dollar a week, and she talked to me like I was dirt. The saloon keeper paid me three dollars a week to clean and help the cook. Same work as at the boarding house but more money, and they were nice to me. So, I worked there."

"And when did you start working the line?" Rad asked.

"I really didn't. Mr. Jackson said he couldn't let me do it since Mr. Smith said I wasn't to do nothing bad. And if there was a good man who wanted to marry me, he'd have to wait till I turned sixteen and Mr. Smith gave us permission. Then Uncle Walter arrived and said I was old enough to work upstairs."

"Well, I'm telling you now that you're not." Beth took a deep breath and eyed Rad. "She looks enough like me to be related. If people ask, we should let them believe she's mine."

He nodded. "Ours."

Shock slipped across Sorrel's pretty face, quickly replaced by speculation. "If I'm yours, can Becky come too?"

Rad chuckled. "You don't want much, do you? We'll talk to Trace about it." He stopped his horse at a fork in the trail. "The Greens have a ranch this way. If we go the other, we'll make the Bar M before dinner."

"Let's visit the neighbors first," Beth said. "We can drop off a couple of posters and pass the word to look for Smith."

Visiting the Greens and other neighbors took longer than she expected. Of course, everything did. She supposed if Rad had arrived in her time, he'd be overwhelmed by how fast things moved. Yet she found herself enjoying the leisurely pace of life in the nineteenth century. At least, she didn't have to look for piles of garbage that might disguise an IED along the trails.

They arrived at the Bar M just before dark, but she still saw the huge log house in all its glory. Hannah Ortiz, the housekeeper escorted Beth to what she thought of as a "master suite," not that she'd call it that when she talked to Rad. He already tried to run the world and she wasn't the woman to let him boss her around. Sorrel happily joined Hannah to find a bedroom for herself.

Beth glanced around the large room where she'd been left alone. The plank walls gleamed a soft gray under a coat of fresh whitewash. A hooked rug stretched across the wooden floor. In the left corner of the room stood a large wooden wardrobe. A matching bureau and a washstand with a china pitcher and bowl filled the remainder of the left wall. A mirror taller than most men was in the right corner, and she wondered how the looking glass got to Junction City when there weren't any real roads to the town. Was it by that steamboat Rad mentioned?

Her jaw dropped when she saw the four-poster bed in the center of the room. The bed had obviously been built in Junction City, from pieces of cedar—like the table and chairs on the right wall. The new furniture still smelled like the woods. She gaped at the pillows piled against the headboard and the bright patchwork quilt on the large bed.

She turned as the door opened and he entered, carrying their saddlebags. "So, why do you have the biggest house in the Territory, Marshal?"

"Have to do something when days get short, and memories get long." He closed the door and leaned against it. "But I reckon we'll find something else to do next winter."

"Oh, I'm sure we will." She slipped out of her coat and draped it over one chair, following it with her shoulder holster and pistol. She began to unbutton her blouse. "Then again, who says we have to wait that long?"

———

He wasn't a 'wet behind the ears' schoolboy, so why did watching her undress stir him this much? It wasn't as if she hurried. Three buttons undone, followed by the next, then another. If she kept up this pace, it'd be a week before she finished. He dropped the saddlebags by the bureau and strode to her.

"Are you trying to kill me, Missus Morgan?"

She smiled up at him, then tiptoed up to brush her mouth across his. "I don't know. Am I?"

His hands tightened on her waist, and he pulled her to him. "Either you get that blouse off now, or I will. And you'll have to sew those buttons back on again."

"Sweetie, I can do a lot of things." She laughed, then nipped at his ear. "But I don't sew buttons."

He bunched one hand in her hair, pulled her head back. "Learn."

His mouth claimed hers in a fierce kiss. With his free hand, he cupped a breast and felt her nipple harden against his thumb. He wanted her and he'd have her. A lot sooner than she thought. He lifted his head. "If you want to keep that shirtwaist, take it off now."

Her blouse fell to the floor, followed by the skin-tight, black chemise, and the strange contraption that bound her breasts, the one the author of her books called a 'bra'. He groaned and trailed a line of kisses down her neck to her nipple and drew it into his mouth. She sighed, arched against him as he sucked.

She tangled fingers in his hair and tugged, "Hurry."

He lifted his head. "If you ask me nicely."

He wrapped an arm around her and drew her back to the table.

Hooking a chair with one foot, he sat down and pulled her onto his lap. He unfastened the divided skirt, pushed it out of the way. He slipped a hand into the front of her drawers. All woman, all his. Wet, hot heat, and his finger eased inside her.

She clutched at his hair when he added a second finger and then his thumb found her. He began a slow in and out rhythm, just like he would later when he had her. She liked it. He knew that by the wet, hot heat that surrounded his fingers. And he kissed her, long, slow tormenting kisses that satisfied neither of them, as she moaned, gasped, and finally screamed in delight.

His heart raced and he looked down at her. She opened dark green eyes and stared up at him, still lying in his lap. He lowered his head and worked his way down to her breasts, sucking first on one nipple, then the other. She arched up to meet his mouth and her hips spasmed as his fingers moved in and out, starting all over again.

"I'm going to die tonight, Morgan."

He chuckled against her skin. "No, but you're gonna scream a lot." He flicked a nipple with his tongue.

"Want to bet?" She managed to sit up and began to unbutton his shirt. "The road runs two ways."

"Let's see about that." He increased the pace with his fingers, sliding them in and out of her while his thumb rocked into the bit of flesh. "Beg for me, Missus Morgan."

She fell back against his arm. "Stop. I can't stand it."

"Learn." He laughed, sucked hard on her nipple.

She choked back another scream. Her eyes widened, and her hips spasmed again. She twisted against him, crying his name.

His shirt soon joined hers on the floor. The rest of their clothes followed, but they didn't make it to the bed. Before he could get up from the chair, she was on top of him, riding him. He clutched her hips and held on for dear life. Their mouths met, clung in a series of kisses. Rising, falling, soaring, crashing until they soared —he'd never had this kind of pleasure. She called his name in release and he followed.

Afterward, she slumped against him. Arms wrapped around his neck, she leaned into him. "I can't move."

He shifted slightly. "If you stay like that, I'll have you again."

"Promises. Promises." She nipped his ear.

"And again."

"We'll see."

The next time was slower, easier. Then, he took her to the bed and had her for a third time. Tender kisses brushed over sensitive skin, and she moaned at almost every touch. When he slid inside her, it was like coming home. He savored every moment of the climb and so did she.

And finally, for the first time she fell asleep in his arms. He held her, dropping kisses over her forehead, her hair. This was the way he'd hoped it would always be – from the first moment he saw her in the cave. And still holding her, he let the world drift away.

Once again, he woke alone in the middle of the night.

He dressed and walked through the house, looking for her. In the kitchen, he found Sorrel and Hannah at the table with mugs of hot chocolate and a platter of cookies. "Bethany isn't with you?"

"Outside, watching the stars," Sorrel said. "Don't know that they're doing much." She twirled a braid around one finger. "She told us she has bad dreams."

"That's true." Rad looked at the young girl and the woman beside her. "Any ideas what I should do?"

"Wake her up," Hannah said. "It's what Gabe does for me when he's home." She smiled, but it didn't touch her eyes. "Else, I'd be having nightmares of burning to death in that fire three or four times a week."

"And maybe she'll tell you what scares her," Sorrel said. "Something does, or she'd be in here, not out with the dog and her rifle watching for strangers."

———

Over the past few days, they'd visited everybody between the Bar M and the Lazy B, dropping off posters along the way. Beth recognized the area around the other ranch as they drew closer to the back gate. Heinrich Gruber stepped out of the shadows, cradling a rifle across his arms, and smiled.

"Good to see you folks. I sent Mac word that you're here and Prescott said to send you on down."

Beth glanced at Rad, then at Gruber again as he moved to open the gate. "How do they send word? You guys don't have contraptions like mine."

"Signal mirrors," Rad said. "Trace doesn't like surprises. Too many men tried to kill her before Prescott moved in last summer."

"And you?" Beth frowned at him as they rode down the hill to the buildings that made up the Lazy B headquarters. "What did you do?"

"Pretty much collected everybody's guns when they were in town and told Trace to shoot what and who needed killing. Otherwise, she'd never have lived this long."

It sounded like the more things changed, the more they stayed the same. It wasn't what Trace knew, it was who and she had the law on her side. "And covered Trace's back when you could?"

"As much as she'd let me," Rad agreed, "and since she had everyone convinced, she was a man, it wasn't much."

"I still can't believe she fooled everybody." Beth spotted her friend working a horse in the corral. In a long black coat, pants, and cowboy hat, it could be difficult to guess someone's gender. Okay, maybe Rad had a point. If Trace had wanted people to believe she was a man, she might be able to successfully masquerade as one.

Luke trotted past them and greeted the other dogs with a low growl and a bark. Keeping an eye on the buckskin colt, Trace sauntered toward the corral fence, then ducked between the rails. "Well, get off and make yourselves at home. It's good to see you."

Beth grinned and dismounted, holding Tigger's reins. "How are my patients?"

"Getting by," Trace said. "Emancipation broke out of his paddock and got in with my mares, so I'll have a big foal crop next year. Ever since she got those special sticks Fremont made her, Mina's been up and about helping Ma Sims around the house."

"And her brothers? Did they hire on with you?" Rad asked. "We've been passing the word about Smith, but we haven't seen hide or hair of the rest of the Dawson kin."

"Probably won't until you get close to Gunny Creek. Word is the place is getting wild and crazy." Trace gestured to two boys coming from the barn. "Come take these horses and put them up for the law."

"Where did you hear about Gunny Creek?" Beth passed over the reins to Shawn. "Who told you?"

"Mac rode the owl-hoot trail for a couple of years and still has a few friends who aren't all they should be." Trace walked beside Beth toward the Big House. "If he hears talk that I should, he passes it on, so we'll be ready."

"And Prescott?" Rad drawled. "What does he say?"

"He's out with Mac, Olaf, and Lars making sure that we don't have unexpected or should I say uninvited company. Don't say anything to Ma. She doesn't like it if we're inhospitable."

TWENTY-EIGHT

Talents of a Guardian include the Power to Heal those with good hearts, any who ask. However, the health and safety of women and children are a Guardian's main task...

RULES OF CHRONOS

THEY'D SPENT TWO NIGHTS AT THE LAZY B. SHE'D LEARNED TO make doughnuts on a woodstove, and Ma Sims sent along a flour sack of the homemade goodies. Becky was delighted to learn of her older sister's safety and Trace agreed to let the youngster visit the Bar M once Smith had been found and jailed. It was the first step in keeping the promise Rad made to the older girl.

"Now, we head for Gunny Creek," Rad said, taking the trail to the northeast. "Fremont told me to take you to the sheepherders, so we'll stop on the way. Why do you need to talk to Chris Padden?"

Beth debated silently about what to tell him. The truth that there were other time-travelers sounded insane when she thought about it logically. And yet, in an odd way, it made perfect sense.

Why should she and Gary Smith be the only ones who came through a doorway to another world?

Rad didn't ask again. He just stopped his horse, turned the mare to face Beth and pinned her with that steady dark blue gaze.

Finally, Beth said, "Fremont says I'm not the only one who came from the future. He told me to talk to Chris Padden about what I'm supposed to do while I'm here."

"Besides finding that woman-killer and trying to take him back to your time?"

Beth nodded.

"All right then." Rad swung Nell back to the trail. "Let's go do it."

The narrow path wound through evergreens for miles. The land rose in steep terraces, then dropped back downhill. Small clearings slowly increased in size until they entered a meadow dotted with grazing sheep. At the far end of the field, smoke came from the chimney of a one-room cabin. Off to one side was a corral and a shed.

When they rode closer, she saw a smaller flock with new lambs. A pair of shaggy collies came out of the barn barking a cheerful greeting, but they were the only other sign of life.

Rad reined up outside the barn and waited. When nobody appeared, he called, "Padden, it's Marshal Morgan. Padden!"

A small shadowy figure appeared at the edge of the barn door.

"Howdy." Rad kept Nell still. "Is your grandpa around?"

"Out looking for a missing sheep."

Finally, the child came out of the building. The little girl wore pants, a wool shirt, and boots. She couldn't be as old as Becky, but they certainly raised kids to be independent here. Beth smiled, trying to look as friendly as possible. "I'm Beth. What's your name?"

"Nettie."

"Do you remember me?" Rad asked. "I'm the marshal from Junction City and a friend of Trace Burdette's. Would it be all right if we waited for your grandpa?"

"Sure." Nettie came a little closer to Beth's horse. "I can make coffee."

"That would be wonderful." Beth swung out of the saddle. "We can have some of Missus Sims' doughnuts with it."

"Bear-sign?" Nettie's dark eyes widened with pleasure. "I ain't had bear-sign in a coon's age. Gran doesn't have time to make 'em during lambing season."

"That makes sense." Beth signaled Luke to behave when he growled at the male collie. "Why didn't your gran take the dogs to find the sheep?"

"Gran took the others. These are s'posed to watch me." Nettie edged nearer and whispered. "There was a bad man around. He stole one of our horses."

"Really?" Beth pulled a poster out of the saddlebags. "Does he look like this?"

Nettie nodded. "How did you know?"

"I'm a detective and I've been looking for him for a long time."

"And you'll put him in jail?"

"Yes, we will," Rad said. "When did your grandpa leave?"

"Early. It was still dark."

Beth glanced at her watch. It was almost noon. "Then we won't have long to wait."

She helped Nettie put on the coffee and checked the pot of navy beans that had obviously been intended for dinner. Following the child's directions, Beth mixed up cornbread and put it to bake in the oven. While they waited for the food to finish cooking, Nettie cheerfully set the table.

Rad carried in an armload of firewood and checked the fire. "Smells good in here. Your dog just headed off, Detective Morgan. So, Padden should be along any time."

"Good to know." Beth went to the door to watch for Luke.

In a few moments, she saw him escorting a slender, gray-haired woman carrying what appeared to be an armload of something little and white. An ewe trotted alongside, bleating in worry.

Beth went to meet them. As she approached, she counted tiny heads. Chris Padden held at least two, no make it three lambs. Beth held out her hands. "Let me help. I'm—"

"I know who you are," Chris said in a rasping voice, "and I'm not ready to die yet, so you'll just have to wait, *Guardian*."

Beth froze, stared. "I don't want you to die."

"There can only be one of us to serve *Her*," Chris said. "Don't you know anything?"

"No," Beth admitted. "That's why I'm here."

"Well, I'll be—" Chris passed over two of the babies. "Not damned. Not when I've served *Her* honorably for the past forty years. Come along, then. Reckon you're here so I can train you to take my place when the time comes."

Beth followed, her head still reeling from the shock. Why hadn't Fremont told her that *Guardians* served as individuals? He probably didn't know, she thought. He'd just talked about living through an injury that would have killed him. "How long does the training take?"

"Depends on you," Chris said, "and how smart you are."

Beth waited while Chris opened the gate to a stall in the barn and penned the mother. Then they put the lambs in with the ewe. While the sheep nursed her young, Chris brought over an armload of hay.

"So, where are you from?" Chris finally asked.

"Don't you mean, *when*?"

"Well, that will do too."

Beth took a deep breath. "I rode into Mount Baker National Forest on Friday, April 13th, 2018."

"Why?"

"To hunt down a serial rapist and killer." Beth hesitated, then told her story. The words tumbled out, but she didn't see shock or disbelief in the older woman's face.

"That tells me why you've come," Chris said, starting for the barn door. "You're here to track down this man and stop him before he hurts anyone else."

"You're right there." Beth walked beside the other woman. "But you have something else in mind. What?"

"How you opened the gateway to the past." Chris paused. "*She* doesn't come to just anyone who calls."

"Who is *she*?"

Another long look and then Chris shook her head. "You really don't know anything, do you?"

"I was alone except for my horse and dog that day when Smith ambushed me. Nobody else was there, not another woman."

"*She* is the woman in charge. *She* has a lot of names. You'll learn, especially if you pay attention when the witches visit the valley." Chris paused. "You asked for help on one of *Her* special days, but it would have taken more. How did you die?"

———

Rad pulled the cornbread out of the oven and put it on top of the stove to stay warm. He walked to the door and saw Beth coming with the old sheepherder toward the cabin. He took a second look at Chris Padden and recognized the truth. Another woman who dressed like a man. When would he learn not to judge by appearances? He glanced at the dark-haired child by the table. "I'll bet you're a girl too."

"Of course," Nettie said. "What else would I be?"

"Good point." Rad stepped outside to greet the older woman. "Thought we'd stop by on our way to Gunny Creek. You've met my wife."

"You didn't say you married anybody." Chris eyed Beth. "You love him?"

"You're meddling in what's not your business," Rad said.

Red crept into Beth's cheeks, but she met Chris's gaze and said evenly. "Is it important?"

Chris nodded. "If he shares what you do like Fremont did with me, then it matters."

"He shares it," Beth said. "And my father always says, "A

woman needs to winter and summer with a man to know him." For me, I have to know him before I'll love him."

"So, you'll share him with whoever comes along in the next year?" Chris didn't back down. "Not a problem since you don't love him."

"I don't share," Beth retorted.

Rad shook his head. The conversation baffled him as if he'd come in late. He understood his wife. Beth had been hurt so much that she didn't trust easily. The fact she wanted to know him before she admitted what she felt didn't bother him. He'd take what he could get, and he had her. Of course, she had him too.

"And you never said *when* you're from," Beth said. "The *Sixties*? Or the *Seventies*? Is it a case of *"If you can't be with the one you love, then love the one you're with?"* Or not?"

Chris Padden didn't seem shocked by the question. She laughed. "Okay, you got me."

Rad straightened. "You came from the same place Bethany did. I've never heard anyone else say, "Okay." I'm right, aren't I?"

"Yes." Chris started for the cabin again. "Let's eat. Then we have some work to do."

———

They'd spent the last three days talking about what a *Guardian* did. The question Chris asked when they first met still haunted Beth. She didn't remember dying. Smith had shot at Tigger. The stallion reared and went over backward. Had he really landed on top of her? Why couldn't she be sure?

Sitting by the campfire that night, Beth stared at the black sky, counting the stars through the wisps of clouds. She barely slept anymore. She glanced behind her at the sound of footsteps. "Did I wake you?"

"Couldn't sleep without you." Rad sat down next to her and put an arm around her shoulders. "What keeps you awake?"

"I'm not sure. I thought it was the war but that seems so far away. It's Smith. I want to find him, but there's something I should remember, and I can't no matter how hard I try." She leaned against Rad, his solid warmth seeping into her. "And then there's the guilt for not being able to say what I feel for you."

He chuckled and drew her closer. "It's only been little more than a month, Bethany Morgan. You'll say it when you're ready."

"What about you?" She studied his features, trying to read his face in the moonlight. "What do you feel about me?"

"I love you. Surprises you, doesn't it? I've been looking for a gal like you for a long time. Didn't expect you to come so far to find me, but we can make this work."

She slid her hands up to frame his cheeks and kissed him. "I want it to work, Rad. You're the first man I've liked, respected, and wanted."

"Then let love come when it does." He leaned down so their lips met again. "Are you ready to come back to bed?"

"Yes." She stood and let him lead her back to their blankets. He didn't try to make love to her, which she had expected. Instead, he just held her. She faded into sleep.

Rain dripped from the brim of her leather cowboy hat and splashed onto her gloved hand. She peered through the misty drizzle, watching the ground for tracks from the horse ridden up this trail earlier in the day. The silent woods and large evergreens loomed over her. The world held its breath. Everything was quiet, too quiet.

She looked for Luke—she hadn't seen him for so long, at least five minutes. Her gaze had narrowed on a small gray, brown and black shape near the granite boulders. The limp, broken body of Luke. He was d...

The whine of a bullet! She spun Tigger toward the trees and spurred hard! The Arabian leaped forward, but it was too late. The leap changed into a rear! Tigger slipped. He fell. The ground approached. Faster and faster. She threw herself out of the saddle, but the Arabian crashed over backward!

She tried to roll away from him—too little, too late. Her body slammed into the dirt. Her head hit the granite boulder beside the path. She tasted blood, her blood. When she looked up, she saw the stallion falling toward her.

———

"Bethany! Wake up." He shook her, then pulled her even closer. "It's just a dream."

"No, it's not. It wasn't." She turned her face into his broad chest. "He killed me. That's what Chris wanted to know. How I got here. Smith did it. He killed me, Rad."

"No, he didn't. You're here. You're safe. I've got you."

"You don't understand. He shot Tigger. And I died when he fell on top of me."

"Your horse is fine. Honey, it was just a dream. A nightmare."

"More than that. He killed me. And if he knows I made it here, he'll do it again. That's what I needed to remember."

"I won't let him. And that's what you must remember, Missus Morgan." He kissed her. "You have me for always. I'll keep you safe."

"Promise?"

"I promise."

She pulled back a little and he saw the fear in her eyes. "Make love to me."

"What? Why?"

"I don't want to think about dying, Rad. Give me a reason to be happy I lived, to be happy I'm with you."

He framed her face with his hands. "If that's what you want, Bethany."

———

While Rad saddled their horses, Beth studied the leather-bound journal Chris handed her. "What am I supposed to do with this?"

"Read and add to it," Chris said. "That's what I did when my mentor gave it to me before she died. You'll pass it on to the next *Guardian*." She winked. "My teacher always called herself, Chronos. It was as good a name as any."

Beth opened the book and read the first entry. *"To do Her Sacred Work, She chooses a Guardian then creates a hallowed place, despite Time and Space..."*

"It helps to know you're not the only one," Chris added. "At least, it helped me."

"I remembered how I died last night." Beth closed the journal and traced the star on the front with her finger. "He killed me. Rad thinks it was just a dream."

"That's how you'll learn more than I can teach you in our time together." Chris stood and brought over the coffeepot. "The hospital where I worked collapsed in an earthquake and I begged for another chance to help people. I ended up here."

Beth tried to smile at the older woman. "Will the dreams always be so awful?"

"No. From now on, it will just be information *She* wants you to know." Chris filled both their cups. "And there's nothing to be frightened of, but you'll need to take care of Nettie for me."

"I will," Beth promised. "I can't take her to Gunny Creek with us."

"I'll send her to Trace at the Lazy B when Mac or Fremont bring supplies next time. She loves visiting and playing with the other children, plus she goes to school there too." Chris glanced over her shoulder at the doorway. "Marshal Morgan asked me if I'd help you change that bandage before you leave. Shouldn't he be healed by now?"

"Smith bushwhacked Rad, shot him through the lung a month ago."

"I know. You told me that before, but you have the gifts the Goddess gave you. It took less than two weeks for Fremont to heal from a spear through the gut. Have you ever removed the entire bandage?"

"No."

"It's time, isn't it?"

"What if he's not a hundred percent healed, Chris?"

"Then, we wrap him back up like a Christmas present."

TWENTY-NINE

"Chosen by the Goddess, a Guardian serves her whole life long,
guiding, protecting, healing, teaching the weak to be strong..."

RULES OF CHRONOS

SILENCE FELL AS THEY RODE THROUGH THE WOODS. THEY'D SPENT
the previous night at one of Connor Riley's logging camps and
learned where the different crews would be cutting timber. At least
she didn't have to worry about a tree being dropped on her head,
Beth thought.

And she could be grateful Rad had clout. They'd slept in
Connor's cabin, not in the bunkhouse with the loggers. The draft
horses that pulled the logs out of the woods to the river had better
accommodations but as Rad said, the teams were expensive and
most of the men could be easily replaced.

She turned Tigger a little closer to Rad's Appaloosa mare. "I
remember you told me that your mother was a—"

"Lady of the night." A wry smile twisted his mouth. "Personally, I didn't think she was much of a lady. Guess her last customer agreed."

"How old were you when she died?"

"Turned fifteen. Nearly a man grown. I stayed at the orphanage till they adopted out Kyle a couple of months later. Then I lit out."

"Where did you go?"

"The war had started." He glanced at her. "Between the North and South. Lied about my age and joined the Army, a regiment from New York. Fought until 1864 when I was captured. Ended up in Andersonville."

She frowned, remembering history lectures in high school and later the ones in the Army. Almost a third of the Union prisoners of war died in the Confederate camp. "You survived."

"A lot of my friends didn't." He paused, looking through his horse's ears at the trail. "You asked why my house is so big. Winters are long here. Snow starts flying in October and lasts until April or May most years. There's times when I can't ride out to work on the ranch or patrol the settlements. When the past crowds in on me, I add on a room or two."

She squeezed her leg into Tigger's side and moved him closer to the other horse. She leaned over and touched Rad's hand. "This year I'll help. I've driven a lot of nails, and I'm not afraid of hard work."

"I'd like that."

———

Another day, more farms and ranches and even more posters passed out to the people they met. So far, she hadn't met anyone who knew Smith or who saw the buckskin mare he stole from Chris Padden. They also hadn't found the missing Dawson boys and that worried Beth.

Had they run into Smith? Had he killed them and hidden the bodies?

"Where are we spending the night?" Beth asked.

"Should make it to Portage by dark." Rad pushed back his hat and smiled. "You'll like the town. It's nearly as big as Junction City."

"Wow. I'll look forward to being impressed." She hoped she didn't sound as snarky as she felt. When he narrowed his eyes, she figured she'd failed. "Okay, Morgan. Eagleville probably isn't here yet, but it's where I worked at one of the outlying sheriff's offices, and it has approximately fifteen thousand citizens."

Stopping his horse, he shook his head, stared at her. "That's a big city."

"Not where I come from," Beth said, reining Tigger to a halt. "It's considered a small town. There are much bigger ones, like Seattle, Tacoma, and Bellevue."

"I'll be hornswoggled."

"I don't know what that means, but it's hard for me to look at Junction City and hear that it's a big town when it doesn't exist in my time."

"Well, what happened to it? Dahlberg's dead so he can't burn it to the ground."

"I'm not sure, but I'll bet it has something to do with the railroads."

"There aren't any railroads in Liberty Valley, Bethany."

"Not yet, but there will be." She frowned thoughtfully. "If I remember Will's stories correctly, there were a lot of backroom deals when Everett was built. It was a company town and the founders owned railroad companies. They traded off train stations to various settlements to get the votes to make it the county seat, and they bypassed the bigger towns whenever possible."

"Probably because it'd cost too much to buy the land."

"Good point." Beth grinned. "Well, let's hit the road."

"No roads here." He started down the trail again. "Railroads, huh? I'll bet if Trace hears about those, she'll figure out how to make money on the deal."

"More like when," Beth said.

Maybe, she'd invest in the railroads too and in Monte Cristo when the prospectors arrived and began mining gold. She was still coming to terms with the fact that Smith killed her in 2018, so how could she leave here? And if she spent the rest of her life in Liberty Valley, she might as well become part of the community. And the best way to be part of it was to help the area grow and prosper.

They rode in from the south end of town. Signs on the buildings advertised a livery and then a hotel. The next structure was a mercantile, not much bigger than a mini-mart. She spotted the steeple of a church. "So, where are we headed?"

"I have a house here," Rad said. "There's a barn behind it for the horses. Once we get settled in, I'll head for the saloons and pass the word about Smith."

"I'll go with you."

"Be better if you talked to the ministers. They can help you with the womenfolk. We don't want Smith hunting them or their daughters."

That made sense. She grimaced. She'd have to change her clothes and wear the skirt and blouse she'd brought along. The things she did to find a murderer. She ought to receive hazardous duty pay.

————

He'd covered almost twelve miles today trying to stay ahead of the marshal and his damned wanted posters. How had the man known who shot him? It didn't make sense unless Morgan recognized him, but he could have sworn the lawman hadn't seen him. So, who told him?

The buckskin mare stumbled in the mud, and he corrected her with a jerk on the reins. Stupid bitch. She'd been the biggest of the three horses in the corral, so he'd taken her. He hadn't realized she had a gimpy knee at the time. Should have looked closer, but the sheepherder had come out of the cabin, rifle blazing.

He saw the three cedar-shake buildings that made up Gunny Creek and relaxed in the saddle he'd stolen at the last farm. Tonight, he'd have a good meal, sleep at the boarding house. He never robbed anyone here. Why foul his nest?

And he'd go to the saloon first, see how his little red-haired angel was doing. She was a sweet child who never sassed him. He could leave the horse with her, and she'd give him the money to buy a replacement. She reminded him of Vera, who'd been the best wife he'd ever had.

Granted, he'd known her from the time she was a child, and she'd learned to please him at an early age. His little angel looked like the woman he'd lost and acted like her, too, always doing what he told her to do. And she thought he was a hero when he went back to save her younger sister.

He dismounted, tied the mare in front of the saloon, and went inside. Bellied up to the bar was the perverted bastard he'd ordered out of the Territory years ago. Walter Tremont.

The bartender hurried toward the door. "Mr. Smith. I tried to keep her, but she bolted out of here three weeks ago. Caught a ride with a drover headed to Snohomish City."

"I don't blame her." He jerked his head toward Tremont. "When did he come nosing after her?"

"Said he's her uncle and tried to make me give up her wages to him. I refused. She took the money and hightailed it. He says he's waiting for her to come back."

"She won't." And he'd take care of this for once and for all.

———

The sun sank lower, and the moon had started to rise when they rode into Gunny Creek. Three wooden buildings squatted on the only muddy street, two on the left and one on the right. Rad stopped in front of the single long dwelling. "Boarding house. It's clean and the food's good."

"And the rest of the town?"

"Mercantile and saloon. Upstairs is the bordello. Most of the town is pretty much a family enterprise. The boys work downstairs and the girls upstairs. Their ma runs the boarding house and their father's been dead nigh on five years." Rad swung from the saddle and dropped Nell's reins across the hitchrail, not wrapping or tying them. "There's a corral and a shed where the horses can stay."

"Works for me." Beth dismounted, studying his tense figure. She didn't have a lot of respect for a woman who'd pimp out her own flesh and blood. "Or we can ride out and camp on the way home."

"That might be best."

Before matters were settled, she heard a shout from the saloon. "It's the marshal!"

Beth pulled her rifle from the scabbard on Tigger's saddle. "I don't like the sound of that."

"Makes two of us." He reached for his own rifle, and they headed across the street.

"High or low?" Beth asked. "I prefer going in high myself."

Before he answered, a stocky man in his thirties bustled out of the saloon, hurrying toward them. Wiping his hands on the apron that covered his clothes, the bartender said. "We had trouble here. A family's dead."

"Why?" Beth asked. "Were they sick?"

"No. Killed." He stopped in front of them. "It's the Tremonts. And we got the boys who done it. If you take 'em with you, it'll save us the trouble of hanging them."

"Can't hang anybody without a trial," Rad said.

"And we don't know that the boys you have actually did anything," Beth said. "We need to talk to them first. They could just be witnesses."

"Oh no, they did it."

Beth grimaced and left the man to convince Rad. She headed for the saloon. As she stepped inside, she saw a pair of dark-haired teens hunched over a table. Two older fellows that bore a healthy resemblance to the bartender held guns on them. "All right. Why don't we start with names and go on from there?"

"These murderin' swine are the Dawsons and I'm Burt Jackson."

"Okay, that's a start." Beth stepped between the men and scanned the boys. Their clothes reeked of smoke, and she saw a burn across one's hand. "Are you related to Mina?"

"She was our cousin," the younger of the boys said. "and we're hunting her killer."

"Might be a little hard to do since she's not dead." Beth hooked a foot around the nearest empty chair and dragged it over. She casually aimed her rifle at Burt. "Put down your weapon and step away. I've got this."

"And just who the hell are you?"

"My wife and newest deputy, Detective Morgan," Rad said from the door. "She asked you nice. I'm telling you."

The Jacksons backed away to the bar holstering their pistols and Burt muttered, "Didn't sound all-fired nice to me."

Beth ignored them and turned her attention back to the Dawsons. "All right. Talk to me. Names first."

"Liam," the younger boy said. "And he's Dominick."

The older boy managed to straighten in his chair, an arm still folded around his ribs. "Mina lived?"

"Well, they got her to me in time," Beth said. "She's at the Lazy B with your cousins and since she was sitting up peeling potatoes for dinner when we rode out, I'd say she's better off than you."

Liam blinked hard. "Can we see her before the hanging?"

"What is it with you people and hangings?" Beth demanded. "Can't you find another way to entertain yourselves?"

"We're just simple country folk, Detective Morgan." Rad crossed the room with a cup of coffee. "People come from miles around to watch a good hanging and bring picnics and such. But it's still too cold for a dance afterward."

"Maybe, we better settle for the box social and dance that Kate

Riley wants to have," Beth said, sarcasm lacing each word. She passed him her rifle and took the coffee instead. "Then, at least we'll have a new roof on the schoolhouse and won't waste the wood building some gallows."

"There are plenty of trees around," Burt said. "No need to waste time putting up a gallows."

They were a bunch of sick individuals, but she didn't tell them that. She sipped the strong, black coffee and studied the boys again. A bruise covered most of Dominick's cheek. "Somebody hit you?"

"A beam fell when I was trying to drag the folks out of the fire. Didn't know they were already dead."

She nodded. "Start at the beginning and tell me what happened after you rode out to find Smith." Out of the corner of her eye, she saw the bartender stiffen. Oh yeah, he knew something about the man they hunted. She glanced at Rad. "While I sort out this mess, do you want to talk to the Jacksons about the fellow we're chasing?"

He followed her gaze, then went to the bar. "Got some posters for you to look at on my horse. Come outside and talk to me."

When the saloon was empty, the two teens relaxed even more. Beth smiled at them and opted to play, *Good Cop*. If they thought she was their friend, she'd learn more from them and she certainly wouldn't allow them to be punished if they hadn't broken the law. "Talk to me. What brought you here?"

"Following Smith." Dominick leaned forward in the chair. "I swear we didn't hurt anybody, not even him. We caught up with him yesterday at a cabin just over the rise at the north end of town."

"Heard someone scream." Liam continued the story. "And he come out of the cabin splashing oil from a lamp. Then he lights up the place."

"And rides off on a big black gelding," Dominick said. "Couldn't follow him then. We had to help."

"And what happened next?" Beth asked.

"It was so wet the wood barely caught on the cabin," Liam said. "I toted water and put out the fire. Nick dragged out the bodies. Two men and a woman."

"Everybody came running when they heard us hollering and they blamed us for the deaths." Dominick wiped at his eyes. "I swear we didn't do it."

"I believe you." Beth put the empty cup down on the table. "Where are the bodies?"

"You don't want to see 'em, ma'am. He must have spent days with them 'cause he tortured 'em worse than what he did Mina." Liam paled. "Honest, it's bad."

"It's all right. I've seen his work before."

THIRTY

"A Guardian chooses a life partner to be a forever mate, not to follow, or lead, but to walk beside her, sharing the Guardian's fate ...."

RULES OF CHRONOS

THE TALL AND LANKY TEENS ESCORTED HER TO THE WOODSHED behind the boarding house. Even before she opened the door, she smelled death. Of course, she'd expected it after she listened to their stories, but it didn't make facing it any easier. She grimaced, then eyed Liam. "Go tell Marshal Morgan that I need my saddlebags."

The younger boy hesitated. "Maybe Nick should go. If you need help to move them, I can do it."

"So can my husband if you fetch him," Beth said, struggling to maintain her *good cop* persona. She didn't trust Burt or his ilk not to mess with the kid, so she added, "You come back with him and wait outside in case I need something else."

"Yes, ma'am." The boy hurried away.

Beth opened the door and saw three silhouetted bodies laid out on sawhorses. "Are they planning to build coffins?"

"I reckon so," Dominick said. "They didn't tell us. Mostly they talked about hanging me and Liam."

She nodded. "Which one knocked you around?"

"How did—"

"I'm not stupid and I've seen it before." She put a hand gently on his arm. "Now, tell me which one did it."

"I'm seventeen, a man grown. I can take a beating. And this way they didn't touch my brother."

"Okay, that's good to know." Beth shook her head ruefully. "And I guess it keeps me from kicking Burt's butt."

Dominick's mouth dropped open. "How did you know?"

"Because I don't have stupid tattooed on my forehead and he's a bullying son of a—" She paused. "I forgot. The marshal doesn't like it when I cuss, says it's not lady-like."

The teenager grinned down at her. "I won't tell him."

Okay, so that worked. The kid was on her side. She definitely hadn't lost her touch. At the sound of footsteps, she turned and saw Rad. When he handed her the saddlebags, she waited to open them while he lit the lantern he held.

"These folks have been dead a while," Rad said, looking inside the building at the corpses. "A lot longer than yesterday. What did Smith do? Live with them?"

"I wouldn't be surprised." She opened her first aid kit and found the container of Vicks, putting a dab below her nose. "He's a sick puppy. And they're going to be crispy critters too. They probably burned a bit before Dominick got them out."

She offered the ointment to Rad, not surprised when he shook his head. He would have to be macho. Besides, he obviously didn't know what it was, and she hadn't explained the pungent medication would stop the smell from the bodies. "If you start to puke, move outside. Don't contaminate the scene any more than it's already been."

"You're downright spunky, Detective Morgan, but I'm not a greenhorn either."

"Well, let's do it then." She reached in her pocket for the digital camera to take pictures. "You fellows stay here and don't let anybody else inside."

"Yes, ma'am."

Rad glanced at the boys. "So, what do you plan to do with them?"

"Send them to Trace. She hired the rest of the family."

Wishing there was a way to have an autopsy on the three bodies, she walked over to the nearest one. A man in his mid-forties, blond hair saturated with blood. She scanned him with the lantern, using the mental shorthand she'd list in her notes. A battered skull. Brown eyes, one out of its socket lying on his cheek. Big, but with more fat than muscle. Broken right arm. It dangled from the shoulder.

She aimed the lantern at the other two bodies, well into the first stages of decomp. "He died last."

"He was tied up." Rad pointed to the rope burns on the wrists and ankles. "Family was probably killed in front of him."

"Let's not jump to conclusions," Beth said, but she agreed with him. "Why would he kill them?"

"It's Walt Tremont," Rad said.

"You know him?"

"Sorrel and Becky's uncle, or so he said. He claimed to be related to their ma, but his wife said it was the pa that was kin to the Tremonts."

"Curiouser and curiouser."

Beth headed over to the woman. Brown hair and eyes. Five feet, three inches, a hundred and thirty pounds, wearing a long cotton dress, dried blood all over the bib of her apron. By the look of her, she'd been dead the longest. Odd. Smith hadn't spent a lot of time with her. Why hadn't he raped or beaten her to death? He'd just cut her throat, obviously in one quick swipe of a knife.

She glanced at Rad who stood over the younger man. "What do you have?"

"Ash Tremont." Rad picked up the boy's left leg. "Been hamstrung."

"What?" She went to join him at the third body.

"Somebody cut his leg tendons. Wouldn't ever walk again even if he lived." Rad frowned. "Smith didn't even do that to the shaman."

"He wanted to cause major pain." Beth let light from the lantern play over the body. The younger man had knife cuts all over him, none of which would have killed him, but deeper than mere scratches. One-inch stab wounds on his chest and yet they weren't hesitation marks, just pokes with the tip of a knife. More gashes on his legs and arms. She studied his hands. Broken fingers smashed, not fractured. Toes chopped off one foot, broken on the other.

"The Jacksons should have heard him screaming," she mused. "Why didn't they? How far away is the cabin?"

"About five-hundred feet from here."

She nodded, then shone the light on Ash's face. She saw the marks of a gag, now removed. "Duct tape, what every modern serial killer needs in his bag of tricks."

"Duck, what?" Rad eyed her curiously. "What's that?"

"A special kind of tape favored by killers. Most of the time the lab techs have to really work hard to get fingerprints off it."

"Thought the idea of fingerprints was fiction, made up by authors like Mark Twain."

Beth tilted her head to one side. "Do you know many successful writers?"

"Just Kyle and he's still working on his first book."

"Well, my adopted cousin is a published author and she's constantly researching for her stories. That's how I figured out her secret identity. She kept interviewing me about my job and when I picked up one of her books at the store, I realized she was

Destynee LaFleur. Maybe analyzing fingerprints isn't common yet in our line of work, but it will be soon."

"Makes sense." Rad gestured to Ash. "You think he was gagged."

She nodded. "He probably screamed his lungs out when Smith cut him, but nobody heard him."

"And his father watched him die."

"Then it was his turn." Beth sighed, wishing she had access to a forensics team and crime scene unit. So much of the evidence would be lost. "Okay, let's turn Ash over."

"You already know what we'll find," Rad said. "I can do it if you want to wait outside."

"I'm not a greenhorn either, Morgan."

An hour later when they left the woodshed, the Jacksons waited with Liam and Dominick. Beth glanced up at Rad. "We're going to have to stay tonight so we can look at the Tremont cabin in the daylight."

"I know." He closed the door and latched it, before turning toward Burt Jackson. "You can bury the Tremonts now. The Dawson boys will leave with us tomorrow so we can keep them safe from Smith."

"They can stay here now we know they ain't killers," Burt said.

"Smith doesn't like witnesses." Beth passed her saddlebags to Rad but kept the lantern. "He's not getting his hands on them. Now, I want hot water to wash up. Where's the closest place to find some?"

Morning came early. The cabin was a one-room shanty, surrounded by trees and scrub brush. Three horses milled around the corral while a sturdy buckskin mare stood in the far corner. Beth rode Tigger closer so she could look at the loner. Most of her weight was on the back legs and she stretched out an injured right front, holding the hoof up in the air.

Beth swung out of the saddle and dropped the reins on the

ground. This had to be Chris Padden's stolen horse, but what happened to her?

Climbing through the corral rails, Beth spoke softly. "Steady, girl. I won't hurt you."

Scrapes covered both knees. The right was swollen and tender to the touch. The mare winced but didn't bite or even pin her ears back during the examination. Beth glanced past Rad to Burt Jackson. "Did she fall?"

He shrugged. "Yeah, but Ash didn't get hurt."

"Ash Tremont?" Beth asked. "Was this his horse?"

"No. Belongs to Smith, well at least he rode into town on it. He went off with Walt and Ash came for the horse."

"Really?" Rad asked. "How fast was he riding her when she went down?"

"A lope, that's all." Burt gazed at them. "Smith didn't care. He just smiled and said he'd have one of theirs to replace her."

Beth stroked the mare's neck. "If he came at me with that smile, I'd arrest him."

"Good idea," Rad agreed. "Then, you wouldn't end up like Ash Tremont."

"Got that right." Beth remembered the young man who'd been tortured, stabbed, sodomized, and finally beaten to death, probably with the same club Smith used on Mina.

Giving the mare another pet, Beth went back to Tigger. "We'll take the horses with us too. The Tremonts won't need them, and you folks don't care enough to feed them."

"Sounds fair to me," Rad said. "You want to see the house before we ride out?"

"Need to get some pictures of the outside first." Beth opened her saddlebags. She pulled out a notebook and pencil. When nobody was watching, she'd use her camera to take photos, but as Will always quoted. *"When in Rome—"* She needed to 'go along to get along', another one of his famous sayings.

They spent most of the morning searching the place for evidence. It seemed the witnesses were correct about the cause of the attempted arson. Smith had intended to burn the place to hide the murders, but he undoubtedly had no idea that the Dawson boys trailed him this far. Or that they'd screw up his plan.

Burn marks scorched the area around the cabin door, but the nearby well provided enough water to make it easier to put out the fire. She'd taken the time to visit the outhouse and was happy to discover that Smith hadn't left another body in the privy. She wondered what happened to the rest of the Tremont family. Trace said they had three sons, so where were the other two? According to Trace, they were twins and purely as evil as their pa.

When they rode out of Gunny Creek in the early afternoon, Beth led the limping buckskin mare. "Where are we headed now?"

"Have to finish my circuit," Rad said. "The trail forks in about three miles. We'll head west toward Snohomish City. Liam and Nick can take the horses with them and return Padden's buckskin on the way to the Lazy B."

"We'll go slow," Nick said. "If we stay at a walk, we should be there in a week or so."

"Then, we'll meet up at the Lazy B about the same time," Rad said. "Keep an eye out for Smith. If he backtracks, he could bush-whack you."

Beth nodded in agreement. Privately, she figured he would have had enough killing for a while. Three people in a weekend – that was a spree when normally he went for a month between victims. However, it'd be smart for the boys to pay attention to what they saw, heard, smelled, rather than ride into an ambush.

─────

The past week was an endurance ride from hell, she thought as they rode up to the back gate of the Lazy B in the early evening. She'd visited more homesteads, logging camps, and would-be settlements than she'd ever considered possible. She wanted a hot shower, a stiff drink, a huge pizza from her favorite Italian place in Eagleville and a big box of sugar cookies from Captivating Catering. They always made her favorite ones with thick frosting and doggy treats for Luke.

Talk about an impossible dream. She wasn't going to get any of it. She wanted to go home. And not to one more ranch, but to her condo. She'd crash out on the couch, eat her pizza, wash it down with ice-cold beer and pig out on giant cookies while she watched the Mariners play ball on her huge, flat-screen TV. Tears burned behind her eyes. She longed to go home, but she never would again. She wanted Will and her own family. She swallowed the lump in her throat before the sobs escaped.

"You haven't said much in the last five miles." Rad turned his horse to face her.

"You don't want to listen to me whine and whinge." She twisted in the saddle, trying to loosen the aching muscles in her back. "Much less bitch and complain."

A smile crept into his dark blue eyes. "You're allowed. Downright frustrating to ride all those miles, talk to all those folks and never find hide or hair of Smith."

"Got that right." She sighed. "So, when do you make another tour of the area?"

"Usually in three weeks." Rad nodded at Gruber when he came to open the gate. "The other Dawson boys make it here?"

"Arrived last night. Big relief to their family. Miss Mina says they're never going anywhere without her again."

Beth managed a smile, remembering the Dawson family Bible. There was more truth to that than the young girl knew. "Well, that's good news."

"And we needed some," Rad said.

"Trace sent word for you folks to use your regular cabin," Gruber added. "Ride on down and make yourselves at home. Missus Sims will be sending over supper."

After turning the horses over to Nolan Dawson and Sean, Beth led the way to the cabin. She pushed open the door and stopped. In the middle of the room, there was a giant tub filled with hot water. Tears burned again. One streaked down her cheek. She choked back the lump rising in her throat. "I don't believe it. A bath? In a real tub, not that little washtub from last time?"

"Oughta help those sore muscles." Rad carried in their gear and put the saddlebags in the corner. "I'll go talk to Prescott for a while. Bet you'd like some time to yourself."

She bit her lip. He was incredibly decent. And she'd been ready to trade him off for a shower, beer, a pizza, and a dozen cookies. God, she was a bitch, even if he didn't know it. She spun around and grabbed his shirt. She kissed him, hard and fast, then slowed down to make it more tender. She stepped back to look up at him. "You are amazing, and I'll be a better partner."

"You're good just the way you are." He pulled her close. "We've ridden over a hundred miles in the past weeks and you're the only one I know who could stick it out through thick and thin, Bethany. Next time will be easier."

"I'll hold you to that."

THIRTY-ONE

A Guardian renders aid to the helpless, the dying, the unborn.
She celebrates life and grieves with those who mourn...

RULES OF CHRONOS

SHE SLEPT MOST OF THE MORNING BUT WOKE IN TIME FOR THE
noon meal. It still sounded strange to hear lunch called dinner, but
she supposed she'd grow accustomed to it in time. When she
looked at the assortment of children around the table, she saw the
Dawson crew, but Chris Padden hadn't sent Nettie yet. Did that
mean Mac hadn't taken over the supplies or had the older woman
changed her mind? Why?

After they ate, Beth strolled toward the barn in search of Trace.
The younger woman seemed to oversee the local universe – she'd
be able to provide an update. Emancipation stood in the corner
stall, enjoying an afternoon snack while Trace brushed him.

"How's he doing?" Beth asked.

"Good. Thought if you agreed, I might pull him out for a ride.
We could mosey around the place."

"He'd like that." Beth opened the stall door. "Did the guys fill you in on what we found?"

"Yes. Morgan told Zebadiah and he told me. Can't say I'm sorry that the Tremonts are dead." Trace moved to the right side of the stallion and continued to groom the huge palomino Appaloosa. "They weren't fit to shoot if I wanted to unload my pistol."

"They're not all gone. You said they had three boys. We only found one. Any idea where the other two might have gone?"

"Not off the top of my head." Trace considered the question. "Mac might have heard something about those two *cabróns*."

"I haven't heard that word before. What does it mean?"

"Outlaws of low breeding and even lower principles. In Spanish, the word means "goat." We can talk to Mac tomorrow when he gets back from Padden's. Chris sent word by the Dawson boys that Nettie was to come here for a while."

"Does that happen a lot?"

"No, but Doc told me last November that I needed to find someone to take over for Chris. Her heart's going to fail one of these days." Trace sighed. "And when it does, Fremont will lose his woman and I don't know how much longer I'll have him."

Beth frowned thoughtfully as she ran her hands over Emancipation's back leg. It bore the proper share of his full weight. He seemed to be able to move it forward, backward, and to the sides. Chris hadn't said anything about heart trouble during their visit and she hadn't taught Beth everything she needed to know about being a *Guardian*. Could she heal the older woman?

Beth worked her way back toward Emancipation's head, exploring his sides. She wished they had the portable X-ray machine her veterinarian used on Tigger. "Ribs feel all right. Legs are fine."

"And his vision?"

Beth caught the halter and checked out the horse's head. The stallion pricked up his ears and nuzzled her. The tear on the right ear was almost healed and only a large scratch remained. The swelling around both eyes subsided too. She lifted her hand on the left and he blinked that eye. Same reaction on the right.

"He has some vision, maybe not a hundred percent, but at least fifty on both sides," Beth said. "It's more than I expected. I think he'll make a full recovery. That's incredible."

"He had an incredible doctor," Trace said. "You pulled off a miracle."

Beth froze, remembering her time with Chris Padden. The woman said they had the power to heal, but could it be more than advanced knowledge from another time? Were they Goddess blessed? Was that the real answer?

She'd saved Rad from an injury that should have killed him. When she and Chris removed the bandages, he only had a faint scar from the exit wound and there wasn't any trace of the entrance hole. Mina bounced back from a concussion, broken ribs, and a shattered leg. Granted the leg hadn't finished healing yet, but the girl would not only survive, but she'd also walk without a limp. And now this horse, but what about the buckskin mare? Would she be all right too?

I need to read the book.

Chris said it had the answers, but what were the questions?

"Want to ride out with us?" Trace asked.

"Sure, but I don't have a horse. Tigger needs to rest up. It's been a long haul and he's sleeping in the sunshine."

"You can ride Ginger," Trace said. "She's a sweetheart."

"A mare with your stud? Is that a good idea?"

"Day I can't handle Emancipation, they better throw a shovel of dirt in my face."

Beth laughed. "Okay, that works for me."

They didn't ride in the same direction they had the last time she visited. Instead, Trace stuck to flat ground to make it easy on Emancipation. As they wandered through the various fields, the Lazy B began to look more and more familiar. Slowly, the answer came to Beth. She had been here before. Her 4-H club camped on the historic Dawson ranch every summer, but she wouldn't share the information with Trace.

To be honest, it really didn't matter who had the place. If it hadn't been paved over and turned into a shopping mall a hundred-plus years from now, her friend probably wouldn't care.

Beth sat on the porch that night, skimming the book in the glow from the lamp. There must have been at least four women who preceded her. She could tell by the different handwriting. None of them wrote clearly about what she could expect. It was all in rhyme and the poems weren't that great. An English teacher would have sent the writers back to class. There must be a reason for the style. Was it supposed to be easy to remember?

She flipped through the pages to those written by the *Guardian* who called herself, Chronos. What did it mean? Who was Chronos in literature? No, not literature—mythology—Greek mythology to be exact. Beth nodded and petted Luke who slept beside her.

"Time. Chronos represents Time and that means she came here like I did." Beth stroked the dog's fur. "Like we did." She read the first entry again, repeating the words aloud. *"To do Her Sacred Work, She chooses a Guardian then creates a hallowed place, despite Time and Space—"*

Well, that made sense. They'd come through Time to a new world, one new to them anyway, but a "hallowed place?" Could that be the ridge she crossed over?

But, what about Gary Smith? Why would anyone let him enter somewhere sacred? It didn't make much sense to her, but then she wasn't a Goddess. Of course, if there was one deity, who was to say there couldn't be another? And that might explain why he came here.

Something or someone wanted the blood Smith shed. Hadn't Rad told her that the shaman said Smith used the deaths of his victims to open the door to come here?

More questions and she needed to find the answers. She heard the crunch of gravel and looked toward the road to see Trace approach. "You can't sleep either?"

"Not tonight." Trace drew out her tobacco pouch. "Then again, I always enjoy talking to you. I love Zebadiah, but he's not one for a lot of conversation about feelings. Tells me what will work the best and then expects me to do it."

"Solution-based, huh?" Beth smiled and moved closer to her dog, closing the book, and sliding it into her saddlebags. "A lot of guys are that way."

"So, what do you do?"

"Talk to other women," Beth said, "and enjoy men for what they can give."

Trace sat down on the steps and began to roll a cigarette. "What does Morgan give you?"

"Good question." Beth accepted the first smoke. "He makes me feel safe. He watches my back. Haven't had that from a civilian since I returned from the war."

"I know the feeling." Trace lit their cigarettes. "When Zebadiah came home last summer, he was the first man who tried to protect me in years. We argue about it sometimes, but you're right. Having someone to trust who stands with you makes all the difference."

Beth frowned as she smoked. She hadn't thought of that before. When she was in Afghanistan, she had to be able to count on the soldiers who stood next to her. She had. They'd counted on her the same way and now that she was here, she could rely on Rad.

"Trust? I didn't call it that, but you're right." She heard the door open behind them and glanced over her shoulder to see Rad. "We're doing girl-talk here."

He chuckled. "I'll leave you the whisky then and go keep Prescott company, so he doesn't interrupt."

On Saturday morning, they left the Lazy B early enough to make Junction City by dinner time. Trace and Zeb Prescott promised to bring Becky and Nettie to visit in a week or so. The girls would stay until the marshal's next circuit. Beth and Rad would bring them back to the Lazy B on their way to Portage, Gunny Creek, and the other settlements.

"Any more ideas on where to look for Smith?" Beth asked as they rode down the trail. "I'm open to suggestions."

"Steamboat should be in on Monday," Rad said. "We'll see what the captain learned in Snohomish City. We can send word to Matt to keep watching for him. What did Mac say about the other Tremont boys?"

"He said the word was they rode north to Corbetts' Town at the northern end of the valley. Is that part of your circuit?"

"No, they have a town marshal. I don't infringe on Grayson Mallory's territory, and he doesn't come into mine."

"He may want to take them into protective custody," Beth said. "If Smith's decided to wipe out the rest of the Tremonts, they'll be high on his list. Is there a way to send him word?"

"Connor has logging crews near Corbett's Town. He'll let Mallory know. Meantime, when we get to the Bar M, I'll tell Gabe to have the men keep an eye out. Smith may hear that we have Sorrel on the ranch and come after her."

"Why? If he intended to kill her, he'd have done it years ago and he hasn't taken Becky away from the Lazy B." Beth urged Tigger to a faster walk to keep pace with Rad's mare. "For some reason, he didn't want to hurt them. He tried to save them from the Tremonts. I wonder why."

"Sorrel may know. Talk to her when we get home."

"Good idea."

They arrived in town in the early afternoon. Once again, they stabled their horses at Connor's. Beth began to feel almost at home in Junction City. After touring the area, the place seemed more like civilization than the smaller settlements. Cal had dinner, a pot of navy beans and ham on the stove when they walked into the marshal's office. Someone had brought over a loaf of homemade bread and a crock of honey as a treat.

While they ate, he brought them up to speed on what happened while they were gone. A few brawls, a knifing at the saloon, a lost child, Michael Ortiz. He'd played hooky from school and went fishing and was safely returned to the family who boarded him while he attended school in Junction City. Rad shared the news from the various places they'd visited.

Beth dribbled honey onto a slab of bread. If she kept eating like this, she'd gain ten pounds. Of course, she spent a lot more time in the saddle now than she did before, so maybe not. "What happens now? Who writes up the reports for the past month?"

Rad and Cal shared a glance. "That would be the newest deputy."

"I ought to have known better than to ask," Beth muttered, around a mouthful of bread. "Who did it before I got here?"

"Kyle, but he wasn't much good at it," Cal said. "Kept trying to add in extra information, 'stead of just the facts."

"Should have guessed that was going to happen," Rad said. "He wants to be a writer like Mark Twain."

"Maybe, he'd let me read one of his stories," Beth said. "I love a good book."

"Could be," Rad said. "You might talk to him about working for Paul at the newspaper. Kyle isn't too fond of the idea, but it'd give him a steady wage."

"Good idea," Beth said. "I will. Like I said, my cousin is an author, and she always says writing for newspapers and magazines teaches writers their craft."

She spent the afternoon and evening writing up what she and Rad saw during their rounds of the various settlements, including the murder of the Tremont family. When Cal wandered through, she collected additional details for the occurrences he handled in their absence. Of course, there were some things he didn't know and that meant visits to the saloon, the doctor, and even Michael Ortiz.

The next morning, they attended church services at the hotel. The town seemed far too quiet. That afternoon in the marshal's office, she mentioned it to Rad and he told her to enjoy the peace. Next Friday, two logging crews would show up to spend their pay and there would be at least one fight. Since the box social was scheduled for the following day, there would undoubtedly be more fisticuffs.

She carried the coffeepot over from the potbellied stove and filled both their cups, suppressing a giggle at the sound of the word. "Do I have to pack some sort of dinner for us?"

"No, we'll be keeping the peace," Rad said. "Most folks will share with us."

"Good to know," Beth said. "Then, I won't have to listen to you whine about my cooking."

He grinned at her. "Be different if you could actually cook, Detective Morgan. Feel like taking a stroll around town and see if anything's happening?"

"Why not? Maybe, there will be a bar fight at the saloon."

"One can always hope," Rad teased. "Reckon, if I tell you to let me handle it, you'll pull out your carbine and cover my back again."

"Then, I better bring the rifle with me."

"Pin up your hair again and we'll go."

She heaved a sigh. "Being in the middle of nowhere and all these old-time expectations gets tiresome in a hurry, Morgan."

"You'll grow accustomed to us after a year or so, Bethany."

On Monday, while his crew unloaded the steamboat, Captain Jensen came to the office with a message from the marshal in Snohomish City. "Said to tell you that he's keeping an eye out for Gary Smith Senior. So far, the fellow hasn't been seen, but they have wanted posters all over town."

"Could he be hiding there?" Beth asked.

"Definitely, but Matt says he'll start rousting the crib owners next week."

"Crib owners?" Beth frowned at the stocky steamboat captain. Middle-aged, silver blond, blue eyes, barely five-foot-eight. "What's that? Some sort of school for little kids?"

Red crept into his face, but Jensen didn't answer.

Beth turned her attention to Rad. "Well?"

"Low-class bordellos on the waterfront," Rad said. "Tell Devlin to take a posse with him when he hunts rats. He needs to keep an eye out for the Tremont boys if they headed south from Corbett's Town. Smith killed their folks, and he may be after them."

"I'll pass the word. Got pictures?"

Beth nodded and opened her saddlebags. "Trace described them for me, and I've made some adjustments to the drawings, so they'll look older than the last time she saw them."

"These will be propitious," Captain Jensen said, taking the papers. "I'll pass them out on every stop downriver. Pretty useful having a deputy who's an artist, isn't it, Marshal Morgan?"

"Don't know what I did without her," Rad agreed.

Beth eyed him warily, wondering if he was being straight up or just a smart ass.

When he smiled at her, she relaxed a little. No, lying wasn't something he did. If he had a problem with her working out of his office, he'd say so. She had to admit his acceptance of her as another law enforcement officer made it much easier to share a life with him. If he'd tried to keep her under his thumb, they'd have split the sheets weeks ago.

That night, she left him sleeping on the narrow bunk in the curtained-off alcove. Since they were alone, they'd seized the opportunity to make love while Kyle and Cal did the rounds in town. Beth poured another cup of strong coffee and sat down at the table to skim through the pictures on her camera. She avoided the crime scene photos, opting for happier times. At some point, she wanted to sleep tonight. She wouldn't if she studied Gary Smith's victims.

Instead, she scanned the images of the ponies at the Silver Lake Pony Ranch. She'd visited there when she was an Animal Control cop to keep an eye on a rescued old mare, taking treats for the horse and mochas to the equine's new owner. From there, Beth went onto the photographs she'd taken at Nina's barn. She glanced toward the door as it opened, and Kyle entered.

"How is everything?"

"Peace and quiet reign." Kyle hung up his rifle, then headed for the woodstove and the coffeepot. "What do you have there?"

"My camera. Pictures of home."

"Do you mind sharing them?"

Beth hesitated, then gestured for him to come and join her. "This is Nina with Wonder, the horse Trace calls, Emancipation."

Kyle's eyes widened when he gazed at the photo of the petite brunette in jeans and a bright red western blouse standing next to the light-yellow Appaloosa horse. "The screen is so small. How did you hand-color pictures on that contraption?"

"It's a digital camera and you'd have to ask Nina how it works. She's the photographer. I just take photos of what I see."

He stared at the picture. "If she was here, I'd want to know more than that."

"Me, too." Beth heaved a sigh. "I wish I could ask how she's doing since Smith attacked her." She heard the rattle of the curtain and turned slightly to see Rad. "Couldn't you sleep?"

"Not without you." He came to join them. "Tell me about the sister of your heart."

"You'll get tired of my stories."

"No, we won't," Kyle said. "You know about us. We want to know more about you and her."

Shortly after the steamboat left Tuesday morning, she and Rad left town. Hannah's son, Michael accompanied them on a spooky sorrel Appaloosa gelding that he said was named Frog because he jumped around a lot. The boy didn't have any trouble handling the horse he told Beth was a gift from Trace Burdette. This time, Rad took a different trail and they arrived at the Bar M in time for supper.

Sorrel ran to meet them at the corral, braids and skirt flying. "You've been gone forever, and it was so boring here."

Beth laughed and swung out of the saddle. She caught the girl in a quick hug. "We missed you too."

THIRTY-TWO

A Guardian brings to justice those who hurt, maim, and kill.
But allows those who harm none to do as they will…"

RULES OF CHRONOS

HANNAH SERVED A VEGETABLE SOUP THICK WITH BEANS AND HAM for supper. Big slabs of cornbread stacked on a plate took up the center of the table. For dessert, they had dried apple pie and coffee. She seemed a little surprised to see Michael, but delighted too, greeting the boy with a hug. He bore a striking resemblance to her husband, and it made Beth wonder if he and Hannah had Michael, split up, then reunited.

After the meal, Sorrel helped Hannah clean up the kitchen. Michael went outside and Beth heard the steady chopping of the ax. A few minutes later, the boy toted in chunks of firewood and filled the box beside the woodstove. He hesitated, then came to the table where Gabe sat with a cup of coffee across from Rad.

"I'd like to visit the Lazy B for a while," Michael said.

Hannah whirled from the sink. Her hands knotted in the dish-cloth. "Why? What happened in town? Did somebody—"

Michael eyed her, then Gabe. "Nobody said nothing I couldn't handle."

"Anything you couldn't handle," Beth corrected his language, studying the boy. He had been perfectly polite when she talked to him about the fishing episode a few days ago, but he acted like he was ten going on forty. He just didn't seem to understand why the teacher or family where he boarded should care what he did if it wasn't illegal or immoral. "So, what's up with you and the Lazy B?"

"I grew up there." Michael ran a hand through his black hair. "And I miss Trace and my brothers and sisters and Ma Sims and Free and Pedro. And Olaf and Lars. I want to go home for a while."

"Makes sense." Gabe pushed back from the table, patted the boy's shoulder, and went to stand by Hannah who'd swung around to finish the dishes. "Now, how are we going to arrange that?"

"You'll let me go?" Relief swept across the boy's face, and he relaxed. "Thanks, Ma."

Beth watched as Gabe rested his hands on Hannah's shaking shoulders and realized the other woman cried into the dishwater. "Why don't you go visit when Becky and Nettie come here?"

Michael blinked. His green eyes widened with surprise. "Trace is letting Becky come here?"

"And Nettie Padden," Beth added, flicking a glance at Rad. "The girls will come home with us after the social next Saturday. If it's all right with your folks, you could go to the Lazy B with Trace and Zeb Prescott. We'll drop the girls back at the Lazy B when we leave to make Marshal Morgan's rounds through Liberty Valley."

"And we could bring you home when we circle back," Rad said. "That'd give you almost a month. By then, you'll be ready to trade the Lazy B for the peace and quiet of the Bar M for the summer. Maybe, Jack and a couple of the Dawson boys could come back with you. We'll ask Trace and Prescott."

This time when Hannah turned away from the dishes, she appeared in control of her emotions. "That sounds good to me. What do you think, Michael?"

"I like it." He flashed a smile at her and Gabe, before facing Rad. "Thanks, Marshal."

Beth bit back her smile. *Talk about smooth*, she thought. She finished her coffee and stood. "So, shall we walk around the place, Marshal?"

"I'm ready." He rose and followed her toward the back door. "Gabe, we'll ride out after breakfast and check the stock. Do you want to join us, Detective Morgan?"

"Not this time." Beth paused on the way to the door. "I want Hannah and Sorrel to help me make up a basket for the social and it will take days for us to cook up a meal."

"You're forgetting." Rad cupped her elbow. "I ate what you cooked in the cave, and I'd rather have you help me patrol the town. You're wonderful with drunken loggers."

"Pink ribbons on the basket and you're going to buy it in front of everybody in Junction City." Beth lifted her chin. "When I was in the mercantile this morning, the storekeeper, Susanne Prescott told me the entire town would be watching me to see what kind of wife I am."

"The best kind." Rad held the door for her. "You know when to shoot and when not to shoot."

"You're buying it and you're eating what's in it," Beth said. "And no whining."

"We'll see."

"We certainly will."

It was shortly after eight and still light when they returned to the house so she couldn't slip away to their bedroom. Rad headed off to the barn, saying he wanted to check on the lumber Gabe had brought from the mill. Luke flopped on the porch outside the back door. Beth joined Hannah and the children in the kitchen where she found the woman knitting while her son set up a game of checkers on the table. "What are you making?"

"Mittens for winter." Hannah looked up with a smile. "Michael must have worn out three or four pairs last year and outgrew the ones he still has left."

"Won't I need some too?" Sorrel asked.

"Yes, and so will I." Beth glanced at the basket of yarn, skeins of red, blue, black, and green in addition to several cream-colored ones. "Do you have more needles? I haven't knitted in eons. I'll have to see if I remember what I learned."

"I'll enjoy the help." Hannah reached into the basket and handed over a pair of wooden needles, glancing at Sorrel. "What about you?"

"We can knit now and then play checkers," Sorrel said. "Come on, Michael."

"But I'm a boy. I can't knit."

"Don't tell the marshal," Hannah said, keeping her gaze on the gray yarn in her lap. "He told me he knitted his own socks for years until he made enough money to buy them."

"Wow, that's news to me too." Beth focused on casting the first row of dark blue yarn on the needle. "I'm curious to know who taught him."

After breakfast the next morning, the men rode out leaving Michael behind to chop firewood so they could keep the fire in the kitchen stove burning. Dishes done, Beth sat down at the table with Hannah and Sorrel to discuss the proposed menu.

"Hannah, you've cooked for the marshal longer than I have," Beth said. "What are his favorite foods?"

"He's not fussy," Hannah said. "Of course, by this time of the year we're all pretty tired of pork, but we don't eat beef."

"Why not?" Beth asked. "There's a lot of cattle here and at the Lazy B."

"Beef goes to market, Detective Morgan," Michael said. "Gold on the hoof is what Trace calls it and there's plenty of other grub. I could go fishing and bring home a couple of salmon for dinner today."

"Fish would be a treat," Hannah said, "but we'll cook it for supper since the men will be gone all day."

"If I went with him, I could hunt for freshwater clams," Sorrel said.

"And learn to fish." Beth went after the coffee-pot and brought it back to refill her and Hannah's cups. "Then, when Michael's not here, we could send you for salmon."

Sorrel gazed at her, obviously stunned. "But I'm a girl."

"So, what?" Michael eyed her, obviously amused. "It's your turn to learn something new. The fish don't care who catches 'em. And most of my sisters at the Lazy B can catch a salmon near as good as me and Jack. Not the little 'uns, like Becky though."

"Why not?" Sorrel asked, suspiciously.

"If she falls in the river, she might drown. She doesn't swim that good yet," Michael said. "And Pa, I mean Trace, says all the gals have to be able to look after themselves. That means fishing, hunting, and shooting two-legged varmints."

"I knew I liked her." Beth returned the coffee-pot to the stove. "I have a present for you in my saddlebags, Sorrel, and it looks like you need it now if you're going fishing."

"But don't you need me here at the house?"

"No," Beth glanced at Hannah, then added, "We're not even sure what the menu will be, and I don't know what food supplies we have on hand. So, go fishing. Hannah's right. We have to feed the guys when they get back."

Once the two kids left for the river, Sorrel in her new pants and Michael carrying two fishing poles, Hannah led Beth to a small room off the kitchen. Long shelves lined the walls filled with different food staples. She saw containers with several kinds of dry beans, corn flour, cornmeal, store-bought wheat flour, brown and white sugar. Jars of home-canned fruits and vegetables still lined three of the shelves. Dried apple slices were suspended on strings from the ceiling, but Beth didn't recognize the vegetables on their lines or the herbs for that matter. Another cupboard held an assortment of spices.

"In a couple of months, I'll start canning for the winter but only the beans and peas are ready to be picked now," Hannah said. "We still have potatoes, cabbages, carrots, and onions left from last year in the root cellar. The turnips are only good for soup."

"Well, if Sorrel finds clams, we can make chowder today." Beth glanced around the room again. "Where's the meat?"

"In the smokehouse. We have milk and cheese in the spring-house. I keep the eggs there too. We're better off than some folks."

"So, we should be able to come up with some fabulous food in our baskets," Beth said. "What are your husband's favorites?"

Hannah sighed. "He'll eat anything, but he told me once that he misses the tortillas his mama made. I've never found a receipt for those."

"A receipt? You mean a recipe?" Beth shrugged. "No worries. I took a Mexican cooking class. Tortillas are easy when you have all the ingredients."

"A cooking class?" Hannah snugged the ties on her apron. "Why would you take a class?"

"It was when I first came home from the war before I was hired at the sheriff's department." Beth walked over to check out the barrel in the corner of the room and smelled the pungent odor of pickles. She wouldn't share the fact that Will had concerns when she was partying with the only lawyer she actually liked. She and Astra used to squabble over who was picking up which man at their favorite local watering-hole, Billy-Bob's Cowboy Bar and Grill.

As Astra said, 'some women talk too much about their sex life, and most men couldn't handle it.' "I didn't sleep well most nights, so my father suggested I start taking evening classes. Just because I don't cook all the time doesn't mean I can't."

Hannah giggled. "Sounds like the marshal is going to learn to suck eggs."

"And I'm just the woman to teach him," Beth said. "Now, tell me what's up with Trace Burdette. Why do the kids call her 'Pa'?

Rad said she fooled the people around here, but those children lived with her."

"And they kept her secret for years," Hannah said. "Michael told me that they all helped hide the truth once they were old enough to know it. They still have a hard time remembering to call her 'Trace' or 'Missus Prescott.' She'll be the only father and mother that most of them ever know."

"They're lucky to have her." Beth checked out the next barrel. This one held crackers. "My parents didn't want a child, so they left me to be raised by the state. Worked for a while and then I ran off to take care of myself."

"So, you and the marshal have something else in common," Hannah said. "You're both orphans."

"I didn't think of it that way, but you're right."

That night, Beth changed into her favorite red, mesh-style, Washington State University football t-shirt, wearing it and nothing else. She had a husband she planned to jump when he finally got here. She curled up in bed with the second of her cousin's novels, rereading the shapeshifter story of twins caught between an overly romantic alpha wolf determined to gain the affections of a female who didn't want him and the machinations of others in the pack trying to keep them apart.

She glanced at the bedroom door when it opened and Rad entered. "So, how's life out on the prairie? Did you and Gabe organize everything that needs to be done before he leaves for the sawmill tomorrow?"

"We're working on it." Rad removed his boots. "Which Shakespeare play are you reading now?"

"None. It's my cousin, Destynee's book. Lots of humor about mistaken identities and twins who have lost track of each other and have adventures finding one another again."

"Twelfth Night." Rad continued to undress. "Sounds like a well-educated woman to me."

Beth frowned thoughtfully, eyeing the paperback she held

again. "She told me once she had to go to work before she left high school to help support her family, so she couldn't use the college scholarships she earned."

"Not going to college doesn't mean a person can't read books or learn from folks."

"That's true." Beth pretended to focus on the page in front of her and watched him lay his pants on the chair, followed by the work shirt. She wouldn't tell him how much she enjoyed the strip-tease or the sight of his broad shoulders, muscled back, and narrow waist. "She attended a few night classes at the university where I studied criminal justice."

"Is that where you learned all about chasing killers?"

"Not totally. What about you? When did you know you wanted to be a law enforcement officer?"

"Between cattle drives, I worked as a deputy. It was an education." He crossed to the bed and turned down the lamp on the nightstand. "You planning to read all night, Missus Morgan?"

"Not if you can think of something else to do, Marshal Morgan." She handed him the book and it was placed neatly beside the oil lamp. "Of course, we could just go to sleep."

"And what's the point of that?"

She squealed when he tugged the quilt off her. He threw it toward the end of the large bed and sank on the mattress beside her. He snagged her hand in nearly the same moment and pulled her against him until she was lying almost on top of him. "What are you doing?"

"Seeing how long it takes to make you scream."

She laughed and twined her arms around his neck, brushing her lips over his. "Not long if I know you."

"And I've barely started." He kissed her neck. "Have I told you how much I like this nightshirt of yours?"

"Oh, I think I know." She gasped when he cupped her breast. His thumb teased her nipple, rubbing it against the mesh cloth. "That's why I wear it."

"I know." He lowered his head, chuckled, then drew her other nipple into his mouth and sucked.

She tangled her fingers into his thick, black hair, holding his head exactly where she wanted it, pressing into him. His hands slid to her hips. She parted her legs, hoping, wondering how long it'd take for him to find her. She was so wet.

She nipped his ear and the strong line of his neck, then his shoulder. "Come on, Morgan. Now. Do it now."

"I'm cogitating about it, but I haven't heard you beg, only order me around." He worked his way to her other nipple, swirled his tongue around it. "Ask me nicely."

"Are you joking?"

"No." He lifted his head, smiling at her, dark blue eyes filled with amusement. "Are you going to be sweet tonight?"

"Not if you keep me waiting."

"Well, that's honest." His smile broadened. "And you always taste sweet, so reckon I'll settle for that." One large finger slid deep inside her, followed by a second and he began a steady rhythm. At the same time, he tormented her nipples with his mouth, rubbing the t-shirt over her breasts.

She moaned, then kissed the strong line of his jaw, his cheek, his ear. "Don't stop."

"I won't." His thumb found her, rubbed lightly while he kept sliding his fingers in and out. Pleasure slammed through her. Knees buckling, she collapsed on his lap, gripped his shoulders, his arms.

"Take me now."

"Not yet." He lifted her off him, shifted, and pushed her legs further apart. His mouth claimed her, his hands holding her hips, so she was exactly where he wanted.

She arched beneath the intimate kiss, moaning when his tongue flicked into the folds of skin. He licked his way into her, and she gasped when his tongue drove deep. Between strokes, he kept lapping, licking the small bud of flesh, and then he finally drew her clitoris into his mouth and sucked. And she came apart, screaming his name.

When she returned to sanity, he was lying beside her. She ran her hand over his broad chest, turned her face so she could kiss the hollow of his throat below the green stone on his necklace. "How do you know what to do to make me crazy? Have you been with a lot of women?"

"Not that many." He stroked her hair. "I had to do something in the cave while you slept for two days so I read your cousin's books. They were an education."

Heat swept into Beth's face as she recalled the steamy sex scenes in the erotic romances. "Are you serious?"

"Yes, and I'm willing to try most everything she described, but later."

"Well, what do you intend to do now?" She caught her breath when he rolled on top of her. "This is pretty tame."

He laughed and parted her legs with one of his. Keeping his weight on his elbows, he drove deep into her. "Let's see how wild I can make it."

Much later, she rested against him, her arm across his chest. "I'd say you really studied those books a lot, Marshal Morgan."

"Not enough." He cuddled her close. "More men should try reading them."

"Like Kyle?"

"Why would he need them?"

"He keeps asking me about Nina and how I got here. I think he wants to go find her if she survived Smith's attack."

"He's a romantic fool." Rad's hold tightened. "I'll talk to him."

"And do what? Tell him not to go?"

"No. If there's a way for him to find her, he should follow his heart. But if he goes, Smith may be there too, and Kyle *oughta* plan on killing the man before he attacks your sister again. Besides women from your time have expectations and he better know how to meet them. He'd best plan on reading those books."

Beth lifted her head and met the dark blue of his eyes. "I think

I love you, Morgan, and not just because you want to take care of me and my best friend."

He kissed her with a sweet tenderness that warmed her heart.

"Tell me again when you know for sure."

"Of course, if you show me something else you learned from Destynee's books, I might know sooner."

"Let's see."

THIRTY-THREE

"On the 13th day, in the light of the red moon, a Guardian's Power will last beyond the next noon...."

RULES OF CHRONOS

SHE AND HANNAH SPENT DAYS COOKING AND THE HEAVY BASKETS held the best of what they created. Following Rad's suggestion, Beth wore a divided skirt and rode Tigger into town while Hannah and Gabe came in the buckboard, Luke trotting alongside the wagon. Michael and Sorrel rode their horses too. They spotted other family groups on the way to Junction City.

"Looks like everybody's ready to party," Beth said.

Rad chuckled. "Got that right. We'll dance most of the night away."

"Who provides the music?" Beth asked.

"Depends on who shows up, but we can count on Cal to pull out his fiddle. Some of the loggers play banjos, accordions, and guitars."

Beth nearly said it sounded like a blast in the past, then opted to keep that opinion to herself. After all, it wasn't her *time*, but this was her new home and she needed to make friends, not enemies. Besides, this was going to be fun.

"So, what's in your basket?" Rad asked. "Besides Missus Sims' doughnuts?"

"Well, Sorrel threatened me with dire deeds if I went after any of her chickens so there's fried grouse, potato salad, baked beans, and a few other surprises." Beth smiled sweetly at him. "And just remember you have to buy my basket or else."

"Since I don't want to deal with that "or else," reckon I better pull out my money."

"Good idea."

They arrived in Junction City an hour later. Horses safely stabled at Connor's, they headed for the schoolhouse with a brief stop at the jail. All the cells were empty, but Cal and Kyle had cleaned them, so they'd be ready for business if fights broke out. As soon as Michael saw the folks from the Lazy B, he took Sorrel to meet them.

Becky tumbled out of the wagon into Sorrel's arms in a desperate hug. Beth watched the two sisters cling to each other. Somehow, she'd have to see to it they remained together. Trace and Zeb stood nearby, holding their horses and Beth headed across the street to meet them. "What are we going to do with them?"

"I'm not sure." Trace turned and untied a large bundle behind her saddle. "For now, I'm going to the hotel and change for the party. Zebadiah, will you take our horses to the livery?"

He nodded. "I'll meet you at the hotel later, Tracee."

———

The sun rose high overhead. Wagons and buckboards crowded the streets. A wooden floor stretched out in part of the field next to the school, ready for the dance. Baskets and small wooden boxes covered a long table. Before dinner, the children would deliver speeches, recite poetry, and sing songs. Dancing would start in the middle of the afternoon and continue until late in the night.

He saw Zeb Prescott talking with Gabe, Paul, and Connor. Rad went to join the other men. Zeb grinned at him. "How do you like your new deputy?"

"She's doing just fine," Rad said. "However, I may be in trouble. Your sister convinced Bethany to provide a basket for dinner. And my wife's better at shooting than cooking."

"You may have to eat those words," Zeb drawled, "and you ain't the only one. Trace actually made up a basket too. I was hoping Missus Sims would do the honors, but she refused."

Connor chuckled. "Lizbeth's ice cream will make up for it." He winked. "Now, that's a surprise so don't tell her I mentioned it."

"Well, Trace has decided we need an icehouse at the Lazy B and by now, she'll have talked Detective Morgan into having one at the Bar M."

Rad rocked on his heels while he contemplated the idea. He could build one of those out of the small trees on the ranch. Log walls, a good wooden roof, and plenty of shavings to insulate the ice. Cutting ice blocks in the winter wouldn't be much of a problem. The river usually froze over, but so did the ponds on the ranch.

Gabe rubbed his jaw thoughtfully. "Selling the shavings from the mill would make money in the summer when I don't cut lumber. Of course, if we have an icehouse, the children will expect ice cream on a regular basis."

"So will I," Rad said.

————

He'd barely made it out of Snohomish City before the posse found him in that waterfront dive. He'd absconded with an Indian canoe and headed upriver. Once he was far enough away, he stole a horse and took to the woods. What set Marshal

Morgan's tail afire? And how had he arranged to get posters downriver?

The new ones even had pictures drawn on them, and Smith worried about everyone who saw him. He figured he could get the drop on the lawman in Junction City, and that would resolve the problem.

However, the town was full of people, and it only added to his difficulties. Perched on the hill that overlooked the main street, he used his rifle scope to look for the marshal. Children raced around the school, and a glimpse of bright red hair caught his attention. Smith froze. Was it his angel?

It had to be a sign. She and a little blonde girl romped around the cemetery. He didn't mind that. He was glad the two sisters had found each other again. Vera would have liked the company, even if she did scold about proper manners and deportment for young ladies.

———

Loggers carried the benches from the school for the audience. Beth sat between Trace and Hannah. Different students recited various speeches from Shakespeare's plays. Michael gave a rousing rendition of *The Declaration of Independence*. All the children joined together to sing half a dozen songs. Beth only recognized *Sweet Betsy from Pike.*

Finally, it was time for Connor to auction off the baskets. He looked inside them and provided comments on the contents, always claiming he wanted the dinner for himself.

He held up Hannah's basket. "Now, this one is truly special, or as Trace told me, it's *muy bueno.* She even wrote down what I'm supposed to be a-saying. Burritos, tamales, and some dessert called an *empanada.* So, who wants to start the bidding?"

"Three dollars," Fremont Goodman called. "I ain't had good Mexican food in years and I've got a hankering for it."

Hannah fanned herself. "I made that for Gabe," she whispered.

"Well, let my brother win it," Trace said. "And now that I know you can cook like that, I'm coming to the Bar M for dinner much more often."

The bidding skyrocketed to five dollars, then seven, and finally Gabe won the basket at ten dollars. A blushing Hannah went off with her husband to join him for the meal. Trace followed a short time later and finally, it was Beth's turn.

Connor opened the basket and peeked inside. As he enumerated the different food items and the bids started, Beth enjoyed watching Rad try to win his prize. She spotted Michael running down the street from the mayor's house and frowned. Now, what?

She stood and went to meet the boy. "What's wrong?"

"It's Sorrel." Michael gasped for breath. "Some man's got her and he's trying to drag her away."

"Where?"

"At Mayor Riley's barn."

Her rifle was at the jail, but she wore her shoulder holster with the Glock under her black jacket. "Fetch the marshal and send him after me."

Grateful she hadn't changed into the blue satin dress yet and still wore her divided skirt, she headed for the barn behind the mayor's house. She heard a soft yip and glanced over her shoulder to see Luke loping up behind her. So, she wouldn't be going in alone after all. *Good to know.*

She slipped her pistol from the holster and took a moment to remember the layout of the barn. The main door opened into a wide central area with a tack area immediately to the right and a grain room to the left. Stalls lined the east, north, and south walls with hay stored overhead in the loft. She hoped whoever had Sorrel didn't plan to set fire to the structure, especially since the place was full of horses today.

Beth eased inside the door and stood in the shelter of the tack room. A body lay in the center of the barn, and she recognized Christine Padden. What happened to her? Was she still alive?

Beth listened for voices, looked for the girl and the man who held her hostage. Who was it? One of the loggers who'd tried to buy her in the saloon? Burt Jackson or someone else from Gunny Creek? The last two Tremont boys wanting revenge for their dead parents?

"Haven't you got that horse saddled yet?" A gravelly voice demanded.

"I'm trying." Sorrel sounded as if tears weren't far away. "I'm not particularly good at it. The marshal says it's not girl's work and makes his ranch hands tack up for me."

Good girl, Beth thought. *Keep slowing the bastard down.*

She knew that voice. She'd spent hours in one of the interview rooms trying to break him. Gary Smith. She glanced around the corner of the tack room and saw him outside Tigger's stall. Sorrel stood just inside the door, struggling to lift the saddle into place, Gary less than three feet away from the girl.

"I don't understand," Sorrel said. "Why do I have to go with you? The marshal says he and his wife will adopt me and—"

"When his wife finds out what kind of girl her husband brought home, she'll throw you out like garbage."

He didn't sound like he planned to kill Sorrel, but she couldn't count on that. Beth assessed him with a quick gaze. Five-foot-eight, graying brown hair, brown eyes, he'd lost weight, but he'd grown a beard. He wore a long coat and held a knife in his right hand. A rifle was propped nearby.

"Get that flea-bit nag ready," Smith ordered. "Hurry up."

Beth stepped out where she had a clear view, aiming the Glock at him. "Come on, Gary. Considering what I paid for him, he's not a nag. He has better bloodlines than you do."

"Bitch. I killed you. You're dead."

"Oh, you're whining because you're a crappy shot," Beth retorted. "Kind of like being a crappy man. Why don't you come and teach me a lesson?" She grinned. "You know you want to."

He took an angry step toward her, then stopped. "Can't do it here. There's not enough time."

"Then, let the girl go and take me instead." Beth eased closer.

She flicked a glance down at Christine and saw the older woman open an eye and quickly shut it. "I'll go anywhere you say and then we'll have all the time you need."

He narrowed his eyes. "Stop right there. Let me think."

Beth obeyed. "Well, hurry up. The clock's ticking and the boy who escaped will be back with Morgan."

"He should be dead, too."

"Give it a rest, Gary. You're a crappy shot. I told you already. You barely grazed the man, and I was a medic in Afghanistan. He's simply fine."

"Don't call me by my first name. You have no respect."

"Why don't you teach me some?" Beth took another step. She was almost close enough. "You know you want to."

"Quit saying that." He started toward her, then stopped himself. He backed up, grabbed Sorrel's arm, and dragged the girl away from the horse. Knife at her throat, he smiled. "Drop the gun."

"No." Beth stood over Christine. "You'll kill her anyway. You've already got one victim here."

"Thanks a lot." Sorrel glared at her. "You're not much help."

"Hey, I just tell it the way I see it. He'll kill you and then I'll kill him." Beth used her snarkiest tone, keeping their attention on her so neither saw Luke belly-crawling in the shadows. "I promise you'll both have nice funerals. Yours will be better than his. We'll get a real preacher."

"Have to send to Snohomish City for one." Rad came in the side door, pistol in hand. "Let the girl go."

Gary backed closer to the stall. "I want the deal that cop bitch promised me. She comes with me, and we get a head start."

"I don't share my woman," Rad said. "She's not going anywhere with the likes of you."

"Your woman?" Gary looked back and forth. "What are you saying?"

"Oh, you should know other men by now, Gary." Beth opted for a condescending tone. "You screw them, and they think they own you. Come on. Give the girl to Rad and we'll get out of here. You can try to kill me, and I'll try to get you back to Eagleville in chains. Let's see which of us wins."

"I like her deal better than yours, Marshal," Gary said. "You win, Detective. Let's go home."

"Fair enough." Beth headed for him.

"Stop there. Put down the gun."

"Okay. Okay. Keep your pants on." She lowered the pistol, placing it on the ground, close enough that Christine would be able to grab it.

His attention on her, he didn't see the signal she gave Luke. The dog leaped for the knife-hand. Gary yelled when teeth sank into his arm. He kicked at the German Shepherd who didn't let go, but hung on, eighty pounds of canine fury.

Beth grabbed Sorrel and shoved the girl at Rad.

Gary came up swinging. Beth waved the dog away and waded in. She ducked the first punch, but the second landed on her shoulder. She blocked the next blow with a fist.

Her first punch landed in his gut. Her second hit his jaw. He was still coming at her. Front kick to the groin. A side kick to the knee took him down to the ground.

He retched.

She snagged his right wrist, yanked it behind him.

"You'll need these." Rad holstered his pistol, pulled out a set of strange-looking handcuffs.

"Thanks." She shifted so he could fasten them around Smith's wrists since she didn't recognize the old bottleneck style or know how to use them. Rad would have to teach her how to lock them on a prisoner later.

"Gary Horace Smith, you're under arrest. You have the right to remain silent." She continued the formal notice of his rights while she yarded him to his feet, ignoring the odd look Rad gave her. Obviously, he had something on his mind, but he wasn't sharing it.

She shook her head deciding he undoubtedly never heard anything like the Miranda warning before, especially not in 1888.

"Okay, Gary. Let's head straight to jail. Do not pass Go. Do not collect two hundred dollars."

"I'll take him, Detective Morgan. You'll want to see to Sorrel and your friend."

Beth nodded in agreement. She rested a hand on Rad's arm. "I'd have said anything I had to say to arrest him and close this case."

He winked at her. "I know. Does this mean I don't have to eat the dinner you made me buy?"

"No, but it means I'll pick up some bicarb of soda at the mercantile." She grinned up at him. "I do love you."

"I'm going to puke," Gary said.

"Sorry, dude. You already did." Beth reached for Sorrel and pulled her into a tight hug. "Now, go to jail, you worthless sack of crap."

After the men left, she framed the girl's face with her hands. "I'd have said anything to get you away from him."

"I know." Sorrel took a ragged breath, tears filling her eyes. "I was so scared, but when you said you'd let him kill me, I knew you were lying. He didn't. He really thought you'd leave with him."

"He's stupid." Beth dropped a kiss on the girl's forehead. "But you're not. Did you see Luke?"

"Yes, but I wasn't going to tell him that."

"A little help here," Christine called. "Bastard hit me on the head, and you'll want back your pretty pink gun, Detective."

Beth laughed. "Come help me, Sorrel. May as well learn how to nurse folks in case you change your mind and decide to be a doctor instead of a lawyer."

Christine groaned and slowly sat up. "You mean I risked my life for somebody who would plead that loser's case."

"Afraid so." Beth took the pistol and holstered it. "But we have time. Years and years of time, Chris. With two *Guardians* on the job, maybe we can change her mind."

THIRTY-FOUR

"Friday the 13th, a Guardian may use Her Power,
and find what she truly seeks before the Midnight Hour...!"

RULES OF CHRONOS

RAD HADN'T NEEDED ANYTHING TO SETTLE HIS STOMACH. HE'D enjoyed all the food she prepared. Maybe catching a serial killer, rapist, would-be kidnapper, and horse thief made the meal even better. She'd gone to the hotel and changed to her wedding dress for the dance and spent most of the night whirling across the wooden floor in his arms.

Hours later, streaks of dawn lightened the sky. They headed for the hotel to sleep. He held her tight, and she couldn't shift in the bed without waking him. He used the opportunities to make love to her several times. When she finally lay exhausted in his arms, he kissed her, soft butterfly kisses that warmed her soul.

"I won't let you leave me, Bethany Rose Morgan."

"Why would I?" She pillowed her head on his broad chest. "We're here and we're together."

"You told Smith you'd leave with him, and you said before you weren't staying after you captured him. You were going back to your world."

She lifted on an elbow to stare into his rugged features and the navy-blue eyes. "I said a lot of things when I arrived here, Radolf Doyle Morgan. Why is it you only believe those and not what's happened lately?"

"Because I heard what you told him earlier." He stroked her hair. "If you take him back to your world, I'm riding along."

She heaved a sigh. "Morgan, we'll talk about it later. In the morning after we've both had some sleep."

After a late breakfast, she was ready to confront Smith and see about a confession. Word would go to Snohomish City on the next steamboat to send the judge upriver and they'd have a trial to attend.

She slid a hand through the crook of Rad's arm and walked beside him in the direction of the jail. "I didn't mean to hurt your feelings yesterday when we captured Smith. In my world, I don't have to tell a perp the truth. I can say whatever I need to say to get him under lock and key. I never would have let him walk out of that barn with Sorrel."

"I've seen the way you love that girl and she needs a momma. I need my wife, not just a deputy."

"You have one. You have me." Beth drew a deep breath. "You didn't get it, Rad. You didn't understand when I tried to tell you the first time at Padden's. There's no going back to 'what was'. There's only 'what is' and that's here and you."

"So, you're not leaving?"

She shook her head. "I'm here for the duration, Marshal Morgan. I'm your lady and you're my man. There may be times when I do things my way, not yours. We'll get used to that."

"Honey, you said that you're a cop." He smiled down at her. "I reckon in your vernacular, I am too. Sometimes, a body must be willing to be crude to get an outlaw's attention. You were and you caught him."

"And you're good with that?"

"I'll be better when you say that you love me without an audience." He paused. "And you can say it with one too."

She caught his arms, rose on tiptoe, and kissed him. "I'll say it so often in the next fifty years, you'll get sick of hearing it."

"That couldn't happen." He chuckled and pulled her closer. "You must promise to teach our girls to fight the way you did yesterday. And it looks like you can start now."

She stepped back and turned to see Becky and Sorrel coming toward them. "What's up, ladies?"

"It's about yesterday," Becky said, elbowing her sister. "Tell her."

"Tell me what?" Beth eyed the older girl. "Did Smith put his hands on you?"

"He grabbed my arm and said we were leaving, but he didn't touch me the other way." Sorrel took a deep breath. "He didn't say which horse, but I figured if I had yours, you'd come after him. And since everybody around had seen you ride him, they'd know he belonged to you."

"We would have come after you first," Beth said, "and then Tigger."

Sorrel stared up at her, tears shimmering in her eyes. "Really?"

Beth nodded. "You belong to us now, too."

"Told you." Becky tugged on Rad's arm. Her childish whisper was obviously louder than she intended. "And me too. I want to live where Sorry does."

"We'll need to work that out with Trace," Beth said.

"And we will," Rad finished.

"Now, I have business at the jail," Beth went on. "Where are you going to be, Sorrel?"

"With Becky and Michael and the other Lazy B kids." Sorrel pointed down the street in the direction of the hotel. "Ma Sims said it was all right with her if it's all right with you."

"That sounds fine," Beth said. "We'll come get you in a couple of hours."

Once the girls headed down the street, Beth stepped closer to Rad. "It looks like we have the start of a family, and that's not even counting Nettie Padden. Good thing your house is bigger than most."

"Reckon, I'll have to keep building on if you keep bringing home stray children."

"That's the plan, Marshal Morgan. I was on the streets until Will gave me a home and I'll help you make ours a fit one for the kiddoes who need us."

Cal and Kyle sat in the main room of the jail drinking coffee. When Kyle saw them, he stood and went after two more cups. "Smith had breakfast and he was asleep when I checked on him a few minutes ago."

"Well, let's see if we can get a confession from him," Beth said. "If he lawyers up, we'll have to wait until he talks to one. Who will prosecute the case?"

"Connor," Rad said. "He's the Justice of the Peace and generally speaks for Junction City when we have a trial. Kyle, why don't you fetch him? Stop by Vance's office and see if he's about."

Kyle grabbed his hat and headed for the door. "Be right back."

"Who is Vance?" Beth asked.

"The only lawyer in town. If Smith wants another one, he'll have to send word to Snohomish City." Rad took the key from Cal and went to unlock the cell. "Against the back wall, Smith."

Beth heard cussing and the rattle of chains. She pushed a chair forward when Gary Smith entered the room, slightly ahead of Rad.

Smith's hands were cuffed behind him. He scowled at Beth. "Bitch."

"That's Detective Bitch to you." Beth sighed when Rad shoved Smith into the chair. It fell sideways and so did Gary, hitting his jaw on the floor. "Morgan, have you ever heard of police brutality?"

Rad righted the chair. He reached down and jerked Smith up by his shirt front, then slammed him into the seat. "This is 1888. Next time he disrespects you, he'll be swallowing teeth."

"Okay, then." Beth hooked a foot around a chair and sat down across from Gary Smith. "So, let's talk about that Native shaman."

"Let's not." He turned, wiped the blood off his chin onto his shoulder. "I want a lawyer. And *you* can't talk to me without one."

"I hate when this happens." Beth met Rad's dark blue gaze. "He's right. Once he asks for an attorney, I have to stop talking."

"Maybe, where you come from. Not here. If you want answers, we'll get them." Rad took a step closer. "You shot me, Smith, and I'm not happy."

"I still want a lawyer."

"All right." Beth flicked a glance over her shoulder when the door opened behind her and saw Connor. "Mayor Riley, this is Gary Smith Senior. He wants a lawyer, so I guess we're not making any deals today."

"This is my town," Rad drawled. "And we don't make deals with a man who murders helpless women, kidnaps little girls, and steals horses in Junction City. We try him and then we'll hang him."

"Too bad for you, Gary." Beth leaned back in her chair. "Doesn't sound like you made a good choice when you came here. You're going to have your own necktie party. And that doesn't mean a trip to the shopping mall."

"I know what it means. I was born here," Gary snarled. "And I won't be hung."

"Don't bet a lot on that card." Rad rose to his feet. "What made those girls you saved different, Smith? Why didn't you hurt them?"

"Why would I?" Gary asked. "They never did me any harm. Are you really going to take them in, Marshal?"

"Promised I would," Rad said.

Beth grimaced. Why did these two have to bond? She propped her chin on a fist. "Is there some reason why he shouldn't? The girls need a decent home, and the Bar M has lots of room."

"And you won't board 'em in town for school, Marshal?" Gary

asked. "Some folks are just filthy. And those girls been through enough with their kin. They need to be kept safe."

Beth shared a glance with Rad. She'd keep her mouth shut for now while he got the information from Smith.

"When they go to school, we'll be in town with them," Rad said, "provided you tell me why it's so important to you."

"I already told you," Gary said. "They're good girls. The oldest one's an angel. You'll see. They do what a man says, and they'll never sass you. Always called me 'sir' and 'Mr. Smith.'" He glared at Beth. "Don't let her ruin them."

Beth started up out of her chair and stopped when Rad squeezed her shoulder. She subsided into the seat again. The most important thing was to learn whatever the man would tell them, not let her ego get the better of her.

"I'll look out for them," Rad promised.

The door opened. Kyle entered, followed by a thin man in a black suit. "Got the lawyer."

"All right." Beth stood. "We'll leave him to talk to his client."

"We'll take a walk around town," Rad said. "I'll lock Smith up when I get back or one of you can do it when he and Vance finish."

Connor nodded. "You and the detective can write up your reports later. I'll put the papers together for the judge."

Cal rose and went to the desk. "I'll put on another pot of coffee. We'll be here a while. Good thing all the witnesses are in town. We can get their information now and won't have to ride all over the valley."

———

The girls had a terrific week at the Bar M and hadn't complained about the ride to the Lazy B. Sorrel seemed to fit in with the other children and only asked three times when Beth and Rad would return from their rounds. He told her they'd be back in less than three weeks.

"So, where are we spending the night?" Beth asked as they rode out, taking the trail toward Portage. "Padden's?"

"Sounds good," Rad said. "Then, we'll make the cave tomorrow."

"And be back in Junction City in time for the trial."

He nodded. "And we'll arrange for the Jacksons to come and testify when we get to Gunny Creek."

———

Beth couldn't believe the speed of justice here in Junction City. The trial would start tomorrow. She'd spent the morning going over her testimony with Connor Riley and felt far more comfortable than she had with other prosecutors. When the tough were ready to go to court, it was time to go shopping.

Thanks to Trace Burdette-Prescott who ran the town council and Connor Riley, the mayor, Beth had wages as a paid detective in Junction City. Granted, a hundred dollars a month wasn't as much as she earned back in her own time, but she figured it was comparable. After all, things cost much less here than they did 'where' or was it 'when' she lived in 2018.

She scanned the latest merchandise in the mercantile. She needed a new dress, but a gold pocket watch in a display case caught her eye. She wanted a present for Rad and this would be perfect. She glanced at Susanne and the other woman came to join her. "Could I get this engraved?"

"Of course. Prince will be happy to do it."

"Good one." Beth spun as the door opened and she saw Kyle. "What's wrong? Rad?"

"No. Smith hit his lawyer over the head and escaped. Vance needs you. He's hurt bad and Doc's not back yet from Portage."

"Okay, let's go." She headed for the door. "Why didn't anyone stop him?"

"He stole your black coat, wore it out of the jail."

"Wonderful." There went her smartphone, digital camera, and

badge. "We'll take care of the lawyer first and then worry about Smith." Beth started for the door, then turned back to Susanne. "We'll finish our business later. Save that watch for me." She hurried out of the store toward the jail beside Kyle.

Horace Vance had been moved to a bed in an empty cell. Cal had carried in a bowl of hot water and a clean white towel, staying with the younger man. He wiped away the blood streaming from the attorney's temple.

Beth dropped to her knees beside the cot. She took the cloth from Cal. "You're going to need stitches, Mr. Vance, but you'll be just fine."

Cal shook his head and pointed to the dent in the man's skull.

Beth nodded, recognizing the potential of the life-threatening injury. She kept up the soothing chatter. "I need my saddlebags, Cal. Would you send Kyle for them? And find me a needle and some thread so I can sew up this scratch. Head wounds always bleed and scare a person…"

Cal gaped at her then stood. He left the room and she heard him talking to Rad out in the main room of the marshal's office. "That lawyer's a goner. No way he's going to survive what Smith did."

"That's what I thought when he shot me back in April," Rad said, "but if Detective Morgan says Vance is gonna live, he'll live. Now, fetch her the supplies she needs, and I'll go round up a posse."

———

They'd chased him this far, but he had a head start and was galloping up the ridge when they drew close. Beth reined Tigger to a stop, studying the path up the steep hill. Luke sniffed at the trail, then trotted back to stand next to her horse, whining softly. The horse backed up and she felt the tension in his body. Neither animal wanted to go forward, and she didn't blame them, not since all three of them died on the trail on the other side of it in 2018.

She glanced at Rad who sat on his horse next to her. "Let's go home, Morgan."

"What about Smith?"

"He's gone back to where we came from, and I can't go after him. Not anymore. Not since he—" She hesitated, then eyed the oddly shimmering curtain at the top of the ridge.

Somehow, she knew he'd crossed through it, and once in 2018, he'd run smack into John Watkins and Fletcher Gaines. They'd see to it that justice was served. She was the one who'd held out for more from the men, not been satisfied hooking up with them on the occasional basis. She'd wanted love and she'd found it here.

Beth swung the stallion around. "Christine Padden told me that Smith used Vance's blood to open the door to the Other Side. We're lucky the man didn't die."

"You didn't let him," Rad said. "If you hadn't been there, he would have."

That was true, Beth thought, but it was her new job to save lives, and she liked it. "Let's go find Kyle and the posse. He can't keep them busy chasing ghosts for much longer."

"And what happens when folks ask about Smith?"

"He's gone," Beth said. "I'll close the portal so he can't come back. At least, I'll try." Tigger tossed his head and started in the direction of Junction City. "And he can face justice there." She whistled for Luke. "But I'm ready to go home to the Bar M."

"All right." Rad turned his Appaloosa and rode beside her. "I'm with you, Detective Morgan."

———

Beth sat on Tigger, scanning the ridge in the light of the full moon later that night. Luke growled, then stood next to her horse, stiff and obviously on patrol. The stallion backed up, tense, tossing his head. He pawed the ground, trying to turn back. She glanced at her brother-in-law who sat on a strawberry roan gelding next to her.

"You don't have to do this, Kyle. I trust the cops on the other side to capture Smith."

"I want to see your world and know for myself he's back in the hoosegow," Kyle said, a frown creasing his forehead. "If it doesn't work, I'll come home the next time the door is open."

"I don't know that I can open it for you," Beth said. "It may take both me and the *Guardian* on the far end. And I don't know who she is. All I can do is tell you again to see my father, Will Dawson. Tell him that I'm all right and ask him for help."

Kyle nodded. "I'll do it as soon as I arrive."

"Fair enough." Beth leaned over to hug him. "I promise I'll try to bring you home in September 2019. That will give you a little more than a year. You can see to it that Smith gets arrested and stands trial for his crimes. Don't tell anyone other than Will where you come from."

"You've told me three times already. I'll keep my trap shut so nobody thinks I'm more loco than a bedbug."

"Okay then." Beth reined Tigger to the left and concentrated on the hill. The rising moon shone on the trail, and she nodded. "The way is open. Go careful if you wish."

"It's what I want," Kyle repeated. "Take care of Rad and name your first baby after your pa and me." He urged his horse forward, obviously eager for the next adventure.

Beth waited until he was out of sight, and she no longer heard the sound of hoofbeats. Then, she gave him another half-hour before she concentrated on the trail, making it disappear in the foggy mists. Tigger tugged on the rein, tossing his gray head. She grimaced, before she petted the Arabian's neck. She'd sworn Kyle to secrecy when he caught her heaving her guts out at the smell of the camp coffee after she and Rad joined the posse this afternoon.

She didn't look forward to telling the man that she hadn't stopped his brother from chasing a serial killer through the years. She swung Tigger around and headed across country to where the posse had camped for the night. Luke raced ahead, his tail a banner to follow. "Come on guys. Let's go home."

She heard the German Shepherd's bark of greeting before she saw Rad on his black Appaloosa mare. Her husband, her 'forever mate,' her partner in everything, even the weird stuff. A smile leaped in her heart. She waved at him.

"He get off safe?" Rad asked as he rode up to her, stopping the mare next to her stallion.

Beth gazed at his dark blue eyes. "You knew?"

"I saw his face when we caught up with them this afternoon. Kyle hasn't been happy here, especially since I gave him those books of yours. Maybe, he'll find what he's hunting in your world."

"This is my world now." She met him halfway when he brought his horse close enough to kiss her. She rested a hand on his cheek. "You're my world."

THE END

———

Turn the page for a preview of the fourth book in the *Liberty Valley* series, *Hero Spell*!

———

Keep up with Josie Malone and subscribe to her newsletter! https://sendfox.com/josiemaloneauthor

———

Don't miss out on your next favorite book!

Join the Satin Romance mailing list www.satinromance.com/mail.html

HERO SPELL

"Magick, monsters and mayhem – just another day in Paradise…."

AUDRA DAWSON

ONE

Everett, Washington - February 1ˢᵗ

AUDRA DAWSON WATCHED AS HER BEST FRIEND CASUALLY
sauntered into the Fandango Room at Billy-Bob's Cowboy Bar &
Grill. Ginger's curvy body was wrapped in a fringed blouse, green
suede skirt and high heeled cowboy boots. Pink and red curls
framed her face and brushed her shoulders. Her makeup was better
suited to a Saturday night out than an afternoon get together. But
the look worked for her, as the ample tips she made bartending at
Billy-Bob's could attest.

"So," Ginger drawled, as she approached, "how are things
coming along? You look ripe for murder. You look like someone
kicked your dog, then stole your man. Or maybe," she eyed Audra
critically and amended, "like you've been talking to one of your
sisters."

Audra slowly lowered the roll of green crepe paper and tape
dispenser she held, placing them neatly on a nearby table. "Clancy
just blew through long enough to tell me the wedding is off."

"After you made special arrangements for the lingerie shower, she and Kate insisted they had to have two weeks before the ceremony?"

"You wouldn't believe all the begging, conniving and family blackmail it took to get this place, plus the hefty deposit I had to pay. And that's not even counting the big family Christmas and all the extra stuff the twins 'couldn't live without' at school this quarter. I am glad," Audra said with mock solemnity, "that someone who knows their way around duct tape, rope and a shovel, is here to help me bury the bodies."

"That's me." Ginger did a little victory dance, more suitable for a twenty-something than a woman fighting her fortieth birthday. "I'll break out the champagne so we can get good and soused before we clobber them."

"Don't tempt me. This is a damn nightmare."

"More like the day of your dreams. You've been patient. You respected your sister's boundaries while she played holy hell with everyone's heartstrings. Now you finally have a shot at Ethan." Ginger headed for the bar and the bottles of champagne. "Are you going to call him and offer a sympathetic shoulder?"

"Not until I figure out what to do about this shower." Audra pulled out her cell phone and dialed her sister, Kate's number. It went straight to voice mail, so she had to be on the line with someone. "It's me. I need to know what has your tail in a knot. And what the hell am I supposed to tell Mom?"

Thirty minutes later, she hadn't heard back from either sister. She and Ginger were on their second glasses of champagne when the door opened. Her mother came in, followed by her older sister, Marlene.

Darlene Dawson looked around the half-decorated lounge—obviously checking the streamers that weren't hanging from corner to corner, the unfinished party favors that hadn't been arranged in plastic cowboy boots. "What's going on?" She pinned Audra with the cobalt blue gaze that made everyone in the Dawson family 'fess up to a million and one sins. "Why are you slacking? Where are the twins? Shouldn't they be helping you?"

Audra blinked. She'd forgotten all about the two baby drama queens. She had five younger sisters, all of whom saw her as a cross between Public Enemy Number One, General MacArthur, and Dear Abby. "They got tied up with some college thing and said they'd be late."

"Those two have lazy down to an art form," Marlene said. "What can we do to help, Audra?"

'I don't know." Audra shrugged. "Clancy came in and told us the wedding is off. She and Kate have changed their minds. They're not marrying the Killian brothers, not in two weeks, not on horseback on Valentine's Day at the Lazy B, not ever."

"Lions, tigers and bears—oh my." Darlene eased out of a denim jacket and eyed Audra, then Ginger. "Pour us each a glass of champagne, Ginger. Give me your phone, Audra. I left mine at home in my other purse. I need to call and warn the boys' mom before she arrives with her entourage and that gossip gal from the local paper. It'll be okay, honey. Better broken engagements than divorces."

Audra stared at her. At fifty-seven, her mother was more of a realist than a romantic. While she claimed she loved both men who proposed to two of her daughters, Darlene was the first to quote divorce statistics and remind everyone that "happy ever after" belonged in movies and books, not real life. She'd even told Kate and Clancy that marriage was an institution, and they didn't have to be committed yet. Why didn't they live with the guys and never get hitched?

"What do we do now?" Audra asked. "How do we handle it when everyone arrives expecting a party?"

"We tell the truth," Darlene said, taking a filled glass from Ginger. "Your sisters have changed their minds and then we'll have a party anyway. I have a horsy sitter doing chores and I'm spending the night at Marlene's. We can't return the cake or get back your deposit, so we may as well enjoy the afternoon."

"The girls will sort this out sooner or later." Marlene accepted her own glass. "There's too much between them and the boys to let these engagements end today. Believe me, sooner or later, we'll see Clancy and Ethan and Kate and Gavin married."

Ginger brought the bottle of champagne over to Audra and whispered. "I hope not. Snag the guy, quick. You take Ethan and I'll jump Gavin. They deserve to have grown women in their beds, not temper-tantrum throwing twits."

———

April sunlight sparkled off the neatly mown, emerald, green lawn in front of the two-story log cabin that Ethan spent years restoring on the Killian homestead. Audra parked her Ford 150 near the back door and switched off the engine. She'd debated what to wear for hours before settling on black jeans, low-heeled boots, and a black shirt with a Southwest print. She didn't want to look desperate even if she was or as if she was chasing the man who thought he loved her sister.

Even though I am after him, Audra thought, and *I'd be soooo good for him. I'd never do anything to hurt him. I wouldn't break his heart into tiny jigsaw puzzle pieces for fun.*

The back door opened, and she beamed at the big man in the opening. Six foot, six, he wasn't just all muscle, even if he looked like a lumberjack in a plaid flannel shirt, blue jeans, and wool socks. His corked boots waited on the porch. An engineer for Boeing, he had brains too.

Her pulses thudded in excitement as she slid out of the pickup. "Hi, there." She walked around to the passenger side and pulled out the picnic basket. "Hope you're hungry. I brought dinner."

She strolled toward him and watched a smile creep across his rugged features and land in silver-gray eyes. Even with the salt and pepper brown hair, he still reminded her of the boy she'd met so many years before.

"Sweetheart, if you're cooking, I'm starving." He took the basket from her. "I smell fried chicken."

"And the rest of your faves too." She'd spent her one day off a week cooking for him and loved every minute of it. "So, how was South Carolina? I can't wait to hear all about the new plane."

―――――

Ginger filled a glass with Riesling and put it in front of Audra. "Drink up. You're spending tonight with me and I'm driving so you can get snockered. How could this happen? You've given your heart and soul to Xanadu Arabians for the past three years. How did they have the gall to pass *you* over for farm manager when you've been running the place for the last six months since New Year's?"

Audra choked down a swallow of wine, trying to drown her tears. She couldn't cry in Billy-Bob's, not when everything would be reported back to family, friends, and other horse professionals in the county.

"What are they thinking?" Ginger wiped down the bar. "Didn't old man Bergstrom say they had the best breed auction ever with you in charge? They actually turned a profit last year."

"I know." Audra chugged down the rest of the white wine. "I was there, remember? He said I could stay on as Jack Abbot's assistant, that Jack would be glad to let me run the breeding program."

"Jack is a lazy, worthless good-for-nothing, and he's now reached his level of incompetence." Ginger picked up the empty glass and replaced it with a full one. "He'd have you doing all the grunt work while he reaped all the bennies."

"I know." Audra stared into the depths of her wine glass. How could she say she'd miss the horses more than the people at Xanadu, especially the filly she'd raised from an orphaned foal? And the Bergstroms wouldn't sell her the horse she loved. She struggled to swallow the lump in her throat and keep up her professional front.

Taking a deep breath, Audra said, "Jack is a good trainer if he gets close supervision, but there's a lot more to running a purebred horse operation than handling the stock. Bergstrom said that if I went to work at my mom's, he'd sue her because of the non-competitive clause in my contract. I don't know what I'm going to do. My family will freak if I move out of Washington State to find a new position."

"I've changed jobs for years, my dear, so let me tell you the proper response when you get screwed by a boss. Tonight, you get drunk. Tomorrow, you move in with me. And then, we call around and find you a stable management job that's out of Xanudu's reach. As for your family, it'd do them a world of good if they had to grow up and stop dumping on you."

———

Lynn glanced around the cafeteria but didn't see her brother anywhere. Where had he disappeared to now? He was supposed to eat lunch with her and the other eighth-graders because he didn't get along well with kids his own age. Granted, he'd made a few friends with some of the sixth-graders, but Jake was just too smart for his own good. Maybe, things would be better at their new school in the fall.

Carrying the tray with her pizza and salad, Lynn headed for the table where Cassie already sat. "Have you seen Jake?"

"Yeah. He took his lunch and went outside. He said he had some serious thinking to do."

Lynn sighed and put her food on the table. "Thanks. Be right back." She found her brother sitting alone on a bench in the school courtyard in the June sunshine. "Do you want to tell me what's going on with you?"

He peeled plastic wrap from his peanut butter and jam sandwich. "We have a problem."

"I'll say. You're out here when you're supposed to be with me."

"No, Lynnie. We need to cast a spell and I have to think it up."

"Oh no." She shook her head. "Not again. Mom's fine. She and

Sean are getting married and we're going to Eastern Washington in two weeks. And Audra Dawson is doing great at running the farm."

"Yeah." Jake bit into his sandwich and chewed. "She's a hero and she needs one."

"What?" Lynn stared at the sandy blond, blue-eyed demon posing as her younger brother. "You can't do that. Not to a stranger. You can't conjure up a man for our new manager."

"She needs somebody who makes her laugh. A guy who loves her best of all." Jake looked at his watch. "You better go eat your lunch. I'll tell you when I need you to help me."

"I'm not doing it, Jake. No way. No more 'love' spells. Not again."

———

He'd left Pullman at five this morning and he'd arrived in Everett in time for a late lunch. He pulled into an empty slot in front of the veterinary office, recognizing the new white Ford 150 his father had posted pictures of on the practice's website. Joe Watkins eased out of his Jeep, stretching to his full five feet, eight inches, and rolled his shoulders. In faded blue jeans and a Washington State Cougars sweatshirt, he didn't look like the new Dean of the Veterinary Medicine department.

Well, he wasn't the Dean yet, he reminded himself. He'd been offered the position, but he hadn't accepted it. He'd asked for time to think about it. For now, he was home to visit his father, see a few friends, be the best man at his friend's wedding provided he liked Sean's fiancée and attend his high school reunion.

And for the first time in years, he wasn't teaching during the summer session. He'd enjoy the two and a month break, call it a vacation, and think about taking a sabbatical to write the book on equine medicine. Or then again, he'd have enough time off to realize he wanted to go back to school with the kids and take over his department.

He headed inside, scanning the waiting room with its comfortable sofas and chairs. Magazines on the tables, chew toys in a basket in the corner. Some things didn't change, and his old man was one of them. He'd never gone for the new plastic seats. If his patients had to wait, they might as well enjoy their time. And so, could their humans.

A heeler-border-collie pup looked up from where it ripped at a stuffed teddy bear and greeted him with a baby yap. The slender brunette, in jeans and a sloppy sweatshirt flushed. She looked as if she wanted to cringe back in the chair, disappear with the puppy, leash, and all. "Sorry."

"No worries." Joe grinned at her and didn't say a word about recognizing her from the newspaper and TV articles. She'd undoubtedly heard enough about being battered by an intruder to last a lifetime. "Puppy shots?"

"Yeah. It's the last booster and his rabies, too." The woman relaxed a little.

Joe lingered inside the doorway. "Aren't you Nina Armstrong, the gal with the horse rescue place? How's that going?"

She eyed him suspiciously, then inclined her head accepting the questions at face value. "It's fine. Donations are up and horse abuse is down, so everything works."

"Good to know." With the economy the way it was, he didn't believe her for an instant, but wouldn't say so. He nodded at the puppy who kept chewing on the toy. "You have a cute fellow."

"Thanks. Pooka loves Doctor Art. He's the best."

"He's an inspiration." Laughing, Joe crossed to the desk but didn't see Sarah Holmes, the receptionist who'd run the office forever. He walked to the first examining room and opened the door and spotted his dad bandaging a gray kitten's leg. "Hey, is there a doctor in the house?"